Praise for *Washington Black*

"Astonishing … Washington Black's presence in these pages is fierce and unsettling. His urge to live all he can is matched by his eloquence." Colm Tóibín, *The New York Times*

"At the core of this novel, with its searing, supple prose and superb characters, is a visceral depiction of the abomination of slavery. Yet, as importantly, it explores an unlikely friendship, the limits to understanding another's suffering, the violence lurking in humans and the glories of adventure in a world full of wonders." Elizabeth Buchan, *Daily Mail*

"Magnificent … By placing a black slave at the heart and centre of this epic romp, by making Wash the explorer of lands, science and art, Edugyan reclaims long-lost terrain in this ambitious, head-spinning work." *Financial Times*

"Terrifically exciting … An engrossing hybrid of nineteenth-century adventure and contemporary subtlety, a rip-roaring tale of peril imbued with our most persistent strife … Discover what the rest of the world already knows: Edugyan is a magical writer." *Washington Post*

"Suggestive of Jules Verne, Mark Twain and Mary Shelley … a strange, engaging tale" *Mail on Sunday*

"Magnificent and strikingly visual prose" *Financial Times*

"The novel is devastating, precisely because Edugyan is never gratuitous or sentimental … In a story that is escapist, as well as poignant and political, Edugyan enjoys taking her readers where they ar

"*Washington Black* is a rare creation. It is a work of unmistakable literary sensibility, written in prose that is fresh and beautiful, yet it retains a storyteller's skill to shock and surprise ... Edugyan has shown herself to be an important voice and one that promises to become even more so." Amanda Craig, *Sunday Telegraph*

"*Washington Black* is nothing short of a masterpiece. Esi Edugyan has a rare talent for turning over little-known stones of history and giving her reader a new lens on the world, a new way of understanding subject matter we arrogantly think we know everything about. This book is an epic adventure and a heartfelt tale about love and morality and their many contradictions. I loved it." Attica Locke

"A brilliantly absorbing picaresque; a book that combines the unflinching depiction of violence with a lyrical, hallucinatory beauty." Sandra Newman

"*Washington Black* is made vivid by Esi Edugyan's gifts for language and character, and by the strength of her story ... The reader feels honoured and moved to have kept Wash company on his journeying." Erica Wagner, *New Statesman*

"Washington Black's triumph is to make us think searchingly about slavery and racism, while entertaining us in the style of Dickens ... An epic, powerfully imagined continent-spanning tale." *Times Literary Supplement*

'Edugyan's genius here is that she's found an urgent, fresh way of writing the antebellum novel ... A romping yarn, beautifully and evocatively written, the narrative spinning along at a glorious pace." Lucy Scholes, *The National*

"*Washington Black* is a profoundly humane story about false idols, the fickleness of fortune and whether a slave, once freed, can ever truly be free." *The Times*

"*Washington Black* is a gripping adventure and an atmospheric portrayal of 1830s society at both the fringes of the world and the heart of the British Empire." John Boyne, *Daily Express*

Praise for the Booker Prize-shortlisted *Half Blood Blues*

"A thrilling story about truth and betrayal ... a brilliant, fast-moving novel" Kate Saunders, *The Times*

"Edugyan really can write ... redemptive" *Guardian*

"Sid's voice ... is a triumph of vernacular writing and convincingly captures the mood of the late jazz age in Europe ... punchy and atmospheric." *Sunday Times*

"*Half Blood Blues* shines with knowledge, emotional insight, and historical revisionism, yet it never becomes over-burdened by its research. The novel is truly extraordinary in its evocation of time and place, its shimmering jazz vernacular, its pitch-perfect male banter and its period slang. Edugyan never stumbles with her storytelling, not over one sentence." *Independent*

"A densely researched tale musing on timeless themes of jealousy and betrayal" *Daily Mail*

"Edugyan's ventriloquism is a compelling, personal and authentic, her story deeply researched." *Observer*

"Mesmerising … Edugyan has a perfect ear for conversations and the confusions of human love and jealousy … moving … a remarkable novel" *Morning Star*

"Assured, vivid and persuasive … Impressively evocative of period and place, and an effortlessly involving and dramatically unusual second novel" *Time Out*

"Simply stunning, one of the freshest pieces of fiction I've read. A story I'd never heard before, told in a way I'd never seen before. I felt the whole time I was reading it like I was being let in on something, the story of a legend deconstructed. It's a world of characters so realised that I found myself at one point looking up Hieronymus Falk on Wikipedia, disbelieving he was the product of one woman's imagination." Attica Locke

WASHINGTON BLACK

ALSO BY ESI EDUGYAN

The Second Life of Samuel Tyne
Half Blood Blues

WASHINGTON BLACK

A Novel

ESI EDUGYAN

A complete catalogue record for this book can be
obtained from the British Library on request

This paperback edition published in 2019
First published in Great Britain in 2018 by Serpent's Tail,
an imprint of Profile Books Ltd
3 Holford Yard
Bevin Way
London
WC1X 9HD
www.serpentstail.com

ISBN 978 1 84668 960 4
eISBN 978 1 84765 997 2

Printed and bound in Great Britain by
CPI Group (UK) Ltd, Croydon CR0 4YY

1 3 5 7 9 10 8 6 4 2

For Cleo & Maddox

WASHINGTON BLACK

PART ONE

Faith Plantation, Barbados
1830

1

I MIGHT HAVE BEEN TEN, ELEVEN YEARS OLD—I CANNOT say for certain—when my first master died.

No one grieved him; in the fields we hung our heads, keening, grieving for ourselves and the estate sale that must follow. He died very old. I saw him only at a distance: stooped, thin, asleep in a shaded chair on the lawn, a blanket at his lap. I think now he was like a specimen preserved in a bottle. He had outlived a mad king, outlived the slave trade itself, had seen the fall of the French Empire and the rise of the British and the dawn of the industrial age, and his usefulness, surely, had passed. On that last evening I remember crouching on my bare heels in the stony dirt of Faith Plantation and pressing a palm flat against Big Kit's calf, feeling the heat of her skin baking up out of it, the strength and power of her, while the red sunlight settled in the cane all around us. Together, silent, we watched as the overseers shouldered the coffin down from the Great House. They slid it rasping into the straw of the wagon and, dropping the rail into place with a bang, rode rattling away.

That was how it began: me and Big Kit, watching the dead go free.

His nephew arrived one morning eighteen weeks later at the head of a trail of dust-covered carriages driven directly from the harbour at Bridge Town. That the estate had not been sold off was, we thought at the time, a mercy. The carriages creaked their slow way up the soft embankment, shaded by palm trees. On a flatbed wagon at the rear of the caravan sat a strange object, draped in canvas, as large as the whipping boulder in the small field. I could not imagine its purpose. All this I remember well, for I was again with Big Kit at the edge of the cane—I rarely left her side in those days—and I saw Gaius and Immanuel stiffly open the carriage door and extend the step. I could see, at the Great House, pretty Émilie, who was my age, and whom I would glimpse some evenings dumping the pans of wash water into the long grass outside the scullery. She descended the first two steps of the verandah and, smoothing out her apron, fell still.

The first man to emerge, carrying his hat in his hands, had black hair and a long, horselike jaw, his eyes darkened by heavy brows. He raised his face as he descended and peered around at the estate and the men and women gathered there. Then I saw him stride back to the curious object and walk around it, inspecting the ropes and canvas. Cradling a hand to his eyes, he turned, and for a frightening moment I felt his gaze on me. He was chewing some soft-textured thing, his jaw working a little. He did not look away.

But it was the second man, the sinister man in white, who seized my attention. This was our new master—we all could see it at once. He was tall, impatient, sickly, his legs bending away from each other like calipers. Under his three-cornered white hat a shock of white hair burst forth. I had a sense of pale eyelashes, an uncooked pallor to his skin. A man who has belonged to another learns very early to observe a master's eyes; what I saw in this man's terrified me. He owned me, as he owned all those I lived among, not only our lives but also our deaths, and that pleased him too much. His name was Erasmus Wilde.

I felt a shudder go through Big Kit. I understood. His slick white face gleamed, the clean white folds of his clothes shone impossibly bright, like a duppy, a ghost. I feared he could vanish and reappear at will; I feared he must feed on blood to keep himself warm; I feared he could be anywhere and not visible to us, and so I went about my work in silence. I had already seen many deaths: I knew the nature of evil. It was white like a duppy, it drifted down out of a carriage one morning and into the heat of a frightened plantation with nothing in its eyes.

It was then, I believe now, that Big Kit determined, calmly and with love, to kill herself and me.

2

All my childhood I'd had no one; only Big Kit, as she was known in the cane. I loved her and I feared her.

I was around five years old when I angered the quarters-woman and was sent to live in the brutal hut below the dead palm tree, Kit's hut. On my first evening there, my supper was stolen and my wooden bowl cracked; I was struck hard on the side of my head by a man I did not know, so that I staggered and could not hear. Two little girls spat on me. Their ancient grandmother held me down with her talons biting into my arms and cut my handmade sandals from my feet for the leather.

That was when I first heard Big Kit's voice.

"Not this one," she said softly.

That was all. But then some monstrous charge of dark energy, huge, inexorable as a breaker, poured towards us and picked the old woman up by the hair as though she were a boneless scrap of rag, tossing her aside. I stared, terrified. Big Kit just glared down at me with her orange eyes, as if disgusted, and then returned to her stool in the dark corner.

But in the morning I found her squatting beside me in the pale light. She offered her bowl of mash, traced the lines in my palm. "You will have great big life, child," she murmured. "Life of many rivers." And then she spat in my hand and closed my fist so that the spit ran between my knuckles. "That is first river, right there," she said, starting to laugh.

I adored her. She towered over everyone, huge, fierce. Because of her size and because she was a Saltwater, a witch in old Dahomey before being taken, she was feared. She would sow curses into the dirt beds under the huts. Rooks would be found eviscerated, hanging in doorways. For three weeks she forcibly took food from a strong smith's apprentice each morning and night and ate it in front of him, scooping with her fingers from his bowl, until some understanding was reached between them. In the smouldering fields she would glisten as if oiled, tearing up the wretched earth, humming strange songs under her breath, her flesh rippling. Some nights in the huts she would murmur in her sleep, in the low, thick language of her kingdom, and cry out. No one ever spoke of that, and in the fields the next day she would be all scorched fury, like a blunt axe, wrecking as much as she reaped. Her true name, she once told me, whispering, was Nawi. She had had three sons. She had had one son. She had had no sons, not even a daughter. Her stories changed with the moon. I remember how, some days, at sunrise, she would sprinkle a handful of dirt over her blade and murmur some incantation, her voice husky, as though overcome with emotion. I loved that voice, its rough music. She would suck air through her teeth and squint up her eyes and begin, "When I was royal guard at Dahomey," or "After I crush the antelope with my hands, like this," and I would stop whatever task was at hand, and stand listening in wonder. For she was a marvel, witness to a world I could not imagine, beyond the reach of the huts and the vicious fields of Faith.

Faith itself darkened under our new master. In the second week, he dismissed the old overseers. In their place arrived rough men from the docks, tattooed, red-faced, grimacing at the heat. These were ex-soldiers or old slavers or just island poor, with their papers crushed into a pocket and the sunken eyes of devils. Then the maimings began. What use could we be, injured so? I saw men limp into the fields, blood streaming down their legs; I saw women with blood-soaked bandages over their ears. Edward had his tongue cut out for backtalk; Elizabeth was forced to eat from a full chamber pot for not cleaning the previous day's thoroughly. James tried to run away, and to make an example of him, the master had an overseer burn him alive as we watched. Afterwards, in the embers of his pyre, an iron was heated and we filed past the charred horror of him, one by one, and were branded a second time.

James's was the first of the new killings; other killings followed. Sick men were whipped to shreds or hanged above the fields or shot. I was still a boy, and cried at night. But with each new death Big Kit only grunted in grim satisfaction, her orange eyes narrowed and fierce.

Death was a door. I think that is what she wished me to understand. She did not fear it. She was of an ancient faith rooted in the high river lands of Africa, and in that faith the dead were reborn, whole, back in their homelands, to walk again free. That was the idea that had come to her with the man in white, like a thread of poison poured into a well.

One night she told me of her intention. She said we would do it quickly. It would not hurt.

"Do it frighten you?" she whispered, where we lay in the hut. "To be dying?"

"Not if it don't frighten you," I said bravely. I could feel her arm draped protectively over me in the dark.

She grunted, a long, dark rumble in her chest. "If you dead, you wake up again in your homeland. You wake up free." I made a little shrug of one shoulder at that, and she felt it, and turned my chin with her fingers. "What is it, now?" she asked. "You don't believe?"

I did not want to tell her; I feared she would be angry. But then I whispered, "I don't have a homeland, Kit. My homeland here. So I wake up here, again, a slave? Except you won't be here?"

"You come with me to Dahomey," she murmured firmly. "That how it works."

"Did you ever see them? The dead, waked up? When you in Dahomey?"

"I saw them," she whispered. "We all saw them. We knew what they were."

"And they were happy?"

"They were free."

I could feel the day's exhaustion descending on me. "What it like, Kit? Free?"

I felt her shift in the dirt, and then she was gathering me in close, her hot breath at my ear. "Oh, child, it like nothing in this world. When you free, you can do anything."

"You go wherever it is you wanting?"

"You go wherever it is you wanting. You wake up any time you wanting. When you free," she whispered, "someone ask you a question, you ain't got to answer. You ain't got to finish no job you don't want to finish. You just leave it."

I closed my heavy eyes, wondering. "Is really so?"

She kissed my hair just behind my ear. "Mm-hmm. You just set down the shovel, and you go."

WHY, THEN, DID she delay? The days passed; Faith grew harsher, more brutal; still she did not kill us. Some presentiment, some warning perhaps, stayed her hand.

One evening she led me out into her little vegetable garden, where we were alone. I saw the sharp, rusted blade of a hoe in her hands, and started to tremble. But she only wished to show me the little carrots beginning to sprout. Another night, she woke me and led me silently out into the darkness, through the long grasses to the dead palm tree, but this too was only to instruct me not to speak of our intentions. "If any hear it, child, we be separated true," she hissed. I did not understand why we waited. I wanted to see her homeland, I told her. I wanted to walk in Dahomey with her, free.

"But it must be done right, child," she whispered to me. "Under a right moon. With right words. The gods cannot be summoned otherwise."

But then the other suicides began. Cosimo cut his own throat with an axe, Adam punctured his wrists using a nail stolen from the smithy. Both were found bled out in the grass behind the huts, one after the other, in the mornings. They were old Saltwaters, like Kit, believers that they would be reincarnated in their ancestral lands. But when young William, who had been born on the plantation, hanged himself in the laundry, Erasmus Wilde himself came out among us.

He walked slowly over the lawns in his dazzling white clothes, an overseer trailing a few steps behind. The overseer wore a tattered straw hat and was pushing a wheelbarrow. The cradle of the barrow held a wooden post, a tangle of grey sacking. They crossed the grass in the harsh sun, pausing just at the edge of the cane, where we had been assembled. In the hot, bright air, the new master studied us.

I could see the flesh on his face and hands, waxen and bloodless. His lips were pink, his eyes a very piercing blue. Slowly he walked the line of our bodies, staring at each of us in turn. I could hear Big Kit breathing roughly above me and I understood she too was frightened. When the master looked at me, I felt the scorch of his gaze and lowered my eyes at once, shivering. The air was stagnant, redolent of sweat.

Then the man in white gestured behind him, to the overseer. That man twisted the handles of the barrow, dumping its load in the dirt.

A murmur passed through us, like a wind.

Sprawled there in the dirt, in a heap of grey clothes, was William's corpse. His face was a rictus of pain, his eyes bulging, his tongue black and protruding. Some days had passed since his death, and strange things were happening already to his body. He looked corpulent, bloated; his skin had become mottled and spongy. A slow horror filled me.

The master's voice, when at last he called out to us, was calm, dry, bored.

"What you see here, this nigger, killed himself," Erasmus Wilde said. "He was my slave, and he has killed himself. He has therefore stolen from me. He is a thief." He paused, folded his hands at the small of his back. "I understand that some of you believe you will be reborn in your homelands when you die." He looked as though he might say more, but then he fell silent and, turning abruptly, gestured to the overseer at the barrow.

That man crouched over the body with a large curved skinner's knife. He reached around and cupped his callused palm under William's chin and began to saw. We heard the terrible wet flesh tearing, the crunch of the bones, saw the weird, lifeless sag of William's body as the head came away.

The overseer stood and raised the severed head in both hands. Then he walked back to the barrow and took out the long wooden post. Hammering it into the dry earth, he drove William's head onto the sharp end.

"No man can be reborn without his head," the master called out. "I will do this to each and every new suicide. Mark me. None of you will ever see your countries again if you continue to kill yourselves. Let your deaths come naturally."

I stared up at Kit. She was peering at William's head on its spike, the bulge of its softening flesh in the sun, and there was something in her face I had not seen in her before.

Despair.

3

BUT THAT IS NO BEGINNING. ALLOW ME TO BEGIN AGAIN, for the record.

I have walked this earth for eighteen years. I am a Freeman now in possession of my own person.

I was born in the year 1818 on that sun-scorched estate in Barbados. So I was told. I had also heard it said I was born in a shackled cargo hold during a frenzied crossing of the Atlantic, aboard an illicit Dutch vessel. That would have been the autumn of 1817. In the latter account my mother died in the difficult birth. For years I did not privilege one origin over the other, but in my first years free I came to suffer strange dreams, flashes of images: Tall, staked wooden palisades, walls of black jungle beyond. Naked men yoked together and stumbling up rotted planks into a dark brig. Was it Gold Coast I dreamed of, the slave fort at Annamaboe? How could that be so, you ask? Ask yourself what you know of your own beginnings, and if your life is so very different. We must all take on faith the stories of our birth, for though we are in them, we are not yet present.

I was a field nigger. I cleared the cane, only my sweat was of value. I was wielding a hoe at the age of two, and weeding, and collecting fodder for the cows, and scooping manure into cane holes with my hands. In my ninth year I was gifted a straw hat and a shovel that I could scarcely lift, and I had felt proud to be counted a man.

My father?

I did not know my father.

My first master named me, as he named us all. I was christened George Washington Black—Wash, as I came to be known. With great ridicule, he'd said he glimpsed in me the birth of a nation and a warrior-president and a land of sweetness and freedom. All this was before my face was burnt, of course. Before I sailed a vessel into the night skies, fleeing Barbados, before I knew what it meant to be stalked for the bounty on one's scalp.

Before the white man died at my feet.

Before I met Titch.

4

Titch.

I met him for the first time that very night, the night of William's desecration, when Big Kit and I were summoned to the Great House to wait at the master's table.

The strangeness of this request was alarming: a field slave was a black-skinned brute born for hard toil, certainly not a being to be brought inside. We did not know why the master should request us. What were we to him? Kit's despair had over the hours grown into a silent fury at what she could no longer do to herself and to me. She now began to fear the master had discovered her intent, and that he meant us some cruel and grievous punishment.

Immanuel and young Émilie waded down the soft slope and into the sprawl of huts in their clean white-and-grey house clothes to summon us. Kit rose up from where she sat on a stone in front of our hut, shaking her head in anger.

"Don't you send Wash up there," she said. "I go. But you leave the boy."

"The master he clear," Immanuel said. "Both you."

"Hello, Wash," Émilie said shyly.

"Hello," I said, my face growing warm.

"They eat before it get dark," Immanuel said. "You be up right quick. Don't make neither them wait."

I had never, in all my childhood, passed through the shaded grove of frangipani and approached the master's verandah. At dusk I followed Kit up the slope, feeling the pebbles, the cool grass on my feet for the first time. Kit stared stonily up at the house.

The doors stood open. A muscle in my throat fluttered, as if I'd swallowed a moth. I had once crawled under the great chimney in the laundry, twisting my neck to peer up its chute at the square of sky beyond and the clouds scuttling by. But the height of that seemed nothing in comparison with the ceiling here; and at the top, a large glass dome of a window, the faint evening light dropping in a long rope to the floor. Dust was adrift in the air. I saw carved scrollwork over the doors and heavy burgundy drapery, padded green chairs crouching on elegant curved legs. It struck me as impossibly beautiful.

"A fine, fine quiet," Big Kit whispered, nodding. "Listen."

We did not dare enter, not with our filthy feet and clothes, stinking—I think now—of sweat and dirt, insects in our hair. We stood uncertain, unhappy. As we had been summoned, we could not go back to the huts, but nor could we bang on the door to announce ourselves. We stared at each other.

At last Gaius, the house porter, came round the corner. I'd come to know him better in the weeks since Erasmus Wilde's arrival, as he was sent out to the overseers more often with the master's instructions. Gaius was tall, thin, old as driftwood. His gestures were deliberate and slow, and there was a grace to him we all of us in the huts admired and mocked because of our admiration. He had been handsome once, and in the strong cheekbones and clear forehead one could glimpse a kind of regal deportment, a man elevated beyond the ordinary. To my eyes, he was a kind of surrogate master, a man with the speech and breeding of a white man. I feared him.

He was stiff, unfriendly. But not unkind. "Good evening, Catherine. Young Washington."

"Gaius," Big Kit said warily. "Émilie and Immanuel come down to fetch us." She faltered. "What do he want us for?"

"The master?"

"He the one."

"Did Immanuel not tell you?"

Big Kit set a huge hand on the top of my skull. I could feel her tense; I knew she feared the master's wrath. "He say we is to wait his table."

Frowning, Gaius glanced past us at the twilight as though there might be someone else waiting there. "Then that is what you are to do," he said. "I am sure he has his reasons. You will wait in the kitchens until you're called."

Neither of us moved.

At last Kit said, "Our feet."

Gaius stared down at the filth caking our bare feet. Then, quite slowly, he opened his jacket and withdrew from the inner pocket of his waistcoat a huge white handkerchief, handing it to Big Kit. "Clean your feet," he said. "Both of you. Either of you leave footprints on his marble, you'll be sorry."

We wiped off our feet, and then he turned and led us through the grand hall. On the far side, we stepped from the cold marble onto parquet flooring; I had never in my life seen such a thing, angles of wood braided to make a miraculous pattern. The air was cool, scented with mint. I felt my fears diminish a little. Big Kit, true, was not at ease. But I wanted to see everything, remember everything, to carry these wonders back with me when I returned to the huts. White lace, silver candlesticks, wood polished to so lustrous a sheen it looked like fresh bread. We moved past rooms filled with ancient rugs and tall old clocks and strange frozen creatures with tawny claws and outraged eyes. I stared and stared, hardly daring to blink.

"Is real, Gaius?" I whispered. "Them animals?"

Gaius stopped to glance at a huge white owl on a perch in an alcove. Its yellow eyes stared unseeing. It did not move. "They were once alive," he murmured, almost inaudible. "Now they are dead and stuffed. The master is the same."

"He once alive?" I whispered.

Gaius paused and studied me with his inscrutable expression. Just when I thought he would look away, he gave the faintest of smiles. "So it is said, young Washington."

I had known Kit to be fierce, an explosive force. But here, walking the halls of Wilde Hall, she too seemed diminished, cowed, anxious. The change in her frightened me more than the frozen beasts in the hall, more than the strange, gleaming luxury surrounding us. I hurried to keep up as Gaius led us deeper into the house.

At last we entered the kitchen. It was a vast room with silver vats at a boil, a wall of heat shimmering in the air. The cook, Maria, turned startled to us, her face dusted in flour, her sleeves rolled up. There were two serving maids in the back, wrestling with an enormous canister. I searched for Émilie, but did not see her among the gusts of flour and stacks of gravy-stained dishes and large wooden blocks with cubes of peppers and yams. An enormous fire blazed in the great open fireplace, a glistening bird turning slowly on its chain as it cooked. I stared in amazement at the bounty, and felt something I had not known before wash over me—desire.

"Don't you even do it, nigger," Maria said sharply, as my eye caught a plate of pastries near the door.

I looked at her in fear, caught out. Something shifted in her face, softened.

"The time for that is later," she said in a gentler voice. "When you is cleaning up, you can lick at what's left over."

"Is so?" I said.

"But only from the touched food, only when you are scraping their plates," Gaius added. "It won't do for you to eat up the fresh food."

"We get to lick the plates, Kit," I said, smiling up at her in wonder.

THE TWO OF them were speaking as we shuffled in, Big Kit and I carrying trays of rolls and hot dishes of steaming vegetables. On a low buffet at the back wall were the dishes set out for serving that Gaius had described to us. He had warned us to be prompt, attentive, silent. That our hands, in their strange white gloves, should be always present, and our bodies always absent.

I could see how uneasy Big Kit was; she stood quietly furious, as if damning the obviousness of her body, clasping and unclasping her hands. The punishment for our plan to murder ourselves, she knew, would not be gentle. She tried to quiet her face, her gaze slow and inward.

I was terrified too, but I also could not prevent myself from glancing at the master's plate as he ate, thinking of the sauces there, the hot yellow crusts he dropped in boredom.

I had not ever been so physically near to the master. Under the burnished candlelight he looked as he had in the field—waxy and ill, the same colour as the rind of hard cheese that lay on the table before them. His flesh was slack, tired. As I leaned in to pour the water, my hands shaking, a smell of wet paper seemed to come off his body. I noticed dried blood under his fingernails.

And yet it was to the second man that my eyes kept drifting. I had imagined he would be dark, frightening. He was not. His hair was at his shoulders; he wore a dark-blue frock coat. His fingers were long and thin, a jewelled ring on the index finger of each hand. His feet were planted wide and firmly under him where he sat, as though he might at any moment stand from his seat. And yet he sat very still as I poured the tepid water into his glass, and paused in his speech to give me a fragile smile. He ran a spidery finger down the bridge of his nose, large, arched, the nostrils slight as buttonholes, and continued in his low voice. "I have tried passing sulphuric acid over iron filings. I have tried animal bladders, silk stockings. Paper sacks. Even some of the more preposterous ones, to see if some merit was missed in them. But they were all abandoned quite rightfully, Erasmus. I think nothing works so well as hydrogen, simple hydrogen, and canvas. You should see the heights one can reach—why, ten, twenty thousand feet. It is truly spectacular. The world from up there is, well—it is God's earth, man."

The master was chewing and did not glance up from his meat. "But you have not been up."

"Ah, no. Not myself. Not yet."

"So you do not know."

"I have read about it. Others' reports."

"And you imagine you will actually make it across the Atlantic in that thing."

"I will have to undertake some test flights first, but yes."

The master grunted. "Corvus Peak is a miserable climb. You will not like it in the heat of day."

The second man, his eyes a stark green, made no answer.

Now the master raised his face. "You will be wanting for me to spare some slaves to carry your apparatus, I expect. What?"

The dark-haired man furrowed his brow.

"What? Speak up, man."

The man paused, his knife and fork held above his plate. He met the master's eye. "These potatoes," he said instead, "they are most unusual, do you not find? The flavour is passable, but I do prefer our white varietal in Hampshire."

"Well, I am pleased you consent to break with convention and dine at this lesser table." The master wiped at his mouth with the edge of the tablecloth.

"You are too easily offended, Erasmus. It is potatoes."

"*My* potatoes," the master scowled. "Potatoes selected by *me*. It always was your passion to thumb your nose at all of my preferences. You and Father were always alike in this way. Damned judgmental."

I was surprised at this mention of a father, and glanced at the second man. I had not thought he bore any sort of relation to the master, but now the resemblance rose to sight, like a watermark: the brisk, bright-coloured eyes, the oddly plump lower lips, the way each man punctuated the ends of certain phrases with a languid sweep of the hand, as if the gesture were being performed underwater.

The master caught the second man glancing uneasily across at Big Kit, and he laughed a sharp laugh. "What? The sow? My language cannot offend her. She has no sensibilities to offend, Christopher."

The second man set his knife and fork quietly down.

"No matter," said the master, waving a slow, impatient hand. "You were speaking of your improvement on Father's air balloons, the great heights you will reach."

"Well, they are not exactly *air* balloons. But yes—"

"And now you want great weights."

The brother laughed easily, a strange sound. "I do require a second man to ride the contraption with me. For the ballast, you see. It cannot be done alone."

"And it is my great weight you require?" The master's eyes had soured.

"Erasmus, your greatness extends to all of your attributes."

"You are saying I am fat, then?"

The man paused, met the master's eyes.

"Perhaps you require something of lesser weight." The master turned sharply; he gestured at me where I stood. I felt the water pitcher in my hands begin to tremble. I dared not meet his eye. "Why not take a nigger calf up with you? He should be light enough."

"Leave it be, Erasmus."

"Would that be suggestion, or instruction?"

The man took a long, slow breath. "I will never understand why you seek offence in everything I say. It is only the two of us here, and I have come for a limited stay. Would our time not be better enjoyed if we tried to understand each other?"

"Do I lack understanding?"

"What you lack," the brother began, but then he broke off and did not continue his thought. Instead, he said, "I would not have this conversation now, in front of the help."

"They are not the help, Titch. They are the furniture."

The brother exhaled, rolling his eyes slightly.

"You are too soft, little brother. How is it you expect to get through a whole year here if already you are weeping at profanities used before a nigger? Heavens. All Father's regard for you would dry up at once if he saw how soft you are become. Indeed, why did you insist on following me to this wretched place at all, given your convictions? Do you mean to steal away all my slaves while I am asleep?"

The man smiled irritably. "I have asked you to leave it."

I was astonished to see the master suddenly smile also, and start to laugh. "So there is a man in you somewhere after all. More claret?"

His laughter, I believe, was genuine. In that moment I understood I would not ever make sense of the master, for there was not sense to be made.

As he was extending the decanter of claret, he spilled a slow red stain onto the white tablecloth. I watched it spread, like blood, seeping outwards. The colour of it, its deep redness, seemed horrifying and beautiful to me. But Big Kit shuffled silently forward, a large, dark shadow, and began dabbing at the stain at once with a white towel.

The master took no notice.

The brother cleared his throat. "I have gone through three shirts today so far. It is a devil's climate."

The master only gave a slight puff of his cheeks. He had not finished his thought. "This is rough work. It requires veins of steel.

What, was it some fourteen, fifteen years ago only, the Easter Rebellion? Niggers set the whole bloody island afire. Vigilance is paramount, Titch. Why, I went into Bridge Town this afternoon with John Willard, he and I went up to the club."

"The man at dinner the other night? The plump one with the red, sweating face?"

"Nay, the shorter one, the yellow-haired one in spectacles. He was a bookkeeper at Drax but found himself frustrated there—did more hunting down of the niggers than keeping ledgers, I think. He still has strong words for the management there. Why keep feeding a man of fifty who can scarce stand, when a boy of ten can cut twice the cane? said he. Willard is a man of very economical turn, I think. It is a question of wastage, said he. Indeed. The best-respected planter can walk out amongst his slaves with a ledger under his arm and just the sight of it can make a nigger skunk his drawers. He has seen it himself. You, boy. Tell me, would you soil yourself to see my brother here with a ledger?"

I could feel the master's pale eyes on me.

"Boy," he barked.

I did not lift my face. "Yes, sir."

The master made a flustered noise, as if my answer did not please. "My point is, without a little grit, I will have mayhem. My task, Christopher, is to contribute to the grit. I care nothing of your science, so long as it does not interfere with my running of the estate."

"How near are we to Haiti?" the brother asked, distractedly scraping at his plate. "The first lighter-than-air craft was launched from there—the first launch of such a craft in the Americas, I believe."

The master paused, frowning. "Do you imagine this is how I wanted to pass my life? Fussing after niggers' filth, stinking of sugar all day? I did not seek the responsibility out, but it found me all the same. Unlike you, I am not Father's favourite and cannot simply roam about the world dreaming up silly contraptions. I must actually do what family duty demands."

"You are the eldest," the man Christopher said. "It does fall to you, brother."

"At breakfast"—the master narrowed his eyes—"something you said then . . . it comes to me. Tell me—does Mother know you're here?"

The brother paused, and stared steadily across at the master.

"You know she will go out of her wits, don't you? All this time we have been together, and you have said nothing. All this time. Well, you simply cannot keep disappearing on her like this. Where does she think you are?"

"How can I presume to know anything that woman thinks?" The brother shrugged. "Paris, perhaps. London. I might have mentioned something about visiting Grosvenor."

The master faintly shook his head, laughed in disgust.

"She would have poisoned me off the idea, wouldn't she?"

"And so you thought you'd simply catch me at Liverpool and sail out? Just like that? No word of notice at all?"

"Sometimes one needs to disappear a little. It is good for the soul."

"Whose soul?"

"Mine, presumably."

"All this suffering, just for your damned flying rag."

The man gave the master a level look. "It is not a rag, Erasmus. It is a Cloud-cutter."

"And what purpose does it serve? Will it cure mankind of its ills? Will it release me from the bounds of this godforsaken island?" Big Kit was still dabbing at the stain on the tablecloth, her eyes carefully averted, and now the master noticed her. "Leave off with that," he snapped.

Big Kit, nervous, took a few last swipes at the stain.

"I said leave off!" The master reached for his plate and, half-standing, struck Big Kit full in the face with it.

A tremendous crack rang out, blood and shards of china everywhere.

My bones jumped up in me, and I just caught the water urn before it slipped from my fingers. I stared at the master's hands, the fresh blood on his thumb. I wanted to rush to Kit's side but only stood gripping the jug, the lemon seeds inside clicking like teeth.

"Oh hell, I have cut myself," said the master, swiping his hands on the tablecloth. Dropping the broken plate, he turned and strode from the room. "Maria! Maria! Heaven's sake, where are you?"

The silence was terrible. I could hear the blood dripping through Big Kit's fingers, where she held her face.

The second man, the brother, hesitated. At last he stood and came over to Kit, his napkin held out before him. "Here, lower your hands."

Big Kit lowered her hands.

"Turn your head. There. Like so."

The man was taller than any white man I had seen, as tall as Big Kit herself, and I felt his eyes pass over me as he dabbed at Kit's face. "What is your name?" he said to me.

I glanced helplessly at Kit, met her steady, dark eyes, glanced back.

I heard rustling in the doorway, and I dropped to my knees and began picking up the bloody shards of plate. I kept my eyes on the mess on the parquet.

"For heaven's sake, Christopher, leave it," the master said. "Don't make a mess of yourself. They'll clean it up. It's what they do." He sounded almost pleased now, relaxed. "Listen, the custard and tansies will be along shortly. I have some hope that they will be passable. Come, man, sit down."

Big Kit's nose was broken.

I did not cry. Together we mopped up her blood in silence, my eyes on the floor, listening to the master absently scrape his shoes over the parquet to clean the mess off them.

The custards appeared in a warm, sugary glow. While the master ate heartily, his brother pushed his plate away, requesting instead another glass of claret. Night deepened at the windows, and I glanced up to see our reflections there, illuminated and clear, as if some other slaves stood miserable and stone-faced across from us. I searched for my eyes but could not recognize them in the boy who stood in my place, white-gloved, still. When at last the master and his brother had retired, and we had helped scrub out the enormous vats down in the scullery and stacked the steaming dishes to dry, Gaius allowed us to pick through the half-eaten food scraped onto a large platter. I had lost my enthusiasm for it, but Big Kit threw me a furious glance and then began eating fast, scooping the food with two forked-out fingers and chewing crookedly with one side of her mouth. She would wince as she did so, then open her eyes in angry surprise, then lean forward again to scoop up more food. I tasted little. I stared at her nose, refusing to forget.

Only later, as Big Kit and I descended through the blare of moonlight to the huts, did she start to talk. "Don't you never not take what yours," she hissed. "You was promised that food. So you take it."

"He shouldn't have hit you, Kit."

"This?" She lifted her face. The nose was bleeding again. "I thought he throw us in the scullery fire for trying to get back to Dahomey. This, this nothing, boy. You never seen a bit of blood?"

Of course I had. We had lived in blood for years, my entire life. But something about that evening—the gleaming beauty of the master's house, the refinements, the lazy elegance—made me feel a profound, unsettling sense of despair. It was not only William's mutilation that day, knowing his head stared out over the fields even now, in the darkness. What I felt at that moment, though I then lacked the language for it, was the raw, violent injustice of it all.

"Is that it, then?" I said in a rough voice. I turned to look up at her in the moonlight. "We don't get to go to Dahomey together?"

She paused and looked at me, very still.

"Kit? We just give in, then?"

"That's right," she said. "And you forget I ever said anything. Put it out your mind."

I nodded, confused by her anger, feeling I had done something wrong. "Our shirts is a mess, Kit," I said miserably. "We going to get in some trouble for it."

It was then we heard, at the same moment, a rustling along the path behind us. We turned as one, Big Kit stepping slightly in front of me.

But it was only Gaius, still dressed in his fine service clothes, making his stiff way uncertainly down in the dark. When he saw us, he gave a quick, polite nod, his face unreadable.

"Gaius," Big Kit muttered. "Don't tell me they is sitting down to eat again?"

He shook his head. "The master has retired. He is inebriated." When we stared at him blankly, he added, "Drunk. Master Erasmus is quite drunk. How is your nose, Catherine?"

"Still attach to my face."

"Yes."

A moment passed. Big Kit said, "You ain't come down here to ask after my nose. You lost now?" She ran a tired hand over her neck, her shoulder.

"Ah. No. You should go on to sleep now, Catherine. Your night is finished."

She started to turn away, and I with her. Then, setting a big hand on my shoulder, she turned back. "*My* night finish? Wash's night ain't?"

Gaius gave me his strange, cold, unreadable stare. "It would seem not."

"Meaning?"

"Mister Wilde has asked for him. He has asked you to attend to him in his rooms, Washington. This evening. Now. Do you understand?"

I did not. "The master?" I said, staring up in fear. What could he want with me?

"Not the master," Gaius said calmly, "the master's brother, Mister Wilde. The other man at table this evening, the dark-haired one. He wishes for you to go out to his quarters."

"You tell him the boy is sleeping, Gaius," Big Kit said sharply. "You say you never did find him."

Gaius wet his lips. "I can't do that, Catherine. You know I can't."

She stepped forward. "He ain't goin' up."

She stared at Gaius, but he did not flinch, only looked coolly up into her face, waiting. At last he said, softly, "It isn't for us to stop, Catherine. I'll be needed back at the house, but you make sure Washington comes up." And then to me he did something most strange: pinching up his fine trousers, he squatted on his haunches to look me square in the face. "Don't keep Mister Wilde waiting, Washington. He is the master's brother. You do not want him unhappy with you."

"I never give him no reason to be."

"Very good."

"What do he want of him?" said Kit.

"What do they ever want?" Gaius said softly, bitterly. "He wants him to do what he says and not ask why." He rose and started to go, but then he looked back at Big Kit and said, mysteriously, "It's an opportunity, Catherine. The boy has a chance to find safe harbour. If Mister Wilde grows fond of him—"

"Don't you even finish that thought," Kit said, but her voice was low, pinched.

"It gives the boy a chance," Gaius said. His face was lost in shadow, and though I could not be certain, he sounded rather sad.

"Just get, Gaius," Kit said. She took a threatening step towards him. "You just get now."

The man left.

I stood a long while beside Big Kit in the bright light of the moon. At last we started walking. She seemed distressed, and I thought she must be angry because of her nose, because she did not want me to be struck also. To ease her fears I said, "Don't you worry, Kit. He hit my nose, I won't cry or nothing. I be just like you. You see."

But this did not seem to help. In the water barrel behind the huts, I splashed my face and arms, rubbed at my hair, felt the fine coolness of the night-chilled water on my skin. When I opened my eyes, I saw Kit, looming up in the darkness of the hut's shadow. She stepped forward.

"He try to touch you, Wash," she whispered, "you put this through his eye and just keep on pushing."

I felt her press something into my palm. I looked down. It was a nail. A long, thick, heavy iron nail hammered out in the smithy. I stood with my hand open, the nail on it warm from the heat of her fist. I glanced up at Kit, but she was already turning away.

I CARRIED THAT nail like a shard of darkness in my fist. I carried it like a secret, like a crack through which some impossible future might be glimpsed. I carried it like a key.

I walked slowly, my heart pounding. I knew what Big Kit would have me do, but the thought of it terrified me. The path led around to the back field of Wilde Hall and into the unlit waste there at the edge of the trees. The master's brother had taken up residence in an old overseers' quarters—a long, low wooden building with a deep cellar that had been used for storing goods, and had not been inhabited for many years. Some of the slaves would tell stories of past horrors there. Some said on moonless nights cries could be heard from that cellar still.

I was shaking. Lanterns had been lit at the edge of the verandah, and I stopped in the open doorway, peering in, hesitant, afraid to call out. No servant came to greet me. I gripped that nail tightly, staring. In the large whitewashed rooms beyond, not an uncluttered surface was to be found. On every table, on every inch of floor space, in piles, sat strange stick-like contraptions, long-spined scopes with legs like grasshoppers, plates hanging from chains.

At last, when nothing happened, I knocked softly, my hand trembling. A moth battered against one of the lanterns hanging from the ceiling.

"Who is it?" a voice called sharply. "Is that you, boy? Come. Come in here."

I took a hesitant step in. And then I saw him, Mister Wilde, standing at the far window of the long room. He was not facing me; he was bent double, his shoulders hunched. I let my eyes take in the strangeness of his house, the windowsills strewn with velvet-lined boxes, their lids flipped open, gleaming instruments laid out within. Some held wooden cylinders with lenses at each end, like the spyglass used by the old ship's captain who had worked as an overseer for a time—but these were stranger, different. As I passed a dining table, I saw vials of seeds, jars of ordinary dirt, powders in spills across the mahogany. The floor creaked under me as I approached, papers strewn everywhere.

"Mister, sir?" said I.

My fist clamped tight around the iron nail.

And it was this Mister Wilde saw, at once. He nodded from his terrible height. "What is it you have there? A blade? A nail?" He frowned down at me.

I started to tremble. Of course he knew. The masters knew everything.

"Well, set it down and approach. Set it there." He pointed to a stack of papers on the floor beside me.

What could I do? I set the nail down. Knowing the fact of it, there, undeniable, was worth my life.

"Closer," he said, impatient. "Here, hold this steady, like so. We haven't much time."

He try to touch you, Wash, Big Kit's voice came back to me. *Through his eye. Just keep on pushing.*

I wanted to run. But he had already turned his attention back to whatever was before him.

"Make haste," he called. "Tell me, child, have you ever witnessed a harvest moon through a reflector scope?"

My voice seemed to stick to my ribs.

He looked up from his labours and his green eyes fixed me in place. "You must see it to believe it. The moon is not as we think it to be. Here." He shifted to one side. On a golden stand sat a long wooden cylinder angled out the window. The near end was tipped in glass.

"Set your eye here."

I did as I was told. What I saw was a terrible blackness. Kit had explained, as I had readied myself to come here, the unspeakable acts done to boys by the overseers; and as I bent down and set my eye against the cold brass rim of the object, I felt exposed, terrified. I did not know what ugliness must follow, but I understood what Big Kit did not—that I could not fight this man, who was so much bigger than I, that violence was not in my blood. I shut my eyes, and waited.

I felt his breath, soft, near to my ear. He said, "Do you see it, boy?"

What could I say? I did not know his meaning.

"Yes, Mister Wilde, sir," said I.

"Stunning, is it not?"

"Oh, yes, Mister Wilde, sir," said I.

He made a noise of pleasure. "Do you see the markings? The craters? It is an entire planet, son, hanging in our field of gravity. Imagine walking that ground, pacing the edges of those craters. No foot has walked that ground before us, ever. It is innocent of all we are."

He tapped my shoulder then, that I should step back, and squinted his own eye against the eyepiece. And then the strange man laughed.

"But you have seen nothing," he said.

His face was still screwed to the contraption, and now he reached around to a small dial and began to turn it with the tips of his fingers. "It is a reflector scope," he said, "of my own design. Based, of course, on the fine Dutch models of the sixteenth century. But rather more compact, I think. Now, there," he said, stepping back. "Have a look now."

Oh, what I saw then. The moon was huge, as orange as the yolk of a goose egg. And clearly etched upon it were deep craters and ridges, just as Mister Wilde had said. It was, I would later think, a land without tree or shrub or lake, a land without people. An earth before the good Lord began to fill it, an earth of the third day.

I could not stop myself, and breathed a sigh of amazement.

Again Mister Wilde laughed, this time pleased. "Now, boy, tell me. Why does a harvest moon rise thirty minutes later each day, as opposed to the fifty we are accustomed to seeing at other times of the year?"

He regarded me, expressionless.

"Tell me, do you think it is because its orbit is parallel to the horizon at this time of year, so that the earth does not have to turn as far?" said he.

I stared at him, anxious. I sensed that very gently, very faintly, he was mocking me.

"Ah," he went on. "But what a conundrum."

We were both still standing at the open window, but now he turned and began to write very quickly in a large open ledger on a stand at his elbow. He was silent a moment, and then, with his hand still scribbling, he said, "What is your name, boy?"

I lowered my face. "Wash, sir."

"Wash?"

"Washington. George Washington Black, sir."

He looked up from his ledger. "I had an uncle ransomed by the Americans when they were fighting for their republic. Came to quite admire them, he did. Well, young George Washington, shall we cross our Delaware?"

When I continued to stare at him, uncomprehending, he made some further notes in his ledger, chuckling to himself. "Our Delaware," he mumbled happily. He double-checked the positioning of the dial on his scope and wrote something else. He raised his eyes again. "Christopher Wilde," he said, offering, I understood, his own name. "But you will call me Titch. It is what I am called by those closest to me. I was ill as a boy, you see, and became very tiny for a period—in any case, the name stuck. Over the years I have grown to embrace it. It will be strange to you at first, I am sure, but it is a fine sight more fitting than Mister Wilde. Mister Wilde is my father. And, as I have been constantly reminded by my mother, I am not he. Have you brought your things? Are they still on the porch?"

I could not imagine his meaning.

"Did the man not tell you? Well." He gave a quick, faint smile and lowered his hands from the ledger. "You must be wondering what on earth you are doing here at this hour. You are to live here with me, Washington, as my manservant. There is much to be organized, I grant you. But you will find me an easy man to satisfy. Your real task, you see, will be to assist in my scientific endeavours. Do not concern yourself about them now. Not tonight. Tonight we shall get you settled. In the morning you shall clean all this somewhat and then we will set to."

I must have worn a look of absolute confusion, for he paused.

"You do not object to these arrangements?" he said.

The very notion of objecting to anything had never, of course, crossed my mind. I stared at him in horror. "No sir, Mister Titch, sir," I whispered.

"Titch," he corrected. "Just Titch will do."

"Titch, sir."

"Excellent." He gave me a swift, assessing look. "Yes. Yes, you are precisely the size that I need. The weight, you see, that is the key to the Cloud-cutter."

I had hardly dared to breathe, desperately imagining he had forgotten the nail. But no sooner had he finished making this last strange remark than he crossed to the nail and picked it up.

"Ferrous," he murmured, and then peered up at me with an unfathomable look. "We learned to work iron rather late, I have been told. A good friend of mine in the Royal Society believes we worked the purer metals first. It makes some sense, does it not? And yet we do not value iron as we value the pure metals."

He lifted the nail into the candlelight and held it delicately. "This will be of some use, I am sure. It could be used to nail me to my cross."

When I made no answer, he smiled, and the strangeness of that smile, its lack of malice, left me confused. And because I did not understand, I felt a deep, cold fear.

"That will be all, Washington." Distracted, he started turning back to his ledger. But then he paused and, coming towards me, very gently handed me the nail.

"There is a bed in the far room, Washington," he said. "Sleep easy. Sleep well."

5

When I awoke, at first dawn, I was still clutching that nail.

I understood at once two things. First, that I would not be returning to Kit, and our hut, and her dark, powerful presence. And second, that she had known this even then, the night before, as I was being drawn away.

I stood in the half dark of the strange, small room, my skin pimpling with cold, feeling very small and alone. The air stank of sap, as though green timber had once been housed there. I rubbed my bare shoulder, my joints strangely out of place. The linens lay tangled in a grey twist. In all my years I had slept on nothing but a dirt floor, and throughout the night I had kept jolting awake, startled by the soft collapse of the mattress.

The strange house might have been deserted. I arose, and went to press my ear to the door. I took a step back, and stood waiting in the centre of the room with my arms at my sides. For I was alarmed by the calm, waiting for the door to bang open, for the man Titch to bark instructions at me. The minutes passed; no one came.

To the right of the door, on a stand, sat a basin of water. Its surface was flecked with dust, a silvery-green fly floating in it. Just beside the bowl lay a small white cloth, along with a little wooden stick with bristles in it, and a tin with a fanciful picture of cherries. I slid a fingernail under the rusting lid and sniffed: a chalky, scratchy smell, like when two warm rocks are pounded together.

I was an innocent, true, but I was no fool. I understood I was to clean myself and make myself presentable, as the house slaves must do; but these very instruments appeared torturous in their mystery. At last I picked up the linen and, wetting it, wiped at my face.

I was astonished at the brownish-red grime that came off. I scrubbed harder: along the walls of my nose, behind my ears, I squatted and washed between my toes and stood and rubbed the folds of my neck. The water had turned a quite beautiful, quite astonishing black. I stared at it in wonder, my skin tingling.

Still no one came for me. I felt an increasing dread. Surely my presence was required someplace, surely I was late for some task?

I slipped the long fang of the nail under the mattress for safekeeping and went out into the corridor.

"Mister Titch, sir?" I called, my voice too loud in the stillness. "Sir?"

The air was still and hot, and smelled of some nutty substance, earthy and edible, and of freshly washed stone. Peering down the hall, I saw a bright room already filling with sun, dust turning in the white light. A window glowing with sunlight. I entered the room, and the tattered burgundy rug under my naked toes was like some stiff, dead creature. I shuddered. Stepping back, I moved quietly to the next doorway.

And then I saw him.

He stood alone in his shirt sleeves, in the bare kitchen, his back to the window. A plate of greyish eggs sat on the table beside him. How tall and thin he looked, how pink. He was reading an opened sheaf of papers, and in his slender hands he rotated and picked apart the shell of an egg. He did not sense my presence. I was afraid to interrupt him, and so I stood, gaping, nervously observing his thicket of black hair, the way he popped the peeled egg into his mouth, his quick, irritable chewing. He had, I noted, a fine white scar cutting up from either corner of his mouth and across his cheeks to his ears, as if a thread had been set on his tongue and yanked upwards. It gave the impression of a crack.

He looked sharply up.

"Washington," he said.

I flinched, smiling in alarm.

He clapped his hands together, bits of eggshell falling from his fingers onto a chopping block. "Well? Are you quite rested?"

I began to nod in apology, but he was already speaking again.

"Very good, then. Come, come. Are you skilled at all in laundering? No, I'd thought not. I have sent for one of Erasmus's domestics to deliver your livery this morning, and I shall request she take the time to school you in the laundry, among other things. I do not suppose you to have any knowledge of English cuisine? Oh, how blessed you are. That is a joke, Washington. I prefer a French kitchen myself, but I understand it to be beyond the means of Bridge Town. Therefore, we must make do with the English. There *is* one salvation, one meal for which I had all the ingredients: I have taken the liberty of preparing for us this morning a light hollandaise. It is one of my most skilled recipes. My secret? The juice of two limes and a touch of Ceylon ginger. I wager you will taste no finer hollandaise in Amsterdam herself. Now, listen, I brought back many spices from my journeys in the East—these you will find in the cupboards. You must use them liberally. I have grown so dependent—I can eat nothing without them. Everything here has the taste of walking stick." He paused. "I make only one restriction. And that is, you are never to use sugar. I will not abide it. You will find none in my larder, and I want none brought over from my brother's residence."

What was I to make of this stream of language? Mister Titch took me by the shoulder and firmly—if gently—steered me into the adjoining room, which had been set with a large mahogany table and six mismatched chairs. I stared at the two white plates, set facing each other.

"Sit," he gestured, and, seeing my confusion, smiled in vague exasperation and sat himself. "I do not intend to dine while you watch, Washington, hovering over me like a murderer. Sit. It is not a request."

Moistening my lips, I sat at table in the soft, monstrous upholstered chair, across from a white man who possessed the power of life and death over me. I was but a child of the plantation, and as I met his gaze with my own, my mouth soured with dread.

He took up his fork; I took up mine. I held it clumsily, in a loose fist.

An eerie, pale orb of sauce lay at the centre of each of our plates.

Mister Titch began to eat, very deliberately, as if to school me. "Erasmus has loaned you to me for the duration of my time here. I trust this suits you." He paused, nodded with seriousness to the fork in my hand, and waited.

I scooped up a dollop of the hollandaise, ate it. I did not betray my disgust.

He smiled. "How shocked my mother would be to see you seated at table with me." He laughed a single sharp laugh at the thought of her imagined reaction. "Well. I've hardly brought you here only to dine. You shall become my assistant. I am hoping you will have intelligence enough to grasp a few simple skills that will be useful to me."

"Yes, Mister Titch, sir." I had no idea of his meaning; I offered him, simply, what I hoped he expected to hear.

He took up an enormous forkful of hollandaise. "Excellent," he said, his mouth full.

I made no response.

"Your old master, Richard Black—he was our uncle, our mother's elder brother," he continued. "When he passed away, all his estates came down to my brother, including Faith Plantation. Erasmus had hoped, I suppose, that my father might be around to offer his counsel. But Father, he is a true man of science. It is not in his nature to be running estates, getting after tenants' rents, the like. Indeed, even when he was home, at Granbourne, that task had already fallen to Erasmus. Father spends much of his time away on research trips. At this very moment, in fact, he is on an extensive voyage to the Arctic. He has been from home a year already, and will stay away two more at least." He sighed. "I don't suppose Erasmus actually enjoys his responsibilities. But he has a good head for numbers and a winning way with people when he makes the effort, which, I confess, is rarely."

Mister Titch took two swift bites, swiping at his mouth as he chewed. "With Uncle Richard now gone, Erasmus has to run not only our Granbourne, but Uncle's Sanderley, and his Hawksworth also. Faith Plantation, too. It is my brother's plan, I think, to spend most of his time here, in West India, with only periodic trips back to England. It is Faith which needs the most nurturing, says he.

Which simply means that it is Faith that supplies the others their money."

I blinked and blinked, and did not fully meet his eye. I was surprised by his great need to talk, as though he had gone several years without companionship.

"Our family fortunes have been in decline some years now, given the expense of Father's scientific pursuits. But lo and behold, Uncle Richard's entailment has brought us wealth again." He sighed bitterly.

I could understand almost none of this. Mister Titch sensed this, and set down his fork with a frown.

"Yes?" said he.

I said nothing, terrified.

"Go on," he said more gently.

I dipped my head, but I did not speak.

"You are wondering, I think, why I have come when clearly I do not have to be here," he said, though I had wondered no such thing. "Well, now I am come, I wake every day asking that very thing." He smiled. "A joke, Washington. In truth, I wanted to run away, and I needed a place to run to. So one morning I simply packed my things and set out for Liverpool without telling anyone. I knew Erasmus would be sailing before month's end, and I stormed his rooms and made the case for allowing me to join him. The West Indies—how much there is to learn! What a rare and miraculous opportunity! I had done much research about wind currents in the northwestern hemisphere, and it occurred to me that here might be the perfect place to launch the aerostat I'd half-heartedly designed. And so I revisited the designs in earnest, and spent the weeks before the crossing amassing the materials for transport."

He ate several more bites, chewing slowly. "It helps that I require very little in the way of creature comforts to survive—just my instruments, a little food now and again. Shelter needn't be fancy, and I can get on quite well without manservants, providing I have an able assistant at hand. Indeed, before coming here, I was in Istanbul some seven months with only a local boy to attend me. Do you know that in Istanbul the ladies veil their faces? I tell it true. Quite bewitching."

What an odd man this was, who had a mother and yet so little regard for her, and still seemed to me warm enough in his person.

"Now, on to more practical matters," Mister Titch continued, slapping his slender hands together over his empty plate. "Cooking, laundry—these are not to be neglected. But your true work, as I have mentioned, will be to aid me in my experiments. You are precisely the size for my Cloud-cutter. Ballast is key, you understand. I can see by your intelligent eyes that you might be able to learn a fact or two, though I understand my intellectual questions are not so easily absorbed. Yes, we shall get along together rather fine, I think. You will do very well. In fact—" He rose suddenly, and strode over to the sideboard, where he snatched up a paper and came to my end of the table, leaning close.

I could hear the whistle of breath in his throat, smell the cuttlefish stink of soap on his wrists. I thought of the black nail, lying like a fine blade under the mattress.

But Mister Titch only smoothed out the paper on the table before me, the onionskin crackling as he ran his fingers along it. And then he did something wonderful.

From somewhere within the lining of his clothes he withdrew a small stub of pencil. He drew, very quickly, an enormous smooth ball in a kind of webbing. I had never seen anything like it. He sketched in the shadows and the light, and the ball seemed to lift from the page. There were ropes falling from it, and beneath the orb he drew in a fantastical boat, with two fronts, and oars hanging out into the air.

I had never seen such artistry. I stared at the paper in amazement. And suddenly I knew that I wanted—desperately wanted—to do it too: I wanted to create a world with my hands.

When I raised my eyes, Mister Titch's own were shining. "What say you?" he said.

It is a wonder, I thought, an absolute wonder. I said only, "Nice, sir."

"I have been re-engineering it some three years." He took the paper from me and held it up to the light. "My father hazarded a similar design some thirty years ago, but he never troubled beyond an initial conception. My father has, well—he would be much astonished at what I have fashioned here. He thought his own creation too unstable. The gases, you see. But how the science of aerostation has changed since his day. I believe mine will actually fly, and for a goodly distance."

He turned suddenly to me, making a noise low in his throat. "Ah, but of course—you are unlettered. Well, we must attempt to remedy that, if we possibly can. You can hardly assist me without your letters. I will need you to record measurements, equations, outcomes, I will need you to read them back to me in the evenings."

"Yes, Mister Titch, sir."

He paused, frowned at me. "Come now. What did I say about that? What are you to call me?"

"Titch?"

"Very good. All right."

I stared up at his glistering green eyes, the lashes matted, black as the legs of flies. And my smile was a smile of terror.

6

And so began my strange second life.

In the mornings Titch and I would examine the previous day's labours, recording minute calculations, marked at first by Titch and—gradually, increasingly as the weeks passed—by me also, though very crudely. In the afternoons we walked the outer wilds of the plantation examining the flora, and then he would send me home to clean and cook, while he continued alone an hour or so more. Then, in the evenings, I would stutter and flush and mumble pitifully through the words of a simple book, while Titch sat irritably by, sounding them out.

I came to dread those evenings; but the morning's labours were strange, wondrous. We collected rainwater in barrels to test the acidity, caught eels in those selfsame barrels to measure their electricity; plucked green-backed beetles from the pasture's dungheaps to drop into cloudy bottles of serum. Titch baffled me. Never had I seen a mind so afire. In the field he was all eyes, all nose, all knifelike fingers plunging into dirt. He would come away black-tongued, his teeth tinged green from tasting grass and soil. He scampered along ledges, climbed halfway up peeling trees, once walked full-clothed into the ocean to snatch up a rare crab, his shirt ballooning out in the tide. And at each new discovery his eyes would narrow to slits. One afternoon he told me to open my palm, and onto it he dropped a minuscule blue lizard, its heart pulsing through its sides, a bright spot of life in my fist.

He did not ever mistreat me. But it was no kindness; for I knew this must all end, that I would be returned to the cane fields and their brutality someday. And so I did not allow myself to grow comfortable, but instead scrambled after thermometers tossed in the grass, gathered his dropped scopes, carefully folded leaves into the long wooden box he called his vasculum, feeling each evening only relief that I had not been punished.

What he thought of his brother's punishments of the other slaves, he never said. He sometimes stood peering out at the distant cane, watching the machetes flashing against the blue of the sky, his face tired but his eyes tense. If what he saw troubled him, he never spoke of it, would simply return to gathering specimens or making calculations. Only once did he venture any comment to me. We were passing through the field's western edge when an overseer struck the field hand Mary sharply in the face with a rusted prod. It was as though a breeze had passed over her cheek, so still did she hold her body as the blood leaked from her mouth. Titch took this in with tight eyes, staring a long while. I stared too, filling with a slow, remembered sense of panic. Then in a voice so quiet I could scarcely hear it, he said, "My god."

That evening, when the master came to take a port with him, I could hear their voices rising sharply from behind the doors of the study. I stood quietly some distance away, waiting to be summoned. Their voices were vicious and hissing, and I could hear the master complaining of a lack of understanding in his brother. Then all fell silent. The doors opened and, listing slightly, his eyes furious, the master went away.

IF TITCH KEPT one store in plenty in his lodgings, it was paper. He was a kind of maniacal proprietor of papers, and would return from Bridge Town some afternoons with large crates packed full of it. And so, there being no short supply, he provided me a new ream each week, and a fine black drawing lead, and instructed me to practise my letters. I would retire to my room, my stub of a candle burning down, and in the vague orange pool of light I began, then, to draw.

I felt something vital, some calming thing, go through me as I worked. Almost from the first it seemed a wonder to me, less an act of the fingers than of the eyes. I drew whatever I had at hand, and studied the ways shadows created a sense of weight, working without method or training. And yet I was careful to roll the finished drawing into a narrow cone each night, and to hold it over the flame, that it might burn down to ash. For I feared to think what my master might do, to learn of my disobedience.

But no secret can be kept for long. It is one of the truths of this world.

One evening Titch intruded upon my labours just as I was holding a page to the candle flame. Frowning irritably, he asked, "Why do you waste that paper, Washington? Your letters cannot be so wretched as that. Let me see."

My heart was in a twist. Titch, with his sunburnt face, his hawkish nose peeling, slowly opened my soft fist. I did not resist him. And there it was: the sunlight-speckled wings of a butterfly we had observed earlier that day.

Titch stared at the picture.

"I sorry, Titch, sir," I mumbled, terrified.

Titch did not look at me.

"Cassius blue," he said quietly. "But did you really draw this, Washington? God alive. Rarely have I seen nature so faithfully rendered." He peered down at me, looking almost stricken. "You are a prodigy, truly."

My face flushed with heat, and I looked quickly away.

The following afternoon, as we set out into the canopy of trees to examine a small wooden cage he had built for snails, he paused and drew me up short. He reached into his burlap satchel and fetched the packet of drawing leads, the carefully bound illustration boards. "I nearly forgot," he said, with deep seriousness in his voice. "Here is the lot. Do not break them. You will be the chief illustrator from now on. Be faithful to what you see, Washington, and not to what you are supposed to see. Do you understand me?"

The hot rim of the bucket I sat on was biting into my thighs, and I stood, nodding—though I did not comprehend the full weight of his meaning in those days.

Later that evening we retired to the verandah, the fading light beyond the railing softening the green of the fields. Titch had brought with him a stack of several volumes. "What do we feel like this evening? *The History and Practice of Aerostation*? The *Airopaedia*? *Physische Geographie*? I have a few here on marine zoology, if you care to read about aquatic animals. And here are two novels. What about Rabelais, this one—this one is downright ghastly. Yes, this, let us read this."

I had the sense, as I often did, that he was speaking to himself and not to me, and so I did not answer. He pulled two chairs close together, setting a finger-smudged goblet of claret on his side table and a glass of mango juice on mine. He placed into my outstretched hand the dreaded Rabelais.

How little sense those words made to me. I hated those sessions. But I will never forget the feeling of paper in my hands those first months, rough, an unfamiliar thing, like compressed dust. The wonder of it. I would finger the pages, and out would come an abrupt, medicinal smell, like a package from an apothecary's.

On that evening, Titch settled down facing me, reading the letters upside down. "What does this say? We saw this word only yesterday."

I stared wretchedly at the page, its tiny black letters like the awful hothouse nurse's stitches.

"Only try," said he.

I looked at the black blobs, I cast my mind back. "Es-try," said I.

"Nearly, nearly. Only slow it down. Es-tu-a-ry."

"Es-tu-a-ry."

He sat swiftly back, a pleased frown on his face. "How you have surprised me these last weeks, Washington. Your mind. I had not expected it."

It did not then occur to me to question why he had chosen me, if he did not believe me capable of learning; instead I heard only the praise, and I found the edge falling off my fear, so that I could finally hear his questions for what they were, inquiries only, and sometimes I could even answer without stammering.

It was not to last. Titch closed the book over his hand to mark the page and sat with a dim frown on his face. "Who was that large serving woman at dinner with you, that night I first had you called in? I cannot recall her name."

I paused, suddenly wary.

"Come now," he said sternly. "You must know her name. The big woman. The one with the broken nose. The two of you were very familiar, I watched you both all night."

"Kit," I finally murmured. "Big Kit."

"Big Kit. And who is she to you?"

"Sir?" I said, flustered.

"She is your friend, is she not?"

I paused, my face hot. The weeks had passed, and still I'd had no covert words from her, no quiet message through the master's house slaves when they came on their errands, nor from the field hands when I passed them in the long, cool grasses. I felt abandoned by her, cut cold, and I was both wounded and desperately embarrassed.

"Yes, sir, my friend," I said finally, furrowing my brow. "She like what a mother would be, had I one."

There was a pause. "You must miss her."

I kept my gaze on my lap.

"Well. Well." He cleared his throat decisively, giving me time to collect myself. Then he opened the book again. "What are our lives but a series of farewells and returns, no? Now. Sound this one out, this here. Good."

Did I miss Big Kit, did I feel her absence keenly, did I lament my loss of her?

When I closed my eyes, what I felt was the cool weight of her hand on my face in the darkness. The thumbnail on her left hand was yellow and cracked like a seashell, and she had a habit of curling that thumb in against her palm, so that it scratched against my cheek. Her voice was low and throaty, and she had the strange West African manner of lowering her tone at the ends of her sentences, as if she were reaching some fine and wise truth. She would clear her throat between bites as we ate, and there were those who hated this, but I laughed at it when I was very little. She would always hold out the last scoop of her breakfast to me and I would eat it from her hand, like a tamed creature. This would make her grin. She was earthy and powerful and would relieve herself before me without embarrassment. She cut her hair very short with a dulled knife. Her ears were misshapen from years of heavy ornaments in Dahomey. She bore seven scars on her abdomen from seven different spears. There was a gap between her two front teeth that the air whistled through when she laughed. But she did not often laugh. What I knew was that a day would come when she would no longer stand to be enslaved, and on that day she would slaughter many before she carried me off to freedom.

7

Morning rose in a white blaze on the horizon. I stood on the porch with Titch before breakfast, studying the pale wash of sky, recognizing in its haze a day that would only grow hotter.

Titch saw what I saw; he felt the heat as I felt it. And yet he said to me, without turning his face from the boiling sun: "Today we shall climb Corvus Peak, Washington."

I regarded him, waiting. He extended a single insect-like arm and pointed at the haze of Corvus Peak in the distance, its flat grey top. Most great houses were built on their plantation's highest point, but that would have proved impossible here at Faith, on Corvus Peak, which was really a small, steep mountain with very little surface area. At dusk it was often feverishly swarmed by rooks—thus its name. To us field hands, who never ventured there, it was a fearsome watchtower, a place the overseers could go to view our every move from the skies. It terrified us.

After breakfast, as we collected various implements and measuring devices, Titch explained that he meant for us to survey the terrain as a place to assemble and launch his mysterious Cloud-cutter. I glimpsed what I now knew was eagerness in his ruddy, bright-eyed face. I held my tongue, expressing neither my fear of Corvus Peak nor warning of the day's coming heat.

We trudged out into the wide, sun-scorched fields. Titch wore loose-fitting trousers and a white linen shirt beneath a light coat. We both carried several packs strapped across our shoulders. I carried the precious wooden vasculum at my hip. The path to the base of Corvus Peak skirted the fields and then led inland through scrub and rough forest, before losing itself in the scree and dry rocks of the mountain itself. Blades of tall grass hissed at our knees. As we walked, I glimpsed in the distance machetes flashing in the heat. I tried to pick out Big Kit from all the flaring motion, but it was impossible.

In the trees the heat eased, though the insects began to bite. We walked waving our hands and slapping at our necks. Here it was less a path than a trampled line of broken bushes. Titch tied off a green ribbon on the trunks of several trees, though he did not explain his purpose. The hour passed. At last it seemed we were moving uphill; the trees thinned, and the heat started to press its awful weight upon us again. The air at the rocky base of the hill was warm, fungal, smelling of rotting grass. Here we paused, Titch handing me a vessel of warm water tasting of wood, and we ate several hard crackers. Then we rose, speaking little, and began to climb. From this low vantage Corvus Peak appeared little more than a rocky, brush-strewn cliff face. I could not see the great height of it rising beyond.

We scrambled at first rather easily, our footing sure. I followed Titch, watching his footholds, testing my weight before continuing. The dirt was loose and shaled. It poured down around our ankles at each step. Sometimes, when we passed an odd stand of grass, or some clot of small leaves, Titch would call for me to gather them up, crush them into the vasculum, and I would do so, grateful for the rest it afforded. Otherwise he did not talk, absorbed in his own plans. But I was not much frightened of his silences now. I folded small yellow flowers into the vasculum's carved cells, glancing up to watch him plunge a thermometer into the moist earth, squinting against the wind at the rising mercury.

"Thirty-eight point seven," he muttered, frowning. "Let us continue."

What had been loose ground only moments earlier turned suddenly steep. We were scrabbling now on hands and knees, clutching at the crumbling scree, the cases slapping and clattering on our backs. I slipped and fell back several times, Titch pausing and twisting to peer down at me, and we continued. Then an outcropping of rock I set my foot against gave out; the weight of the vasculum dragged me sidelong, and I felt my hands loosen. I plunged hard down some five feet, colliding with a flat bench of rock.

I lay gasping, the breath knocked from me. I pushed myself upright to touch the sting of blood on my lip, my cheek. My shirt was torn; my knees were bleeding. I was frightened that I had broken Titch's precious vasculum, and I immediately began struggling with the strap. In the air beyond, a flock of water birds rose as one, their wings black against the sky.

Titch climbed carefully back down to where I kneeled on the ground.

"Nothing is broken," I said, anxious, holding up the vasculum that he might see.

"It is your bones I am the more concerned about." Titch crouched beside me, slapped the dust from my shoulders. His skin smelled of mint. "There are less painful ways to test Newton's second law." With his thin fingers he reached into the chest pocket of his frock coat and drew out a red silk handkerchief. He leaned in to dab at my cheek. Through the tear in my shirt he glimpsed the mottled sear of the *F* branded into my chest. He frowned.

"We there, nearly?" I asked, in part to draw his attention away.

His voice was quiet, soft. "You are growing tired?"

"No, Titch."

He regarded me. "It is some way yet, Washington. You would like to go back?"

"No, Titch, sir. I am well, truly. We keep going."

He squinted against the sun, slack-faced, his own breathing dogged. The skin under his lower lip pimpled with sweat. The thin scar that ran the length of both his cheeks had gone bright red, like a line of blood.

I began to get to my feet, but he put a hand on my wrist, shook his head.

"I fell climbing Chimborazo, in the Andes," he said. "That will mean nothing to you. It is a grand volcano, perhaps the grandest. Twenty-one thousand feet. So high that it is in snow year-round. It was a foolish ascent, we were none of us prepared. I had climbed in the Pyrenees two years earlier and even then had nearly fainted from altitude sickness. But a theory was circulating then that such sicknesses did not affect one in the southern hemisphere."

He paused, and we sat in the heat a long moment.

"What is snow?" I asked.

"Something you need never know." He smiled down at me. "It is frozen water, which falls from the sky like rain. It is very cold and treacherous underfoot."

"You fell in it."

"We were above fourteen thousand feet when our porters abandoned us. There were legends about the fog and the cliffs of

Chimborazo. We divided the instruments between us, and kept going. At certain points we were obliged to climb on our hands and knees, so thin were the paths. The blood vessels burst in our eyes, our gums were bleeding. Thibodeau, poor man, could not keep even water down. Jorge went blind with headache. It was then I slipped: I just fell, and fell, and kept falling. I managed to brace myself against an outcropping and stop the fall. A broken collarbone: that was the sum of it. It was decided we should all turn back." He smiled. "Corvus Peak should prove slightly less challenging."

Titch ran a long, thin hand across the back of his neck; it came away slick with sweat. I stared up at the haze of sky, my eyes narrowed in the brightness.

"From the cold to the heat," Titch said quietly. He got to his feet.

"Titch, wait." I opened a burlap sack filled with oversized plant specimens and drew out two fistfuls of stringy palm leaves. Titch looked in gentle perplexity at me. I held both hands high.

"Put these in your hat. It will help."

"In my hat? It will help with what?"

"The heat, sir. Titch. The heat."

He looked at me some seconds, half in thought. Then he upended the hat from his sweat-darkened head and began to line the crown with the leaves.

WE REACHED THE flat red expanse of Corvus Peak's top sometime beyond late afternoon.

But it was not flat; it extended in rough, broken slabs, all of it covered in a long, yellow, burnt grass that lay flat in the hot wind. There were no trees.

Oh, how different the world did look from that height. Imagine it: my whole life I had lived on that brutish island and never had I seen its edges, never had I seen the ocean in its vastness, the white breakers rolling in upon the beaches. Never had I seen the roads, with their tiny men and tiny horses, the roof of Wilde Hall winking in the light. The island fell away on all sides, green, glittering. There were birds in the grasses of Corvus Peak, and as I walked they would rise in a wave of song, scattering into the sky. The sun was already descending, the shadows lengthening beyond us. I walked to the southern cliff edge and stared at the glittering blue ocean, its pricks of light there like thousands of cane-knives. I joined Titch where he stood on the eastern edge. In the dusty light I saw the manicured fields of Faith Plantation, white lines cut into the earth. I stood shaken, confused by the incontestable beauty.

"We must not linger, Washington," Titch said, as though unmoved by the spectacle. "Lest we find ourselves climbing back down in darkness."

He strode back to where we had set our instruments down and fumbled with a sack. He waved the folio and the leads at me.

"Come now," he cried. "I want you to draw what you see. The topography is most important. Draw it from several different vantages."

Titch withdrew the longest measuring rod from his satchel. Pacing to and fro like a penned animal, he began muttering, scratching down distances. "Twenty paces by seventeen. Yes, yes indeed," said he to himself. "This will do very well. A rise of sixteen inches at the south corner and a drop of three inches at the north. Fair ground. She will launch perfectly."

But as I surveyed the terrain, a slow feeling was growing in me, a feeling I could not account for. I watched Titch at his exertions. And as I began to draw what I saw with a clean accuracy, I realized I was troubled by the enormous beauty of that place, of the jewel-like fields below us, littered as I knew them to be with broken teeth. The hot wind snapped at my papers, and in a kind of ghostly sound beneath this I thought I heard the cry of a baby. For the few women who gave birth here were turned immediately back into the fields, and they would set their tender-skinned newborns down in the furrows to wail against the hot sun. I craned out at the fields; I could see nothing. Far out at sea, a great flock of seagulls rose and turned, the late afternoon light flaring on the undersides of their wings.

8

TITCH COULD NOT BEGIN HIS EXPERIMENT WITHOUT ONE last element, he said.

"Workers, Washington," he explained to me. "Carriers, draggers, lifters, haulers, strong arms and strong wrists. We cannot carry the apparatus on our own, can we?"

And so we found ourselves in the entrance of Wilde Hall, quietly sweating. The air smelled of tea leaves, as if the house rugs had been recently cleaned. Titch had grown impatient; I watched him pace the scuffed parquet, the wood creaking faintly under his steps. He would then return to me and pause to lay a soft, tentative hand on my shoulder. His eyes kept drifting to the far corridor. Time seemed to slow, distend around us.

I do not know how long we waited. At last a silhouetted figure flitted distantly across a corridor. Titch called out to it.

His voice seemed to drift off into the shadows. There came a pause, then Gaius materialized from some unseen place, his uniform crisp as an English envelope. Seeing him, I thought he must possess more bones than the average man, so full of knots and angles was he. I imagined I could hear the light crack of his joints as he approached.

His fine, hard face stared up at Titch, betraying nothing.

"What is the holdup, man?" said Titch, his face red and tense. "We have waited fifteen minutes now without explanation. Or refreshment. Is my brother unwell?"

"No, sir."

Titch snorted. "Well?"

"I did not know you were here, sir. I daresay Master Erasmus has not known of it, sir. Have you been received?"

"Would I be standing here if I had? Where is he?"

Gaius glanced at me, and for some seconds it seemed he did not know me. How did I appear to him now, after all these weeks away with Titch—had I changed at all? He gave no indication. I longed to inquire after Big Kit, but it was not possible. Abruptly, Gaius gave me a terse, almost invisible nod with his chin. To Titch, he said, "Master Erasmus is regrettably occupied this afternoon. We have been instructed to inform any callers that—"

"I am no caller," Titch snapped. "I am his brother. Remind him for me."

"Sir," said Gaius, with a deferential dip of his head.

"Tell him if he does not greet us, he will very much regret his next dinner with me."

"Very good, sir," said Gaius.

But he had not moved, and stood still with his face averted. I understood he did not wish to risk the master's wrath. A long silence passed.

"Oh, hang this," Titch muttered. "Where is he? Is he upstairs? Come along, Washington."

He strode from the reception hall deeper into the house. I jogged along behind him, past a sitting room heavy with velvets, the chairs undersized and delicate, the sideboards monstrous with detailed scrollwork.

We descended a wide, curving staircase and emerged into a corridor half-filled with shadow. At a small table against one wall stood a girl with a stringy rag in her fist, wiping at a blackened candlestick. I did not at first recognize her, with her newly softened posture, but then she turned, and I saw the beige richness of her skin, the strong cheekbones. It was Émilie, her face framed by the crisp white bonnet hovering like crumpled paper upon her hair. She paused at the sight of me, then shyly lowered her eyes.

My face grew hot and I glanced instinctively down, and that is when I saw it: her rounded belly, pressing against the starched fabric of her scullery whites.

I could not keep the shock from my face; I stared and stared. It was a common-enough occurrence at Faith for a woman to be taken with child, though actual births were rare, given the conditions in which the mothers toiled. But this I had never expected, Émilie being just eleven, and beautiful and inviolate and God's own angel. It was a slap to me that the father might be any man on the land, even the master himself. I watched Émilie's stilled hands on the brass candlestick, and I felt a wrenching inside, a sadness so bracing I had to look away.

Titch sensed nothing of our discomfort; he was impatient to get on with his day. "Well?" he demanded. "Where is he?"

Émilie turned and glanced very deliberately behind her at a door left ajar. A blade of light fell from it. Inside was a small, narrow room, a laundry, stinking bitterly of soda and wet wool. And at the far end of it, facing us but hunched over a creaking table, stood Erasmus Wilde.

He was wielding a large, black, hissing artifact, built of iron, leaning his weight into it. I saw, as we neared, that he was pressing it across a blue cotton shirt. It was then he glanced up.

But how astonishing to see him like that, engaged in so low a labour, his face strangely attractive in its distraction, the full bottom lip, the eyes colourless as a glass of water. I glimpsed a sort of brittle prettiness in his features, a delicacy.

But then the master smiled a sudden, tight smile, and the moment passed. "Christopher," he said softly. "You have been waiting."

"I have."

The master shrugged. With two hands he lifted the iron monstrosity to one side of the shirt. "I instructed that Gaius boy to dismiss you. I ought to crush his skull and find better help."

"He did warn us you were occupied," Titch said, wrinkling his forehead. "Do not fault him. I had not realized how pressing your business was."

"Ah, very droll," said Master Erasmus. But he did not smile. "You are surprised to see me so engaged?"

"Nothing surprises me," said Titch. "It is my iron constitution."

"Wonderful," said the master. "Amusing."

We stood, no one speaking for a long moment. Steam gasped from the iron's underside.

"Well?" said Titch.

"I am waiting to see if your wit is quite worn itself out. Now what is it you want of me?"

"Not laundering, certainly."

"That is what your nigger calf is for," the master said pleasantly. "Why else did I lend him?"

Titch nodded, raised his eyebrows in mock surprise. "Now

you have struck on my very purpose. I am here because I require more hands."

"Indeed," said the master. "For your balloon contraption, I assume?"

"My Cloud-cutter, yes. It is as you foresaw."

The master tipped the black-faced iron up and spat onto its surface; it gave but the faintest hiss. The smell of rusted metal filled the room. "You have killed my heat," he said distractedly.

"I ask but fifteen men only. I will accept strong women among them, if it would serve you better. Fifteen workers, Erasmus. And I will need them only for the time it takes to transport and assemble the cutter on Corvus Peak. A week. Perhaps two."

"Corvus Peak?"

"Its altitude will do nicely, I think."

"Corvus Peak is no small expedition, little brother."

"Which is why I ask for the additional labour."

The master pursed his lips. "This Cloud-cutter, as you call it—remind me, now. It is rather dangerous, is it not?"

Titch paused. "Dangerous?"

"Mm."

"Anything is dangerous without proper precautions. Riding in a carriage is dangerous."

"Hardly to the same degree."

"It will be tethered at each ascent, Erasmus. And only myself and the boy will go up in it. I expect the risk should prove minimal to any others."

"The boy is my property." This the master said without even a glance at me. "Did you not tell me once this contraption could prove explosive?"

"Previous models have, yes," said Titch, a wariness entering his voice. "Not my own design, not this design. The gas is relatively stable, so long as it is carefully handled."

"And you trust the niggers to handle it so."

"The men will be supervised, brother."

The master spread his empty arms wide, shrugged. "Regretfully, it cannot be done," he said simply. "I cannot lose fifteen niggers. The field hours alone make it impossible. No."

Titch did not appear surprised. "How many?"

"How many what?"

"How many men can you spare?"

"I tell you it is considerable revenue that would be lost. I could part perhaps with one."

"Not sufficient. Did you not say that while I was here I would have use of some of your resources for my experiments? Did you not say that?"

The master grunted. "I did not mean to the detriment of profitability."

"Profitability," Titch scoffed.

Master Erasmus made a sharp gesture at me. "Watch your tone."

"Do you believe them capable of understanding, then?"

"I believe them capable of mischief. I believe them capable of malice."

The bolts of the ironing table creaked plaintively as the master began to fold his shirt. In the dust-swarmed room I could suddenly hear the high, nervous humming of Émilie at work in the outer hall.

"Twelve, then," said Titch.

"Two niggers, no more."

"Ten men."

The master gave a long, tired exhale, as if struggling to keep his patience. "We are not exchanging apples in Madame Aileen's orchards, Christopher. We are not seven years old."

"Ten men and women, Erasmus, and I shall ask nothing more of the field labour."

"Ten niggers, then. But only at the end of their workday."

But that is our time, I thought. The sole waking hours that belong to us. I remembered those short hours as the calmest time of day in the huts. We all of us would gather to eat, tell stories.

Titch was shaking his head. "That is un-Christian, brother, the Negroes need their rest like anyone. What good would it do them to work for me in the dark? There would be injuries. And what good would they be to you during the day, tired from working twice, half of them injured—"

"And so?"

"Nine, then. But relieved entirely from other duties for the duration of my project."

"You seem rather sanguine about how hard you will be working them yourself, Titch. Where is your famous conscience now?"

"I will be answerable to that. Will you lend them?"

"Five, was it?"

"Nine."

The master sighed. He frowned at his iron, pausing a long while. He seemed to be slowly recalling something. Clearing his throat, he said, "Yes, nine, so be it. You are nothing if not persistent, little brother. Listen to me, there is a matter of real importance I have been meaning to raise with you."

Titch cocked his head, peering down at his brother. He waited.

"Five evenings ago I received a letter postmarked Kingston. What business could be coming from Kingston, said I. Well, it seems cousin Philip could be coming from Kingston. He threatens us with his imminent arrival."

"Philip?" Titch's eyes narrowed, and he fell abruptly silent. It was as if he had been told a visitation were upon him, as though a ghost, not a man, would appear. "Philip is here? Whatever for? Philip. My god."

"Indeed."

"Did he write of his purpose? He would not have sailed for pleasure."

"Nothing gives him pleasure. I'm sure we shall learn of it soon enough."

"Philip in Kingston." Titch closed his eyes, a faint line of worry rising between them. He shook his head. "And this is the first you are hearing of it? It is a mighty risk he takes, waiting so long to inform us of his arrival."

"Ah." The master smiled a cruel smile. "He did write some weeks ago, but I did not believe his intentions serious. It appears I was mistaken. He did not move so fast when we were boys."

Titch frowned at his brother, said nothing.

"Fat as a Liverpool wharf rat, he was." The master laughed. "And so dour, so morose. Good god, I hope the poor man doesn't attempt to kill himself. I would rather he killed me—I'd no longer have to suffer his moods."

"He comes by it honestly, in any case," Titch said a little sharply.

"Well," said the master. "I shall require you to collect him in Bridge Town when he arrives."

"Consider it done. Is that all?"

"And I shall require you to lodge him."

Titch stood blinking some moments. "Have you not a single room to spare among the five wings of Wilde Hall?"

"They are all under repair, brother."

"I see."

"He will eat and eat and brood and eat and he will be sick every morning. I have not space enough for the drama."

"Erasmus."

"I could always lodge him with the niggers," the master grinned.

Titch did not smile at that. "He is to stay how long?"

"I am told three months. I do not believe it."

"He will not last a fortnight," said Titch thoughtfully. "Deliver me those nine men and you can consider the matter settled. I will welcome Philip with a full plate and bottles of wine."

"He does love a spectacle, our cousin," said Master Erasmus, distractedly running a hand over his pressed shirt. "Now, may I continue with my day unmolested?"

THE FOLLOWING MORNING Erasmus Wilde delivered, as promised, nine wasted slaves, his sickliest possessions.

Titch began the venture by granting them a day's rest, offering them a simple meal of maize and cod and clean, cooled water. Then, the next morning, he set them the task of cutting a workable trail through to the base of Corvus Peak, and only then did they begin to carve out a path halfway up the scree. A rough pulley system was constructed and set into place for hauling the instruments and heaviest objects the last of the distance to the top. Titch now spent his days among them. I would see them always from the corner of my eye as I worked at Titch's various ongoing experiments. I would be fishing worms in a field, my nape stinging with sun, and I would see by the side of my eyes women and men flickering on the slope, carrying on their heads rolls of wicker, baskets of cloth, newly forged iron bolts that winked against the blueness of the sky. And though they were far away, I imagined I could hear them talking, the scorch of their bronzed voices. I thought of Big Kit. But she was not among them.

Of the nine, most of whom knew me and who averted their eyes from my person, I spoke only to James Madison, "Black Jim" as he was known. But when I asked after Big Kit, if she had no secret missives for me, he stared silently back with dark, pebble-like eyes. I understood then that to his thinking I had been swallowed whole by the white man's world as even Gaius and Émilie were not. My eyes burned with the shame and anger of his rejection. The pain of it was bracing.

Slowly the trail was cut, and the strange, monstrous parts of the Cloud-cutter began to be transported towards Corvus Peak. I watched as heavy crates were hauled away by four people at a time, as sacks filled with iron ingots were thrown over shoulders. There were long ropes of varying thickness, and boxes of glass instruments that could not be dropped, and tarpaulins and oilcloths and great twists of fabric. I observed it all in wonder.

But all work ceased on the morning of Mister Philip's arrival, for Titch did not trust his workers beyond earshot. The night before, Titch had eaten in preoccupied silence, and then, exhaling harshly, glanced at me in surprise and asked me to dust and make up an extra room. I felt a sudden dread; I had feared from the first that this odd, peaceable domesticity with Titch must end. I understood now, no matter his cousin Philip's temperament, there would be less tolerance and more severity with another white master in the house. I felt a rope of fear uncoil in my stomach.

We set out in the carriage after breakfast, Titch insisting I ride inside with him. "You do not take up very much space, Washington, it is all right. Do close the door firmly." He wore on his face the pinched gaze of a man meeting a punishment directly.

"Is he so *very* bad, Titch?" I asked.

Titch smiled in alarm. "Bad? Oh, Washington, have you been troubled all this while? Heavens no. Philip is a fine sort. A little melancholy, it must be said—well, *very* melancholy—but on the whole a rather sporting fellow."

Titch fell to staring out the window at the passing fields; he did not appear entirely at ease. The carriage bumped and rattled along the roadway. He fixed his green eyes on me. "We three, Erasmus, Philip and myself, we played together and entered society in the same years. But a distance grew up between us as our lives and duties took over."

Titch's shoulders swayed as the carriage rounded a corner and began a slow descent. The sun was baking in through the windows. They did not open.

"Philip is very decent, very decent." He smiled to himself, a distracted, sad smile. "For a long time now he has refused to shake hands, so frightened is he of being touched. Molecules, you see. He believes there are molecules about that will make him ill. My mother is the same way. No, Philip is lovely, on the whole. Only somewhat low-spirited, perhaps, and with a hearty appetite. If I hesitate, I suppose it is only from a general dread of company. We all of us wish for it, in our solitude, but on the eve of a great visit, we shudder."

He drew out a slow breath, and in the silence there was the clatter of hooves on the dirt road. It was a beautiful day, the light blaring out over the rustling crops.

"Mine is a strange family, Washington, stranger than most, I think." Titch clasped his hands in his lap, his hat upended on the seat beside him. His dark hair was mussed. I glanced out at the passing slave huts, dirt-hued and roofless. "I think I mentioned that Mother and Father are not well-suited. It is not the fate of my class to marry for affinity. We all have our duties, and must fight for our freedoms." He looked at me, and blushed. "Well." He was silent a moment. "My father takes a mechanical view of the world. He believes that man can know everything there is to know if only he can unlock nature's secrets. And he has discovered much, it's true, but the one thing that has defied all his powers of inquiry is my mother's heart. He simply cannot begin to understand her. This I have much sympathy for, as I cannot fathom her either. She is almost irrationally headstrong. She claims it is because she was born in the north of the country, where the rain is very cold and does not let up all year."

I tried to imagine the cold north of Titch's country. I could not. "Is that where your cousin is from also?"

"Ah, indeed, no—Philip is my father's cousin's boy, our second cousin. For many decades now their branch of the family has resided in London. They keep townhouses in Grosvenor Square."

"He is from London," I repeated.

Titch reached forward, squeezed my shoulder. "It does you no credit to fret so, Washington. Philip is a gentle-enough character. You shall see."

+ + +

As the carriage entered Bridge Town, I sat up higher on the bench, pressing my brow to the hot glass. I had not once visited its streets; such a privilege was granted only to select slaves, never a field cutter. I stared in wonder. So many buildings. Their wooden slats silvered from decades of hurricane weather, and before them, pale, brightly dressed people bustled through the streets. Swells of dust boiled up off the roads. Horses trotted past, heads low in the heat, flies swarming. We clattered past a sailor on a street corner blowing through some bizarre knot of pipes, while beside him a second danced along to his own fiddle, his fingers flying like shadows over the strings. We stopped in the sudden traffic; through the carriage oozed the stink of overripe fruit carted in from the port, and of immense slabs of tuna starting to turn in the heat. At a passing market stall I glimpsed their fishy eyes, fissured with blood as they gawked on beds of cool leaves.

All this I wanted to remember, on that first trip into the town; all this I wanted to hold in my mind to draw later. The carriage rattled softly under us as the horses jogged across a kind of boardwalk. And then you could not help but see it, your eyes rising: there, above the hills of the town, among the dark trees, flashed an endless white swarm of enormous windmills. I leaned forward, pressing my hands against the glass.

"But you have seen windmills, Washington, powering your own sugar mills," Titch said, surprised at my interest. "I suppose it is that you have never seen so many all at once like this. Well, it is a monstrous spectacle."

Bridge Town seemed to extend forever, to my innocent eye. I kept trying to imagine the rooftops I had glimpsed from Corvus Peak, but could not do so. As we descended towards the water, I saw groves of lemons, limes, oranges. I glanced up. Gun batteries loomed over the entrance to the harbour. When at last we reached the wharf, Titch swung open the carriage door and unfolded himself down into the street. He set his hat carefully on his head.

"No need for you to brave this heat, René," he called to the driver. "I shall fetch my cousin myself."

Out he went into the throng of people, his elbows slightly raised the better to get by. I climbed down and brushed off the folding step to stand at the carriage door; it would not do to be seen waiting inside, seated like a master's son. I saw we had pulled up on the landward side of a wide wooden boardwalk. Piers, platforms and gangways ran alongside the harbour, great wooden vessels moored high overhead. Everywhere people called out, their voices bright and harsh; luggage thundered down gangplanks; sweating black porters hoisted above their heads crates of pale new wood. There was everywhere much colour, and great motion.

We waited. René stood with a hand on the harness, near the horses. He did not speak to me.

At last Titch was wending his way back through the crowds, his arm around the shoulders of a dark-haired man. I felt my heart flutter into my throat; my legs seemed to thrum. For though the man shared Titch's finely boned face, the same black hair and jade-coloured eyes, he was far thicker through the waist, and his face was set differently, so that he appeared flinty, and cautious. I did not like the look of him.

Behind them came two porters, rolling the visitor's large leather trunks. I stepped forward at once and began instructing them about how and where to set each on the carriage's roof. Titch's cousin took no notice of me, but stepped past and into the carriage, waving his hat before his face for the heat. The flies were biting. And I saw that while the man was portlier than Titch, he was by no measure enormous. All their talk of his eating had given me to think he'd be gargantuan. He was not even half of Big Kit's girth. His arms, awkwardly thin, folded oddly out from his body. A strange creature indeed.

I double-checked the knots to be certain the man Philip's baggage would not be lost during the dusty ride back to Faith Plantation. Then I scrambled back down and climbed up into the carriage. I swung the door shut with a satisfying bang.

Mister Philip stared. "Rides in here with you, does he?"

"Excuse me," said Titch, gesturing to me. "This is Washington. My assistant."

"Washington?" Mister Philip said with soft displeasure. "I'd rethink that name if I were you, Titch. Makes a mockery of the poor creature."

"I did not choose it, Philip. It is his name."

"Well, rename him, then, for goodness' sake. However did he get such a name?"

"My uncle Richard, I imagine," said Titch. "Richard Black. Indeed, most of the slaves were given fairly benign names, but others seem to have been christened rather queerly. René, after Descartes, Immanuel, after Immanuel Kant, Émilie, after Émilie du Châtelet."

I jolted softly at her name. So many weeks had passed since I'd last glimpsed sight of her at Faith that only now, in the cloistered warmth of our carriage, did I realize I had given up searching. She was clearly no longer at Wilde Hall. Where had she gone, then, so heavy with child? Was the baby now born? I understood I would likely never find out, for those who disappeared from Faith were never, not ever, seen again.

"Richard Black," said Mister Philip, shaking his head. "Heavens. The man was a lunatic." Mister Philip flitted his green eyes at a lady passing outside, her bonnet reeling back from her face in a slap of wind. He glanced suddenly back at me. "What a smell in here."

"It smells fine," frowned Titch.

Mister Philip shrugged, crossing his legs, shifting his bulk. "I did always find that lot insufferable, the Blacks. All their hymns and sermons. I should sooner suffer a charnel house than visit good Felicia Black's dinner table yet again."

"I thought them rather clever. Bookish branch of the family."

"Well, you can keep them."

"Heaven keeps them now."

"Heaven does. Making better use of the afterlife, one hopes. Lord knows they wasted their time down here. Cornelius Black wore out his miserable knees in their little chapel."

"Blasphemer," smiled Titch.

"Ought to have worn out his wife's knees, that would have been heaven. Or holier. If you take my meaning."

"Good god, man!"

"Come now. You wouldn't argue your aunt Amelia hadn't a heat to her cheeks, would you?"

Titch was very studiously examining the dust on the rattling pane. "She was very handsome, yes."

"Died looking like a sack of chicory, what. But in her prime? Oh." Mister Philip closed his eyes theatrically. "Your failing, good cousin, was always a lack of appreciation for the world's bounty. You would rather suffer the grotesque than know beauty first-hand."

Titch laughed. "The grotesque?"

"All your scientific nonsense. It's a pity, really."

"Some pity. My father and I are satisfied enough."

"Yes," said Mister Philip, and something shifted in his face. It was difficult to say, but he looked almost guilty. "Well. In any case. I see you are in fine health. Erasmus is well too, I hope? I am ever so eager to see him again."

"Erasmus has business at another plantation. Indeed, he will be the whole week away, even two, perhaps. He truly did want to be present at your arrival, but I understood it was a matter of some urgency."

"I see," said Mister Philip, and I thought I glimpsed a dim anxiety beneath his easy, relaxed smile. "Well." He was silent some moments. "Well."

Titch glanced from the window back to his cousin. "And how is my mother?"

Philip sighed. "You are sorely missed in Hampshire, Christopher. It took the poor lady an age to ferret out your whereabouts. Erasmus, apparently, sent along a letter. Said you'd gone soft-witted and chased him all the way to this godforsaken wasteland, instruments in tow. I cannot say she took it very well. Nearly went half-mad herself."

"So then she is fully there," Titch muttered, but a flush rose slowly in his cheeks. "But she is generally well?"

"Your mother is forever ailing and she will outlive us all, I daresay. Outlive England herself, perhaps."

Titch smiled. "A fine observation from you, man. Have you not her same fear of molecules?"

"It has passed," Mister Philip murmured, "the molecules."

We rolled onto Broad Street, and I raised my face to see a series of large hardwood cages, silvering and flaking in the sun. Within them, slaves sat or paced or rested their sun-sore faces against the bars. The ground at their feet was strewn with cast-off clothes and their own horrid waste, and drifting slowly by we could smell the obscene yellow reek of it.

Mister Philip did not ask about them. But I knew these to be runaways. The house slaves had often mentioned this makeshift street prison with a dark pleasure at having witnessed it. No man would raise his face, and I was relieved to catch no one's eye. I stared at a short, thickly built man, his muscles draped in stained rags. His face was expressionless, as though he had outlived his urges, or lost the very memory of desire. He might yet be retrieved by his master, and maimed, and allowed to live.

I flattened my palm against the sun-warmed pane, a dark apparition of a boy gliding by in his fine service linens.

"Such a dreary place," said Mister Philip, yawning against his fist. "I cannot imagine how you tolerate it."

I COULD NOT have described him so then, but Mister Philip was merely a man of his class, nothing more. His great passions were not passions but distractions; one day was but a bridge to the next. He took in the world with a mild dissatisfaction, for the world was of little consequence.

He was often, it is true, in a grey, grey mood. On these days he could be silent for hours, as if mulling over a problem of exquisite difficulty. He liked to walk the scrub hills with Titch on our collecting expeditions, but he would bring a shotgun, and attempt to hunt as we went. This shotgun was a source of some teasing from Titch, as Mister Philip took much finer care of it than even his own appearance. In dress he was expensive but hastily tossed together, always some button or string dangling. His gun and his stomach were his chief obsessions, and in the nurturing of these he was fanatical. He had little hunger but much appetite, and was thoughtful but decisive in his requests for dishes. He would eat fried plantain and sweet potatoes by the pound, would graze on salted cod and turtle stew. He ate cassava topped with raw oysters, marlin eyes stewed in hollandaise. He devoured glass after glass of mobbie, bowl upon bowl of custards. In the mornings he slept late; in the afternoons he would be found slumped in a cane rocking chair on the verandah of our quarters, a lemon water in his hand. He spoke little to me, beyond soft commands. But one day, as I sketched alongside Titch before a dish of Scotch bonnet snails, he glimpsed my drawing and, grunting, took the paper from me, holding it out in amazement.

"You have seen this, cousin?" he said.

Titch glanced up, smiling. "Washington has a rare gift, does he not?"

Mister Philip shook his head. "You have put ideas in a slave's head, Christopher. You should be more careful. No good ever came of it."

"You sound like Erasmus."

"I have read my Gibbon. You would do well to read it again."

Titch frowned. "The Romans did not collapse because their slaves learned to draw."

Mister Philip returned the paper to me. "Everything begins somewhere."

Despite his general mildness, I feared him, of course. He wandered the halls of Titch's residence with the lost expression of a ghost, his exquisite frock coats straining across his chest, the heat plastering his hair to his forehead.

"Boy," he would call softly to me in the evenings as I kneeled polishing the dark mahogany floors with coconut husks. I would freeze in the rope of light from the nearby window, feeling the shudder of his steps crossing the boards. He had never struck me, but the possibility floated between us like a thread of music. "You are not an artist when it comes to food," he said gently, like a disappointed father. "This night's chicken was not good. Too much salt, too much ginger, what. You must do better tomorrow."

I nodded, even as his dark form retreated.

As the days passed, however, I began to understand that he would not make blistering use of his fists, as the master would. In fact he seemed, on certain afternoons, to be startled by the sight of the labouring slaves, as if their shadows were a sudden darkness marring the picturesque island holiday he'd imagined for himself. "Well," he'd say somewhat cheerlessly, sounding strained, "no progress without blood, I suppose." Then he'd turn rigidly from the sight, as though a chill had entered him, and make his slow, considered way back to Titch's quarters.

Over the weeks, my fear of Mister Philip eased, though my wariness of him remained. Some nights, when the eating proved too much, Mister Philip would remove himself to the east-facing sitting room and collapse upon a chaise. On these occasions I would creep into the room with my leads and tattered sketchbook. There he'd lie, his mouth slackening back to reveal a dark-pink gullet, wheezing out the smell of sweet milk. And I would begin to draw his form, starting with the ferocious roots of his toes, stockingless and gnarled on the rug. Then I would go up, up, ending in the white, chick-like down at his temples.

These sketches were some of the softest I ever drew. True, I had done technically better ones, ones in which a flower looked so powdery it seemed the paper might break apart at a touch. But these secret etchings of the glutton were strangely vivid, underlit with a tenderness I did not understand. I showed them to no one, Titch least of all.

Each night in my room I tore them up, burned them piece by piece in the candle's flame.

9

AND SO THE WEEKS PASSED MUCH AS THEY HAD BEFORE, except that we had among us an unending hunger in the form of a living man. The master finally returned from his business across the island, but he came back ill and shivering, and shut himself away at Wilde Hall. When his newly arrived cousin and his brother came to call, they were turned gently away by Gaius. There were rumours of putrid fever, of the master's possible death. I prayed they were true.

My nightly readings with Titch continued, broken occasionally now by Mister Philip's brooding presence, and I struggled still to identify the words without difficulty. I could take only the most rudimentary dictation in the field, but Titch was pleased with my progress. I realized then that he had selected me with only the barest hope of my actual success, and seeing now my abilities, he felt happy, confirmed in his choice.

The men and women continued their labours on Corvus Peak, hauling the crates and lumber and ropes up the crumbling hill. We would inspect their progress daily, Mister Philip accompanying us in the heat some afternoons, Titch with a satchel of instruments slung over one shoulder, me with our provisions in tow. At last, on an infernal afternoon, all the pieces of the apparatus were collected in their entirety, finally ready for assembly.

Titch was in excellent spirits. He kept slapping at the back of his neck with a cloth he had brought for the task. "We shall have to celebrate, cousin," he called breathlessly back to Mister Philip. "Look at this sight." He turned grinning to me. "Wait until my father hears about this. He swore it could not be done." He placed a damp hand on my shoulder. "What a great venture lies in wait here."

"A blasted fool venture," gasped Mister Philip as he came over the crest.

There, on the top of Corvus Peak, lay dozens of crates and boxes and coils of rope. There was the bright wicker frame like an enormous toppled hat stand; a heap of odd beige cloth; rolls and rolls of new wood for the gondola, pale as skimmed butter. I crouched in the hot dirt, unslung our bag of provisions, began to massage my shoulder. All had been carefully arranged in a semicircle around the flattest expanse of the peak, and there, in the centre, lay the colossal rubberized mass of the aerostat itself. We had in the previous days carefully examined every inch of its surface, Titch and I, seeking any imperfection or possible leak. I did not, it is true, quite comprehend the nature of his Cloud-cutter, but I understood his directions well enough.

I shuffled closer to Titch, lowered my voice. "I do not doubt your father would be most impressed."

Mister Philip was standing with his hand at his chest, peering around him in mild interest. He mopped at his sweating face. "What do you imagine Erasmus would say to see all this mess?"

With a tight smile, panting softly, Mister Philip drifted off to examine the view from the western edge of the peak. Titch began pacing, muttering and frowning against the dreadful sun. It was a windless day, and up here the heat felt as clotted as smoke. He touched a black-streaked handkerchief to his glistening brow.

"The Arctic is a very great distance?" I said.

Titch walked some paces, and the light fell differently upon his body, so that he looked now dark against the glaring blue of the sky. "A very great distance, yes." He coughed. "Father is renowned for his specimen collection, most of which he donates to Montagu House." I could hear the stifled pride in his voice. "He is a Fellow of the Royal Society, you know, and the recipient of both the Copley Medal and the Bakerian lectureship. High, high honours."

Titch moved past me, kneeled beside the rubbery cloth. "This canopy we shall attach to that frame over there. From the bottom of the frame we shall hang our gondola, mounted with the navigational wings and oars."

"And they will keep it in the air."

"They will give it direction, allow it to steer its course. What will keep it in the air is the gas. The hydrogen."

I looked at him, curious. He had spoken very little about the hydrogen gas.

Titch was rooting through the light wooden parts of the frame, the rods clicking against each other like knuckles. I fingered the rigid fabric. The cotton had been coated in a thick rubber film, giving it the feel of something once alive, of corpse flesh.

"That is the envelope we shall fill with hydrogen gas. The gas, you see, is of lower molecular weight than the surrounding atmosphere, and that is what will allow for ascendancy." The skin at the edge of his hairline was purple as a bruise from the constant sun. "Here, look, shall I give you a demonstration? Philip!" he called out.

His cousin turned, raised a hand to shield his eyes.

"Shall I give you a demonstration of the gas?" Titch called.

Mister Philip waved a hand, trudged stolidly back over.

"You must wait over there," said Titch to his cousin. "And you, Washington, you wait there with him."

I joined Mister Philip some fifteen paces away, while Titch kneeled beside a large metal canister outfitted with levers.

Mister Philip turned slowly to me, as though it pained him to move in the heat. "Where are the sandwiches, boy?" he said.

"I beg your pardon, sir?" said I.

"The sandwiches. Where did you set them?"

I glanced back, towards where Titch was working with the hydrogen gas chamber. Some five feet from where he kneeled the provisions satchel lay in the dry yellow grass. Looking up at Mister Philip, I found him staring expectantly at me. I glanced at the fields below, the rows of bright cane, hearing the levers clink like a tray of rattling glasses. From this height the trees appeared spindly, like thread on the landscape. We had ascended Corvus Peak several times now, but each climb filled me with wonder all the same. I went at a quick half run towards the satchel, thinking I could collect it and be returned to Mister Philip before Titch was ready to begin his display.

But from behind me came a great whoosh, and I turned towards Titch in surprise, the air exploding suddenly in a glistening swarm, as if a cloud of glass bees had burst forth. Then my face was afire, and I was lifted and thrown back in the shuddering milk-white flash of light, my head striking the ground. A distant roaring filled my ears, a sound as of great wings beating the air.

Then all went silent and dark.

✦ ✦ ✦

How long did I remain in darkness? Little felt familiar to me, and I turned on my right side, my ribs aching. My breath was loud in my ears. I felt a cool pressure on my eyes; I could not open them.

Then I heard the sound of feet approaching, a door opening. I turned my face from side to side.

"Is this Dahomey?" I called out softly. "Are we there, Kit?"

There came a long silence.

"Kit?"

"Wash," said Titch, and I tensed. For a moment I feared I was between worlds, that my death had not been complete and I'd been left suspended and weightless, lost. "How are you feeling?" he continued, and I knew then I was unmistakably still at Faith, all of me, and that I had not died.

The bed buckled, and Titch shifted his weight. He did not talk, merely breathed there in the dark. Then, clearing his throat, he said, "I am afraid there was an unforeseen complication. I had supposed the altitude sufficiently poor in oxygen for a demonstration. I was wrong." And very softly, in halting language, he told of how he had released the hydrogen into the atmosphere, and how the air began to boil, and then a sharp blast hurled both of us clear. Titch's frock coat had caught fire, but he had scrambled to his knees and managed to shrug it free in time, suffering but the mildest of burns on his wrists and hands. Then he had looked across, his ears ringing, and seen me. It seems, in my confusion, I had turned to face the very brunt of the explosion.

"Your body," said he, quietly, "was mercifully unharmed."

I tried to speak, but paused, alarmed. The skin of my lips felt seamed shut, so that I could not open the right side of my mouth. I raised a tentative hand to my bandaged face.

"You are rather lucky. The explosion might have killed you."

I said nothing. Swallowing was painful.

"What were you standing so close for? I sent you back to observe with Philip. He was not harmed. You should have been with him. I sent you back, Wash."

And then I remembered Mister Philip, his desire to eat. I remembered the flash of light, the pain like a sunrise in my skull.

I could feel now a weight on my neck, a strange blunt numbness. When I turned my cheek, I noticed a damp spot on my pillow, pus or blood. I tried to wet my lips. "The sandwiches."

"What's that?" he said softly. "What did you say?"

I tried again to moisten my lips; they began to throb. "He asked me to fetch the sandwiches."

Titch was silent some moments. "I see."

I stilled my lips, hoping the pain would subside. It did not. With great difficulty, I said, "I want to see. I want to know what is there."

I heard Titch breathing quietly there above me, considering. "It is too soon. Be patient. Let it heal."

"Please, Titch."

He paused. "Wash," he said softly. "I should not."

"Please," I said, my voice breaking.

What did he hear in me then? More silence passed. Finally I felt him bend close and, with his rough fingers, begin to unwind the gauze.

Oh, how painful this was. Such a moment I will never in all my life forget. First the creaking of the pus-encrusted bandage, the catch of it on my raw flesh. Then the final unpeeling, the rush of light and air. My left eye winced at the brightness of the room.

But in the right I saw shadows, as if the bandage were only partially shifted.

I could see Titch's face, lined, sun-browned, his bright eyes creased and old. He gave me a weak smile. "Science has left its mark on you now, Wash. It has claimed you."

"I would like to see myself, Titch."

"I will not lie to you. It is a grave change."

"May I see?"

"You should wait."

"Titch."

He hesitated, then went out, returning some minutes later. He held the small mirror some six inches from my face, my image shivering there before me.

What a grotesque creature peered back at me. I raised a hand, and shuddered at the touch of my cheek. It felt like meat. The right side had been partly torn away. I could see into the flesh of my cheek, a strange white patch marbled with pink, like a fatty cut of mutton. Old black scabs edged the wounds, along with fresher ones, clots pale as boiled oatmeal. My right eye was full of blood. I could still see foggily by it, but the pupil looked lunar, bluish white. I saw it and thought of the raw, cursing eye of a duppy.

Titch cleared his throat. "I am told it will continue to heal. I am told it will improve with time." He took from his pocket a white handkerchief and wiped under my eye.

"I am crying?" I asked. I did not even feel it.

"The wound is weeping," he said gently. "That is all."

✦ ✦ ✦

I HAD BEEN wounded many times before, though none were so grievous as this. The last time it had been Big Kit herself who had done it.

It had happened during the cooler months, when her crab-yaws would flare up and she'd be taken off the great gang to toil with us weaker beings on the second gang. We were working the fields together when she accidentally cut me with the tip of her machete. I told her to be mindful.

Her eyes, with their curious orange colour, narrowed. "How that, boy?"

I swallowed. "Your knife, Kit. You clip my leg."

I remember the strange stillness in her face then. The driver was somewhere to the left of us, crying hoarsely out there. In the dry, hot field, a smell like burning sugar filled the air. Kit was standing with her head cresting the tops of the cane, staring down at me with a calm, wholly possessed expression.

My heart stuttered in my chest.

She took a heavy step forward; suddenly my breath was knocked from me, a vicious pain raged under my ribs. I staggered backwards, gasping, and hit the ground with my ears ringing. I could smell the heat radiating from the soil, tasted blood in my teeth. In the fierce sun I watched the shadows of the women pass over me, calling out to each other. Then, very slowly, I was lifted onto a wooden plank, and I felt myself being carried across the bright fields.

Three cracked ribs. Her kick had been that harsh, that swift. I refused to tell the overseers who had done it, and in this way Kit was spared. But the pain was immense and suffocating, and I was several nights in the hothouse before returning again to our huts.

She avoided my eye as I was led in, my chest still in bandages.

That evening, as I drifted into sleep, there came a touch at my face. I heard soft weeping, and realized with alarm it was Big Kit. She was running a cold palm across my forehead, whispering.

"Oh my son," I heard her say, over and over again. "My son."

I understood then that she had not meant to strike me so hard, and that my days away had pained her greatly. I closed my eyes, feeling the coolness of her skin on my brow.

10

The weeks crept past. Confined so long to my bed, an old ache rose in the ribs Kit had fractured; I kneaded them. My burnt face began to knot and blacken, and I could see more by my right eye. The pain faded, and slowly the dark silhouettes of objects came into view. Titch bade me rest, anguished over his miscalculation, though he did not say it aloud.

While I drifted in and out of sleep in my sickroom, a basin of cool water beside the bed, Titch returned to Corvus Peak, to repair his apparatus. Some evenings he would come to tell me of the progress, relaying to me the careful measurements and construction of the cutter. I turned my face to the wall, listening in silence, not speaking. As I grew stronger, I began to rise and walk to the small library, and there I would take down Titch's volumes on aquatic life and stare quietly at the illustrations. I sometimes tried to read the words but would falter at their difficulty. Instead, I poured over the lustrous watercolour sketches, the roaring vividness of them. My favourite was a tome on the nudibranch, a kind of mollusc that sheds its shell after the larval stage. They were creatures of wild and varying colours, ethereal and beautiful.

At last, one day I walked out onto the porch, squinting in pain at the blazing sunshine, and peered east towards Corvus Peak.

And there I saw the eerie, otherworldly orb of the inflated Cloud-cutter, the long cables holding it fast, the great monstrosity of it hovering there. I turned and went back inside.

I feared my eye would not recover; I feared my face in all its new grotesqueness. But most of all, I feared that I had been burned beyond use, that I had been made a ruined creature.

Titch would not hear of it. He came to me, patient, gentle, and I found his solicitousness so strange that I did not know how to understand it. He told me that I was much improved, that soon I would return to my duties. He said my absence was much felt. He said he had not had a competent sketch in weeks.

I made no answer.

He then broached a question clearly troubling him since he'd first come to me after my accident. "When you first opened your eyes that day"—he hesitated—"you imagined you had died and woken up back in Africa?"

I was silent some moments, then slowly I began to explain of our ancient beliefs, of how a figure killed in captivity would in death be returned to his homelands.

Titch was very still, listening with great attention. When he spoke, it was with much gentleness. "But you were born here, Wash. This is your homeland."

I told him that Kit had willed to bring me with her, to Dahomey.

He paused. "I did not expect this of you, Wash."

I said nothing, pained by his disapproving tone.

"That is nonsense, Washington. When we die, there is nothing. Only blackness. Forever and forever."

Something wrenched in my chest, and I had the panicked feeling of wanting to push everything away. I turned to the wall.

It was a kindness he felt he was offering; he was doing what he thought was a goodness.

MISTER PHILIP WAS another matter. His first sight of my burns turned his face full white. I stood before him in the dark passageway, my knees touching each other, and I felt myself begin to tremble. He shook his head, solemn. "You are an ugly thing now, aren't you," he said, but there was no malice in his voice. He looked instead aggrieved, as if the sight of me caused him great emotional pain. "You should not have walked into the proximity when Mister Wilde instructed you otherwise," he said softly. "When you are told to do something, it is best you do it. It is for your own safety, boy. Though I daresay you will not make such a mistake again."

"Yes, sir," said I.

"Very good," he said, though he was still clearly suffering some disturbance. "Run along with you now."

I did not know if it was guilt he felt, or some unrelated grief. But being Mister Philip, he soon enough turned his concerns to the cooking. To satisfy his anxieties Titch had one of his brother's kitchen slaves sent over. The woman who arrived I knew only by name, and though I would catch her glaring at me with a hard kind of pity, when she spoke to me it was curtly and in evident disgust. She was called Esther. She bore a long white scar across her right cheek and over the bridge of her nose like a line of paint.

Mister Philip spat out the first dish she made, a fish soup, kicking back his chair and leaving the room. Her second dish, a breadcrust stuffed with cod and root vegetables, he dropped on the floor in disappointment. Her third dish he pushed rudely from the plate onto the table, and her fourth dish he forced her to sit and taste.

At last Titch would not stand for it. He held out a long, thin arm at Mister Philip, halting him before he rose from the table. "Tomorrow night you shall eat precisely what I eat, cousin. Or I shall send Esther back to Wilde Hall. And then it will be hollandaise every night."

But in the event, Mister Philip was reprieved. An invitation arrived, to dine with Master Erasmus, who had finally recovered his strength after suffering several long weeks of fever. How disappointed I was to learn of his recovery; how many lives his sudden death might have spared. For I imagined that, whatever new arrangements Titch would have had to make at the plantation, the life would surely have been more merciful. But it was not to be.

The master looked thin, thinner than usual, and paler in the face, dark rings around his eyes. But he seemed in fine spirits, and welcomed his guests with a sharp tongue. I accompanied Titch at his urging, and stood burnt and gruesome behind his chair. But he had instructed me to tend to nothing, to not strain myself. For there were other slaves in attendance, some field hands brought in to serve, and I was reminded as I watched them of that night long ago, when Big Kit and I had served here, in this room. There was an older slave, a tall, heavy-set, grey-haired woman I did not know, along with a small boy, and I saw in them a glimpse of how we must have looked. The older slave had suffered some horrific brutality upon her person; the bulb of her right shoulder had been crudely severed off, so that she seemed always to be shrugging. She walked with a lurching gate and kept glancing at me, so that I felt uncomfortable. When my eyes did drift to her, I noticed how careful she was with the child; she would take the heavier dishes and leave him with the easier task, always, just as Kit had tried to do for me. She smiled gravely at me once, when her back was turned to the masters, such a quick flash I was uncertain I'd even seen it. I turned away from her, trying not to remember my Kit.

There was among these slaves a frightened air. I watched their shadows fall across the white tablecloth as they shuffled past, trying to bump neither the table nor each other. A vague scent of sweat and soil came off their skin, the soft green smell of fresh-cut cane. The boy spared no glance at me, the monster, the burnt creature. In the foreground, like a carriage, the masters' conversation rattled on.

"Have you given any thought to redecorating, cousin?" said Mister Philip, not bothering to lift his face between bites. "There is a fine German proportioning to the room. It would not be difficult."

The master frowned. "To what end? So the niggers could track their filth through it?"

"You might send for a decorator from London. I know a man, a brilliant eye. Redecorated half of Grosvenor in thirteen months."

The master gave a long, luscious yawn, and a hank of his cloud-white hair dropped across his brow. "Christopher," he said, turning to his brother. "I will say, I am shocked to find you still in residence, after all these months. You have the fighting spirit, little brother. You may actually see out the year."

Mister Philip scraped his plate. "Mussels were a tad overdone, what."

"Well. Things are progressing so well with my cutter," said Titch, tipping back the last of his wine.

"Indeed?" The master drew out the word, and it was impossible to say what he thought of the matter. He turned abruptly, his bright eyes seeking me out. He studied me a long moment, then turned very slowly back to the table. "What did he do, anyway, for you to punish him so?"

"It was an accident, brother."

The master made a gesture of concession. "It is difficult to hold one's temper in check when dealing with them. I know it myself."

Titch stared irritably across at Mister Philip. "Philip was present. Why do you not ask him?"

Mister Philip was absorbed in running a finger along his empty plate to lick. "What?"

"The accident. The boy's face."

"Oh, yes. Quite. Damn shame, that."

"Tell me," the master continued, "in his state, what is the point of your keeping him?"

"And what would you have me do?" said Titch.

Mister Philip set down his fork. "Very well, very well," he said quickly, and he wiped his oily fingers on a fold of the tablecloth, leaning back in his chair. "Christopher. Erasmus. There is something I would speak to you both about."

Titch turned to Mister Philip in mild surprise, and I could not help but do so myself. Was he truly going to lay bare his role in my disfigurement?

Mister Philip glanced down at his plate, as though steeling himself. "It concerns your father." He made a nervous clearing of the throat. "Your father," he repeated, then fell silent.

"Yes, well, out with it," the master said sourly. "What of him?"

Mister Philip glanced down again, as if all he wished to say were scripted on the dull patina of his dinner knife. The tall, maimed, grey-haired slave began refilling his glass, and he gestured sharply for her to stop. She melted at once back to the wall.

"What is it?" said Titch.

Mister Philip hitched back his lips. "Your father has, I fear, passed away."

I shifted my heels soundlessly on the floor, I stood up straighter.

The master was frowning at his cousin. "Passed away."

"I regret to tell you, yes. There was an accident, at his outpost in the Arctic. I do not know the particulars."

Titch was blinking very quickly. He seemed to be searching for words. "I do not understand." He glanced in perplexity at the master, turned once again to Mister Philip. "You are telling us our father is deceased?"

"I am sorry," Mister Philip said with a look of anguish. "Indeed, it is the very reason for my visit. I bring a letter from Granbourne. Your mother has written all the details. I shall fetch it for you after the last course."

Titch and the master looked silently at each other. The master's face, already sunken with illness, had turned a deathly pallor.

For some moments the only sound in the room was the dry rag of the slave woman wiping down the sideboard.

"Five weeks," said Titch in a voice so pale he was barely audible. He lifted his drained face. "Five weeks you have been here. Eating my food. Taking my leisure."

"I meant to inform you at once. I did." Mister Philip hesitated. "But I thought it wrong to tell you, Titch, without also telling Erasmus." He turned to the master. "But you were from home when I first arrived. And then, when you returned, you were so ill you would allow no visitors until this night. This is the first opportunity I've had."

"You withheld this deliberately," snapped the master. "You vengeful, duplicitous bastard. You are getting your revenge. You are worse than a dog. You are shit."

How strange to hear the master damn a white man so. I lowered my face, did not dare look at him.

"It was not deliberate, cousin. You cannot imagine how it has oppressed me, not being able to speak it."

"My pity for you is boundless," the master hissed.

"I only meant that—" Mister Philip stopped, dropping his gaze to his hands. "I am very sorry for you both. It is hard news indeed. And I do sympathize with your fate—having to leave Faith when you are only just settled. How dispiriting."

"Leave Faith?" said Titch.

"Naturally, Erasmus will have to leave Faith." Mister Philip glanced uneasily across at the master. "You are needed in Hampshire, Erasmus, to sort out your father's affairs, to run Granbourne on site for some time, I imagine. A year. Two. Until such time as everything is settled. Your mother has written it all in her letter, I am sure. She gave me to understand that you are to return with me. Indeed, your passage has already been booked."

The master turned a harsh eye upon his cousin, but some of his rage had eased. He seemed to be weighing the sudden reprieve of a return to England.

Titch stared without expression at the tablecloth, his skin drained of all colour in the yellow candlelight. Behind his chair, the slaves flitted back and forth like vapours.

"But what of Faith, in my absence?" said the master, his voice calm.

"Well, Christopher is here, what. Your mother thought that perhaps he might manage things in your absence. What a blessing, said she, that he has run to precisely where he is needed. It is God's hand. Erasmus will return and sort out Sir James's affairs. Faith, said she, might be passably run for two or three years by Christopher. Hopefully he can do it profitably; we have no doubt you can do it profitably, cousin. In any case, Erasmus will untangle any messes upon his eventual return."

The master was evidently mulling this over. "It is an idea," he said.

"It is all in the letter," said Mister Philip.

Very quietly, Titch backed his chair out, causing the child slave to scurry out of the way. With his mouth set very tight and his eyes distant, Titch took the napkin from his lap and placed it on his gravy-stained plate. Without looking at anyone, he started for the door.

"Oh come, brother," called the master. "Please come back. Such grave news, Christopher, we must weather together. Let us comfort one another."

But Titch did not turn. We all watched him go, the slaves with their heads gently bowed, Mister Philip looking solemn and remorseful. When Titch passed me, I lifted my head, but he did not look at me.

He left the door standing wide.

I felt I should follow, but did not want to draw the master's attention. I watched the old grey-haired slave turn, and meeting her powerful golden eyes I was suddenly flooded with pain, horrified and confused.

It was Big Kit.

How could I not have known her? Had I not all these months prayed for her deliverance each night, imagined for her a life beyond the blood-blackened fields of Faith? When I had first come to live with Titch, it was Kit's iron nail that had kept me from despair; waking into darkness after the gas explosion, it was Kit I had believed at my bedside, her hand on my brow.

She was much changed, it was true, maimed terribly, grown thinner, the hair at her temples silver as flies' wings. Aged, now, as though decades had separated us. But I was the more changed; that was the uglier truth.

I gripped anxiously at my hands, staring at Kit's tall figure. How solicitous she was with the boy. I saw now how she kept a careful eye on his posture, his manners. I knew instinctively what this meant, the great angry love she held that boy inside, like a fist. I tried to imagine what he might be like. He could not have been older than six or seven years, I thought. I wondered at the sudden pain coming up in me.

The master and Mister Philip stood from the table; Mister Philip placed a steadying hand on his cousin's cowed shoulders. He instructed Gaius that they would take their port and pipes in the drawing room. I tried to catch Kit's eye, but by then she had been instructed to leave, and so I watched her retrieve a fork from the sideboard and turn, slouching from the room with the boy following.

I stared after her diminished form, a dryness in my throat, feeling desperate.

Just then there fell a twisting grip on my collarbone, and I glanced up at the veiny, shifting eyes of the master.

"You are still here, nigger?" said he. I could see deep into his wet scarlet mouth, and felt very afraid. "My brother is gone. Off with you, boy, go on."

11

I FLED.

When I returned to Titch's residence, I found the rooms dark, not a candle burning. But under the closed door of Titch's study I saw a crack of candlelight. I paused there in the hallway, listening, but there was no sound from within. I left him to his grief. I knew from what he had told me that his father had been everything to him, the very heart of his life.

I left him there and, making my way through the darkness, undressed and went to bed in silence.

In the morning I rose early. In the quiet of the house I collected a bucket and went out to fill it with water. I walked to Mister Philip's door and left the usual porcelain bowl of water and clean towels on the pier table in the hall. Then I went to Titch's bedroom and did the same. When I opened his door, though, I found his room empty, the bedding untouched.

I found him at last in his study, slouched over the mahogany desk, his chin smeared with fixative dust. I was met with the chemical smell of ink and damp skin. The room was silent and heavy; the drapes had been drawn crookedly shut. There was the soft tapping of a moth stunning itself against the locked window. A tower of pages lay piled by Titch's elbow, the paper warped with ink and sticking in waves against each other like French pastry. What he had been writing I did not know; I trusted it had to do with his father. I set a soft hand on his shoulder and he gave a start. Raising his head, he turned to me in tight-browed grief.

"Wash," said he.

"You fell asleep," I said. "It is morning."

He was in his shirt sleeves, and he drew the cuff of his left wrist across his mouth.

"Can I fetch you anything?" I said.

He shook his head. "Such a person, such a mind. I still cannot believe it. I simply cannot fathom it. Gone, truly? I—" He shook his head, glancing sadly at me. "He did not have the opportunity to see my Cloud-cutter."

"He would have been very proud," I ventured.

"And to stay on and run Faith?" He shook his head, his expression faintly contemptuous. "They must know it is madness." He ran a nervous hand through his dark hair, and with his skin drawn slightly back like that, the white string of his scar was visible, like a harness rising from either side of his mouth. "Much as I love my mother, she is of difficult temperament. She really is too ecstatic. As a child, I found my father always from home, and I did not understand his constant absences." He shook his head.

I said nothing, stood quietly there.

He frowned softly. "But it would seem I have no choice in the matter."

I was silent some moments more, not knowing what to say. "I must begin preparing the breakfast."

"Philip will be hungry," he said, his voice edged with contempt.

Then he seemed to check himself, shook his head. "It is not Philip's fault. None of this is his doing."

I was surprised he should be so forgiving of his cousin's concealment of such news.

"I am sorry, Titch. About your father."

He looked suddenly fragile, fear and resignation in his face. "Well."

I began to move towards the door, feeling somehow disturbed. I feared I had overstepped my place, perhaps. But Titch called to me before I reached the hall. When I turned, he gestured me back to his side.

"I wanted to show you this," he said.

He squared the sheets before him. I leaned into the plank of light falling across his desk. There were three blackening banana peels piled by his inkwell, folded neatly. I squinted at the page. *Preliminary Remarks Regarding the Theory and Practice of Hydrogen-Powered Aerostation in the West Indies.*

I made a noise of surprise. "It is finished, then? But that is wonderful, Titch."

"Look closer."

Then something caught my eye. Beneath the title, in a clean, fine hand, he had written, *Authored by Christopher Wilde, Esq., & Illustrated by George Washington Black.*

I glanced up at him, uncertain.

Titch gave me a sad, weary smile. "You are a man of science now, Wash. Or so you shall be, when this paper reaches the Royal Society." He paused. "That was your Big Kit last night, at dinner. Looking very poorly, it's true. But it was she, right there before us. Did you see her?"

I felt the blood rise to my face; I did not wish to tell Titch that I had not recognized her, nor that when I did, I was horrified to find her so disfigured and ill-used. I did not wish to tell him of the other boy, of the hurt I felt seeing them so close.

I must have looked startled, for he placed a gentle hand upon my shoulder, softened his expression. "Our science is not the sum of my work here," he said quietly. Thumbing through his papers, he drew from beneath our treatise a thick sheaf. I leaned in: *Catalogue of the Injustices and Cruelties Borne Upon the Persons and Minds of the Enslaved Negroes on a Barbadoes Plantation in the West Indies.* I looked at him in some alarm.

"I did not simply run away," said he. "Well, yes, it's true, I did run away, but not for need of personal freedom." He glanced in caution at the door. "My dearest friend Samuel, in London, he said if there is any possibility of your travelling to your family plantation, do so. He asked me frankly to make notes on all I saw. You see, we have colleagues, Wash, many of them, greatly interested in seeing an end to all this, in seeing you, your people, free. A group of us are gathering notes, recording each and every cruelty we observe. These reports we will eventually hand over to a very influential friend in Parliament." He paused to measure my expression, then with his long, jointed fingers flipped through the pages to the end. "Look, see here. I have just this evening added your Kit to my notes. Her wretched condition will not fail to move. I also expect your own scientific work will prove useful."

I did not speak, so surprised was I. I could not fathom when he had had the time to make his observations, never mind to record them.

The skin around his eyes tightened. He shook his head. "Negroes are God's creatures also, with all due rights and freedoms. Slavery is a moral stain against us. If anything will keep white men from their heaven, it is this."

Only years later would his phrasing strike me. In that moment I only thought with horror of the master's discovery of these reports.

"I shall ask my brother to release you permanently," said he, weighing my expression. "Does that please you?"

I made no answer, so shocked was I.

"You would rather remain the property of my brother?"

"Oh, no, Titch, I would rather be your property," said I, eagerly. I did not understand the pained look that crossed his face.

"Well," said he. "Well. We shall talk more on it again, Wash. Yes."

But he seemed troubled, somehow, and in my innocence I could make no sense of it. I had thought I was saying what he wished to hear.

"YOU ARE JOKING, brother. Look at the creature. He is a monstrosity."

The master raised his long pheasant gun to his shoulder and, squinting his right eye shut, let off a shot, grey smoke rolling from the barrel. "Damn," he said, scowling. He lowered the gun, massaged his shoulder, glanced back at Mister Philip and Titch. They were the three of them out shooting that day in the scrub and hills at the base of Corvus Peak.

A full week had passed since Mister Philip's announcement. In those grim days Titch had kept firmly to his rooms, only emerging to dine alone in the evenings long after Mister Philip had retired. Then one morning the master arrived at the house, and in my fear

I rushed to fetch Titch, who consented, finally, to sitting down with his brother.

They spent an afternoon out on the verandah, talking over glasses of warm rum I replenished by the hour. In those sad hours of reminiscence some healing seemed to take place. Mister Philip wandered out to join them, and the three sat gently laughing over the escapades of the late Mister Wilde, his eccentricities and brilliances.

The next day they decided to go hunting, and it was here that we found ourselves, deep into the scrub under Corvus Peak.

"No, it would be cruel to remove him to England," the master continued. Recognizing that his father's death would allow him to return home, he had been in the brightest of moods, as though some well-thought-of dog, not a father, had died. "What good would come of it? In any case, it is I, not you, who will return to England. And I certainly have no use for him there."

I felt a heat rise to my cheeks. Titch had not mentioned the possibility of England to me.

Titch hesitated. "Events do not have to unfold as Philip dictates. It makes far more sense for you to stay here and look after Faith, while I return to Granbourne. Think of it. It is this plantation that affords the other homes their luxuries. What if something were to go wrong?"

"It is your mother who dictates, not I," said Mister Philip.

But the master was not finished. "A nigger slave at Granbourne." He levelled his pale eyes on Titch. "Come now, man. The proper servants would eat the poor creature alive. They are rather proud, you know."

"Which servants, exactly?"

The master raised his weapon. "A position at Granbourne, at Hawksworth, Sanderley—all are positions of stature, such as they are. You must know this."

"I think you are rather more familiar with servants than we," said Mister Philip, smiling.

"Erasmus is a great collector of knowledge," said Titch tartly.

"Knowledge about certain servants, perhaps. Maids and such."

The master frowned at the teasing. "It is a privilege to serve a great family."

"A great family's cock," said Mister Philip.

Titch smiled despite himself. "I'd think they would care more about fine treatment and solid pay than position."

"Erasmus does all the positions," said Mister Philip.

"Oh, don't be so naive, Christopher," snapped the master. "Everyone cares about their station."

"I do not," said Titch.

"Because you do not need to. No, I will not let you have the boy. You may continue to borrow him for the duration of your stay here. Then, upon my return, if he is still alive, you will give me back my worker." He shook out his trigger hand. "Tell me, have you had a chance to examine the ledgers I had sent over? You will have to understand how to read them, eventually."

Titch frowned across at Mister Philip.

"I understand you will have much studying to do, Christopher," said Mister Philip.

"I have not yet decided," said Titch. "If I will take over the running of Faith, that is."

"You speak as though there is another option," said Mister Philip.

"My mother can manage perfectly well. Indeed, what recourse

has she had in your absence, brother? Surely there are trustworthy tenants. Solicitors. Accountants. Others she can rely on."

"Mother is old, Christopher." The master lowered his gun and, setting the stock on the rocky ground at their feet, held out his hand for a flask of wine. I hurried forward. "It is one thing to engage others for a period, and quite another to rely upon them indefinitely after a master's death. It must be stressed to all the tenants that order still reigns at Granbourne. I must go. I cannot allow you to go in my stead. You will make a shambles of it."

"You cannot allow it?"

"No."

Titch laughed a sharp, angry laugh. I had not heard such a sound from him before. I looked quickly up, but he was staring out at the sky and I could not see his face.

"Erasmus's passage is already booked," said Mister Philip, and there was something beseeching in his voice. "We will return at month's end. Before the wrathful winds begin in earnest."

"One may wait five weeks to mention a death," said Titch, "but time is now of the essence."

The master shook his head. "I do not understand your sharp tone, Christopher. We shall not disrespect Mother's wishes, that is the end of it."

Now Mister Philip stepped forward and for the first time, seeing him and Titch together, I noticed the startling physical disparity between the two. There was a power to Mister Philip's broad shoulders, a strength that dwarfed my master. Mister Philip set a thick hand on Titch's shoulder, and it struck me as somehow threatening.

"I promised your mother I would bring him back," Mister

Philip said. "It is my honour on the line here also, cousin. Think of me in this."

"Ah, yes," said Titch. "I should not wish to sully your name."

The master was blinking. "Do not think for a minute that I do not share in this grief, Christopher. He was my father too. You mustn't take it out on me. I am only concerned for the future of the estates, as should you be."

Mister Philip crouched, resting his knee against a slab of yellow stone. He raised his gun and fired. The air shuddered with a great, violent punch, and we all glanced out at the bleached sky. The brown silhouette of a grouse clapped onwards, its wings beating, untouched.

"Damn it all," Mister Philip muttered.

"Is that how you are taught to shoot in London, cousin?" laughed the master. "And for a man who takes such prodigious care of his gun . . ." He shook his head.

"Your bag is as empty as mine," said Mister Philip. "Only Christopher has had any luck."

"It is the trained eye of the man of science," said the master. "Luck, nothing."

Titch looked away.

Mister Philip coughed, spat a long yellow thread into the grass. He squinted against the sun at Titch. "Think of your mother, man. She is quite vulnerable now—every cheat will try and take advantage. If only on a practical level, it is dearly pressing for Erasmus to return. Just until arrangements for the estate might be made."

Titch did not answer.

"He is cross that I do not make the burnt creature a gift," said the master. "Look how sullen he is become."

Mister Philip smiled. "Why do you not buy the creature from Erasmus?" He turned to the master. "What would you sell the boy for?"

"Let us leave it be," said Titch quietly.

"Why is he of such value to my brother?" the master mused. "You do not imagine he has formed an unsavoury attachment?" The master paused, feigning shock, then looked over at me and called, "Is he unnatural with you, boy? Do you make the beast with two backs?"

"Leave him be, Erasmus," said Titch.

Mister Philip tsked. "Oh, just sell him the boy and be done with it. If it will bring him peace of mind—"

"I think not," interrupted the master. "No."

"He is of no worth to you. Look at him."

"Rather the contrary." The master folded his long, thin fingers over the mouth of his gun, shrugging. "Titch has taught the creature to make fine illustrations, and that is of enormous use. Dr. Quinn will come from Liverpool this year. For a heavy sum I've promised him access to ten of my slaves for his experiments. Putrid fever, you see. He's trying to invent an inoculation against it. Surely he will be in need of faithful diagrams."

Suddenly Mister Philip dropped to one knee and, swinging his gun to his shoulder, fired, letting off a second powerful thunder and the stench of metal, a cloud of ghostly brown smoke. In the distance a smudge plummeted from the sky.

The dogs were loosed, disappearing into the brush at once, barking in frenzy.

"There, that is how it is done," cried Mister Philip, beginning to laugh. He swung his gun down and rose heavily, turning to his cousins. "Did you see? A fine shot indeed. A London shot, I should call it. A London shot."

THE VERY NEXT day the weather turned.

The sky blackened, went dark as tea. But then the afternoon passed without rain, and the clouds drifted gently out to sea. The following day was the same. All this Titch watched with a judging eye, making the long trek up to the Cloud-cutter most mornings. I dutifully recorded his anxious observations as best I could, in my rudimentary language.

The men and women laboured here and there all across the Peak, their pale clothes grass-stained at the knees, calling to each other in our pidgin tongue. I stared at the cutter, the immense punctured lung of it, the netted rubberized skin hanging from it. It was, I knew, a thing of wonder and beauty. It was true that the season was coming to an end, true that the hurricane days would soon be upon us. But Titch did not want to accept this.

"Can you not put a tarp over it during the bad season?" I said. "It will be an enormous labour to have it all brought down again, only to have to carry it back up after the storms pass."

He gave me a curious look then, and I understood he was surprised that even I had condemned him to stay here into next winter.

Still, it was a kind of relief, for me, to observe Titch animated again, moved by his own work, absorbed in its problems. In the immediate days following the news of his father he had gone into a grey stupor, wanting to talk neither of his father's death nor of England. Now he was at least interested, though still quite worried about how to manage under the insistent pressure from his family.

He kept mumbling how devastated he felt that his father would never see this, the work of his life, their shared passion for flight made whole by his own hands.

"Do you know what should be done?" he said, his eyes wide and distant-looking. "Some commemoration should be made for my father at his place of rest, in the Arctic. Someone ought to travel out there and erect a marker for him. Peter, his assistant, is his only companion up there, and Peter is not a man given to sentimental gestures. My father did so much to enlighten men about the world. Can it really be that he will pass from it without so much as a shudder?" He glanced at me. "It is not natural. It is not right."

Without awaiting an answer, he bent again to his measurements, and we passed the morning in silent work. Some hours in, I thought I heard a cry in the distance—hoarse, resigned, like some final expiration. I raised my face, squinting down into the roiling cane.

These cries had been a feature of my life in the field; how shocked I was to realize how rarely I now heard them. My face flushed with the pain and shame of it, the half-healed skin throbbing.

Titch lifted his face to the sky, and decided then we would go down early. We did not speak, but drifted down through the dry yellow grass, disappointed, tired.

TITCH AND I had nearly reached the base of Corvus Peak when we caught sight of a silhouette shivering in the bleached afternoon light. Titch paused, placed a hand on my chest to stop me walking. We squinted at the figures, the woman's dress fluttering against her skinny calves, the bow-legged child beside her, their faces cancelled in shadow.

Yes, there was the white scar across the face. Esther. She trudged stolidly forward in her starched kitchen whites, gripping the child by the shoulder, a viciousness to her mouth despite her expressionless eyes. The boy I did not know; he walked beside her, wiry and thin. He was chewing on a strand of sargassum weed, which he spat nervously out as he reached us.

"Esther. You will be looking for me, I trust." Titch studied the boy. "Good morning, son."

"Sir," came the response, the boy's face trained on his shoes.

His shoes had been polished to a high shine and looked two sizes too large. He moved in them awkwardly, like a creature trapped in mud.

"Well? What is it?" Titch held his hat in place in the soft wind. "What has happened?"

Esther stood before him, blinking. "Master Erasmus is sent over your new boy, sir." Her voice was beautiful, I realized suddenly, low-pitched, musical.

The darkening clouds were moving past us overhead. Titch stood frowning against the warm wind. "But I have not asked for a new boy," he said slowly.

"Yes, sir."

"Do inform your master that I am quite satisfied with my present boy."

She lowered her face but did not move.

"Esther? Did you not hear me?"

"Master Erasmus gives you this boy in exchange for that one," she said stubbornly. "He wants the burnt one back, Master Wilde, sir."

I turned quickly, glanced at Titch.

Titch appeared unruffled. "That I had already understood. This is a discussion for your master and myself to continue. He ought not to have involved you, Esther."

"Yes, sir."

"You may tell him to expect me in the coming days. We will discuss it further."

Glaring at the ground, sounding now almost frustrated, Esther said, "Master Erasmus was quite insistent, sir, if you will. He will not have this boy back. He orders you to send over the burnt boy at once."

"Orders me, does he?" A tightness had crept into Titch's voice. "Does he also state the consequences of my non-compliance?"

Esther said nothing, just raised her hard face with its passionless eyes, its white earthworm scar. I knew the master would beat her if she returned with Titch's message. I watched but said nothing.

Titch too seemed to understand. He sighed, taking the boy by the shoulder. "Let us go now to Wilde Hall, then. Esther, you will return with Wash." He handed me his sack of instruments. "Please take these back to the house, Wash, and begin preparations for lunch." He looked warily at the boy, who kept his head bowed. "And what is your name, son?"

A pause, then in a whisper: "Eugenio, sir."

"Eugenio. Let us go back to Wilde Hall."

They set off in the direction of the master's house. Watching them go, I thought they looked very much how Titch and I must appear together, two awkward forms pouring through the darkened fields like shadows.

+ + +

How do I explain the events that followed? I have weighed that afternoon in my mind these seven years and found myself unable to give a clean accounting of it. I was young and terrified and confused, it is true. But it is also true that the nature of what happened isn't fixed; it shifts and warps with the years.

I do not know how long Esther and I trod through the brush, only that the late afternoon air was cooling pleasantly, and that we did not speak. She seemed neither preoccupied nor uneasy; her silence was marked by a held-in rage that I have only now, several years later, come to understand as the suppression of will. For she was a ferociously intelligent woman, and it strained her to have to conceal it. She sometimes spoke as no slave should speak; the scar on her face was some testament to this. In Titch's household she found tolerance and a patient ear, though even he sometimes grew irritated and urged her to remember her place.

She kept her face forward, breathing softly with the exercise, the hem of her dress snagging on passing weeds. Occasionally her damp arm would brush mine, but she did not move away. Above us, the birds wheeled blackly in the starched light. I stopped to clutch a fistful of wildflowers, the petals crumbling with a satisfying reek like burnt parsley. I was trying to still my mind, trying not to dwell on the master's alarming request to have me returned to him. A fine shiver went through me.

Then, as from nowhere, a voice called out.

"Boy! You! Boy!"

We paused, turning in the blanched light to see him striding full towards us. We did not look at each other. I watched instead the glint in his thick hands, the freshly oiled steel that had been engineered to survive every destruction, dark and blunt and final.

Mister Philip and his gun. He moved sluggishly in his beautiful clothes, the gun in his red-knuckled fingers, an intensity to his eyes despite his calm expression. I paused, awaiting his approach, my heart thudding.

He reached us breathing heavily. His voice, when he'd called out, had sounded threatening. Now, pausing before us, he appeared blurred, rundown, diminished, as if a soft grey air had settled upon him. His black hair was matted across his forehead, and fine blue veins stood out at his temples.

He studied Esther a long while, so that it became uncomfortable. "Run along with you now," he said finally, but with no force.

She tipped her chin back, surveying him without expression, her white scar like a string tied about her face. Without looking at me, she turned and continued alone back to the house.

I glanced quickly past Mister Philip; Titch was very far now, so that I could no longer see him. I peered nervously up at Mister Philip. He was frowning, his eyes glassy and reddened as with drink.

Terror cut through me; I swallowed it down. "Titch has bade me return to the house, sir. If you go that way yourself, sir, I can bring some refreshments out to you on the verandah, if you please."

Mister Philip was staring behind me at the distant scrub as though he had not heard. I turned; there was nothing to see, only the dry yellow grass rattling in the dusty air, Esther's fading silhouette. Slowly, he looked down at me, smiling in a tight grimace. "Here, boy. Gather this up."

Nervously, I reached for the provisions he held out. "This may not be the weather for a hunt, sir," I said, thinking perhaps I might disrupt whatever plan he had in mind, though I knew it was too forward of me to speak it. "Titch believes it will rain."

His face darkened. "You have some audacity to address me so."

I lowered my face, awaiting a blow.

He merely gestured for me to follow him, mumbling. "When the slaves forget they are slaves . . ." He shook his head.

We walked in silence, me following his lope through the fields towards the scrublands fringing Corvus Peak, the hunting grounds. I was terrified; I could scarcely walk for the fear. What did he mean by all this? If he intended to hunt, where were the hounds? I only hoped Esther would alert Titch to what had happened and that he would come in search of me. Mister Philip's provisions were heavy, and though I did not dare set them down, I would lower my head every few paces to take the good cool air on my neck. I would raise my face and stare out to the scrublands, trying not to look at his gun.

"PERHAPS IT IS easier for you."

I looked warily across at him. "Sir?"

Mister Philip did not answer, merely sat heavily on an outcropping at the base of the mountain, awkwardly balancing his gun on his round thighs.

Less than an hour had passed, though it felt a lifetime, and we sat in the scree at the base of Corvus Peak, the crickets already creaking in the darkening air. All this time he had not taken a single shot, not even raised his gun. His stride had slowed and slowed, his wide shoulders rounding, his eyes growing hazier, more distant. He was pensive, grave, and the few glances he spared me seemed nearly apologetic, as if he regretted the outing. He carried his gun low at his thigh, and every time he changed hands I would stare uneasily at his fingers, then look away and count the blades of grass under my breath.

By the time we had settled in the rocky outcrop, I was beyond frightened. I could barely hear his voice, which in any case was quiet and thoughtful, hollowed out almost, as though he were thirsty. An unnatural stillness had come over me, like an extension of fear. The rock on which I sat bored painfully into my thighs. I could smell the wild lemongrass in the last of the day's heat, feel the bite of mosquitoes on my shins.

Across from me Mister Philip stared out at the distant tamarinds, their tops bowing in the dull wind. There were red fissures in the whites of his eyes, and under the mountain's shadow his skin appeared grey. I noticed the flaking red knuckles, so strange on a man of leisure, and the mesmerizing whiteness of his teeth; I saw the oddity of a body used for nothing but satisfying urges, bloated and ethereal as seafoam, as if it might break apart. He smelled of molasses and salted cod, and of the fine sweetness of mangoes in the hot season. I eyed him uneasily.

He glanced at me from under his darkened brow. "Perhaps it is easier for you," he said again. "Everything is taken care of for you. You needn't worry about what the coming days will hold, as every day is the same. Your only expectations are the expectations your master lays out for you. It is a simple-enough life, what."

It was as though he had spoken the words to determine their truth. He shook his head irritably.

I stilled my face. I said nothing.

He exhaled harshly, dragging the gun up his thighs. I looked at his hands, the pallor of them on the dark metal.

"I am sorry." His voice was so soft I barely heard him. He gestured with his chin. "Your face."

I stared, feeling the soft tremor of my hands in my lap.

"I was in Vienna, some months before coming here," he continued in the same hushed voice. "In Vienna, the bread is a wonder. Everyone says Paris, but the true artistry is to be found in the Viennese dough. It is their yeast perhaps, or their manner of kneading it." He stared quietly down at the gun. "There was a very fine cemetery there, at the edge of a church. I'd grown tired that day, the light made my head ache, and I sat on a bench beyond the surrounding wrought iron fence, and ate my bread." He moistened his lips. "The streets were utterly silent, deserted. But after a time I heard the clopping of a horse approaching, and raised my face.

"The horse's flesh—there was something wrong with it. It glowed pink through the white pelt, diseased. A rather miserable four-wheeler dragged along behind it, the broken spoke slapping along the cobblestones. There was no driver."

He paused, staring a long while in silence at his hands. "Curious," he murmured. "Curious. Unsettling. I watched the horse trot by, a knot of flies at its face. The noise of its hooves on the stones faded, the scrape of the broken spoke. I shall never forget the eeriness of it, the sound." He shook his head.

"Some minutes later, a man appeared from round the corner of the cemetery. The owner of the horse, I presumed. He neared slowly, at no hurry. He was short, and very poorly dressed. His frock coat was green, his trousers yellow, the dress of someone from another century. I recall vividly he was chewing on a carrot. As he neared me, he started to tip his hat, but then he paused, staring at me. He had small eyes, ugly eyes.

"I bid him good day, but he only kept staring. Finally he said, 'I just passed your grave. I just passed your monument.'

"I imagined he was jesting.

"'Come,' he said, waving the carrot at me. 'I will show you.'

"I followed him into the cemetery. He brought me to a small cedar grove sloping away from the main path. And in that place, I came face to face with my stone likeness."

Mister Philip paused, staring still at the length of gun on his thighs. "There I was, carved in stone: the same hair, the same eyes, same mouth, same chin. Everything. I studied the gravestone. The man had died fifty years earlier, on the exact day of my birth."

He shrugged in resignation. "What is the truth, I ask you?"

I shifted on the rock, saying nothing.

"Who is the ghost in that tale?" Mister Philip glanced up, and the deadness of his eyes dried up anything I might utter. His pupils were large, black. He stared as if struggling to see through me, as if I were a sudden obstruction.

Oh how I wanted to run from all this, to quit the dark, weed-strewn grove, its oppressive trees already silvering in the dusk. Above us a flock of gulls screeched, keening towards the sea. In the soft breeze, the grasses began to rattle.

Something was wrong. All at once Mister Philip rose with the gun swinging upwards in his fists, his shadow black and blunt against the failing sun. How did I know what was coming? I threw my hands over my face, as if to obscure the horror, my heart stamping in my ribs, and though I opened my mouth to yell, no sound came out.

A GREAT, SHUDDERING blast, then all went white, the explosion dying sharply out. The sky emptied itself, the seabirds disappeared, and on the air the reek of fresh meat and chalk was pungent. The grasses wrestled to and fro, and in the brisk wind I felt a wetness on my face, smelled the sudden iron stink of blood. I was clutching myself on the outcrop, my body cowering in a ball, and I could not move. I listened for his breath, listened for any sound or movement. I felt small, wet shards on my arm and raised my face, staring in the dusk at the muck on me.

It was teeth, or pieces of bone, other parts of his shattered face. In horror I swiped it away and stood, shivering—not from the sudden violence, which had been with me since birth, but from the terrible fact that I alone had been present at the death of a white man.

Brushing at my clothes, I felt myself almost choking, and I did not look directly at what I could glimpse by the side of my eye: the whiteness of his large open palm, the dull grey sheen of his boots. And yet, leaving, I could not help but glance back. The flesh of his face was folded viciously away from the skull, like leather freshly cut. In the distance, a rook called out.

I ran.

TITCH AT FIRST did not understand a word of it.

"I was just now coming in search of you," he was saying when I rushed into his candlelit study from the fields. "But what's this?" said he, rising immediately, his face blanching. "Dear god, Wash. Come, come—you will need to be examined at once. My god, that is a great deal of blood."

I could hear myself speaking but had no sense of my words. I was vaguely aware of the room's warmth, its faint smell of fresh-cut hibiscus, its flickering candlelight and the odd bright spot on the wall that always looked as if someone had just that minute scrubbed it clean. I sensed my teeth tapping harshly against each other, and I tried to regain control of myself.

Titch sank onto his haunches. "Where is the injury?" he said, examining me. "Show me the wound."

My teeth were chattering painfully, but I managed somehow to make plain that it was not my blood.

Titch stiffened. "Wash," he said quietly.

Stuttering, I made to explain. And I watched as his confusion turned to slow disbelief. His lips parted gently, a slow frown growing on his drained face. Abruptly, he rose, wrenching a tense hand through his dark hair. He stood some seconds staring at the balding rug.

Then, quite suddenly, he began to breathe noisily through his lips, rubbing at his forehead. I could not discern his thoughts and this panicked me beyond everything; I wanted to tell him again that I had done nothing, that I had been forced to watch, that Mister Philip had wrought his vicious end himself. This Titch already knew; this I had already said many times; and yet I wanted to emphasize it, to confirm that Titch truly accepted it.

"Esther," said he, his expression unreadable. "She came to Wilde Hall while I was with Erasmus. She informed us both that you had gone away with him, with Philip."

I was still shaking softly, and did not answer.

"Why would he take you along?" he said softly.

Still I said nothing.

He stared thoughtfully at me. "Where is he?"

I moistened my lips, but it was some while before I could speak. "At the hunting grounds, still. In the scrub of Corvus Peak."

"You must take me to him at once."

I blinked and blinked—how could I will myself to go back there?

He closed his eyes a long while. Opening them, he looked faintly surprised to find himself still in this room. He came forward and placed a hand on my collarbone, his palm cool and gentle. "I cannot find him unless you show me."

I breathed out; I knew I could never return there.

"Wash. Please."

And so I found myself walking to the door, and I stood waiting as Titch pulled on his frock coat to go out into the soft evening air. At the threshold he frowned down at me, uneasiness in his waxen face.

I followed him out. He moved slowly, stiffly, and in the reluctance of his gestures I saw Mister Philip's own slow passage through the grass, his steps ghostly, belaboured, as though he were savouring the rustle and cries of those green fields one last time.

12

From a distance the body looked whole. And yet, as we trod across the damp night grass towards the twist of clothes in the clearing, its desecration was obvious. It was as though a trunk of clothes had been split open in the field; bits of fabric hung off nearby branches. It shocked me to notice it; I could not recall seeing this before, I remembered nothing beyond his maimed face. The rags were like the radiance of some terrible star, bright and emanating from something already extinct. I thought suddenly of the night Titch had summoned me to live with him, the awe in his slender face as he bade me observe the pure surface of the moon.

He had been silent the long walk to the hunting grounds. Seeing his cousin's dark form in tatters there, his face filled with anguish. But he did not cry out; he spoke no words at all. With damp eyes, he circled the mess in the clearing to retrieve from deep within the high grasses the gun.

I could go no farther. A vicious itch had broken out in the crooks of my elbows and knees; my breath caught in my throat. I could see the ruin of Mister Philip's torn red face, the explosion of teeth and bone like bloated rice on the blood-slicked grass. And I could hear again the thin horn of his final cry, the moist thud of his body, as though a damp blanket had been thoughtlessly thrown. I heard also the strange punctuation of his phrases with that word, *what*, and the faint hiss of his gun being dragged through the grasses. I saw his hands on the barrel of that gun, I smelled the vile brown stink that filled the air. And I saw his weariness as he walked through the field, as if in his last minutes he were picturing the late morning hours spent on the verandah's rocker, the honeyed light pooling on his skin, the warmth and the ease of it.

I could not bring myself to touch him.

OF COURSE, THAT night I did not sleep. I pinched my eyes shut, but the images kept coming. Breathing hard against the sheet balled in my fist, I felt my heart would explode. Horrifying as the act itself had been, I understood it as Titch was not able to. Death by choice was an opening door; it was a release into another world.

What I did not understand was why Mister Philip had involved me. He had offered apology for my face; the decency of that gesture had been undermined by the utter destruction his act had now wrought upon my life. For though I was very young I understood beyond all doubt that his death must mean my own. I would be blamed; Titch could do nothing to shelter me. The master would discover the accident, and my presence at it, and I would be killed. My only hope was for a swift, unsentimental hanging, or an axe to the back of the head. I could only pray he would spare me the agony of grotesquely drawing it out.

Thinking I heard a noise, I raised my head, turning from the wall. But the room was silent, smelling of freshly washed stone and my own sweat. There were, I knew, only some hours till daybreak. I lay my head back down, thinking with bitterness of the great journey denied me and Big Kit when she could not kill us, the voyage back to her Dahomey. For I had come to believe that all Titch had said about death—that it was an ending, a blackness—applied only to deaths not chosen, which meant of course to killings. When I pictured myself being cut down by the master's hands, severed brutally from the world, a taste like unripe apples filled my throat, and I saw the blackness Titch spoke of, the finality of it.

There it came again: a low silver tinkling in the hall, the hiss and drag of something being slid across the boards. I shifted onto one elbow, swung my feet down onto the floor. Finally I padded out.

It was Titch: fully dressed, barefoot, his boots folded up under one arm. He was creeping from room to room in the house, the dancing incandescence of his lantern cutting the dark. My heart was stamping hard in my chest. I followed him into his bedchamber.

"Titch?" I hissed.

He whirled, and stared at me a long, dark moment as though he did not know me. Then he nodded. "There you are," he whispered, though from his tone I understood he was somewhat surprised to find me there. He lifted the lantern higher. I exhaled at the sight of his strained green eyes, the red skin beneath them raised like wax seals.

"What are you doing?" I said.

"Lower your voice," he whispered. In the gauzy yellow light I could just make out his form cutting through the room. I heard the unsticking kiss-like sound of the tacky varnish on his armoire doors. Then came the muffle of clothes, the lisp of papers. The room was humid.

"Titch," said I. "What is happening?"

"We are leaving, Wash. Keep quiet. Do not wake Esther."

"Leaving?"

"For Saint Vincent. Or Saint Lucia. Any other island. Whichever way the winds will take us."

I was beginning to understand. "Titch."

"Go now, Wash. Dress yourself. Take only what you most value; we will find everything else anew. But be as silent as you can."

"I will be in chains before we even leave port."

"We will not take a boat, of course."

I paused. "You cannot mean the Cloud-cutter. In all this darkness? The Cloud-cutter?"

He shoved something into what appeared to be my journeyman's sack. "I have your sketching leads and your notebooks, some clothes, your magnifying lens." He slapped it anxiously against my chest. "You may collect one or two things more. But think of the weight as you do."

I stood quite numb in his doorway.

"Heaven's sake, Wash," he hissed. "Be quick about it."

Hearing the bite in his voice—he who rarely grew impatient—I felt suddenly cold. I heard then what must have been there all along: the vague hiss of wind in some cracked window.

"Victuals are already packed and on the porch," Titch whispered. "We can take little, given the weight. But they should do us fine until landfall."

Suddenly it became real, and I was filled with a sort of disbelieving terror. I shuffled nervously in the doorway. It struck me then, all he was risking to save me. "Please, Titch. I will accept whatever punishment awaits. I will hand myself over to Master Erasmus."

He turned sharply to me. "Get dressed. Make haste. We have not time at all."

When still I hesitated, he said something that has stayed with me all these years. "I am not doing this for you alone. I will not stay in this awful place. This is not a life for me."

Did he say this because he knew my mind? Because he knew I would not decline, if he were to risk his life regardless?

I frowned. "Do you truly feel the Cloud-cutter is ready?"

"If it will not rise now, it will not rise ever. I have been inflating it all night. Now, enough, enough talk. Quickly."

I hesitated.

He turned fully to me in the dark. "Esther has already revealed that you went away with him—you understand she despises you, don't you? She will do everything she can to implicate you in the death. Not that Erasmus will actually believe you responsible—but he will most certainly pretend to as a means of forcing me to hand you over. Consider, Wash—he had already requested your return even before this misfortune. What do you imagine will befall you now? What do you imagine awaits?" He paused, his voice going quiet. "Sadly, you are caught in an ugly game between brothers. More than a game, now." He exhaled slowly, harshly. "You are welcome, of course, to choose your own path, but in doing so ask yourself what is just. Look at the truth of this matter, and ask yourself what is rightful."

I faltered; his tone was flat, but still his words unsettled me. I stepped forward into the stain of the lantern light, and I took up my bag.

In the hot, mulchy room a silence passed; then he raised the lantern to his face and blew out the light.

✦ ✦ ✦

And so we fled, staggering under our sacks in the grey half-light.

The moon had dimmed. Titch relit the lantern and dropped a cloth over it, and we walked by the weak orange light, stumbling over the path we had traversed so many times. In silence we fumbled and scrambled our way slowly up towards Corvus Peak. I could see the mountain, black and alien against the grey sky. I felt an increasing dread, thinking of Mister Philip's body nearby, for in the end Titch had not been able to collect up the remains, so that we'd only covered the outrage with a blanket he had brought. On the desk in his study he'd left behind a note detailing the suicide and a map where his cousin might be found.

I feared we must be discovered; I feared the master must have some manner of guard or watch that would alert him to our passage. But Titch did not seem to share my fear; he walked steadily, distracted, weighed down by the seriousness of what he was about to do. As we neared the scrub edging the mountain, I searched and searched for the blood-marked blanket but could see nothing in the darkness.

When we reached the peak, we slid our packs off, our legs trembling, our faces damp with sweat. A wind was blowing; the Cloud-cutter roared, creaked, leaning into its ropes. The wind was warm, unpleasant, with the scent of iron and rain in it. I watched Titch's dark figure move to adjust the canister of gas in the blackness, grunting and cursing softly. The canopy hung high above me, a scorch against the lighter sky.

Titch called to me urgently, and I clambered into the wicker-and-wood gondola, its oars stretching like antennae into the sky, its four odd wings creaking like rudders in the wind. How terrifying it all looked, in the dark; a great hot fear of death went through me.

As Titch was double-checking the bolts and knots, he paused to give me a strange, quiet look. But I said nothing, and he said nothing, and in the silence he turned back to his preparations.

"Well, Wash," he said at last.

"Well," I said, terrified.

Then, without another word, he adjusted the canister. A higher column of fire surged upwards into the canopy, and the fabric began to shudder and shake. The shaking was terrible. My teeth rattled in my skull. I stared in fascinated terror at the broad black mouth sucking up fire.

The air stank of char and smoke, of burning oil. Finally Titch leaned over and severed each rope in its turn. All around me I could hear the hissing of the grass as the wicker basket was dragged across it—a vicious, final sound.

In the half-light I could just make out the hollows of Titch's face, his eyes blacked out, only the white shards of his teeth distinct and visible. I felt a give in my belly; I clutched at the oars of the Cloud-cutter in dread. The air around us began to howl; the sky rushed towards us. We were rising.

I can barely describe the sight of it. I saw the threatening sky below, a great red crack of light, like a monstrous eye just opening. The sky was still black where we were, but the wind was already hurling us seaward. I watched the half-cut cane fields in the faint light, the white scars of harvest glistening like the part in a woman's hair.

What did I feel? What would anyone feel, in such a place? My chest ached with anguish and wonder, an astonishment that went on and on, and I could not catch my breath. The Cloud-cutter spun, turned gradually faster, rising ever higher. I began to cry—deep, silent, racking sobs, my face turned away from Titch, staring out onto the boundlessness of the world. The air grew colder, crept in webs across my skin. All was shadow, red light, storm-fire and frenzy. And up we went into the eye of it, untouched, miraculous.

PART TWO

Adrift

1832

1

The squall struck us not an hour out from the island. It fell upon us with sudden force, roaring, and I stumbled back against the oarlock, my arms outstretched as the small craft swung wildly from its ropes. Titch hurled himself across the Cloud-cutter and, fumbling with the ballasts, hollered at me in the darkness. But I could see very little, only the pale, lithe shape of his face, the shadow where his mouth should have been.

I think now that he was not so surprised as I. As we had sailed out into the blackness, I recall how he tapped at the barometer and exclaimed softly to himself; how he shuffled about on his knees in the bed of the Cloud-cutter, sifting through our packages; how he separated the least necessary into a pile at the stern. And I have not forgotten how, in the moments after the storm struck, Titch at once took up that small pile and hurled it over into the darkness.

He leaned in close to me, the winds flattening his hair, crying out, "We must try to get above it. We must go up!" He stabbed upwards with his fingers, as though I might have any notion as to how to manage this.

A strong wind suddenly buffeted us, and Titch was thrown backwards, seizing one of the guy ropes at the edge of the drop to steady himself. "It will not do, Wash! It will not do!"

I shut my eyes.

I felt us descending, plummeting through the storm. The rain came on now and it lashed at us, the coated fabric of the balloon crackling under the onslaught. Titch brought us down, the covered lantern still fixed madly to the prow of the Cloud-cutter. I gripped the edge and peered up over, could see now the distant, black, roiling waves of the ocean below us. We were falling fast.

"Titch!" I shouted. "Titch!"

He did not hear me, and I grabbed for his arm, gesturing at a far swell. A light seemed to be shimmering off the crests of the waves, and then it was gone, lost, everything so dark that I did not know if I had imagined it. A cavernous blackness rang out.

Titch leaned into the guide ropes, drawing the aerostat with all his might towards that darkness, steering us in. From between the wide, mountainous swells I glimpsed a leaning spike of wood. A silhouetted ship hove into view, rolling almost on its side, and then it crested and rode foaming down the swells to disappear again. A moment later it rose up. I swallowed and, turning, stared at the madman leaning soaked into his ropes. For I understood: Titch was aiming us directly for that ship.

We struck the mast at an odd angle and tilted, then smashed downward in a great splinter of wood. We lifted again and crashed again down, before the Cloud-cutter was dragged across the deck with a hissing screech, hopping gently into the air, then turned over upon itself in a bellow of splinters.

Dazed, I shook my head. Something warm was pouring over my face. I felt myself hanging upside down, and knew I was tangled in the Cloud-cutter's ropes. And then I saw Titch's face in the rain, upside down, shouting at me, and then I could see nothing again but darkness.

The Cloud-cutter groaned terribly, and started to slide towards the edge of the ship.

"Wash!" Titch cried. He was pulling at the ropes with a frantic energy, but I could not be freed. I could feel the Cloud-cutter pull away in the wind, light, boneless. My stomach lurched.

"Wash, free your hand!" Titch was shouting. He had set a boot against the Cloud-cutter's prow, was leaning with all his might.

The ship rose again, vertically, coasting up a wall of water. I was staring upside down into the darkness, and it seemed the world had gone mad.

Then out of the rain and wind a figure appeared behind Titch, staggering. It shoved him to one side. A thick, bearded brute of a man, spray flying from his beard, dragging beside him an axe. He heaved back and swung, chopping the knot of ropes pinning my throat. I collapsed forward, free, onto all fours, gasping into the rain.

The deck was slick, cold. I half-lifted my face.

I could hear the man hollering something in a guttural tongue. Titch too was shouting.

A sudden gust of wind dragged the balloon crackling up into the air over the black waters. The Cloud-cutter lifted upright and scraped sharply backwards, making a terrible shriek. I watched it smash into a row of barrels in the fore-rigging and ricochet up, and then suddenly it was sucked out into the storm, leaving only wreckage and blackness. All the while the rain, silver by the ship's lanterns, sliced painfully down upon us.

2

And so we did not die.

The burly man with the axe proved to be the ship's captain, a German by birth, an Englishman by chance, who went by the name of Benedikt Kinast. He was sixty years old at least, with pulsing red hands and extravagant wrinkles. He dragged us down, soaked, gasping, out of the storm and into the swaying, creaking hold of the ship. There were sailors moving rapidly in the shadows, tying ropes fast, working at the hatches. At each sudden shift of the vessel a great dunk of water poured in through the hatch, sloshing at our feet.

There was a single lit lantern hanging from a nail on a beam above Mister Benedikt's head. He turned on us in the swaying light and swore. "You cracked the mizzen and damaged my victuals," he bellowed. "What business have you, anyhow, being out in a storm like this, in a contraption like that?"

"It was a Cloud-cutter," said Titch.

"I do not give a shit what you call it. You don't drop it on my aft-deck. Who are you?" he said, turning on Titch.

"I might ask you the same, sir," Titch replied. "And your vessel, in fact, did not *damage* my Cloud-cutter, but rather destroyed it. Entirely. I might suggest you owe me for the expense of an entire new *contraption*, as you call it."

The captain wiped at his wet beard with a big red open hand. He glanced over my shoulder. "Mister Slipp, get back and lash the barrels fast. I won't have more damage this night." His eyes fixed again on Titch. "I was on course here, steady as the fucking stars. You fell on *me*."

"Captain!" a second man called from above. "Cutter's like to give!"

"Fix it fast, you bastards!" he roared.

"We, Captain, were in complete control," Titch continued smoothly, as if the burly man had not just shouted. "We were flying low to keep out of the storm. *You* sailed into *us*. Where were your deck lanterns, sir? How is it you sail so unmarked?"

"A goddamn storm," Mister Benedikt muttered. "A balloon in a goddamn storm."

Titch's head was bent forward to keep it from striking the low ceiling, and he reached up now with both arms to grip a beam for balance. He said, angrily, "One would be forgiven, sir, for mistaking this for a smuggling vessel. Who else sails at night, without lights?"

"You'll want to watch your bloody mouth."

"You mean my bloody mouth, *sir*," Titch snapped.

The two men glared at each other as the ship swayed; both were leaning into their thigh muscles to keep in place. My stomach lurched. The captain was powerful, all spit and outrage, an extension of the storm itself.

"You're a bold one, aren't you?" he said. "You have a name?"

Titch remained silent.

"Don't care to say, eh?" said Mister Benedikt. "Someone after you, then? Pair of fugitives?"

"Christopher Wilde," Titch said, looking leadenly at the man.

"Son of James Wilde, Fellow of the Royal Society, recipient of the Copley Medal and the Bakerian lectureship."

Captain Benedikt puffed out his cheeks. "Royal Society."

"My friend here calls me Titch."

Though the storm had not abated, still something had shifted, eased, between us three below decks. Captain Benedikt turned an angry smile on me, and grunted. "Friend? Ain't you property, boy?"

Titch let go of the beam he had been clutching for balance and set a hand on my shoulder. "Indeed, the boy is my property," said he, and I was rattled to hear him speak these words. "He has shown himself an excellent scientific illustrator, and so, rather than wasting his talents in physical labour, I've made better use of him as a personal assistant. He has quite a gift for expressing aeronautical methodologies in ink. You and your crew would be wise to treat him with the respect he is due. There are powerful men in England studying our latest report with interest."

Mister Benedikt chewed at his pipe stem. "Oh, give off," he said. "Looks a plain old nigger slave to me."

"The first rule of science, Captain, is to doubt appearances and to seek substances in their stead."

The ship rolled, turned, rolled. "Substances my arse," Mister Benedikt said, paying the movement no mind. "You still owe me a ship's worth of repairs, Christopher Wilde, and we'll be talking to the substance of that right enough."

My scalp was bleeding. Captain Benedikt had handed across to me a large red handkerchief cold with salt water, and when I pressed it to my head, the wound at once started to sting. He explained that a ship's surgeon was on board, though violently ill in his cabin. He scowled and told us to find our way aft to the fellow, and to keep out of the way of his bloody sailors.

"Go on," spat Mister Benedikt, "the both of you. I won't have you expiring on my damned deck. Go."

"Where do we find this surgeon?" Titch asked, his knees shifting as the ship ascended another swell.

There was a crash and the sound of men hollering from above.

"Do I look like a man with the time to offer directions?" Mister Benedikt roared. Nevertheless, he said, "Straight along past the hammocks and up the first ladder. You'll know it by the bile between your toes." He turned to go, muttering and shaking his head. "It's a goddamn barque, you can't walk far without finding open water."

Titch gave me an exhausted look, and I could see the toll the evening's events had taken. He led me on, into the darkness of the ship, falling against the narrow walls, ducking his head as he went. A single lantern swayed on a hook near some webbing, and the shadows crawled across the walls. A sealed wooden box slid the length of the cabin; it splashed up against the far wall, then rolled back in the ankle-deep surf.

An image of Mister Philip's wrecked face flashed in my mind, and I was overcome with a sick sort of panic. It seemed inevitable to me we'd be found out; that the stink of blood was on me still.

The old surgeon opened his cabin door at the second knock. I caught my breath, staring. I did not understand the nature of the joke. For it was Captain Benedikt who stood before us, groaning, his coat changed and dry now, his hair drawn tightly back from his pained face. He wore the same beard, coughed the same damp cough. "What is it?" he barked.

"Captain?" said Titch.

Then I saw the missing fingers on the man's left hand and shook my head, confounded.

He stepped back, gestured us in with his chin. "I take it you were sent here to be examined? Come, let me have a look at you. You are the gentlemen who fell upon our deck, no doubt. Come in, do. My brother will be cross if I do not at least bandage that cut on the boy's head."

"Look at him, Titch," said I, astonished. "He is the very image."

"They are twins, Wash," said Titch.

"I trust we are," the surgeon said. "Or there is more mystery to my origins than I can account for. Will you sit?" The surgeon gave us a weak smile. "Theo Kinast, sir, ship's surgeon and general source of sailors' misery," he said to Titch. "And you, boy. Hold yourself steady so I can see to that gash. Though from the looks of it the cut is nothing to your past injuries. What a ghastly burn."

I gripped the edge of his narrow bed frame as the floor shifted under us. I clenched my teeth as he poked at my wound, though I knew better than to speak or cry out.

The doctor muttered as he worked. "Gave the lads quite a scare, you did, dropping like gods from the sky. Some of them are quite superstitious." He coughed, turning to Titch. "Now, what is your name?"

"Christopher Wilde, sir."

"The nigger called you Titch."

Titch frowned. "The boy is called Washington. And yes, he did call me Titch."

The surgeon eyed us both, grunting. "Well, Mister Wilde, what do you mean by flying about in this weather? What were you flying away from?" He poked some sharp thing at my scalp and I let out a cry. "Stop it, now," he said to me, but not unkindly. He glanced wearily at Titch. "The lads tell me my brother believes the boy a fugitive. Believes that you, sir, are stealing this black away from his rightful master."

"I am his master," Titch said patiently. "As I explained to your brother, the boy is my assistant on the plantation. I was launching a prototype of my aerostat."

"And which plantation would that be?" said the surgeon.

"Hope, on Saint Lucia."

"Why would a planter venture out in such a fashion, leaving his plantation to the whims of others?"

"I am not the planter—I oversee the slaves who operate the mechanized tools. I am trained as an engineer, you see. I was given full use of the plantation's resources, as well as some few days off to make a successful launch of my aerostat. If I'd triumphed, the Cloud-cutter would have proved an invaluable tool in our daily operations there. This boy you see here was granted me as an assistant. He has played a crucial role in the assembly and launching of my aerostat."

"The balloon that is now at the bottom of the sea," said the doctor.

"It is not a balloon," said Titch.

The surgeon smiled tiredly.

"What is progress, sir, without error?" said Titch.

"Hold still," said the surgeon. But he leaned back and gave me a curious look. Above his beard he had a long, needling nose and deep-set black eyes. His brow jutted outwards like some awesome precipice. And despite all, his dark eyes seemed to me soft, restless, thoughtful, with a kindness so rarely granted to one like me that, meeting his eyes, I shivered.

The morning waters were calm. The ship smelled of tar, of vomit and salt water. Again I had not slept; I lay in a twist of blankets beside Titch on the planks of a tiny, unfurnished cabin. Titch had been so tired he'd begun to snore as soon as he'd lain down. In sleep he looked easy, emptied of all striving, like someone granted a clemency. I recalled his lie of the night before, the chill it had sent through me to hear him claim me as his property. The ruse had of course been necessary, but still it felt eerie to me, like a sudden breach of reality. Most strange, I think, was that in a parallel life—or perhaps even a prior one, before his moral awakening—Titch's story might have been the truth.

He stirred now, his bones cracking softly, his face pale with exhaustion. He sat up, rubbing at his cheeks, and for a moment I glimpsed in him the anguish of the earlier evening. Catching my eyes on him, he gave a slow, sad smile. "We have made it away, Wash," he murmured. "What a miracle."

I returned the smile, but could not help but think of Mister Philip, and of the master. I knew Titch could not possibly fault me for all that had happened, but still I felt uneasy at having been the sole witness of his cousin's brutal death, and for wrenching both of our lives off course. I was terrified also of being found out by the Kinasts. Did the brothers have some method of detection to discover where we had come from, what we actually were? What would they do with us then? The boat rose gently under us on the swells, and I got up in silence to clean my teeth and face.

Moments later Titch and I found ourselves at the small breakfasting table in the captain's quarters, facing the ship's surgeon, none of us with any appetite. Captain Benedikt was nowhere to be seen. "My brother is rough in his manners, but he has a generous heart," his brother explained. His eyes were ringed, his skin ill-looking. "He tells me you will accompany us to the next port. Indeed, it is either that or leave you for the sharks." He gave a sharp little chuckle. "Do not worry, you shall have no trouble in finding a vessel in Haiti to take you back to Saint Lucia. Unless you wish to accompany us as far as Virginia, which I imagine you don't."

Titch paused, gripping his metal cup tightly. I saw something pass across his face. "Virginia," he said slowly. "You sail the triangular trade, then?"

"We are not illicit slavers, if that's what you mean," said Mister Theo, sparing me no glance. We waited for him to elaborate, but he spoke no more.

I thought Titch would leave it, but he said, "So what is your enterprise, then, sir?"

Mister Theo shifted uncomfortably. "Rum, molasses. Sugar. Goods from the Indies. We trade them in Virginia for hemp—for hemp and tobacco, I believe." His face darkened in embarrassment. "I sail with the ship, you understand. It makes no difference to me where she goes, what she carries. I am paid the same."

"By your brother."

"By the gentlemen underwriting this journey, sir. My brother is the captain, not the owner."

"It must be an unusual living."

"I do not do it regularly," Mister Theo said. "I am a chiropodist, principally. I am along on this voyage as a favour to my brother, that is all."

"A chiropodist," Titch said, interested. "That is the study of feet."

Half-rising from his rough wood seat, Mister Theo reached for his glass of rum, licking the rim in a bright flash of tongue. "Very good, sir, yes. Of course, my training is the regular training of the surgeon. I am satisfactorily qualified for this task. My specialty is rather my own."

I knew this man was not being forthright with us, and though I could not conceive the nature of his dissembling, I believed his claim that they were not slavers. It would have been difficult on such a ship to conceal so grotesque an endeavour. In any case, it seemed unwise to question him further, we who had our own dark business to conceal. The wood beams in the ceiling creaked as the ship moved, and we could hear the shouts of sailors on deck and the sounds of feet passing overhead. Through the small port window, pale light drifted in. The shelves held hide-bound charts and sea annals. Mister Theo took down a chart and unrolled it, gesturing to Titch to study the location with him.

"I have a very dear friend in Virginia," said Titch, and I glanced up at him. "It is in fact quite serendipitous for me that you are headed there. If it wouldn't be too much trouble, might we accompany you the entire journey, to Virginia? We have money enough for our keep, and we will try to be as useful as possible."

"But have you leave to be so many months away from your post, sir?" Mister Theo said flatly, though it was clear he was suspicious.

"I do not. But the reunion in Virginia will undoubtedly prove crucial to redesigning the Cloud-cutter. My friend is a great aeronaut. I shall write my employer at once explaining the situation. I am sure I will be given leave."

Mister Theo cleared his throat as though taking it in, but I sensed he did not believe Titch. "This I must discuss with my brother. You realize we are many weeks, many stops yet from America?" he said, stabbing with his ruined hand at the chart. "Your contraption, your Cloud-cutter—what was your destination, before the storm struck?"

Our silence was marked, uncomfortable. And so I blurted, "What happened to your fingers, sir?"

"Wash," Titch said softly.

Mister Theo studied me, rubbing his beard. "They were removed, boy, with a knife. A gift from the French, during the wars. It was a very hot knife. And a very unwelcome gift."

I HAD NOT known twins before, and the sight of them together all that first day left me uneasy, as though a cloud had passed in front of the sun. Titch and I walked the ship, we rested, we perused the minuscule library of books and charts, we slept. We neither of us mentioned his cousin, nor his brother, nor the danger of discovery that held us fast like a leash. On the second day I awoke before Titch. I paused in the thin morning light and watched him sway in the slung hammock he had now been given. I slipped out of the cabin and made my way to the upper deck. My head was sore, but the wound was not serious. The light was radiant, and very white, and I stood in the sudden salt air feeling a cool wind on my face, my clothes rustling around my body. The blue sea stretched out as far as the eye could measure, in all directions, as if the world had been swallowed by water. There were sailors at work, coiling ropes, clambering up and down the rigging, washing down the deck. I saw two men—carpenters—sawing down boards and nailing into place a makeshift barrier at the railing where the Cloud-cutter had gone over. If not for such evidence the storm would have been but a hallucination. The ship cut its quick wake through the waves, the sails fore and aft swollen with wind.

Beyond those first days I saw little of the captain and his brother, the surgeon. This was as great a relief as it was a worry, for much as I feared being interrogated about the true nature of our appearance here, I did not like to think of the Kinasts furtively discussing us, secretly making plans to turn us in.

All this I tried to put from my mind as the days became weeks, but I never let my guard down, watching, observing. Some evenings I would take out my papers and leads and attempt to sketch the twins from memory, trying very hard to recall their differences so as to make them distinct. But at this I always failed. In life they were discrete as cane fields, each with his own character and history and way of talking. Yet when I sat down to draw them, they became one pale face, one beady, judging set of eyes. They defied my every attempt to get them right. Disturbed, I began instead to make sketches of the open water. I would walk slowly to the railing and stare out at the roiling waves. When we reached port in Haiti, I stayed aboard with Titch and sketched the sailors hauling huge crates through the air with ropes blackened with sea plants.

The long, slow weeks at sea turned me inwards, brought unwanted ruminations. Peering over the great rambling township of Habana, I thought of Mister Philip's abrupt death and the unknown scenes that must have followed. But I also thought much of Big Kit, and of Gaius, and of all those I had left behind at Faith. It was a wonder to me that a world of cruelty and hardship existed, even now, only some miles away. How was it possible, thought I, that we lived in such nightmare and all the while a world of men continued just over the horizon, men such as these, in ships moving in any direction the wind might lead them? I thought how Titch had risked everything for me. I knew he had preserved my person despite the death of his own flesh and blood, and I knew, too, how strange it felt to be alive, and whole, and astonishingly worth saving.

I felt burdened by such thoughts and so did not notice until the last moment that I was no longer alone. I turned to see Titch standing behind me, running his long fingers over his ruddy face, blinking sleepily in the brightness.

"It is a fine day for sailing," he said with a tired smile. He looked past me out at the empty and endless waters, and then raised his face and stared up the tall mizzen-mast to the small figures scrambling about in the sunlight.

"Imagine this life," he said. "Scurrying about like monkeys. Look at them."

I looked.

"We shall be arriving in America in some few days, I expect," Titch said.

I studied his face as he said this. I knew that he was not telling me all there was to tell. I lowered my voice. "Do you suppose they know?"

Titch shrugged softly, turned to me. "It is impossible to say. But what they do not know, and what they must never discover, is which island we came from, which plantation."

I stared at him, nervous. "And shall we stay in Virginia, when we arrive there?"

He smiled sadly at me. "I am afraid you will not wish to once you have seen it, Wash, believe me. I expect there will be many ships leaving from there. Though we may be best served by a ship out of Baltimore." When I looked at him curiously, he added, "It is only a short ways farther along the coast. It is a big city, a city of ships."

I nodded. "And then where will we move on to?"

"It is a large world." He gave me a long, searching look. "Have you eaten anything? Let us go down and find ourselves some breakfast. I fear the ship has been awake for hours, there may be little left."

CAPTAIN BENEDIKT NEVER deigned to speak to me—he would stare out past my head if I neared him. But his brother, Theo, seemed eager for a listening ear, and as the *Ave Maria* neared the coast of Florida, I came to learn more of the Kinasts' strange story.

Their father had been an officer in the Hanover Foot Guards, and when George II declared war on France in 1756, the elder Kinast was conscripted to cross the Channel and drill with the English regiments. The twins were babies then, only just months old; they journeyed with their mother to Maidstone, Kent, where their father had been stationed. In the years to come, the boys found Kent suspicious, sunless, unfriendly to any who spoke a broken English as they did, having learned the tongue from their mother. English words clotted in their mouths like a shadow German. Their frost-white hair and identical faces were mocked by the local children.

When cholera took both of their parents in the final year of the war, Mister Theo and Mister Benedikt were left alone in their narrow, dirty rooms; they wandered the streets with a pack of urchins prowling for food. One week later the doctor who had cared for their parents appeared, having learned of the twin boys left orphaned, and took them home to his grand house.

"That was a charity we were not used to," Mister Theo explained to me. "I think you will understand me, boy, when I say the world cares nothing for a child alone in it."

"What of your parents?" I asked quietly.

Mister Theo looked slightly to the side. "They were buried in a pauper's grave, like all of the dead that summer. We never saw them again. And the dead have no compassion for the living."

The English doctor and his wife were childless, and they raised the boys as their own, seeing to their education and introducing them to the worlds of their choosing. Mister Benedikt had wished to join the army, as their father had done, but in the end enlisted in the Royal Navy and served out five years before taking his leave and entering the merchant trade. Mister Theo studied medicine in Edinburgh and later in London, the nature of the human foot driving his studies. He was interested in the shape of the bones and the manner of human ambulation, but had discovered the profitable nature of chiropody to be somewhat less intriguing.

"One lances a plantar's wart, boy, or extracts an ingrown toenail, and there the thing sits, glowing in the basin like some hideous barnacle," he said, a brief smile playing at his lips. He took three swift drinks from his flask, his fingerless stumps looking red and raw. "And this is the labour of a man, day after day, as he lives out his life. How does that strike you?"

After a long moment of trying to muster my courage to speak, I remained silent.

"One night I agreed to treat my accountant—a fine man," Mister Theo continued, "and as he settled into the chair, it seemed to me all the outer world had quieted. I readied the scalpels—as I had done every day of my working life—but my hands were stiff, stupid, and I could see the poor man's nervousness. I mustered my composure, boy, and I cut into his heel. He screamed."

A shudder passed through me.

"It was from that moment that my interest in feet began to decline. I cannot explain it. Inside the basin lay a putrid muck, I could *smell* the rot as if I had not witnessed just such foulness week after week. And from that day on, at each procedure, I heard a great echo rolling inside of me, a great thundering echo. As if I were half-mad."

I nodded.

"And then, after a time, at last, I stopped hearing it. And when I stopped hearing it, that is when it happened."

I hesitated. "What happened, sir?"

"What always happens. A woman."

"Do they happen?"

"If you are lucky, boy, that is all that happens."

I did not understand his meaning. "That sounds terrible, sir," I whispered, fearful still of venturing an opinion to an unknown white man.

He gave me a sharp, swift look. "Does it? Ah. Well, perhaps I am not describing it right."

THE *AVE MARIA* was a brig-rigged ship of one hundred and fifty tons, but heavy for its size. It had been outfitted in England, its hull reinforced for northern waters.

All this Mister Theo told to me as though it might make some impression. She cut a sharp line through the waves, sailed straight as a compass. I saw less of Titch as the days passed, but would glimpse him studying some arcane text in the ship's library, or deep in conversation with the captain, and I would leave him be, knowing he was likely trying to aid our case with the Kinasts. And so I wandered the tarry decks, clambered up the ladders to sketch from above, wandered among the barrels and nettings to make sketches from below deck. I had, from the very first day, found myself entranced by the crew, who all seemed of an age, and spoke little to each other, but, almost like a single organism, understood what was needed and where, and worked as one. They mopped, polished, tied, retied, folded, unfolded, let out and drew in all of the bolts and buckles and crates and sails and ropes and pulleys of the ship with a fixed concentration I found hypnotic. I set myself the task of sketching everything on the ship, its berths and small cabins, the lower hold. And all this time we sailed nearer and nearer to the land of freedom, the land I had been named for, the great, impossible America.

On the sixty-eighth day Titch walked to the stern where I sat with my face in the sun. He smiled.

"You have been keeping busy these weeks," he said.

"I am like a cat," said I. "I roam everywhere and am not seen."

He glanced squinting in the light, then turned back to me. "I have been speaking to Captain Benedikt," he said quietly. "Our conversation was pleasant enough, all about our origins and family. He asks a great deal after you. After the *F* he has seen on your chest."

I tried not to look alarmed.

"We will make land at Norfolk," Titch said, as if this was some reassurance.

It meant little to me, of course. Titch explained we would be entering Chesapeake Bay, and would therefore soon be leaving the ship. We would also, however, find ourselves subject to the laws of American freedom. "Freedom, Wash, is a word with different meanings to different people," he said, as though I did not know the truth of this better than he.

"I shall be glad to see my friend," Titch said thoughtfully.

"Who is he, this man in Virginia?" said I. "You have spoken of him these weeks as your colleague. He is an aeronaut?"

"Among other things." The ocean around us was a pale blue, the sunlight glittering upon the wind ruffling Titch's hair. "You shall find him a most interesting man."

ON THE NIGHT before we struck land, I stood on the upper deck peering west, towards what I imagined must be Virginia. The air was different. I could smell the mulchy scent of the cliffs, the farmlands beyond, and something else, an acrid tang which I did not know. I stood gripping the rail loosely in one hand, my face upraised, my eyes closed in the near darkness as the ship rose and dipped in the swells. Then I heard a strange crackle behind me, almost as of leaves rustling. Startled, I turned to observe a jagged silhouette fluttering in the weak glow of a lit pipe.

It was Mister Benedikt. He stood at the bulwark with his pipe clenched between his teeth, watching me with unblinking eyes.

Nervous, I lowered my eyes and made to slip by.

"You have been speaking to Theo," he said suddenly.

I stood there feeling quite naked. "He has been speaking to me, sir," I said almost inaudibly, again lowering my eyes.

"Spirited, aren't you. Rather like your friend."

I said nothing to this, my eyes still lowered.

"The friend that you purport is your master."

I tipped my chin up, looking openly at him, though my hands were trembling.

He seemed to take no notice of my nervousness. "And how do you like *Ave Maria*? A fair ship for her nature. Cranky somewhat." He nodded as if in agreement with himself, turning towards the darkness. "She was a privateer, but the bloody navy revoked her letters of marque two years back. Her size never troubled her. She's no smaller than a sloop, and twice as fast. Used to be, at least. What's that look, boy? She sails the Atlantic trade now, she does." Mister Benedikt gave me a quick, dark look. "Not slaves, as you've seen. Sugar and tobacco. It's profitable enough, for them that can keep the wind at their back."

I did not understand why he was suddenly speaking to me so. I thought of his brother, how Mister Theo described him as a man with a good heart despite his gruffness. I wondered if this was the good heart addressing me now.

He paused as a night crewman stepped across the deck and made his way aft. "Look at that, boy. All my sailors are the same age, give or take a year. Did not you wonder about that? Did it not strike you?"

I did not answer.

"They're all of them orphaned boys. Whole bloody crew. Took them on myself when their orphanage was shut down and they were all to be thrown into the streets. First time I knew I was in the right, I was nearly drowned in a pinnace at Abu Shehr and five of the lads leaped into the waves to rescue me. Five of them. That was an era ago. All my other men are gone and these wee ones are still here. What does that tell you?"

In my fear I was a long while to speak. "You are well regarded by them, sir," I said softly.

"Aye." Mister Benedikt smiled a thin, vinegary smile. He spoke very quietly. "I know you are a slave run away. And I know your Mister Wilde is a thief for having procured you."

I stood very still. This he had said when we first crashed upon his ship; it was no new discovery.

He eyed me in the darkness, the boat rising and surging in the wind. "Saint Lucia my arse." He shook his head. "You were far too southeasterly for Saint Lucia. No, you are a nigger slave from Barbados, or from Grenada."

My heart was pounding so hard it was as if I would be knocked from my footing. A thin, invisible mist sprayed off the water.

"What are you?" said he, his voice suddenly softer.

I raised my face, terrified.

"Are you a human creature?"

He reached out and touched the burnt half of my face, drawing his rough hand sharply back almost at once, as if scorched. I was too surprised to move. I stood stunned by the feel of his fingers. His touch had been cool, and gentle, and somehow, though I would never have thought it, filled with an impossible sadness.

3

Norfolk stank. Its docks stank of tobacco, of lead, of crushed reeds and especially of cotton, white bolls of it glowing like plucked eyes on their boughs. It stank of unwashed deckhands and mutton stew and offal steaming in the gutters along the harbour streets. It stank of mud and turpentine and stale perfumes oozing from the pores of the prostitutes in their greasy dresses. The pungency of it all after the long days at sea left me light-headed, and I stared all around me, slack-jawed, like a simpleton.

For what a grand city was Norfolk, despite all! The bustle and the clatter, the swarm of men at work, the scurrying about the streets, the towering three-storey brick warehouses facing the shipyards. How I longed to draw all this! There were horses pressing through stalled carts, and wagons with huge open beds, their drivers lolling drunkenly as they hollered casual profanities. Titch had told me of the fire that had burned the city in 1804, but I could see no evidence of it.

In the end we needn't have feared the Kinasts, or so we came away believing. Certainly they had guessed at our history, but it became increasingly clear that Captain Benedikt cared more about having been lied to than about the actual substance of that lie. He was a man with his own fate to meet, and neither he nor his brother wanted to be waylaid by complications they had not themselves taken on. And so they asked only that we be discreet in departing their ship, and that we not mention their vessel or their names when speaking of how we'd arrived on American soil. They saw in our desperation something of their own childhood losses, and they did not want to hurt or make trouble for us.

Titch said, "It is still best to be cautious, Wash, to place as little trust as possible in strangers. Men forget themselves too quickly, and a mercy is often the first thing revoked."

And so Titch and I stepped from the plank into port, stunned by the vast roar, the waters teeming with ships. Smoke rose from oily fires along the docks. Nets filled with crates were swung out over the black depths. And everywhere men walked their own destinies, uncompelled. So this, I thought in wonder, this is America.

Ah, but not all men went about in such freedom. Not men such as myself.

Titch and I drifted through the crowds at the darkened quayside, trying very hard not to be noticed. He believed if he made the correct inquiries he could find this "most interesting man" he had mentioned, a great friend and associate of his father's, one Mister Farrow. We walked circumspectly as he considered his options. I had a bundle of sailor's clothes and a hock of salted ham tied to my back, for we had been given goods, along with a few bright coins more, by the irritable Captain Benedikt, to better acquaint ourselves with the world of America.

Titch left me at the sunlit corner of a busy thoroughfare. He crossed the street to inquire at an inn that doubled as a postal office, passing into shadow. I watched him go, tall, rumpled, clutching a paper with his acquaintance's address on it. Then I turned aside to wait under a shopfront overhung with a rotted wood sign, its purpose illegible, its interior in shadow. When a man with a tall white hat walked out of the next doorway, I raised my face in surprise. A harsh sweetness filled my nose, the very smell of my old life.

Sugar.

I stepped forward, cupping a hand and pressing my brow against the grimy display window. Boxes of bright, lumpy candies, yellow and golden and green, red candied discs on sticks, twists of black licorice that I had seen on my sole trip into Bridge Town. White fleeces of sugar frozen and set out in cones of paper. An early sun had warmed the pane, and against my face it felt like a human hand. I thought of Big Kit's slow, soft palm.

"Take your face from there, boy!"

For a moment I felt myself between worlds, and I stayed where I was, my face pressed against that good warm glass.

I was struck on my side, and I stumbled, and gasped in shock. It was not the pain but the surprise that took me. A pale-eyed man with bleached mutton chops stood scowling. He wore a white apron, his shirt sleeves tied off. His teeth were orange in the front.

He made a curious shooing motion with his hand.

"You shove off now, nigger," he said. "You don't go pushing your goddamn nose up against my window, you hear?"

In the street a carriage rolled by, its wheels grinding over the cobblestones. Men and ladies pressed past, taking no notice.

I took a frightened step back.

He lifted his chin and peered over my back at the ham. "You steal that there, boy? You a runaway? Who you here with?" He took another step towards me. He was not a large man, but he lacked fear, and I had known such men on Faith Plantation. They were the most brutal. "What happened to your face? Someone burned you up right good."

I was so frightened I closed my eyes, as if he might then disappear. I did not know where Titch had gone to, but I understood, in that moment, the terrible bottomless nature of the open world, when one belongs nowhere, and to no one.

I felt an awesome blow to my chest, and then another, and waiting to be struck again I felt only the absence of pain; when the third blow did not come, I opened my eyes in astonishment.

Titch shoved his way between us, his necktie askew, his hat in his hand as he gestured angrily down at me. "What is the meaning of all this?" He glared down at the small confectioner from his towering height. "What is this?"

"This your boy?" the confectioner said, uneasy.

"What has he done?"

The man cleared his throat, drew the back of his hand along his jaw. "My apologies. I had him mistook for a runaway."

"Mistaken."

"Come again?"

"The word is *mistaken*. And yes. You were."

Just then a man in a cutaway strolled into the confectioner's store. The shopkeep frowned and gave me a black look, saying, "You get your boy here some proper sack for carrying your goods. Looks like a fugitive, going round like that." He nodded and, turning, stepped inside.

My terror was such that I desperately wished to sit down right there, in the muck of the street. But Titch slipped a hand under my elbow and, with a saddened expression, steered me clear of that place.

+ + +

TITCH DID NOT at first make mention that anything was wrong.

With a queer lightness of voice he explained how he had acquired directions to his associate's address. The man's name was Edgar Farrow, and he was the acting sexton of St. John's parish. The parish lay some ten miles to the west, in the rolling fields and woodlands along the course of the Elizabeth River. We walked awhile in the morning sunlight, the birds brisk and loud. Titch sank into preoccupation, not talking.

"You are nervous at meeting Mister Farrow again?" said I, guessing at his thoughts.

"I have never in all my life laid eyes on him. He started as my father's associate, actually, from the Royal Society. Our own correspondence began only some years ago, but it very quickly became constant, fervent. His mind, Wash, oh, it is an absolute wonder. Brilliant. Brilliant." Titch exhaled heavily from the walk. "Do not be alarmed by him. He has some rather idiosyncratic notions about the nature of the world and is seeking to learn how far they might go. In this, I expect, he is no different from any of us." He paused. "Except his interests are not chiefly aeronautical. He is a necropsocist. A scholar of human decay." And then, I suppose, in case I was not sufficiently disturbed, Titch added: "Mister Farrow has made a reputation for examining the ways and conditions under which human flesh rots."

I gave Titch a look of displeasure. "He is a man of the Church."

"You are correct," he nodded, mistaking my meaning. "I think you will find him a man of many contradictions."

We continued walking, the sun high and hot.

"You are uneasy," said Titch.

"No," said I. "Yes, perhaps."

"You are thinking of Philip," he said quietly.

I nodded.

Frowning slightly, Titch came to a stop on the red dirt path, taking from inside his pocket a tattered paper. "I did not want to show it to you. It was mounted in the postal office." Glancing warily at me, he began to read:

A Reward of One Thousand Pounds will be paid for the capture of GEORGE WASHINGTON BLACK, a Negro Boy of small stature, his countenance marked with Burns; a Slave for life. His Clothing is a new Felt Hat, black Cotton Frockcoat and Breeches, and new Stockings and Shoes. He may be travelling alongside an Abolitionist White Man not his lawful owner, with Green Eyes and Black Hair, of tall stature. Whoever secures the Murderous Slave so that I get him Dead or Alive shall have ONE THOUSAND POUNDS Reward.

JOHN FRANCIS WILLARD, acting agent for
ERASMUS WILDE
Faith Plantation, Barbadoes, British West India

I stood very still on the dirt path. I stared at the paper in Titch's hands. What senselessness came over me then, what shock.

Titch took my arm, led me into the shade at the foot of a dogwood in flower. Above us, in the clear skies, tiny birds dipped and trilled.

"The postmaster was a talkative sort," Titch said. "I asked after the man who had posted it, but he said he had given no name. I asked for a description of him, and how long ago he had come in. He said it was very recent, some days ago only. Described him as brown-haired, tan-complexioned, tall and rather plump, with brown eyes."

I glanced sharply up, waiting for him to say what he knew.

"The description fits no one I know—a random man. But then I realized I recognized the name on the poster, the acting agent. John Francis Willard."

"Who is he?"

"My brother hosted a series of formal dinners when first we arrived in Barbados. John Willard was twice in attendance."

"He is a slave catcher?"

"Rather, a self-described righter of grievances." Titch pinched his eyes shut, as though struggling to recall. "Very cultured, soft-spoken, manners beyond reproach. I remember he'd been the book-keeper on a neighbouring plantation before becoming frustrated with it all. I understood he'd begun hiring out his services as a kind of transnational bounty man." Titch shook his head. "It was odd, hearing him speak of it. It seemed woefully out of character. He talked of travelling large distances to catch men who had done nothing more than rack up gambling debts. He talked of tracking down errant slaves who'd made it off the island. He described the job with great obscenity, as if it thrilled him to be beyond the law of any nation. He recognizes no jurisdiction, you see, and he is never held to account." He frowned, muttering. "I understood he'd done some terrible things."

I fell silent, staring at my hands.

"Wash," said Titch.

"A thousand pounds," I breathed. I could not imagine such wealth.

Titch made a soft grunt. "I had thought something of this order beneath Erasmus," he murmured. "Men are rarely what they seem, I guess."

I said nothing. I stared at the iridescence of a fly scuttling across the hock of ham in my half-open sack.

"It is a considerable sum." Titch shook his head. "And you know this is not the whole of it. Willard will already have been paid to begin the hunt, even if only in expenses. I expect if he delivers he will be taking away all this and more." He turned to me. "You do understand that my brother does not actually believe you responsible, do you not? That all this is merely a means to get at me?"

If this was meant as some consolation, it failed miserably. A fierce nausea began to chew through me, as if some feral thing had lodged in my gut. "Can you not simply take me to England?" I said, my voice pale, thin. "Will I not be safer there?"

Titch eyed me uneasily. "This is a bounty, Wash. The law means nothing to a thief-taker out for his reward. And the reward, frankly, will be a lure to many. It is grotesquely large."

I thought and thought. "Can you not simply pay it out yourself?"

"Pay off Willard, or some other madman? How would that work? He would simply pocket it and keep after you for the second thousand. And how many would we need to pay off? I have not such great funds at my disposal." He shifted on the gravel, cleared his throat. "I am the second born, I have a small living only. I have not access to the family purse as my brother does."

We sat a good long while in the heat, not speaking. When by chance a rickety cart passed, we were invited by the ancient driver to clamber up. Titch rode on the bench in front, I in the rear bed with a sack of leather and nails at my back, the large hock of ham set flatly down in the straw. The cart was drawn by a shaggy grey mare, with a single bloodshot eye rolling back at us. The driver, his cheek full of tobacco, leaned over and spat, wiping the back of his hand along his mouth before shaking the reins. On we cantered. I feared the driver would wish to speak for the company, but he said nothing, just spat occasionally and kept his own counsel.

It had happened so gradually, but these months with Titch had schooled me to believe I could leave all misery behind, I could cast off all violence, outrun a vicious death. I had even begun thinking I'd been born for a higher purpose, to draw the earth's bounty, and to invent; I had imagined my existence a true and rightful part of the natural order. How wrong-headed it had all been. I was a black boy, only—I had no future before me, and little grace or mercy behind me. I was nothing, I would die nothing, hunted hastily down and slaughtered.

I watched as the green crept past in the sun, the great warm fields of springtime Virginia. I was startled by the vastness, the endless stretch of earth. When we passed a small grove, I was overwhelmed by the smell of tiny white flowers, the watery, soft perfume they gave off. I glimpsed, too, slaves in the fields, and as I stared upon their bodies, I was flooded with guilt and fear for myself.

At last we were set down at a fork in the road. The driver gestured us on eastward. With the sun already lowering at our backs, we walked the grassy roadbed with our shadows stretched out before us.

Just then we came around a bend in the slope and saw it: St. John's.

It was a small white clapboard church with a single low spire, and a weather-bruised fence enclosing a graveyard to one side.

There was a figure in black walking bow-backed among the graves as we climbed the hill. Titch took the ham from me and paused at the gate.

"Mister Farrow," he called. "Mister Edgar Farrow, sir."

The man tilted back the wide black brim of his hat, frowning. "We'll buy nothing from you this day," he called back. "But I can offer you shelter for the night."

Titch smiled. "Oh, we're selling nothing. But we'll take the shelter all the same. You won't know my face, Mister Farrow, though you might recognize my hand. I am Christopher Wilde, sir. We have corresponded on the potential for pressure shifts in aerostat ascents and its effects on the human body, these past two years now. My father, James Wilde, is your associate in the Royal Society."

I saw the man straighten then, and lift off his hat. He looked suddenly rail-thin, with a large oblong head and limp black hair. He was balding somewhat, and beneath his heavy brows his eyes were round and black, ringed from a lack of sleep. His lips were bloodless, his expression flat. He came towards us quickly, skirting an opened grave.

"Christopher Wilde, in the flesh," he said in a serious voice. "You are not in the West Indies, sir. Where is your Cloud-cutter?"

"At the bottom of the ocean, I fear," Titch laughed. "We are put ashore here, sir."

"Bottom of the ocean? What has happened to you, then?"

"A storm."

"'Tis indeed the season for it," said the sexton, muttering. Then his eyes dropped on me, his black gaze unfocused. He gave a series of methodical blinks, as though he did not notice my standing there. He frowned suddenly in distaste, though when he spoke, it was with a curious lack of emphasis. "It is the season for storms, yes," he repeated slowly. "And all manner of strangeness shall be blown in. Come, both of you. Let us speak inside."

4

"Come in, come in. I orient the graves towards the east, towards Jerusalem," he was saying, "that they may welcome the Resurrection." He shut the door of his living quarters with a sudden bang, locked it. The room felt dim, cold. I thought I could smell the wet soil on his palms, under his fingernails. Behind this, in a kind of green haze of scent, lay something sour and sharp, like a vat of pickling juice or vinegar left out too long. I wrinkled my nose. "Of course it is all nonsense, Mister Wilde, all superstition and foolishness," the sexton was saying. "Still, it keeps the parishioners satisfied. It would not do for them to find me wanting, and start asking questions."

He paused beside the little black stove and, retrieving a small piece of firewood, turned to me with a dark look. "Now, who is this you have brought me?"

"George Washington Black," said Titch, "lately of Faith Plantation."

"And a boy who can keep his tongue, I trust?"

"That he is. I'd stake my life on it."

I glanced sharply at Titch, surprised he would so easily reveal our particulars to this stranger. As if the gravity of the broadsheet had not yet sunk in.

"Do not be so hasty, Mister Wilde, to stake your life on anything. It is a lesson I have learned through much trial and error." The sexton made a curious clicking noise with his tongue, twice, and then turned on his boot heel and crossed to the far side of the room. "This, gentlemen, is where I sleep and eat and ablute. That door there leads to my offices, where I conduct my studies. Through that passage is the church. And this door, gentlemen," he said, stamping twice with his heavy boot, "leads to the cellar."

"We appreciate your allowing us to stay, sir," said Titch. "It is a fine, honest house."

Mister Edgar took a step towards me. "Mister Wilde has no doubt told you I am a man of solitary habits, and peculiar."

I hesitated. "He has said you study the dead, sir. That is all."

Mister Edgar raised his eyebrows at Titch.

"The boy has eyes in his head," Titch said, allowing himself a smile. "This he would certainly have discerned for himself."

The sexton studied me; again he clicked his tongue twice. "The boy, yes," he said in his soft voice. "I do not much care for childhood. It is a state of terrible vulnerability, and is therefore unnatural and incompatible with human life. Everyone will cut you, strike you, cheat you, everyone will offer you suffering when goodness should reign. And because children can do nothing for themselves, they need good advocates, good parents. But a good parent is as rare as snow in summer, I am afraid. Well." He smiled sadly. "It is possible I have some prejudices in this respect."

"You are an orphan yourself, are you not?" offered Titch.

A shadow played across the sexton's face, darkened his wide, pale forehead. We were still standing just inside the doorway, awaiting some further invitation that was not extended. My glance drifted to a darkening yellow square of muslin nailed over the lone window. Dusk was already descending outside.

"Sometimes," Mister Edgar continued, "when there is a baptism, I will stand in the nave and look upon the babe's face at a distance. I almost cannot bear it: the soft skin, the tenderness, the eyes so guileless and trusting. I would almost wish the innocent to be stricken at once, there, in God's house. To keep such purity intact. From the arms of God to the arms of God."

Titch was looking at the man with a curious expression. "Well," he said at last. And then nothing more.

Mister Edgar smiled slowly. "But why do we stand here? You are my honoured guests this night. I shall fetch you some bedding. Come in, come. The two of you will sleep here, if that suits."

He left us with the candle and walked to the trap door to the cellar. Hauling on a large iron ring set into the floor, he disappeared down into the darkness. I was surprised that he had not taken a light with him. We could hear the distant clank and shirr of objects being moved in the earth below us.

Titch had taken up the candle and he held it high, turning slowly to survey the room. He did not speak. He went through the narrow door to the sexton's office and I followed. The strange pickled smell grew stronger.

And then, from around Titch's left shoulder, in the candlelight, I saw it. A tall brass washbasin, with curving sides in the French style, and lying inside it in a bed of dark water was the thin, elongated form of a human arm. It was white as mould, with greyish veins running the surface, and a string had been tied to the wrist to elevate it. The hand was small, a woman's hand, and in the candlelight it appeared very white and bulbous, the flesh swelling. I saw that the thumb had been opened, and some metallic object had been inserted into the cavity.

"What is this?" I whispered. "Dear god."

"It appears," said Titch softly, "to be a severed arm."

I swore; I shook my head in disgust. "But where is the rest of her?"

"We shall not stay long." Titch had already turned and was leaving the office. He set the candle down where it had been before, at the edge of the small pier table beside the front entrance.

"Must we stay at all?" I said. "Titch?"

"Hush."

"He is a madman. His faculties have been damaged."

"I had said he made a study of the dead. This I did tell you."

"You have brought us to the house of a lunatic."

"Hush," Titch hissed again.

"It is not right," I protested. "Look at what he has done. I would rather risk meeting your Mister Willard in the city than stay in this abominable place."

"He is not my Mister Willard," said Titch.

But just then Mister Edgar materialized, his face pale in the shadows, his eyes black and unreadable. "My gentle friends," he said in his low voice. I felt my heart tremble; I did not know how much he had heard, how long he had been there. "Let us settle you in and then we shall feast."

IT WAS A fine, simple dinner of potatoes and string beans, along with our salted ham. I watched Mister Edgar with a quiet gaze, trying to determine the nature of the man. But Titch vouched for this sexton, and so I did not allow myself free suspicion.

Mister Edgar cut at his pork with great energy, then stabbed the cube of meat and started to chew. "I knew you were coming, Mister Wilde," he said around his bites. "During my morning prayers I had the sense. Or rather I felt it, sir, God infused the knowledge into my flesh." He smiled, chewed, smiled. "I did not foresee the ham, though."

"Our host has made a study of the flesh, Wash," Titch said to me. "He speaks of it as if it carries knowledge."

"Because it does," Mister Edgar said quickly. "Why, I could speak at length about you and your habits and your very life history, boy, through a cursory study of the markings on your body. Our bodies know truths our minds neglect." He squinted his eyes powerfully. "You were clearly burnt by a sudden eruption of fire, a spontaneous explosion. One can see by the feathering at your earlobe that you made a turning motion at the very moment of incandescence." He turned suddenly to Titch. "And you, Mister Wilde, that scar about your mouth."

Titch paused, looking uneasy.

"It was clearly caused in boyhood, between the ages of four and six," Mister Edgar continued. "A very thick wire, of tempered iron likely, was pressed into your mouth and yanked back, like so." He raised his thin, pale hands at either cheek and drew them sharply back. "You were dragged about in that fashion some two, three minutes before the wire was finally removed from your gullet. Much damage had been done to the epidermis, the basement membrane and the dermis, but the subcutaneous tissue remained mercifully intact."

I could see the orange light of the lantern reflected in Mister Edgar's eyes; he stared at me a long, thoughtful moment. His chair creaked.

"Remarkable," Titch said, though he did not sound at all impressed. Then, very abruptly, he cleared his throat, and began to speak of our adventures. He described the storm, and the plummet of the Cloud-cutter onto the deck of the *Ave Maria*. His mention of this ship's name was a shock; in my alarm I did not look at him. Only when he began to talk of his cousin's death and the bounty on my head did I turn to him in quiet horror.

Setting down his fork, Titch slipped the broadsheet from his pocket and flattened it across the grease-stained tablecloth. Mister Edgar scrutinized it with his large black eyes.

"Willard," Mister Edgar murmured, shaking his head. "How will I know him, if he turns up?"

"He has blond hair, and wire spectacles. His eyes are very large, and very blue." Titch paused, thinking. "He parts his hair very severely, so that it appears almost painful. And one of his eyes doesn't focus right, it lists all about, and is very disarming."

Mister Edgar took this in with great attention. "I daresay it would be a long way to travel for one black boy."

"I imagine it would be made very much worth his while."

Mister Edgar frowned. "I trust no one knows you are here."

"I did mention it to the captain of the *Ave Maria* that we would seek out a scientific colleague just beyond the city. The particulars I did not offer."

"I fear your stay in Virginia will be short, then."

"Yes." Some unspoken suggestion passed between them, something I could not discern the meaning of. I felt suddenly frightened again, agitated.

"The plantation is your father's, is it not?" said Mister Edgar.

"It came down through my mother's line, from her brother to mine."

"Even so, you might alert your father to what is happening. Perhaps he might intervene."

Titch looked weary, his forehead lined and heavy in the amber light. "You have not heard, then. My father passed away. Some eight months ago."

Mister Edgar made a curious face. "Passed away?"

"In the Arctic. His assistant wrote to my mother. My cousin Philip came to Faith to deliver the news."

Mister Edgar sat twining and untwining his long fingers on the table, his eyes glassy, unnerving. He stood abruptly from his seat and crossed the small room, returning with a dog-eared ivory envelope on which his name had been penned in a fine hand. This he set before Titch.

Frowning, Titch slid the papers from the envelope and began to read. I stared silently across at Mister Edgar, at the crooked set of his lips. He did not appear to be smiling, exactly; there was a kind of unhappy mirth to his features, like someone greeting a long-unseen aunt at a funeral.

The blood had left Titch's face. He looked up slowly. "Perhaps this is Peter's hand. His assistant." He sounded almost irritated. "Was it not very similar, their penmanship?"

Mister Edgar took the pages from Titch, flipping through them with his long, bony hands, then parting them in half. In silence he set the two thin stacks side by side on the table. "Here you have your father's letter, on the left. And here you see the one written by his assistant, Peter House, mailed alongside your father's."

Leaning into the orange candlelight, we brooded over them. The cursive was markedly different; the one by Peter House was tighter, blunter, harsher, leaning fiercely to the right as though in the onslaught of a strong wind. Titch ran a finger along the blue trace of ink.

"But as you say," Mister Edgar allowed, "perhaps your father's was written well before his death, and House only posted both much later."

Titch was staring at his father's letter with a grimness about his mouth, chewing at the inside of his cheek. "The penultimate paragraph," he muttered, sounding dispirited. "He references my having been nearly a year at Faith." He raised his face, aggrieved. "This is very recent, sir."

"I have no explanation," Mister Edgar said softly. "But as men of science I am certain we can ferret it out."

Titch kept passing his hands through his hair, a deflated expression on his face. How painful all this was proving to him; he was in total bewilderment. It was obvious the death of his father had crushed him, and now the possibility of that father living still was crushing him. It strained his wildest hopes, opened up the wounds of his grief.

When I placed my hand on his shoulder, he smiled tiredly.

"Let us leave it all for tomorrow," said he. "Perhaps there is more sense to be made by daylight."

"Indeed," said Mister Edgar.

With a great sigh Titch rose from his creaking seat. The impossible occurs so infrequently in this world, even to those who would devote their lives to studying it. But anyone could see: he ached to believe.

✦ ✦ ✦

After we had washed up, dragged the table to one side and upended it, Titch and I set out our bedding before the fire. We then drew the makeshift curtain between our side of the room and the sexton's, effectively cutting ourselves off from the door to the outside. For we were in the back half of the room, with the cellar trap door in the corner, and I could not help but notice Titch's uneasiness as he lay down his head.

I could hear Mister Edgar breathing and clicking his tongue as he moved about on the other side of the curtain, drifting in and out of the small room where the lady's arm was being dissected.

"Do you suppose he truly is alive?" I whispered.

Titch rolled over. He said nothing.

"Perhaps you might write to his assistant, Mister House. Surely he can clarify everything?"

"Let us speak of all this tomorrow, Wash. It is late."

Despite his agitation Titch fell at once into slumber. I myself could not sleep. I confess the strange figure of Mister Edgar Farrow left me feeling wary and afraid.

More troubling for myself, even beyond the unsettling idea of Titch's father surviving his own icy death, was the person of John Francis Willard. Who was he? Though a child, I did not picture a monster—he was no creature all teeth, all vicious blue eyes behind mangled wire spectacles; his voice was not slow and reptilian, his hands not huge black claws. I knew the nature of evil; I knew its benign, easy face. He would be a man, simply. And it was his very anonymity that would make it impossible to see him coming. When I tried to set it from my mind, to close my eyes, I saw his pale, expressionless face looming, and I did not want to live past this night.

I must have dropped off then, for I opened my eyes onto blackness, my breath ragged in my ears, the air now so cold I could almost see it in the darkness. It must have been sometime past midnight, for the fire had burned down to nothing.

What had awoken me? The cold?

But then I heard it, again: a rattling sound, like the loose handle on a metal bucket. That is what it sounded like: metal clattering against metal. I wrenched myself upright, listening.

Someone was there, breathing in the dark.

I reached across to shake Titch awake, but my fingers met only empty bedclothes.

"Who is there?" I hissed. "Mister Edgar?"

There was the creak of a hinge, and the click of a glass door shutting in a lantern, and then a weak orange light spilled across the floor. It was held aloft by the sexton. In his other hand he carried a shovel, blade up. He was dressed warmly in a wool coat.

"Did I frighten you, boy?" he whispered. "Do not be alarmed."

"Where is Titch?" I pleaded. "Where is Mister Wilde?"

"Come," said Mister Edgar. "I will take you to him."

You will find it astonishing that I rose that night and went with him outside, into the cold air, to walk in the darkness among the gravestones. I find it strange, myself. For I was yet but a child, and half this man's size, and no part of me did trust him.

He led me to the edge of the opened grave. There he unshuttered his lantern, and in the sudden slant of light I saw a small wooden ladder standing upright in the grave. At the back end of the grave a square of earth had been scraped clear, and the rough wooden top of a box—a coffin—was visible.

"It is quite all right, boy," the sexton said softly. "Your Mister Wilde is down there, if you care to join him."

I backed away, alarmed. I did not take my eyes from the man.

He smiled, a toothless black smile in the light of the lantern. "Oh, it is not a grave, child," he called to me. "It is a doorway and a passage. It is the way to the future. Do not be frightened. We all must descend before we may arise."

"Where is Titch?" My voice sounded small and tremulous, even to my ear.

But the sexton had already turned and was climbing stiffly down into the grave, the lantern swinging in his fist. When he had vanished entirely, all I could discern was a low orange glow rising from the earth where he had gone. I felt the darkness press in around me. The light in the grave dimmed.

"Mister Edgar?" I called, uneasy.

After a moment I crunched through the grass, until I reached the edge of the grave. I peered in.

The grave was empty.

THE SEXTON HAD quite disappeared. But as I looked closer, I understood that what I had mistaken for the boards of a coffin had been lifted clear and dragged aside, and now stood leaning against the wall of the grave; for they formed a lid of some kind. I saw the top of a second ladder within the hole, extending into the earth. The orange glow of the sexton's lantern shone weakly from the shadow, as though he had entered that small hole and was even now moving away from me.

I did not call out again. I went quickly down the ladder and kneeled at the edge of the tunnel, lowering my face upside down. I could see very little. The second ladder stretched down a narrow earthen drop, and I could just make out the opening of a low passageway. The air was cold and sour, and I pulled the front of my shirt up over my mouth as I went down into it.

I paused at the base of the ladder. I could hear voices, though I could not discern what they were saying. The tunnel was square-cut, the soil surrounding it black and moist. I went doubled over into that passage with my knees out before me, cautious.

I had not gone ten paces when I reached a large rock. I climbed over it, and found myself crouching in a bright pool of lantern light.

"Is that you, finally?" said a voice.

It was Titch.

The space was low, too low for standing—a long, narrow chamber dug out of the earth and shored up with timber on the sides and across the ceiling. The floor too was built of boards, and looked dry enough. Seated at the far end with the lantern between them were Titch and Mister Edgar, and two runaway slaves.

I knew what they were at once. You will wonder how I knew them with such certainty. But what sort of mistake can a boy make who has lived his life among such people, and never dared dream of freedom himself, but heard the rumours, the whispers, the mutters at night of escapes? I knew them by the whites of their eyes and the tremble in their fingers; I knew them by the stillness of their shoulders, as if their very breath did not belong to them.

"Come, Wash, come closer," Titch said quietly, waving me close. "We have much to discuss and little time to discuss it."

Frowning, I crept slowly forward. There was a slop bucket in one corner and the smell coming off it was foul. I saw two satchels and a roll of bedding against the far wall. I saw the way the two runaways looked at me, suspicion and pity intermingled. And though I felt strangely ashamed, I stared boldly back at them, powerful men both, with thick necks and scabbed knuckles.

"They are leaving tomorrow night," said Titch quietly, seeing my gaze. "This is Adam, and this Ezekiel."

The two runaways said nothing. Ezekiel was shorter and thinner, with tired, kind eyes; his companion had about him a rougher look, as though a nasty hand had only ever been offered to him. He stared at me with a hardened expression. I did not speak. I looked now questioningly at Titch, now at Mister Edgar.

"They will be in the north before the month's end, Wash," Titch continued. "Free men. Men with their lives ahead of them. They will be in Upper Canada, and that will make them British subjects."

"Well," the sexton said, "not exactly. Rather, an act was passed some years ago—any enslaved person who reaches Upper Canada will be freed upon his arrival."

"You are a smuggler," said I. I had heard the stories on Faith Plantation of a certain distillery in Bridge Town, the rumours that the barrels contained more than just rum. We had given it little credence. Big Kit would snort and laugh and scowl. "Oh, them white folk is just so eager to help they poor black property out this life, I don't doubt it," she'd say with a twist of her mouth.

Titch leaned forward, a light frown on his face. "It is a great risk, of course. Adam and Ezekiel are in immediate danger also. They are being hunted even now."

I regarded them with interest, wondering at Titch's sober tone. Ezekiel kept his head lowered, his eyes fixed on his scuffed shoes. But I knew he would be a man of intensity and courage, simply by the fact that he had made it this far. Adam had a hardness in his eye, as though he had killed before. I had known a man like that at Faith, a leather worker whom we all believed had murdered a housegirl. That leather worker was found with a knife in his chest one morning down by the well.

Titch cleared his throat. "It seems surely a risk worth taking," he said. "Does it not? Wash?"

And then I understood. But I did not want to. "What are you saying?" I asked.

"Lower your voice, boy," said Mister Edgar. He glanced uneasily at the tunnel behind me.

I paid him no heed.

Titch regarded me a long moment. "I am telling you to go, Wash, to save your own life."

I stood there surprised, not speaking.

Titch shook his head. "I am going north, Wash. To the Arctic."

"But—"

"I will never be satisfied until I find out what happened to my father. See his resting place with my own eyes." He paused. "Wash, listen to me. Do you understand what all this is?"

I only stared at him. I had thought we would continue our journey together. "I'm not stupid."

"Of course not."

"You are telling me if I don't go with them I will likely die."

The runaway Ezekiel raised his face at this, and the pity there made me flush hotly. Still, I could not stop myself. "But it doesn't have to be so. I do not have to die."

"He is my brother, Wash. So long as you are with me, he will be near. And he will not relent, he is too proud. Your best chance is to disappear among the Loyalist communities, in Upper Canada. Among your people."

I glared at the two runaways, as if this were their doing. I recalled suddenly something Big Kit had said—that free men had total dominion over their choices; that they controlled every aspect of their lives. Nothing happened that they themselves did not sanction.

I met Titch's eye boldly. "If I am a Freeman, then it is my choice where I go."

"It is."

"Even if that means hiding in the Arctic."

Mister Edgar glanced at me in puzzlement.

I suppose I believed there to be some bravery in this choice. I suppose it struck my boyhood self as an act of fidelity, gratitude, a return of the kindness I had been shown and never grown used to. Perhaps I felt Titch to be the only sort of family I had left. Perhaps, perhaps; even now I cannot speak with any certainty. I know only that in that moment I was terrified to my very core, and that the idea of embarking on a perilous journey without Titch filled me with a panic so savage it felt as if I were being asked to perform some brutal act upon myself, to sever my own throat.

I stayed firmly seated on the boards, grim, resolved. Titch gave me a pained look, obviously taken aback, confused by my choice. But he did not say any word more.

5

WAS THAT A TURNING POINT? NOT AN EVENING SINCE that fated night in Virginia have I not revisited the choice. What would my life have looked like had I gone with those men? What happened to them, in the end—did they use their freedom wisely or foolishly? I do not know what fate met Ezekiel and Adam, what they left behind, whom they dreamed of as they slept at night, or if such longings dulled or faded with the years. I know for myself they have not. I miss all those I had once known as friends. And there are few of them still alive.

Titch and I returned to Norfolk from Mister Edgar's churchyard the following morning. There seemed little sense in remaining, and Titch was eager to find a charter heading to the Arctic basin.

It was anger I felt, betrayal. I could not have said it at the time, so strange was the sensation to me. But I did not speak to Titch the entire journey back to Norfolk, nor would I meet his eye. I understood he had been seeking safety for my person, some assurance of my deliverance. And yet to my boyhood sense of justice it felt like a casting off. I chafed at the idea that he desired to rid himself of me, I who had been his most faithful companion. An outlandish conclusion in retrospect, perhaps, but you must remember that I had been raised on chains and blood, suffering for even an unmeant kindness. And into that life had walked Titch, and he had looked upon me with his calm eyes and seen something there, a curiosity for the world, an intelligence, a talent with images I had until then been unaware of. I did not know what lay on that route to Upper Canada with those men; I had already some notion of what a life with Titch could be. It was a choice. I had only moments. I made it.

Would I choose so again? Well, now that is a question. I will only say that if I have acquired any wisdom from Big Kit, it is to live always with your eyes cast forward, to seek what will be, for the path behind can never be retaken.

We sought our passage north and were eventually taken aboard the *Calliope*, a vessel of some lesser tonnage than the *Ave Maria* but newer in her fixtures. She was captained by a man called Michael Holloway, no slaver but still with a strong code of distinction between Negroes and whites. He had been born and raised in Chattanooga, with little good to say of the place. He was short, but stocky and bullish. He did not drink and kept instead always a steaming snifter of tea by his side.

His second, a fellow named Jacob Ibel, was strangely free of the captain's prejudices, though the men had been close since boyhood and indeed were raised in the same street. He spoke to me as if I were a human being and often came in search of me to play whist and pinochle. He had a thick black moustache and a very pale, grey mouth, as if his lips suffered for sunlight. I liked him very much but did not trust either man.

Before boarding their ship, Titch had us stop to purchase clothing, provisions and equipment with money given him by Mister Edgar. We set sail two days later by light of dawn, under the push of a strong wind. As we stood at the railing, the ship groaning mournfully from port, I noticed on the boardwalk the figure of a short-statured man there, staring out at the boats, at me.

He was portly and fat-bellied, his light brown hat battering softly across his forehead. He wore an impeccable dark suit of clothes and though his eyes were blurred by the distance, I imagined them cruel, hawkish, without mercy. My breath caught in my chest; I gave two quick tugs at Titch's sleeve. By the time Titch leaned out over the wet railing to see, the man had already turned into the crowd.

WE WERE CLEARING the chop of American waters, working our steady way north, when the sun at last rose fully. Titch and I were accommodated in hammocks. Though I did not ask, he explained that the captain had accepted his offer of substantial payment to make a detour in their plans and drop us at an outpost in Hudson Bay. He grinned at this, his eyes bright, his lips crooked, and I found myself, however reluctantly, smiling back.

And so what followed was the long, languid rising and falling of the vessel, day after day, as we continued our journey north. It did not occur to me that some part of Titch despaired to discover his father alive, or that he might be frightened of Mister Willard. I trusted him yet, for I was still but a boy. I believed that only in his keeping would I be safe.

Was it happiness I began to feel, unexpectedly, as we set out from Norfolk? All around us lay the green swells of the ocean, and the swoop of white seabirds in our wake. The high sails crackled with the wind, and the days, the days were still fine and not yet what they would soon become.

✦ ✦ ✦

We were somewhere off Labrador, in black waters, when Titch at last raised the question.

"Is it not early in the season to be sailing north?" he said one day, at luncheon in the captain's quarters. It was, as always, the four of us: Captain Holloway, Mister Ibel, Titch and myself. The captain had softened somewhat and would now suffer my presence, though I was never invited to speak and it was clear my burns disturbed him still. It was Mister Ibel who always addressed me, in his mild, laughing way. We had been sailing into colder climes some days now and the sun was low in the sky. I had taken to wearing all three of my shirts and a thick coat provided by the bosun at all times, even while I slept.

"Early, aye," said the captain, cutting a bulb of sausage. "We aim to be the first in these waters."

Titch took a sip of rum. "I know very little of such matters, gentlemen. But I do understand the ice retreats haphazardly. Is it quite safe?"

"I never heard of a reward without a risk," said Captain Holloway. "Did you ever hear of a reward without a risk, Ibel?"

"I never did," said Mister Ibel.

There was the rasp of knives on plates. Titch shook his head. "What sort of expedition is it, gentlemen, that you are embarked upon? If I may inquire?"

"It's a no-business-of-yours sort," said Captain Holloway.

Titch nodded. "That is true."

"I think it hardly matters now, Michael," said Mister Ibel. He furrowed his brow. "We are at sea. Surely it hardly matters."

The captain stroked his beard, scowling.

"We are seeking the wreck of a whaler," Mister Ibel said abruptly, taking his friend's silence for agreement. "The *Magnolia Lion*. She was crushed in the ice off Baffin Island some two Novembers ago."

Titch expressed no surprise. "But surely it will not still be there? Surely the ice has carried it north?"

Captain Holloway narrowed his eyes. "So you know how the ice moves, do you?"

Titch shook his head. "Only *that* it moves. I do not know the currents."

"It doesn't matter," said Mister Ibel. "The crew unloaded the barrels before they set out. They took them to a small island near the wreck and buried them under a shelter. The oil will be precisely where it was left. Islands do not move, Mister Wilde."

"Aye," said Captain Holloway.

Titch smiled, a quick, happy smile. "Then you gentlemen will do very nicely for yourselves, I expect. It might prove a most profitable undertaking."

"We aim it to be so," said Captain Holloway.

"An old man came to my attention, more than a year past," said Mister Ibel, "a man with an unfortunate swelling in his knee. He was, it seems, an old friend of my father's. Also a seaman, he was. He had been trapped in the snows and suffered a severe frostbite. His toes had already been taken from him. This man, this Mister MacBane, was a Scotsman shipped out of Yorkshire on a whaler, the aforesaid *Magnolia Lion*. He told me of the wreck, and of the oil, stranded in the white wastes, and of its worth. I thought no more of it."

"Until . . . ," prompted Captain Holloway. He waved a rough hand at his friend.

"Until I was summoned to his bedside. His leg had grown worse, had grown septic from an injury suffered in a public house one night. Mister MacBane was dying; I could see this at once. He was attended by an ancient widow, a woman in black, his sister. Agnes was her name. I pitied him; I asked if there was nothing I could do for the man. She left me alone in their second room while she tried to speak to her brother, and it was there I noticed a curious handwritten map."

"A map to the wreck," said Captain Holloway.

"And to the barrels of oil," said Mister Ibel. "Although I did not know it at the time. Agnes returned to me and saw me reading it. She told me of its import. She said she could explain the markings and that her brother, a navigator by trade, had kept a precise eye as they struggled south on the constellations. She said his map was accurate. She said any ship could find their way to the oil that knew where to look."

"All this she offered to you?" said Titch, interested.

"All this she offered to me, with the condition that I concede a portion of the profits to her."

"I should be very interested in his directions," Titch said. "How did he annotate the stars in their seasonal displacements?"

"Oh, maybe we'll just take out the map and give it over to you," scoffed Captain Holloway.

Titch raised his shoulders in a shrug. "I have no desire for money."

"Seven hells," said Mister Ibel. "Everyone has desire for money, sir."

"So you are sailing to the wreck," Titch said. "You mean to steal the barrels?"

"Not steal," Captain Holloway said sharply. "Claim."

Titch raised an eyebrow.

"Aye, there's the beauty of it," said Mister Ibel. "The insurance is already paid out. The company's men *can't* claim it now."

"But would it not belong to the insurance company, then? By rights?"

Captain Holloway snorted. "Not by the laws of salvage. It's a wreck. Any vessel can collect flotsam and jetsam."

"Do barrels of good oil stacked under a shelter count as flotsam?" asked Titch.

From the expressions on their faces I did not think it likely.

"You are missing the cardinal point, Mister Wilde," said Mister Ibel with a dry smile. "Let them try to collect it from us. We shall have them sold at a profit before any claim can be made."

"And that claim wouldn't be worth the shit in a gull, neither," said Captain Holloway, grinning.

"A lengthy court dispute, to what end?" agreed Mister Ibel.

"Well," smiled Titch, taking up a last piece of hardtack from his plate. "I should think we are exceedingly lucky to have met with you, then. First ship of the season indeed."

And he took a great happy bite of the hardtack and sat crunching it, smiling at each of us in turn, immensely satisfied.

THE AIR CLENCHED to ice, stinging our cheeks. It began to pinch. Sailing, we glimpsed in the passing black waters eerie, exquisite cathedrals of ice. I had not ever seen ice before, not in its immensities: I stared into the refracted light like a creature entranced. How beautiful it was, how sad, how sacred! I attempted to express the awe of it in my drawings. For it felt very much as though we were leaving the world of the living and entering a world of spirits and the dead. I felt free, invincible, beyond Mister Willard's reach. We sailed past the mouths of glaciers; enormous, violent bergs were calving, rocking in the foaming water. We sailed slowly along those channels, half in dread of some underwater collision.

Whales surfaced, snorting thick gusts of spray, then sliding back under the cold waters. I walked the deck, dressed heavily in all I had brought, clapping my hands for the cold, a small black boy bundled until he was quite rotund and waddling. The sailors laughed and called me their penguin and their mascot, and when Mister Ibel showed me an etching of a penguin in a book, I too laughed.

On our third week out from Norfolk we passed a battered brig sailing southward. Mister Ibel muttered some quiet imprecation, and Captain Holloway spat, but we did not slow down, did not hail them. Titch explained they would have wintered over somewhere in the Bay and would now be eager to return to warmer waters.

"They will not have taken the captain's barrels, then?" I said.

Titch smiled down at me, his breath visible in the cold. "I expect not, no."

We did not speak of it, but with every league through those waters a sense of lightness, of freedom, took hold in us. It was as though the great emptiness allowed us to forget. Sometimes our eyes would meet, and we'd give a quiet laugh, with no sense or reason for it.

And so onward we went, northward. Titch had arranged our passage to a trading company's outpost on the western line of Hudson Bay. The weeks passed, and the sunlight lay dazzling on the ice, the snow dunes sculpted into strange feathered shapes by the wind. Seeing them, I began to feel strangely solitary, alone. It seemed we all did, for the four of us, Titch, Captain Holloway,

Mister Ibel and I, seemed to turn away from each other in that icy climate, as though the cold had entered more than just our flesh; as though we longed for a solitude unreachable in the tight confines of that ship. My mind kept casting itself back, and I found myself thinking of Mister Willard, of Mister Philip, of my long years at Faith—the way the red dust would gather in my throat, the itch of sweat in the small of my spine as I hacked at the cane, the feel of Big Kit's hot hand gripping my shoulder in affection.

FINALLY WE NEARED the Bay, and the trading post.

The black waters were calm and still speckled with chunks of ice. Titch bade Captain Holloway and Mister Ibel good fortune, heartily shaking hands. Then we climbed into a small cutter that rocked as we disentangled ourselves from the rope ladder.

We were rowed towards the miserable, leaning wood shacks that made up the post.

Inside the trading post a young white-haired trader greeted us, reeking strongly of whisky. He leaned his thin arms on the plank before him, the skin at his wrists cracked and scabbed with rash. He narrowed his glassy pink eyes at us. "Who did you say?"

Titch stepped forward, his clothes rasping with ice. "James Wilde, the Englishman, the naturalist. He was said to have died at one of the westernmost outposts. I am not certain it is so."

The trader swiped at his running nose. "What?"

Titch frowned in impatience. "Wilde. James Wilde. Surely there are not so many gentleman naturalists in these parts?"

The trader grunted; he peered roughly at us. "Is it he you are meaning, or some other body?"

"Wilde," Titch said sharply. "Wilde. Now if you will direct me to the location of his last encampment, I will be grateful."

The trader stared silently at us, his eyes a fierce pink in the hazy glow of the lanterns.

Titch glanced at me in exasperation, then back at the man. "Did you hear me?"

Without speaking, the trader turned suddenly around, and in a loud bark called to a lone man standing some paces outside in the snow. "Him," said the trader, slurring his words at us, "he knows the way like he knows his own arse. He won't take you wrong."

Titch looked nervous, caution in his eyes. He watched as the dark figure absorbed our glances, suddenly aware of our attention. Slowly, like a shadow unattached to any entity, he began to drift towards us.

"He won't take you wrong," the trader repeated. "He and the old hermit have an understanding."

"An understanding?" Titch murmured in distraction, his gaze still fixed on the man crunching closer through the snow. He appeared to be a tall Esquimau with a long knife tucked into his belt.

The trader ran a thick, rash-riddled wrist under his leaking nose. "This one's his slave, I think. Or his wife. It's something like that. Been here so long he's half-savage himself. You can't think like a savage and still be a man."

He said this cheerfully, not sparing me a glance.

Titch, to my surprise, thanked the man, and began to walk backwards over the snow.

Without another glance the man returned to his drinking.

I rushed after Titch. In dread I watched the far-off man approach, his thick, slow steps puncturing the crust of snow. I glanced up at

Titch, hoping for some sign that we might run, but he only paused in the cold, brutal air, his eyes narrowed against the wind.

How alarming the stranger was! How large and spectral. His oiled caribou skin creaked with ice, the reek of old frost and mud coming off him. He was tall and reed-thin, his cadaverous cheeks chapped with wind, a livid beard of grey hairs raging from his face. His complexion was mottled with fleshy brown moles, and to the right of his high-arched nose stood a vicious, glistening boil that looked painful and full of poison. His eyes were as grey as his hair, and they regarded Titch with a blunt, vicious judgment that unsettled me.

And then all at once Titch was gripping the man's hands, and with a look of shock and even anguish the man grabbed back at him, and they held on, laughing quietly to each other. The man's laugh was like a seal's bark, sharp and pleasant. He did not speak and Titch also said nothing.

It was Peter House himself. By chance he had been at the outpost collecting goods. I watched Titch step away from him and begin to make strange, elegant gestures with his hands. The man gestured back, slapping at his chest and torquing his fingers into wondrous shapes. His hands were wrinkled, with a spray of grey hair matting the knuckles. Titch nodded and nodded his understanding. I stood like a simpleton, staring at both in wonder.

Titch blinked viciously, swiping at his eyes. But I could see he was relieved, even happy, and I knew then that the death was a lie.

Before I could say any word, Peter House was frowning down at me, assessing me with frank, pale eyes. He smiled brusquely so that I almost did not see it, and reached for the sack in my hands, which held all our provisions. Then he turned and began crunching through the sullied snow towards a sled in the distance, the pack slung over his shoulder.

"Peter will take us to the camp," said Titch as we followed him. "Wash, my father is alive. He is alive."

Hearing it spoken aloud, I shivered at the eeriness of it. "But did he tell it to you, the man?"

"Peter is dumb, Wash, he does not speak. He talks with his hands."

His voice was tinged with relief, and yet there was an air of exhaustion and sadness to him, as if the revelation had drained all his energies. He placed a cold, thin hand on my shoulder, staring ahead at the awaiting sled. In the distance we had not noticed the dark-faced Esquimau guide standing there. At our approach he acknowledged us with quiet, intelligent eyes, and took the pack from Mister Peter to lash it fast to his sled. Then he bade us climb on, like baggage ourselves.

The guide cried out a command to the enormous dogs. We lurched sharply forward, and then we were on our way, into the great, echoing domes of snow.

6

AH, BUT THE COLD. I DREAMED ABOUT THAT COLD FOR years after. It had a colour, a taste—it wrapped itself around one like an unwelcome skin and began, ever so delicately, to squeeze. My healed ribs started to ache. I could not catch my breath.

We journeyed in a strange sled-like contraption drawn by a team of wet-jawed dogs. Titch, Mister Peter and I sat in the bed of the sled; the guide stood behind us, crying out hoarsely to his creatures. The long blades of the sled jounced and bumped across the packed snow. I listened to the runners scrape and hiss as we went. We were wrapped and blanketed until we could not move. In all my life I had not dreamed such a place possible, had not thought snow could be so solid, so vast. The knifing winds carved it into towers, sharpened it to precipices and chasms. And all this, I thought, squinting through raw, frozen eyelids—all this is only water, nothing more.

I had been warned by Mister Ibel that snow was white, and cold. But it was not white: it held all the colours of the spectrum. It was blue and green and yellow and teal; there were delicate pink tintings in some of the cliffs as we passed. As the light shifted in the sky, so too did the snow around us deepen, find new hues, the way an ocean is never blue but some constantly changing colour.

Nor was the cold simply cold—it was the devouring of heat, a complete sucking of warmth from the blood until what remained was the absence of heat. When the wind stirred, it would scythe through the skin as if we were the cane and the wind were our terrible reaping.

North we went, north and then west, and then north again. We stopped to rest the dogs; our guide tethered them to stakes he had driven into the ice, to keep them from attacking each other. They sat, hunched white mounds of fur ruffling in the wind, their eyes slivered shut. I made a quick, vivid sketch in pencil, wondering at their ferocity. Our guide passed us a small cube of what Titch explained must be blubber. It tasted rank, oily, but I did not complain.

And all the while we spoke very little about what we were venturing towards, or what we were leaving behind. I thought of my life at Faith and it all seemed a figment, a distant, vicious dream.

We had left in the dark hour of the morning, and we rode swiftly all day, stopping on occasion to rest. We finally arrived very late in the afternoon, as the darkness was descending again. I had observed an increasing uneasiness in Titch as we travelled, as though he were not yet ready to meet with his whole and living father. I understood we had arrived when our guide drew the dogs to a halt at the centre of five large snowdrifts, the blades of his sled hissing to a stop. Mister Peter stepped down from the hold, his beard full of ice, and began unpacking the wooden crates that made up our backrest. Titch and I shifted uncomfortably, not speaking as the sled was gradually disassembled.

My tongue felt huge and cold in my mouth. My voice creaked after the long, frozen silence of the sled. "Are we here?" I asked Titch hoarsely. "Is this your father's camp?"

For I saw now they were not snowdrifts at all, but domes of ice, five of them, arranged in a rough pattern. I was astonished to see these habitats; fear cut through me, as though I was gazing upon the site of a resurrection. As we slid down from the sled, struggling to our feet, I glimpsed hides draped over the entrances. Mister Peter made rapid gestures with his fingers, then pointed to the third dome.

"They are called igloos, Wash," Titch said through his oiled sealskin, his voice wavering, nervous. "The ice acts as an insulator. It keeps the inside perfectly warm."

I doubted this very much. But I had seen enough strangeness to understand the world was unfathomable. Titch, I knew, would find such a notion unscientific, but it mattered very little to me from where I stood, a child of the tropics, half-obliterated by a cold that made my mended ribs ache. I turned and studied the darkening snowfields around us. Mister Willard felt like a haunting from another life entirely. Truly, we were at the ends of the earth.

Titch was already crunching through the snow towards the third dome. He paused at the entrance, and as he glanced back to Peter, I glimpsed the uncertainty in his face. But Mister Peter and the Esquimau were already disentangling the dogs from the harnesses, staking them in a row.

Titch hesitated a moment longer, then squatted down on his hands and knees to draw the hide curtain to one side and crawl through.

I ran over the snow, slipping, and slid to a stop abruptly at the entrance. My heart clapping in my chest, I drew a breath and went in too.

The inside was bright but smoky, a stink of burning fat in the air.

"Hello?" I heard Titch murmur. There was a clatter from within, and then stillness. "Is anyone here?"

I remained crouched on my hands in the entrance, straining to see past Titch.

And then I glimpsed him, a man rising from the shadows: like a figure from myth, the great patriarch of the Wildes, Fellow of the Royal Society, recipient of the Copley Medal and the Bakerian lectureship, the man whose learning had kindled his son's mind and never burned down, the man who had drawn us north through icefield and hazard, against what odds, oh, that man, whose very treatise on the icy nature of comets once left the Sorbonne in chaos, whose learning could be expressed in twelve languages, who admired the jokes of the Tartars and the salads of the Inca, who had instructed his three-year-old son to scoop when his hand held a knife and to cut when it held a spoon, for no person ought to assume a tool's use is determined by the tool, the man of a thousand lifetimes, who had set his heavy English leather boots on the soil of five continents, and collected the mud from each—I saw him, and I kneeled dripping in the low entrance, staring. For he was short, fat, and under his scraggly whiskers was a face very much alive and quite brutally ugly.

He peered out at us, a light frown on his hard, round face. I saw he had his four front teeth out, upper and lower, and in their place were wooden ones.

✦ ✦ ✦

I COULD NOT shake the sense that we had come to meet our own deaths.

Titch was in a paralysis of astonishment. He hugged his father, held on with a kind of anguish, while Mister Wilde patted at his back, openly embarrassed by his son's affections. Then, swiftly disentangling himself, Mister Wilde gestured for us to follow; sparing me no glance, he slipped gracefully out through the igloo's entrance. I trailed after Titch, and Titch followed his father, his steps ambling, sloppy, like those of a drunk. More than once he almost slipped, so numb with shock was he. How I felt for him, in his state. To actually witness his father alive, after months of believing him dead—I could hardly fathom the distress of it.

We were led back outside to the fifth igloo, where inside we found a group of Esquimaux eating some pale, whitish repast. They raised their faces to us, their eyes gliding past Titch to fix on me. What an improbable creature I must have seemed to them, a boy black as the winter sea and ruinously burnt. They followed me with quiet eyes, chewing.

Only when we'd settled in amongst the men did Titch attempt to speak.

Mister Wilde raised a sharp hand. "I know why you are come."

Titch hesitated, glancing at the other men there. "I do not think you do, Father."

"You are come," said Mister Wilde, his bright eyes wide and light-filled, "because you believed me dead."

Titch and I glanced quietly at each other. The days of nervous anticipation had exhausted us both, and in the flickering brown light of these cramped quarters Titch appeared haggard, used up. The heat in here was most oppressive, smelling blackly of animal fat, the main sound that of the other men's jaws working moistly. The men were part of Mister Wilde's small encampment here, for though he and Mister Peter craved isolation, it was impossible for two white men to live alone in these plains. Mister Peter came and went with his Esquimau comrade, and together they supplied Mister Wilde with all the goods and tools he needed from the outposts. One sensed Mister Wilde had little to no communion with the Esquimaux himself—they were a necessity only, insurance against death. Mister Peter was his intermediary, and indeed the only man with whom he seemed to converse. They sat in the near silence of the igloo, their active hands casting shadows in the warm orange light. With Mister Peter he was affectionate and even tender. He touched him a great deal, even once tugging the greying hair at his nape softly. Titch often looked at his own hands as they spoke. He grew flustered and appeared flushed in the unnatural light. Mister Peter stayed but a short while, then left again with one of the Esquimaux on an errand.

"I knew there was much rumour," Mister Wilde said when Titch attempted once again to explain the full impact of the fraud. "I was first made aware of it when Peter received a letter from a colleague in Mexico asking after my death. We did not think much of it until a second letter arrived from Germany—a friend in Heidelberg lamenting my passing. But I had no notion of the rumour reaching you and your mother. It seems I rather underestimated the intrepid nature of human stupidity. I am horrified. If I'd anticipated how widely it would spread, I would of course have sent word dispelling the falsehood. In fact I will need to post a note to your mother at once."

"But who concocted the lie? How did it reach us?"

"Has the altitude impaired your hearing, boy? I have just said I do not know."

Titch was silent.

His father's top lip twitched painfully over his wooden teeth, and I realized he was attempting to smile. "I do thank you, Christopher, for the sentiment you have shown in coming all this way, though you see now it is a fool's errand."

Titch stared down at his hands, and for some moments the only sound was of the men shifting in their thick clothes.

Then Titch said, "Please do not mention I have come here, when you do write to her."

"Stolen off again, have you?" Mister Wilde chuckled, scratching at his chin. "Ah, Christopher."

I listened sleepily to their halting voices, and it was as though both belonged to ghosts, so gauzy and hollow were they.

Abruptly I was awoken, and Titch and I were given heavy furs for sleeping and a small dish with a seal-fat candle for light. The floor was laid with furs and wooden planks underneath, though I could not imagine where wood had been procured in this wasteland. Perhaps from a trading vessel at the outpost.

Stacked against the far walls were wooden crates with numbers burned into them; these we did not disturb. I lay down, and almost at once felt a wash of exhaustion come over me.

"Titch," I mumbled. "What did you think when first you laid eyes on him? You must have been very shocked, and very happy."

"Rather more shocked than happy, I think. Indeed, it is difficult to get beyond the shock. And being again in his presence, I am reminded of how—well, how complex he can be." He shrugged. "I don't know."

"I did not think his camp would be so big."

"Yes."

"He has been here a long time, hasn't he?"

"A lifetime, I think. Even before he came here, he was here."

"What will we do now, Titch? Will he hide us here? For how long?"

"Sleep, Wash," Titch murmured. "There will be time enough to discuss it."

"Mm," said I, and wrapped myself deeper in the furs.

"Go to sleep," he said again.

And I did.

THAT IGLOO, THAT house of ice, proved indeed a warm and inviting refuge. I awoke cozy and satisfied, and in the easy blue warmth could not wager how late I had slept. Titch was already awake and gone, his furs neatly rolled and set at the foot of his sleeping pallet.

It had snowed in the night, lightly, and I saw where Titch had brushed the sleet from the entrance of our igloo. I could make out the trace of his boot prints leading to the second igloo. I discovered him sitting cross-legged inside with his father, the two of them eating some grey, rubbery breakfast.

"Wash," Titch said with a cautious smile. "Come in, do. The repast is nourishing, though bitter. Take it in your fingers, like so."

I watched him eat and smile, but I caught a slight shudder as he swallowed.

"Is there nothing else?" I said.

"It is not fancy, boy," said Mister Wilde, "but it is enough to keep you alive in a place that wants to kill you. Eat it and keep your wits."

I glanced at the old, unkempt scientist, but I could not determine if he was joking.

The grey substance had been cut roughly into cubes. I stuck out a tongue, licked at it nervously.

"Do not taste it, Wash," laughed Titch. "Two quick chews and a swallow and there you have it."

"The taste grows on you, boy. I did not care for it either at first. But after all this time I do not mind it so." Mister Wilde chuckled.

"And who introduced you to this delicacy?" said Titch. "Your man?"

"Peter?"

"Your Esquimau, I mean. The one who brought us here on his sled."

"Hesiod? But he is not our servant." The smile eased from Mister Wilde's face, and he gave Titch a strange, disapproving glance. I was beginning to recognize the sudden shifts in his temperament and to dread their swiftness. "I should think you of all men would understand that, Christopher."

Titch flushed. "Hesiod is not in the employ of you and Peter?"

"He comes and he goes at his choosing. There is no word for 'servant' in his tongue. The idea would not make any sense to him." Mister Wilde frowned and tapped some yellow powder into the ice in front of him. I watched as the yellow seeped through the surface, blooming. "Hesiod is not of the local tribes, Christopher. His people are much farther west. He finds our company more agreeable to the degenerates at the trading post."

"Why degenerates, Mister Wilde?" I asked quietly.

He belched quietly. "Eh?"

"Why do you call them degenerates?" I said again.

"Because they are. They are drunks and petty schemers and they whore out their women to the sailors." He said this brusquely. I had seen the men in their kayaks during the off-loading of the *Calliope* and I was not so convinced. Aside from the trader, no man I had yet encountered here seemed anything but dutiful and industrious. But I kept my thoughts to myself.

"Hesiod is a curious name," I said instead.

"It is not his name. We call him Hesiod because some of the men here consider him a great poet. His true name is unpronounceable." Mister Wilde stretched his mouth into a grimace and, baring his wooden teeth, uttered a long string of guttural grunts and squawks. "That is the closest I can get to it."

"Fascinating," said Titch. "It rather resembles the language of the natives of Borneo."

"Ha!" said his father in disgust. "Listen to the glottal stops and tell me that again. The Borneo tongue! You have no ear for philology, Christopher."

"I should stick to aeronautical studies," Titch said, his cheeks colouring.

"Is that what you were pursuing in Barbados? Lighter-than-air constructions?"

Titch looked somewhat startled. "Erasmus wrote it to you?"

His father shrugged. "He only said you were there wasting his resources. He did not tell me the nature of that wastage." He chuckled. "Ah, you boys. Always chafing at each other. Now we are speaking of it, I haven't had a letter from your brother in months."

Titch frowned. "He thinks you are dead, Father."

"Ah, that he does. Right."

I watched Titch shift, clear his throat as he prepared to describe his work, our work. But before he could speak, his father was talking again.

"Peter is my true assistant, not Hesiod," Mister Wilde said to me, as if he would have the truth acknowledged. "Been with me these, oh, twenty-two years now. It is he who sorts out the particulars of our experiments. Transports the apparatuses, collects specimens, keeps us from walking into the northern wastes and never coming out. He has been for years my truest companion." As he spoke, I saw a look of mortification pass over Titch's face; only when his father paused did he glance up.

Mister Wilde gestured a thick, leathery hand in my direction. "Much like what you have with your boy here. Companionship."

"I should think not," said Titch archly. He glanced outside at the men passing silently by. "It seems a waste, does it not, to be unable to communicate with all these men, to learn their stories, their histories? You are a man of languages, Father. Why have you not attempted to learn theirs?"

But Titch's father had already turned and was rummaging through a low stack of leather-bound books, their paper warped.

Now Titch cleared his throat, and spoke to his father's back. "Father, you will not believe how it was we managed to arrive here. Do you remember when I improved upon your sketches of a cutter tethered to an aerostat? Some three, four years ago?"

"Where did I put it?" Mister Wilde muttered, still sorting through his books.

Titch gave me a quick, uneasy smile, looked again to his father's back. "My Cloud-cutter, I called it. Do you recall?"

His father rummaged and rummaged, muttering. "Oh. Right—

that damnable craft. I remember it. Do not tell me you have actually attempted its construction?"

"Better than attempted, Father—Washington and I completed it. We built it, and launched it from a hilltop at Faith."

His father turned sharply, his eyes wide and critical. "And where is it, then?"

Titch's eyes flickered to his lap, and he gave a series of fleeting, tremulous smiles. "At the bottom of the sea, I am afraid."

"But we should have remained airborne had there not been a storm," I broke in, shyly. "It was circumstance only, sir. She was as sound and viable a craft as any. You would have been proud to see her, sir."

Mister Wilde glanced from me to Titch, chuckling into the scraggly black tangle of hairs at his chin. "Well, I do hope you are better haulers than aeronauts. Peter left early this morning. I will need you to carry my instruments."

THE DAYS PASSED. The hours were short and dark and fleeting, with nightfall coming swiftly. Titch did not mention the Cloud-cutter again, and his father did not ask after it. Instead, they spoke of their family life with a curious detached air. There was a distance, a wryness, in Titch's manner that did not resemble the man who had grieved at the news of the death, on Faith Plantation. I understood this to be his father's doing—that Mister Wilde was a man with a broken apparatus in place of a heart. It was not, I came to believe, that he did not love; only that he loved intermittently.

They spoke for hours. I listened. I learned of a life and a world I would never have imagined for Titch. I heard stories of his mother, accounts of their travels to Paris. I heard tales of a greenhouse on their estate in England filled with poisonous flowers. And I heard, most strangely, about Erasmus Wilde as a boy, how Titch and his brother would swim naked in the lake on their property and then run through the halls of their house still without clothes, startling the servants. I heard about the night when Erasmus and Titch painted their bodies with the notion of being African priests and made a bonfire in the courtyard out of the dining room furniture, chanting and singing in the firelight until their mother threw buckets of water on both boys in horror. I heard how Mister Wilde had taken Titch to witness an aerial ascent in Norwich from Ranelagh Gardens, the balloon a perfect incandescent orb in the sky before its slow plummet into the sea. I heard how Mister Wilde stood explaining the idea of gases even as the balloonist drowned in the waters, how Titch had begun trembling at the sight of the accident and was not able to stop until halfway back to Granbourne. I heard also of Titch's tenth year, how he had been ill and frail and lost half his body weight, of how in these bleak days his brother had nicknamed him "Titch," on account of how tiny he had become. I heard how the doctors had insisted on bloodletting but his mother had prevented them.

"She saved your life, son," said Mister Wilde, suddenly tender. "A brilliant woman."

I looked at him curiously, trying to imagine this stout, unwashed, ugly man with his wife. I could not. He had begun to reminisce now of his wife, Abigail Wilde, remembering her youth in Liverpool and how, when they had first met, at a ball, they had spoken until sunrise about the complicated imprecisions in hand-copied maps and the lack of standard Continental measures. He had known from that moment that the solitude he had lived inside for his entire youth might not be his fate. Titch said nothing to this, I noticed. He said only, "Erasmus and I used to watch her as she sat for her Italian lessons in the afternoons. She was the most beautiful creature we knew."

"You were children," his father said. "You knew nothing of beauty."

"Children know everything about beauty," Titch countered softly. "It is adults who have forgotten."

7

Some days the wind hissed across the icefields, the snow blowing in sideways. Mister Peter carved his way out of the camp every morning and returned at nightfall. I imagined it was to the outpost that he was going, but I was not wholly certain. Watching him, I understood him to be a sensitive and intelligent man, quietly pragmatic in his solutions. I could not fathom why he'd elected to surrender his life to the unpredictable whims of Mister Wilde.

Also in the mornings Titch's father worked at his experiments in the fourth igloo, a space he had devoted to the microscopic study of various kinds of ice. He spoke at length of the tiny creatures he found in the icy waters, and he showed a carefully tagged box of loose bones, describing the monster they had been taken from. A walrus, he called it. He showed me a long, spiralled horn and said it came from a sleek white whale that lived beneath the ice.

One day I sat sketching a specimen. And though I had made many a sketch before, I was suddenly astonished at myself—at what I could create with these thin, tremulous fingers with their nail beds lined always in dirt. The image seemed less a drawing than a haunting, a vision of the specimen's afterlife, set down in a ghostly lustre of ink. How far I had come these long months; how much I had grown in both art and life.

I sensed a breath at my neck, and turned to find Mister Wilde peering unexpectedly over my shoulder. I jolted, then turned to face the small man, surprised as always to find his face nearly eye to eye with mine, his fish-scented breath rasping in his throat. He bore the same bright green eyes as Titch, but his were smaller, flintier, with odd pinpoints of light in the irises. He stared down at my hands and paper, and it was as though his eyes were finely dissecting every stroke of my sketch.

"Hm," he said, sounding both surprised and unimpressed. "There is talent there."

Then he smiled at me, and it was like a flash of violence, all wooden teeth and gums. Seeing it, something shrank in me. I felt both his intense awe and his mockery, as if he were watching some insensible creature perform an unnatural act, as if a hothouse plant had learned to speak.

I left off drawing in the afternoons, and instead would walk with Titch and his father, checking the various small cages and traps Mister Wilde had set around the perimeter. They were, without fail, always empty. One afternoon we came across the deep-set tracks of a polar bear. We followed them for several hours, and when we reached open ice, the trail vanished. Mister Wilde came to himself then; he glanced at the darkening sky and his eyes filled with alarm. We hurried for miles back to the camp, arriving just as everything went black on the horizon.

All this I observed with real interest. But my true study remained, I understand now, the curious person of Titch. He was, I feared, becoming increasingly lost within himself. I suppose there must have been a deep love between him and his father, a love I could get no sense for because of its reticence. But as with most loves, it was shadowy, and painful, and confusing, and Titch seemed to me overly eager and too often hurt.

I could see a sadness coming over him, a kind of slow despair. I understood he was anguished over his father—over his failure to ever impress the man, over how to explain that Philip had killed himself and that we were now in hiding. Each night, as we lay in our furs in the close darkness of that igloo, I listened to Titch breathing, and felt the increasing dread in him, like a heat. I was worried.

Finally I could no longer hold my tongue. "You must tell him, Titch," I said into the darkness. "He has to know what has happened."

"Do you suppose it was a trap, all this? That Erasmus and Philip concocted the falsehood of my father's death so that Erasmus could get away from Faith and trap me there?"

"But that is madness. Consider that your father was aware of the rumour also. No, I do not think it likely."

"Yes, you are right," he muttered.

"Please do tell him everything, Titch."

He lay there breathing heavily in the dark, and did not speak.

THAT NIGHT I dreamed, for the first time in months, of Big Kit. We were standing at the edge of the cane at sunset and there were tiny flecks of insects feeding in the darkening air. A haze of pale light was furred around Kit's head, like a halo, and I could not make out her face. She reached forward and held my hand, and her touch was terribly cold. I gave her a pair of thick fur-lined mittens. Then somehow we were standing in the snow, the world so white around us. Kit's face looked wondrous to me, dark, sombre, beautiful. I studied it.

"You be my eyes, Wash," she said to me.

And reaching up and with her fingers, she forcibly pressed her own eyes in. A wide blue light shone out from the sockets.

I felt—and this is the peculiar truth—a sense of peace and well-being come over me. I understood a great gift of trust was being extended to me.

When I awoke in the darkness, I was crying.

I DID NOT accompany Titch the next morning when he went with his father to the camp's perimeter to inspect the cages. Rather, I walked to the edge of the encampment, the eyes of the men there trailing me, and I made vivid, detailed sketches of the igloos.

When at last Titch returned that afternoon from his father's observation igloo, he sat a long time in the dim light of our shelter, staring at his mittens, not troubling to remove his heavy clothes. I too was dressed for the outdoors, for I could not get warm enough, and I had been fumbling with a needle and thread trying to sew up a small hole in the thumb of my mitten. I glanced across at Titch, but did not speak. For a long time we sat, unmoving, while the weather blew past outside.

At last Titch stirred, rubbing at his reddened face. "Do you know what a family is?" he said bitterly. He turned and met my eye, studying me some moments. "You do not know what a family is, because you have never had one. That is why you think it matters."

He shifted on his knees and, pulling his pack from beside the low ice shelf, began filling it with provisions.

"You have told him, then?" I said nervously.

Titch continued to stuff our provisions into his pack.

"What did he say? Titch?"

Still he did not speak, only shifted on his creaking knees in the dim light.

"Surely he is not casting us out? I hope you did emphasize it to him that I was nothing to do with it, the death. And that Mister Willard—"

I let my voice falter and drift off.

Titch had paused, was leaning back on his haunches, measuring me. "Do you know what he said, when he learned of Philip's death? Do you know what his words were? 'The boy was too thoughtful for his own good.'" Titch laughed in misery. "That is who we are dealing with, Wash. That is the man who is my father."

I hesitated. "Does he understand about Mister Willard? Does he understand what he means to do?"

"He seemed reluctant to inform either Erasmus or my mother of his being still alive. He keeps saying he would not like to startle them. I believe he sees some advantage in their ignorance. If they believe him dead, he does not have to be troubled by them just yet—he can simply continue on with his research, with his life here with Peter." He moistened his cracked lips, frowned. "I have explained that Erasmus cannot be pressed to remain at Faith without proof of his still being alive. I have explained how my word alone will carry no weight. He pretends not to understand. 'Far be it from me to interfere in your brother's business dealings.' This he *actually* said. He is fully aware of where the resources funding his research originate." Titch spat angrily at his boots. "This is who my family is, Wash. This is my blood." He shook his head. "It would not surprise me at all to learn that he is the very source of the falsehood."

I stared at him only half-comprehending, my heart shunting in my chest.

"I am not staying in any place," he said bitterly. "Do you understand me? I am not staying in England, I am not staying in America, I am not staying in the Indies, and I am certainly not staying here."

A dread came over me then. We had reached, it seemed, the very summit of the earth; there would be no better place to hide. I tried to smile. "There is nothing in any of those places for me either. Where shall we go, then?"

But Titch had turned away from me again and was silent. I felt a sudden misgiving. I studied the jagged outline of his profile, saw in the dim light the white line of his scar trailing like a fine hair from the side of his mouth. I felt there was more he was not saying, something that had driven him beyond anger, caused him to despair. Whatever else they had discussed, it had raised in him a deep anguish.

"Titch," I said gently. "I will go wherever you wish."

When he looked at me, his eyes were red.

"I will go wherever."

"You are steadfast, Wash." His expression was unreadable. He clasped my hands in his heavy mittens, the two of us kneeling in the small igloo, the smoky residue of the seal fat in the lamp darkening the air. "No matter how changed I am," he said at last, "I know that you will know me."

I stared at him, uncomprehending.

"Your life is not my own. Do you understand me? I did not ask you to accompany me here." He cleared his throat. "What I am saying is, we are north, Wash. It is not Upper Canada, but you will be safe here." He turned to me, and I saw the anguish in his eyes. "I have made arrangements with Peter. He will see to your safety. I have left you money, provisions."

"What are you saying, Titch?"

He crawled from me then, taking up his pack of supplies. Shoving it ahead of him and out of the entrance, he wriggled out after it, into the blistering cold of the day.

THE SNOW WAS blowing in at a sharp angle; the wind forced me sideways when I too crawled out of the igloo. All was very white, dazzling. There was a barrenness to the odd light coming down through the snow. I hunched my shoulders, squinted into the white. I could see Titch's crooked silhouette leaning to one side to counterbalance the weight of his pack as he started south. His boot prints were already filling with new snow. I did not hesitate; I drew my hood tight around my face, clenched my teeth and floundered after him.

Here again, as in Virginia with the sexton Mister Edgar Farrow, I felt Titch was trying to liberate himself from me. And again he would do it under the guise of granting me safety.

How terrifying, to think of having to make my way alone here. Look at the white wastes. The impossible cold. I was thirteen years old, with no one at all in the world. And so I crunched stubbornly after him through the deep snow, my legs stiff in their heavy hides. I did not hurry; I struggled only to keep him in view.

After a time he paused, clapping his mittens together and looking all around him as the snow came down harder. I stood some paces away, panting.

"You are like a ghost," Titch hollered to me. "Go back."

The roar of the wind and snow was increasing. It would be sometime past mid-afternoon by now, but the light had not dimmed, only shifted. We stood in that obliterating whiteness, as though the world had vanished.

"You will not leave me, Wash," he shouted. "Even when I am gone. That is what breaks my heart."

I did not understand. Yet it seemed to me he meant to kill himself by going into the snow. "Let us both turn back," I called out helplessly. "At least until this weather has passed. Then we can make our way to the trading post together. To go farther in this is madness."

I could not see his face, only the fur rippling at his hood. He shouted, "Go back, Wash."

I turned, pausing. I could not see our footsteps in the snow—everything was white, raging.

"If you cannot find the path," he shouted, "stay where you are. You will be found."

"We should both wait here," I shouted. "We should wait out this weather."

Titch slung his pack down into the snow between us.

"Yes," he cried.

He was facing me, but took several steps backwards into the storm.

I struggled with the pack, swung it awkwardly up, stumbling back into the snow. "Wait," I shouted. "It is too heavy."

"Yes," he cried again. But he had turned his face into the wind, as if listening. He started to walk out into the whiteness.

"Titch," I shouted at him.

He entered a white void, and the roaring oblivion of that place closed around him, ate him whole. And so it was that he walked calmly out of his life, and was lost.

PART THREE

Nova Scotia
1834

1

I BEGAN TO CRY; THE TEARS FROZE AT ONCE AND PULLED like sutures at the skin of my cheeks. Titch's tracks had already blown clear, and I peered behind me, or what I thought was behind me, to find the white air churning. I turned and turned, my eyelids burning, my nose already dead and numb. A panic cut through me. I understood that I would not find my way from this place, that I would die.

What happened? I have little recollection: a hand on my arm, a sensation of being dragged, half-carried backwards through howling wind. The snow all around. And the light, how it seemed to break and dissipate into smoke, and the taste of frost in my mouth, like rust. How much of that was real?

I awoke in a smoky orange warmth. I rose up on one elbow, heard the rasp of my sealskin against a sleeping pallet. Mister Wilde was seated in the half-light of a smouldering lantern, sharpening a stake with a rude steel knife. I sat up.

"You'll be sore for some days, boy," said he, smiling bitterly. "But you'll keep your toes and fingers."

"Titch," said I, my eyes fixed on the stake. I swallowed. "Is Titch—?"

He paused in his work, studied me with bright, hard eyes. "My fool of a son," he began angrily. But he did not continue.

I shook my head, shivering. "Is Titch . . . is he still out there? In the storm? Mister Wilde, sir—"

But the old man continued carving methodically, slowly, at the stake. In the dim light I thought I caught something in his face—a downward turn of the mouth, a softening of his ire—that told me he understood more of Titch than I.

I grew uneasy; I became sharply aware that Titch was this man's most-loved son.

"Was it you who pulled me to safety, sir?" I said at last.

He sat back on his haunches, regarded me a long moment before answering. "Not I," he said finally. "Peter. You were born with a ring of luck around your neck, I will say that, boy. An hour more and you would have been buried in ice." He went grimly back to scraping at his stake, his hands wrinkled and trembling. "The men have been out now some hours. I expect word to come soon." He coughed, scratching at his whiskers.

I stared at Mister Wilde, his face stubborn as an Old Testament god's, his eyes ferocious and damning, an old man stooped in a bad light, carving away at his worry.

My voice, when next I spoke, was soft. "How long has it been, sir? How long have I been asleep?"

He did not reply.

The hours passed. Mister Peter and the Esquimaux returned without Titch and rose again at first light to go back out. That day came and went and still there was no sign of him. I could see Mister Wilde growing more and more restless; he slept little and ate less, his hands working constantly at some small task. He did not visit the traps anymore, preferring instead to whittle at some object and stand guard at the entrance of his igloo, his eyes always on the horizon.

Then one morning he had had enough. He gathered all his tools of survival into a large green sack and, stepping his withered, bowed, hairless legs into a freshly oiled caribou skin, he set out under the enormous weight of his bag into the snowy wastes. The Esquimaux tried to discourage him, but he would not hear of it, roaring at them to be gone. Mister Peter gestured for them to let him go, and then, with a tenderness that was quite moving to me, though I could not explain it, he followed, keeping some fifty paces back, to ensure old Mister Wilde too would not be lost.

Mostly what I felt at the time, though, was worry. When every night the searchers had returned without Titch, my stomach twisted, and I'd sat fingering the edge of my tattered pallet, praying for his safe deliverance.

Several days passed before Mister Wilde and Mister Peter returned together, loping slowly over the scoured, bright plain. I could hear Mister Wilde's breath before he even reached me, so raggedly did it pass through his lips, which were cracked and raw.

"You did not find sign of him?" I asked as he reached me at the mouth of the igloo.

It was as though I had not spoken. He passed me by, his face still fixed in a grimace against the bitter air, his body trembling softly. He entered the igloo, and I followed. In the smoky dimness he began to strip off his caribou skin and all the woollens beneath, crouching there bare-chested, his white ribs heaving. The sight of his sweat-laced skin shocked me, the ugly grey hairs matted there. I lowered my eyes.

"A damn foolish boy," he cursed. He began to wipe himself down with his cast-off clothes. "Always running away. Even as a child. Always hiding in some tree or ditch or another before deciding to come back." But I could see by the suppressed pain in his face that he did not believe his son would come back, not this time.

I turned my face away. For I understood in that moment I had well and truly been abandoned, and that no one but myself would see to my safety now. Titch, out there in the snowy wastes, would not be returning.

Mister Wilde cleared his throat. "I daresay you will be all right," he said quietly. I startled at the rough grip of his hand on my shoulder. I peered up at him.

The pity in his eyes surprised me, the gleam of something there. It was not anger. He turned and began to dress in silence. I sat with my back resting against the igloo wall, my knees drawn to my chest.

"We have provisions enough," he continued. "We have food. Clothing." He coughed a racking cough, grunting against his fist. "Your sketch of the whale's horn the other day was very faithful, very pretty. Perhaps you will do some more." But he shook his head then, as though exhausted by these words, and, muttering something, turned away.

Some hours later he fell very ill. In the igloo he shared with Mister Peter he lay on his pallet, his thin, hairless old man's body bundled in furs, shivering. At times he would half-rise and fling the furs away, his face ablaze and damp with fever. Then he would claw them back into place. Mister Peter came and went with a dull lantern, the rope of light swaying over the snow. To his companion he brought all manner of soups and potions and tinctures meant to kill the infection.

But the days passed, and as Titch failed to return, so did his father's health. Though Mister Peter showed little emotion, as if nursing his friend was only one more duty, a restlessness crept into his pale eyes, and his body seemed to tense, contract. His gestures became abrupt. I went every morning with him to check the traps at the perimeter, but it was only to distance my mind from my troubles; we collected nothing and spent most of the hours walking silently, gazing out at the hardened cataracts of ice.

In the afternoons I watched over Mister Wilde as Mister Peter made his trips to the outpost. The old man lay there with his eyes pinched shut, breathing shallowly, his thin body bundled. What a shock he appeared: the inner hollows of his eyes dark blue, his cracked, bleeding lips upturned as though at some private pleasure, a smell like young butter coming from his skin. Observing the fine grey hairs lining his ears, I went and fetched my leads and sketchbook.

As I drew, I thought of Titch, of his lying alone out there. It seemed impossible that after all these days he should still be alive. I turned my mind to John Willard, and to Philip, and in a vision I saw him again—the abomination of him on the dark grass at the mountain's base. It struck me that his single vicious gesture had granted me my new life. For Titch would never have risked taking me away were it not for the danger in which his cousin's death had placed me. I would surely have continued on at Faith. And what would that existence have looked like, after Titch's departure? A return to the fields, to the huts where I had come to be even more despised and pitied, a twisted black Englishman. To Big Kit, who had already replaced me with another. And all this only were I lucky enough to survive the master, when I was returned to him.

I glanced again at Mister Wilde, and paused. I could no longer hear his breathing. His face, turned towards me, had stilled, as if an invisible film had been stretched tight across his features. One yellowing arm was flung across his body. He was dead.

His fabled death was now a true death; the new order Titch had sought to prevent was now reality. I stood in the cold as Mister Peter and the Esquimaux gathered up Mister Wilde from where he'd lain and carried him away. The hours passed; in the warm, dim glow of the igloo I sat staring at the thumbs of my torn mittens.

I did not want to stay in that place. All my life I had known only the warmth of the Indies, the fresh salt of the sea air. I felt shuttered up, boxed in, shuddering with a cold no blanket or animal hide or fire could keep out. Mister Peter and the Esquimaux would, I knew, do their best to keep me safe, but with both Titch and his father gone, I did not know for how long. And so, as the hours passed, I began to collect up my belongings, and in the evening, when Mister Peter returned, I told him of my intention to leave.

He had lost his dearest friend, the companion of his life—and yet that man was as stoic and as kind as when I had first laid eyes on him. He bid me take whichever of the Wildes' possessions I most desired, and to the leather-bound treatise on marine life I selected he added several hand lenses of Mister Wilde's. He also gave me the skin full of money Titch had left for me, and much good food and provisions. When finally I was ready to go, he gathered me up in his arms and crushed the breath from me. Then he and Hesiod propped me aboard a sled, and whipping at the dogs, they led me off into the cold white wastes.

At the outpost Mister Peter slapped my pack on my shoulder and gave me a stern look. I was turning from him when he gestured for me to wait and pulled suddenly from the folds of his clothes several small scopes. They were Titch's self-made models, compact, with odd dark gears for knobs. Mister Peter placed them in my open mittens; then he gave me a strange clap on the side of my head, not hard, and was gone.

2

TITCH HAD SPOKEN MUCH OF THE LOYALISTS; IT WAS TO them I resolved to go. I believed I would be safest among them. And so, after several weeks at that northern outpost, cowering away from the drunken traders, I finally managed to arrange passage on a vessel sailing for the Maritime isles. How frightened I was, how terrified to be a small black boy alone at sea. I stayed out of the captain's path, fearing he might sell me to a passing ship bound for the Slave States. I was terrified also of meeting John Willard or his agents, convinced they would discover and kill me. One evening, as I sat eating a greening rind of cheese, a wrinkled-faced sailor approached. I stared in dread, awaiting a fatal blow. Instead, he hefted me up with his thick, bread-like hands and tied me with an end of spun rope to the rigging. There he danced, taunting me, until I agreed to stand treat a quart of rum. After that I spent little time on deck and spoke to no one. I hid in my quarters, feeling beneath me the slow heave of the boat, and paging through the one book I'd carried away—Titch's fine leather-bound tract on sea creatures.

The sailors talked of many islands, of free ports. But it was a life among the Loyalists, in Nova Scotia, that I most desired. I travelled south, then east, crossing the dark waters, journeying overland by cart and carriage; and I arrived finally at Shelburne, with high expectations. But I found that the free, golden existence once described to me had been used up, crushed, drained to the skin by all who'd come before. Shelburne was wet and dreadful, its mud streets teeming with the tattered and the grey-faced, displaced roamers from last century's American war. There was little land and fewer supplies, and the black-skinned were given the worst of it when they were given any at all. I worked for a time in a small-scale fishery. But my years on the plantation, and my memory of John Willard's agent on the docks, had twisted something in me—I was everywhere uneasy in my skin, and this made me irritable and nervous and desperately melancholy, though I could not then have expressed it so. The fear, the fear was always with me. And not just of Willard's agents—kidnappers generally roamed the coast, and in the rainy, grey dusk they would stun a freed man in the street and drag him half-conscious onto a ship bound for the Southern states, to make of him a slave again.

This was not the only hazard, though it was the worst of them. White men were everywhere aggrieved, and they would sometimes rise up against us black devils, the miserable black scourge who would destroy their livelihood by labouring at cheaper rates. One night I stood on the edge of an overcast tavern, drinking some fermented brew from a dirty tin cup, when someone crept up unseen behind me, like a piece of broken-off shadow, and closed his hands about my throat. We tussled and fumbled in the street, debris flying, when finally I managed to grab a fistful of pebbles and pressed them into his eyes. He cried out and I ran off, and though bystanders later told me he was only a local tough, an old defrocked Anglican priest known to many as a brawler, I could not shake the feeling of having escaped John Willard himself, and I grew even more watchful, and solitary.

Such were the times. I saw myself grow flint-like, and bitter, and fill with a restlessness beyond all sleep. Out walking one afternoon, I picked up a discarded piece of tin in the street, and peering at my reflection there, I saw in my eyes a lightlessness, a methodical will for violence. I knew I must move on, or kill, or be killed.

I was not yet sixteen years of age then. I had run through the coin Peter House had given me long before. And so I gathered my belongings and moved on. In those drifting days I often gave my name as Joseph Crawford, as if I might hide inside the spectre of another man. But finding myself never able to answer to it, and uneasy in my skin besides, I dropped the ruse and became again Washington Black. I settled on the edge of the Bedford Basin, in a sleepy township on a quieter shore, finding, in due time, work as a dishwasher and a laundry boy. I still struggled to continue to sketch, though my interest in it had waned; it did not afford me the solace it had once done, making me feel instead sad and drained. After a time I found work as a prep cook, and discovered I had a gift for it. By the end of 1834 I was working as a chef in a dining hall popular with disbanded soldiers and out-of-work fishermen flooding in from Newfoundland. But I cooked always behind a curtain, unseen, my scarred face being, the owner feared, repugnant. The schedule was demanding, and after some months of this I gave up drawing altogether, finding no extra hours in my day. Though I did not know it then, I had begun the months of my long desolation. I became a boy without identity, a walking shadow, and with each new month I fell deeper into strangeness. For there could be no belonging for a creature such as myself, anywhere: a disfigured black boy with a scientific turn of mind and a talent on canvas, running, always running, from the dimmest of shadows.

MISTER WILDE HAD told me I was born with a ring of luck at my neck. Luck is its own kind of manacle, perhaps. I do not know when it happened, only that it gradually crept over me until one day I woke to a burning certainty: I needed to better my circumstances, or I would die.

I was a child no more; I was already a young man of sixteen. And so I found intermittent work at the docks. This work was a choice made in strength—for *I* governed how much I worked, and spent the rest of my days as I wished. I recalled what Big Kit had once said about freedom—that if he did not feel like working, the free man tossed down his shovel. If he did not like a question, he made no answer. And I was trying my best to live up to that ideal, to be my own free man. But it was quite an awakening, to leave behind Titch's coddled world and meet again with the brutality of white men. To be called nigger and kicked at in disgust like a wharf rat. My colour was already one burden; my burns made life unconscionable. One night I was held down in the alleyway behind a drinking establishment and beaten and urinated on by my laughing white colleagues, men with whom I daily worked.

Rarely, by then, did I think of Titch. But sometimes at night I would remember his face, or his voice; and I would wonder at his possible survival in all that snow, though I knew it a hopeless thought. Given his empty beliefs about the afterlife, his confusion over his cousin's choice, it surprised me that he too would end things so. It made me feel that perhaps I had never understood him.

It was in my lowest of days that the miraculous occurred. For I was hired on to unload a sailing vessel in the dead of night, and while rowing a crate ashore I noticed shapes in the black waters. I caught sight of a sudden current, a sudden flash. Then from farther off came another flash, and then another, tight explosions of green and yellow, as if comets were being detonated there.

I leaned over, staring. The sea was smooth as a wooden table, and yet I could see upon its surface an odd translucency. The ship's light caught it, and oh, oh, what a sight drifted there, what alien and wondrous beings! For I observed now a wide, transparent green orb, pulsing, and beside it a yellow one, and then another and another, dozens of glistening suns flaring all about in the dark waters.

I had seen jellyfish before, in visits with Titch to the beaches near Faith. But never in such numbers, and never so vibrant, so glasslike. The black of the sea was far-reaching, as though no light could penetrate it. And yet here these creatures floated, fragile as a woman's stocking, their bodies all afire. My breath left me. I leaned over the edge of the little rowboat and watched the sea pulse in a furnace of colour.

The dock master was shouting at me, cursing my laziness. I came to; I started to row again, the oars turning and scattering the light.

Later, back at my boarding house, I dug out my papers and paint, and I sketched for the first time in months. I sat in the fragrant glow of a tallow candle and attempted to capture what I'd seen in the waters. I could not. It had been a burst of incandescence, fleeting, radiant, every punch of light like a note of music.

3

And so I awoke to myself, my boyhood long behind me. Somehow I had become a stranger in my own skin. How was it I had let all wonder, all curiosity, seep from me? I was amazed. I sought out and found permanent employment as a delivery man for Fummerton's Dry Goods. I worked only from mid-morning to late afternoon, which afforded me time again for sketching in the fine salt air.

How surprised I was to see how poor my drawing had gotten after years of rest. It struck me how grand my talent had once been, how innate and eerie. At just eleven years old—untrained, a slave—I'd been able to sketch the most luminous tree frogs and wind-blown palms and human feet, feet that frightened with the brutality of their hair and bones and speckled flesh. I would now have to practise what had once come so naturally to me; I would have to retrain my hand. But the prospect did not trouble me. Rather, I felt grateful for the return of the simple urge to draw, at the feelings of calm and peace it brought.

And it was perhaps these feelings of renewal that allowed me to open myself to a kind of friendship. His name was Medwin Harris, and he had care of the rooming house I moved to in December of 1834. He was a long-time resident of Nova Scotia, his family having arrived as refugees at the Melville Island prison—once used for American prisoners of war—back in 1815. He had tried for a time to live away, working as a waiter in a moss-strewn, picturesque hotel edging Niagara Falls. Amazingly, his wages and conditions there had been equal to those of his white colleagues, but still he had abandoned his post, and come back to these soils of his boyhood. He became caretaker of the shabby, rundown rooming house I lodged in, and he was proud of the appointment, speaking of it like a triumph of the will.

"You shall find me here long after the rats have run off, boy," he'd say to me with a grin. "Look for me in the rubble."

And then he would spit on his boot and rub the toe to a shine with his handkerchief.

To call him a friend is perhaps inaccurate. Rather, we drank together, and occasionally got into trouble together. When the dark thoughts came on, of Big Kit, or of Titch, or of Philip, I would seek Medwin out in his rooms, and his joking would lighten my spirits. I did not ever mention John Willard, and he never offered any intimacy of his own.

Medwin was tall, much taller than myself, with thick, brutal forearms and a neck wider than his head. He was five years my senior, or so he told me, though given his history I suspected he was somewhat older than that. His gestures were quiet and even meek, and there was something so jarring in the contrast between his looks and his modesty that he seemed eerily watchful, as if he was quietly and constantly taking your measure, which perhaps he was. I will say that he often gave clever, useful advice, and that he understood my silences as even Big Kit had not. But it is also true that there was something in him I did not fully trust.

He was not a bad man, I believe. But I sensed he was not a good one either. There were few men in that place, in those years, who had not learned the hard way of living.

When I heard news of the English establishing an apprenticeship system in the Indies, a measure proving that slavery truly was ended—or so I then believed—Medwin and I went out to celebrate.

We sat in a filthy establishment, drinking the dreck someone had likely brought in from an illicit distillery. It was a fine, clear evening, the reek of the sea plants so strong that it filled even the inner rooms with a rotted, blood-like stench. Medwin's people being American, it was no great occasion for him, but he could see what it meant to me, and he stood me a drink.

"Well," he said, raising his glass.

"Well," said I, raising mine also.

And then we sank into a kind of silence, Medwin whistling lightly under his breath, glancing all around at nothing much.

I was overwhelmed by thoughts of Faith, of Gaius, and especially of Big Kit. What would her life become, now she was well and truly free? Would she roam the world as I had roamed it, alone, with no salve for her troubles? Or would she find her way? Where would she go? Could she ever be found? Would she even want to be? And then it came to me, the idea that she had not survived, that she was dead. I do not know why I thought it, but now it had entered my head, it settled leadenly there, like an ache. When I sipped from my drink, I found my hands were shaking.

If Medwin noticed, he said nothing. Instead he stretched back in his chair and, drawing his threadbare handkerchief from his pocket, began to worry its edges with his thick fingers.

As from nowhere, our table was flanked suddenly by two dark-faced men. In the thin yellow light of the sparsely hung lanterns I could see the black gleam of their foreheads, their twisted, damp mouths. I did not know them; one man was shorn bald and bowed in one leg, the other quite short with enormous hands unfitting for so small a body. Yet for all their oddity they looked upon me like I was a creature of repulsion.

"You seen this nigger's face?" the taller one slurred to his friend.

"Fuck," said the friend, and I could smell the vomit on his breath. "Christ."

"Who let this thing in here?" the first man called out, trying to focus his eyes on me. "Shit."

"Like some shit dragged behind a cart."

"Hell, nigger. You should have prayed they killed you."

Across from me I could feel Medwin begin to smile.

"This comical to you?" the shorter man said.

"Look at him grinning away like that. Like a imbecile."

"You find this amusing? Best you get the hell out this place before I break your fucking neck. Beat you shitless."

"Why am I wasting my breath on this here filth?"

"Filth. Both of them."

"Waste of breath just to say it. I'm done talking."

"What?" said Medwin so suddenly that the men paused, as though momentarily sobered.

The tall man moistened his dark lips. "Said I'm done talking, nigger."

"What?" Medwin said again.

"You got shit in your ears? I'm done talking."

Medwin smiled across at me. "Don't sound like he so done talking, do it?"

I closed my eyes, sensing the coming rush, like a pressure. Then I heard Medwin smash his glass on the table ledge, and I glanced up in time to watch him drive the jagged edge into one shocked face, then the next.

4

SUCH WAS THE WAY OF THE PLACE, AT THAT TIME. THERE was a quiet lawlessness to it all that was often grotesque. The viciousness between the races was bracing enough, but almost as dreadful was the way blacks sometimes treated one another, as if all they had endured in cruelty would be paid back doubly on their brothers. Sometimes it felt as though I had not travelled very far from the rundown huts of Faith.

I tried to avoid all conflict. It was difficult with a friend like Medwin, who sought out fights as he sought out food, as a life-blood. Though I still did delight in his company some days, I kept more and more to myself, and began to go out into the raw spring dawns to draw.

Each morning, I would gather my satchel of leads and paints, and a small collapsible chair with an easel attached that I myself had fashioned, and I would walk the quiet dirt road behind my rooming house towards the dark inlet. At that hour, in that place, the street belonged to me alone; there was only the scrape of cats in the side streets, the rattle of loose doors, leaves hissing in the gutters. John Willard, Philip, Titch—all of it seemed another life. I would make my way towards an inlet just beyond the headland, out of sight of the town, hearing the hush of the water's slow creep up the seaweed-choked rocks long before I came in sight of the strand.

How radiant the world was, empty and silent like this. Often, at that time of year, the tide was still receding. Carefully, I would remove my shoes and, still clutching my belongings, lurch over the cold, damp rocks, the air smelling of wet weeds. With the sun just piercing the horizon, the light was hazy and filmy, the sand seeming to stretch on into oblivion. The seafoam stirred whitely at the edge of the water. It was here that I set down my tools. I would turn up the legs of my trousers and, with a sharp intake of breath, step in.

The tide pools were most alive at first light. The hazy air seemed to gild all that lay within, the anemones glowing pink as human flesh, their tentacles open and pleading. Small soft-shelled crabs with lively little eyes, and sometimes a sea pen, its quills magisterial. Some days, if I waded farther out, I would find pansies or green sea urchins, large crabs, polyps magenta with toxins. The jellyfish were shy here, a mercy—for many carried poison in their harpoons, and at the first touch of danger they would spring-launch them, and stun a man senseless.

It was on so quiet a morning, the water bitterly cold, that my life was to take its next sudden turn. I had waded in mid-thigh—my rolled trousers drenched, stones and broken shells biting into my bare feet—when I felt something like a presence. I turned; I was quite alone, I could see no one behind me. But then the light shifted, and I caught a distant silhouette on the shore. Gradually a figure took shape. He was standing about a half mile from where I'd set down my equipment.

I must admit to feeling some alarm. But when the stranger began to set up an easel on the sand, I relaxed somewhat. I did not believe a man who had read John Willard's poster would go to such elaborate lengths to snare me. In any case the silhouette looked rather shorter, rather more plump than I expected a bounty man to be. I watched uneasily as the man drew out his instruments and began very leisurely to paint.

These early ventures had become my one pure pleasure; the sense of freedom was intense. At the easel I was a man in full, his hours his own, his preoccupations his own. It bothered me that some stranger might show up to destroy it. All morning I did not make to approach him; nor did he walk in my direction. I scratched down my sketches in haste and left early.

But the next morning there he was again. Grumbling, casting angry looks in his direction, I gathered my tools and stamped away without any sketches at all. The inlet felt tainted; even the air seemed to stink. When the next morning I again discovered him there, I understood even this would be taken from me. I raised my hand in an exasperated gesture towards him before wading in. He paused, and put a hand to his eyes to see me, and then he raised his own hand in a friendly wave—or so I believed, he was so very far away.

I took it as a reproach. Who was I to deny a fellow artist his own pleasure at work, his own sense of freedom? I too possessed nothing of worth but these hours. We might even, in another life, have been colleagues. And so every dawn we would greet each other from across the long strand, before growing absorbed in our respective work. I began to think it strange that this person with whom I now shared my intimate hours should remain unknown to me, a stranger so absolute that I would not recognize him in the street. I began to wonder, too, what sort of work he was embarked upon. But I did not wish to complicate matters.

In the end it was not I who overturned the delicate balance. One morning, when I had pulled from the sea a hermit crab and sat sketching the silver arc of its shell, a shadow dropped across my paper and a voice, raw and soft, said, "Oh, how beautiful. What a talent you have, sir."

I turned on my creaking wooden seat, grimacing against the early sun, and saw her face for the first time.

She had dark, foxlike features, and vaguely narrowed eyes. She smiled at me. She wore an oversized beige pair of trousers, rolled up to the knees. Her tanned calves were quite bare, strong and rounded. I raised my eyes: beneath her large-brimmed man's hat her black hair was pinned harshly up at her nape, as if it were shorn. She was very short. Her left hand was cocooned in a plaster cast stained with soot, as though she had long ago broken her arm and could not be bothered to remove it. With her good hand, which was stained with paint, she gestured at the half-finished anemones I had left to dry beside my easel in the sand. "You should see my own reproductions. They look rather more like something down a man's trousers, I fear."

I must have looked startled, for she laughed then—an odd, whisking sound—and said, "I have shocked you. Forgive me."

"I am not shocked," said I.

"Taken aback, then. You really must forgive me—I am too plain-spoken." She held out her tiny hand, and a moment passed before I thought to take it. "Tanna Goff."

"George Washington Black."

"Of course you are. I would have expected no less. First the Delaware, then the Labrador Sea."

"The joke is new to me."

"My goodness, you are polite," she said with a dry smile. "Unfortunately, I am not. Please, George Washington Black, do forgive my forwardness. It's just—well, have we not been sketching side by side every morning these two weeks now? I thought it only correct that we were acquainted." She shrugged cheerfully.

I glanced down the beach—her easel stood eerie and abandoned. "I had thought you were a man all this time," I said. I saw her expression and immediately felt foolish. "It is the distance between us," I continued. "I do not mean to offend you. That is, I would not mistake you now—"

But she was smiling a most strange smile. "Oh, good Mister Washington Black, I am wearing trousers—it is only to be expected. You have not insulted me. In any case, many have said much worse, standing closer than we are now."

In the embarrassed silence I searched her face: her skin was golden, with darker freckles peppered across her nose, her eyes exquisitely flinty and intelligent. She was not a white woman, or not entirely; from where had she come? Her doll-like stature made her seem vulnerable, childlike. But she was not vulnerable. She was strong of speech, and of a seemingly knowing age. I could not say for sure, but she seemed some years older than myself, nineteen perhaps, twenty, her face shrewd, her lips red and full and moist-looking.

"I don't suppose you could teach me to paint like that?"

I paused, startled by the suggestion. "Forgive me, Miss Goff, I do not think—"

"What? You cannot think me beyond all hope yet—see my sketches first, then tell me I am beyond all hope."

I hesitated; that had not been my meaning at all.

"I do not mind paying some fee."

"Oh, no, absolutely not." I shook my head. "I do not wish a fee."

"We shall work out some payment," she said with a smile.

"A payment?"

"So you agree, then. You will teach me. Wonderful."

Staring into her sharp face, her brown front teeth edging over her lower lip, I felt a kind of despair, sensing the solitary mornings of the world fade from me, and grow dim.

WHAT AN ODDITY, to work alongside a stranger by the wind of the sea.

Alongside a woman.

I knew so little about her. But I would rise at my usual hour, and walk now with even greater uncertainty through the streets to find her already standing at the shoreline. She would turn and wave with her good hand, then wait with her round, childlike arms tucked into the gentle folds of her skirts. For since that first meeting she'd begun to dress in more feminine attire—though even this was not "proper," the fabric much less voluminous than the accepted fashions. I would reach her and with a quiet greeting lay down all my instruments on the sand and set to rolling my cuffs. Together we would wade into the waters, and I would point out all manner of crabs and fish and limpets and slugs and worms and starfish, and she would wrinkle her freckled nose and narrow her eyes as if trying to commit it all to memory.

How can I describe these mornings? She was comical and blunt, with the loose tongue of a sailor and a rough, unbeautiful voice. She had, most strangely, been born in the Solomon Islands, though she did not say how she came to be here, on the desolate shores of Nova Scotia. She had five half-brothers, all older, and her mother had passed away in childbirth with her. This she offered cheerfully, but I could see it unsettled her still. Her wrist she had broken two months earlier, and she was impatient with its progress, for it did not seem to be healing.

"You can imagine how it has set my drawing back. Better to break both legs than this." She gave a light smile. "If one must break something, that is."

"I imagine it is very limiting," said I.

"It is a tether." She shrugged. "I could never accept any restriction on my freedom of movement, you see, even as a child. I have always been this way. Sometimes it has served me poorly, but . . ." She shrugged again.

She wanted to know all there was to know about me. Indeed, the intensity of her interest dismayed me, so that I grew flustered and embarrassed. I could not fathom what it was she thought she glimpsed behind the knotted flesh of my face. Sometimes when I spoke she'd stare on with quiet ferocity—but it was not pity I sensed there, nor morbid fascination, but something like a greed to fully enter my consciousness. The wrecked visage I was forced to carry like an unwanted warning to others was to her a known thing, a familiar mask. She seemed to see beneath it something of her own suffering and recovery—the acceptance of a life-changing wound, the will to go on.

Yet despite all her prying I kept my past my own, and spoke instead of the different manipulations of watercolours, how best to thicken and thin them, when to better use chalk pastels and what paper most readily accepted both. All this she took in like a model pupil, sometimes scratching down notes, and she would laugh at her own mistakes, a sound hoarse and strange.

I was not a person to make a study of such details, but I noted the gentle pores on her long throat, the unnaturally black hair of her long eyelashes. I watched the slow morning light creep across the folds of her golden ear, and felt myself uneasy.

I was surprised at how much I came to enjoy her company. So dazzling was her talk that more than a week passed before I discovered she was already familiar with the many varieties of invertebrates, had in fact a keener and more thorough knowledge of sea creatures than I. Her broken wrist was even a result of her having cracked her arm on a crag of rock while on a shallow-sea dive right here in the inlet. My face burned with the embarrassment of having attempted to school her.

"But you did ask me to teach you," I said, confused.

"To draw, George Washington, to draw. The whelks and such I know like my own voice. It is the artistry to depict them in which I am wanting."

"Oh." I looked away, chastened.

And it was then that she placed her hand in mine. I was so rattled that I flinched. But I did not draw my hand away.

"You will show me," she murmured, and I turned to her surprised, startled, and roused beyond all my senses.

Her eyes were narrowed, and across her freckled face passed a lazy, intimate smile. More shocking to me than my own desire was the sight of it reflected in her clear tan face. I had never before experienced such strong feelings from a woman, the rawness of her want, the openness. In those seconds a sense of wholeness came over me: I felt the broadness of my shoulders, the force of my height, my blunt, low voice. I was pieced together, suddenly, a man intact.

She let her eyes drift to my right cheek, and her face softened. "Your scar," she said quietly. "How did you get it?"

I looked into her eyes, sharp and judging, her smile tremulous, the teeth tobacco-stained. I could smell that tobacco coming off her body, the scent of her sweat and the essence of some flower, lavender perhaps. I felt the clench of her cold hand in mine, her skin rough as new wool, her warm breath, and the quick, dull pulse of her heart beating through the fabric of her dress. I stepped forward and I felt her close, and a surge like water went through me, something rushing and hot, and I wanted so much to take another step forward, into her, but I heard my breath then sharply in my ears, and a terror rose up in me. I glanced quickly at the beach shacks in the distance, my fingers grazing the coarse cloth of her dress as I dropped her hand.

She turned her face to the dark houses also, her smile wry and sad. I heard only the ocean between us, the static hush of the water.

"To alter the viscosity of the paint," I said, and my voice sounded odd, not my own, "some use ox gall. I myself prefer glycerine, but—" I paused.

She looked thoughtful, and a long moment passed before she reached for her sketchbook to make notes.

5

"White woman ain't but the devil. Don't you do it."

"She is not white," I answered. "At least I do not think so. And to whom are you referring? What white women do you know?"

Medwin only raised his palms, shrugging.

I was seated on the crooked wooden staircase of our rooming house, a drink in my fist, taking Medwin's counsel in the fine night air. Behind us, wild Irish sea shanties roared from one of the larger rooms, and there was much hooting and laughter.

I had only just begun to speak of Tanna when he cut me short.

"As if you ain't been through hell on earth enough, boy." He gave his head a shake. "You lost your damned mind? How do you suppose she even here, man? You think she just wish it and, poof, in a puff of smoke, here she is? Ain't you said she from the Solomon Islands? Something ain't right in all this. How she explain her being here?"

"She didn't."

"Well, then," he said, looking profoundly satisfied.

"Your powers of detection are immense," I said sourly. "You should start charging a fee. Set up a booth with a little pink awning. Help ladies find their lost hats."

"Listen, boy, it's this kind of stupidity finds you waking with your throat cut. It's this kind of witchery gets your bowels shot out." He coughed harshly against his fist. "Now just consider the particulars, won't you? You a man with a face like a goddamn lobster salad, can't barely make passable, sociable conversation. What the hell she want with a boy like you?"

I gave a resigned shrug, as if to say I wondered as much. I had had little experience with romance, it is true. In all my years I had loved but one girl, chastely—the housegirl Émilie, at Faith Plantation—and lain with two others: one a fine, fine lady, the other a prostitute, a fact unknown to me until all was over and done. The fine one, a girl called Vivian Hatcher, I had met at the dockyards when she'd come to bring a hot lunch to her father. Her father and I had been fellow dockworkers for weeks, but I knew nothing of him beyond that he hailed from Macon, Georgia, and had fought alongside the English in their Revolutionary War and was now breaking crates for little pay. Vivian was a quiet, dark-faced girl of fourteen, with a slow, open, thrilling gaze. We spent the afternoons in the grassy knoll behind her rooming house, eating maple sweets from a crackling paper sack and touching each other. Her father, when he learned of it, threatened to crush my skull. I understood at once that the quality he despised in me was the same one that had drawn Vivian in: my scarred face. He called it a "bloodied butcher's board."

Medwin poured another finger of gin into my chipped glass and we sat in silence, him drinking, me turning the full glass in my hands.

"She knows all there is to know about molluscs," I said. "If you can imagine."

"What I can imagine is your body hanging from some good old oak," said Medwin, lapping at his empty glass. "What I can imagine is you dragged behind a horse cart. I do not care if she knows the secret to distilling angel-water, you stay right clear of the lady, you hear? Don't you go back to that beach."

I took a quick sip from my glass, shuddered.

Medwin gave his gravelly laugh. "Made that one myself. You like it?"

"As much as the company."

"That good, huh?" He chuckled. "Hey, listen, now I'm seeing you—a man come on by looking for you. White fellow. Short. Ugly. Well, uglier than you, which is to say considerable."

A rope of fear uncoiled in my stomach. "What did he say?"

"Not much. Real silent type. At first I thought he come to make trouble, to rustle me up for those brothers I cut the other night, but he was only making inquiries. Odd fellow. Got this real soft voice, like a widow's or a kid's. Kind of high-ish. Body ain't look like much—I could've had him on the ground in a minute, boy. That said, there was something about him I wouldn't cross."

"What did he say?" I said again, my voice quiet.

"Well, nothing. Just asking after you. When I said I didn't know you from Adam, he asked when you might be returning. Real quick bastard. I said again I did not know you but that you certainly sounded like a type I would never allow through the doors of my distinguished establishment. I told him to get the hell out and good fucking luck with the search."

I glanced up at him, trying to appear natural, failing terribly. "Thank you."

"It's bad, what he got on you, ain't it? *Bad* bad. Won't pry about it, though." He shrugged, and gestured at my glass. "Anyhow. You got time for another?"

THAT EVENING, AND long into the next morning, I lay in bed with a dread heart. My sleep had been restless and tortured; I had awoken in a damp tangle of blankets, frightened.

I wanted to do what I'd done every morning for weeks: I wanted to gather my belongings and go to the shore, go out to her. I wanted to re-create yesterday, when she had placed her cold little hand in mine; but this time, I wanted to take her against me, press myself into her thighs, let her feel me, my desire for her. I wanted to put my mouth on her long, golden neck and feel the blood pulse under my tongue. But I could now not even leave my rooms; somehow, when I had most forgotten him, John Willard had found me.

I did not know beyond all doubt that it was him. But neither could I say with certainty that it wasn't. The softness of voice Medwin had described, the small stature, the unsettling manner—it was too familiar, so that I lay flat on my back on the damp sheets, breathing raggedly.

But why did he still hunt me, after all these years? How was it that I still held value for Erasmus Wilde? Years had passed; the slave trade had long been abolished in West India; slavery itself was now ended there too, though it still darkened America. Surely the grudge did not hold? But the mind of an evil man is never legible. I only knew that I was now too frightened to leave my rooming house, and that what I most wanted in the world was to touch the fine strands of Tanna's pinned black hair.

I cannot now think of how I managed it. But, shivering,

reduced, I rose from the bed and began to pack my tools. Fighting back much terror, I was able to leave my rooming house that morning, to walk beyond the creaking door towards the beach.

The strand was deserted.

I scanned the rocky sand in the distance: only the shadows of trees, silence. My hands trembling badly, I set up my tools and waited, watching the horizon as much for Willard as for Tanna herself. No one came. After an hour I gathered my things and took the back roads home. There, staring nervously out the window, I ate a quick meal of boiled eggs. I was due that morning at my employment, delivering packages for Fummerton's Dry Goods. I was determined to keep this post, and this required showing my face rain or shine, whether I had ten deliveries scheduled or none. And so I tucked an ivory-handled kitchen knife into my waistcoat and lowered my hat to go out.

The day passed without event, though it kept occurring to me that Willard had only to order a package under a false name to lure me to him. Pushing aside the twine, I scanned the names penned on the thick paper wrappers. Mrs. Stephen Blatch; Mister Raymond Grimes; Mister James Smith. This last seemed suspiciously benign and as I neared the door of his grungy rooming-house flat, I felt the nausea rising. But he was only a wilting little person of thirty years, his hair thinning badly, and he accepted his package of sugar like a man slapped, gazing in shock at my wrecked face.

After work I dropped into bed, the knife beside me, exhausted from hours spent in tension and watchfulness.

Again the next morning Tanna did not appear at the strand. I did not stay long, and later only left my house to go deliver packages. When, the next day, she also did not show herself, I became disconsolate, and cursed myself for having so callously dropped her hand on that now-distant morning. For the whole encounter had come to seem a dream, as if in the madness of my solitude I had invented her—a figment to tear myself open, to destroy my freedom and peace of mind and wrench me off course. And then, suddenly, I began to connect her appearance in my life with Willard's arrival. I asked myself if she was somehow working for him, sent to weaken my vigilance so that he could get at me. Was the thought so stupid? Yes, I decided, it was. I lay there picturing her as she'd been on the shore that last day, the play of light across her fine golden cheeks, the air smelling of rotted weeds and salt.

Days passed. There came sometimes a knock at my door, but I never answered. I knew it was likely only Medwin, but I did not want to risk it. Towards the week's end I ran out of food and stayed the next two days together in bed, fasting. Finally, when my head began to spin and my muscles to shiver, I rose and walked weakly through the back roads to an open-air fruit stand a quarter mile away. I stood there scrutinizing the crowd, searching the bodies and faces for any likeness of Willard. I did not think I saw him, and went finally to choose some fruit. I was sorting through a basket of gooseberries when suddenly the air browned with tobacco and lavender, and I lifted my face. What were the chances? And yet it was she, Tanna Goff, tiny and sensuous in her slack dress, a distracted look on her face as she studied a cartful of wormy green apples.

People were glancing at her, some laughing quietly at her strangeness, yet she did not seem to know it. The early evening light gilded her skin, so that her whole face was illuminated. She seemed relaxed, and with some of her severity now gone, there was only the fine intelligence of her eyes, and the obvious bodily pleasure she took in being out in the fresh air.

How could I disturb this quiet, this peace? And yet it had been nearly a week, and with each waking disappointment my anguish had grown. And so I straightened my cuffs and, with a quick moistening of the lips, ambled through the small crowd.

But a queasiness rose up in me before I reached her, and I stopped. What would I say to her? What was it I desired? She would think me a child, foolish. Before she could catch sight of me, I squeezed between a stand of potatoes and a rickety apple cart, and fled.

6

I WAS A COWARD; I ADMIT IT. BUT EVERYTHING TROUBLED me then, nothing was right.

Some days later, at Fummerton's Dry Goods, I was handed a sack of flour, a bag of sugar and a bolt of lady's fabric to deliver. It was a common-enough order, nothing remarkable. But the name on the package arrested my eye.

Mister Goff.

I realized I had never given any thought to her living situation. Mister Goff. I felt something dim in me, go dark. So there was, in the end, a husband.

It took me nearly an hour to reach the shack at the edge of the red dirt lane—twice the length of time it should have done. I took uncommon roads, always watchful, tense. I felt sick, and recognized it was as much from fear of who I would discover at this address as it was of Willard. Finally I reached a small saltbox house painted pale blue, surrounded by tall, wild grasses and bramble pulsing with purple chokecherries. Someone had flung a strange iron contraption on the porch, its front wheel tilted askew. I mounted the creaking steps, scraped my boots on the straw mat, which was fraying so badly that loose strands of it flitted across the worn porch boards.

I dropped the knocker, hearing a man's muffled voice behind the door. Then, with a suddenness that caused me to step back, he answered, his pale face grimacing against the brightness. He was rather old, and short, and stocky, and as he peered up at me I saw his eyes were dark, unblinking and seemingly without pupils, the eyes of a fanatic.

"What, then?" he said, his teeth very small and false-looking. He was searching my face, and seemed now wary, nervous.

"Delivery, sir." I glanced at the package, as though I had not memorized it already. "For a Mister Goff?"

He frowned down at my hands, then turned and barked into the darkness behind him, "Your parcels are come." He grimaced in frustration. "Is this it? Is this all?" Before I could make any response, he had stepped back into the dark reception hall.

I felt a ghostly sense of recognition then, as though I had stood on this porch before, delivering just these items.

He waved a distracted hand, bidding me come in. I hesitated, then stepped into the modest hall, the air inside cool and smelling faintly of lemons. He had a funny little stride like a child's, full of quick steps, and very swiftly he led me into a parlour full of old and desperate furniture: in one corner, under a grimy clerestory window, sat a chair with a broken leg glued back on in slightly the wrong spot; the red silk cushion on the threadbare settee was vomiting feathers. But it was the boxes strewn all about that I marvelled at: recklessly tossed there, they held dried starfish, large crabs, other sea fauna. On the pine desk tucked under the far window, a tiny, brown, desiccated seahorse was in the process of being pinned in a box.

He walked to the desk and, with his plump, coarse hands,

shoved a stack of books onto the floor. They flew down in a clatter, their pages flapping open. A veil of dust radiated from the rug.

"Go on and set them there," he said, gesturing at the now-cleared space. "Pantry's a mess just now."

I did as asked, and stooped to retrieve the books. I turned a spine to read the title. "Oh, but this one is wonderful, sir," I said, forgetting myself. "You would do better than to treat it so."

He eyed me sharply. "Like that one, do you?"

I had pored over many such books in the library at Faith, during those lazy days of healing from the blast. I peered up at him. "It is a favourite. Do you also know his *Cnidaria and Cephalopoda Past and Present*? It too is very fine. I confess I have not read it, only looked at the illustrations, but I found them mesmerizing. I do believe the author does his own sketches. He is frightfully talented—a fine, clear hand. I will say, though, that I do not believe he has ever out-done his watercolours in the *Resplendence of Nudibranchia*—"

My voice trailed off, seeing the old man's face. I rose slowly.

"Why, you are *that* Goff," said I, softly. "You are G.M. Goff. Is it not so?"

He stood grimacing, and it was some moments before he grunted his assent. For he was a greatly celebrated marine zoologist, a man whose books I had studied with a religiosity and fervour rarely given to anything. His shading was unconventional, so strange as to sometimes feel wrong, his oddly drawn observations made gorgeous by the threadlike clarity of his line.

"Take an interest in science, do you?" His voice had softened somewhat. "What is your area of study?"

"Marine life, sir, though I shrink to say it before a man of your accomplishment."

"What a rare and fortunate meeting this is, then," he said, and though he did not cease to frown, I understood some part of him was pleased. His eyes were so dark in his face they looked depthless, like night waters.

"But why are you here, sir? I rather pictured you in a manor house in England. You do not reside here?"

"Ah, research, my boy, research. I am collecting specimens. Then it is back to England. There are some fascinating crinoids to be found here."

"Indeed," said I, a little too forcefully. The light shifted in the room, grew sootier, as though a cloud had passed over the sun.

Goff wiped his ink-stained palms on the front of his black waistcoat. "Well. Well. You are an interesting and knowledgeable young man. Forgive me—your name?"

"George Washington Black."

"George Washington," said he.

"Black," said I.

"Indeed," said he.

"My acquaintances call me Wash."

He paused, turning something over in his mind. "This will seem unorthodox. But my daughter and I, we do so suffer for kindred company. I have two delightful sisters, one in England, one in France, but here we find ourselves quite isolated and alone. In any case, Tanna and I were thinking of taking a boat out upon the sea tomorrow noon. It being a Saturday, perhaps you are free to accompany us? Nothing dangerous, of course, just a rowboat and a good lunch. We're recording observations for my new book." He grunted. "Perhaps you are otherwise engaged. So late an invitation."

I had heard only one word: *daughter*. His daughter. I breathed out in relief. "There could be no finer way to pass an afternoon, sir."

I watched a strange, crooked smile pass over his face.

"Ah, splendid, wonderful. Tomorrow, then, at the cove. Let us say twelve o'clock." And then, frowning and mumbling to himself, he took his seat at his desk, as if I had already gone.

I PAUSED IN the brisk sea air. At the water's edge a small rowboat lay tilted deep in the sand, and I watched from a distance as two figures lumbered awkwardly with it, the woman attempting to guide the oars with a bandaged hand while the other—unmistakably Goff, in his dark suit of clothes—pushed against its side, trying to right it. Behind them the sea heaved in bright waves, the foam white and radiant.

I walked slowly towards them. It was a bitterly cold day, the sky very blue and clear. I listened to my boots sludge through the damp sand, the loose clasp on my portfolio clicking. The air stank of rotted sea tubers, sour and appalling. John Willard and his vengeance felt very far away.

I was still some way off when the woman raised her head, and even at that distance, even beneath the wide-brimmed bonnet, I could see her: the dark, freckled face with its faintly stained teeth. I stood there in the sand, my heart clapping in my chest. I could hear nothing, not even the sea.

Catching sight of me, she did not smile but only stared angrily, until I looked away. Goff's face, though, brightened into his crooked smile. "What prodigious timing," he said, offering his large, rough hand. He had on his face today a curious pair of spectacles, so that his already probing eyes seemed to pulse. "Come, Mister Black, do help us."

"Good day," I said to them both, awaiting some introduction. Tanna did not answer; Goff made no move to present her. I took my place at the side of the boat, began pushing.

"Brought some paints, have you?" said Goff, nodding at the portfolio I'd set down in the sand. "My daughter here will sketch on my behalf, though she is still a novice, and did indeed fracture her wrist some months ago. Until last week she had been coming down early mornings to attempt to paint the tide pools. She is a bold girl, my little Tanna. It was weeks before I even realized she'd been leaving the house early. When I did, I insisted upon accompanying her, for safety. And do you know what? She would rather stay at home than have her freedom compromised."

I glanced at Tanna. She gripped her bandaged hand with the long, slender fingers of the other. She did not look at me.

I turned to Goff, expecting again some introduction.

He peered at me with his quiet black eyes, his irises swimming behind his finger-marked spectacles.

"Well, let's get on with it," he said.

Tanna spared me a glance by the side of her bonnet; she appeared irritated.

But to feel her eyes on me, even in annoyance, sent a pleasurable shiver through my body. I lowered my face.

What a strange journey we embarked upon that afternoon, full of anguish and desire and wonder. I took out my paints and papers and made sketches of passing fish, which Goff admired with surprised grunts. I had improved much these last months, so that I was drawing quite as well as my boyhood self. It was still strange to think of my complete proficiency at that age, the boy I'd been, the near man I was now. So much had shifted within me.

For lunch Tanna had brought along a late breakfast, and by the thin light of the overcast sun Tanna unwrapped it, wordlessly passing us boiled eggs and black bread and cold smoked salmon. Goff and I took turns paddling out, and then all at once we were floating on what seemed the heart of the sea, only water to be seen for miles, the reflection of the beach shacks on the surface long ago sunken away.

"You have no children, young man?" said Goff.

I paused; it seemed vaguely absurd, given my youth. "I do not."

"Ah, well, children are a blessing, though I understand not everyone finds it so. My daughter here was born on my journey to the Solomon Islands when I travelled there to study *Pterois* some twenty-odd years ago. Her mother, oh, what a fine woman she was—fiery, strong-willed, a good thinker. Tanna here is just the same, takes after her soundly. I did not plan to bring her away with me from the island—as if I were collecting her along with the lionfish and such. I did not like that she should grow up so divorced from her society. But her mother had passed on, and it did not seem right to abandon her. In any case, she has been my salvation. You cannot imagine what tremendous help a daughter is. She is as passionate about marine life as her old father here, a true partner in my studies."

All this Tanna listened to without betraying the slightest pleasure or distaste. I was aware of her soft breathing, the way her legs moved beneath the fabric of her skirts. Our knees scraped accidentally, and so fierce a heat rose up in me that I shamefully had to cover my lap with my hat until the urge passed. Her hair was pinned up as usual beneath her bonnet, and not for the first time I wondered that so free-spirited a soul would choose to wear her hair in so ugly and restrictive a fashion. I imagined her in a half-lit bedroom, night at the windows, unpinning it to fall in soft black strands at her shoulders. The wisps at her temples smelling of tobacco.

The conversation passed amiably enough, though only Goff and I spoke; Tanna sat chewing quietly, in silent profile to us. Goff seemed oblivious to his daughter's mood. Licking his fingers, he spoke of the dorids of the Salish Sea, which had a striking ring of retractable gills on their backs; he mused over the muscular contractions of cuttlefish, which so impossibly shift their colour from yellow to red to black; he talked with sweet regret of having escaped the sting of the Irukandji in the green waters off Oahu, as if he had cheated himself out of an honourable, beautiful death.

"Death is a wildly differing event, dependent on the society," he continued. "When first I arrived in the Islands, I was deep in mourning. My youngest sister, Miranda—there were three, you see, Henrietta, Judith and Miranda—well, she had just killed herself, swallowed some toxin or such, poisoned herself." He shook his head, and I shuddered at this mention of suicide, thinking suddenly of Philip. "Telling a group of islanders of my life, I found myself speaking of her passing. Well, to my utter consternation, they all began to laugh—great, deep, racking peals of laughter. I was shocked. I thought they must have misunderstood me. And so I tried again to explain. This only made them laugh harder.

"It was I who had failed in my understanding, you see. Life holds a sanctity for them we can scarcely begin to imagine; it therefore struck them as absurd that someone would choose to end it. A great ludicrous act. In any case, it was then I recognized that my own values—the tenets I hold dear as an Englishman—they are not the only, nor the best, values in existence. I understood there were many ways of being in the world, that to privilege one rigid set of beliefs over another was to lose something. Everything is bizarre, and everything has value. Or if not value, at least merits investigation."

I thought it wonderful for a man of science to speak so. Staring at his bright chewing face, I realized how profoundly I liked him.

Which is not to say that I liked his manner with his daughter, who all this time said nothing, and ended lunch by picking up her quill and papers to make notes of the observations he called out, his voice echoing off the flat waters.

"And so what do you work on now, sir, if you can tell me?" I asked, to dispel the awkwardness.

Goff was standing in the boat, a stunned crab turning in one hand like the innards of a clock, a mop of algae in the other. "I am exploring the discrepancy between the factual age of the earth and so-called evidence of His creation. It is more a philosophical investigation than one of strong conviction. I am simply curious to see if the evidence exists that would entirely dispute creationist theory." He glanced distractedly down at me from behind his water-pocked spectacles. I waited for him to continue, but he only narrowed his eyes at the muck in his fist.

I paused, wondering at the contradiction with his earlier statement, that all beliefs had value. "It sounds an enormous endeavour, sir. What sort of evidence, in particular, are you gathering?"

Muttering to himself, Goff kneeled suddenly, tossing the winding gyre of the crab into his daughter's lap.

She peered at it unsurprised, gathered it up in a soft fist.

"My father, you see," said Tanna flatly, speaking for the first time that day, "is collecting New World specimens for a small exhibition in London."

I stared at her, perhaps too intently, and she met my eye, and for the longest while we only looked at each other as the boat rocked softly beneath us. Her face was calm, placid even, but there was an air of irritation beneath the stillness. She sat holding the anxious crab in her good hand. I did not speak. Goff might have been an ocean away.

Finally Tanna frowned and, reaching her hand over the edge of the boat, gently deposited the little crab back into the sea.

We passed the next Saturday again in each other's company. Little by little, as they began to bicker softly, regularly, I realized the Goffs' intimacy was a complicated and uncommon affair.

She had softened a little, but only a little, and she would allow herself a dry joke every once in a while. These jokes went unremarked upon by her distracted father. What an agony it was, to see them together: old Goff, earnest and probing and high-minded and utterly oblivious; Tanna, sharp-tongued and brilliant and stifled and yet somehow devoted to that self-absorbed man. It was clear to me that both were intelligent, kind people, but careless with each other's feelings, and poles apart in temperament. I liked both immensely; I hated their way together.

Perhaps it was jealousy, I reasoned—perhaps all my dislike amounted to that. After all, she possessed a father as I myself never had, and whatever annoyances the bond caused her, its consolations would no doubt be the greater. And looking back now, I suppose jealousy did play its role. But he was also truly cold and abrupt with her, and in these moments I disliked him violently.

It did not help that I could sense old Goff's disapproval of me. He liked me well enough as a dabbling scientist, but when he caught me looking in fascination at Tanna, a grimness came into his rough fanatic's face and he'd take his seat heavily between us. I could not blame him; my desire was terribly plain, as, I imagined, were my origins as a slave. He was not a man of prejudices generally, but rather of this one prejudice in particular, as it related to protecting his blood. For though he was self-absorbed and grandstanding and took her for granted, Tanna was clearly his most meaningful tie to this world, and he would shelter that bond from all that might destroy it.

I respected him, I did. But I could do nothing to quell the desire I felt for her. I would stop constantly throughout my day, jolted from my work, to wonder at the cruelty of my attraction. It did not seem natural to me, to ache after someone I could never be with; that is how little I understood about the human heart. I did not want it; I could not stomach it. I was besieged by dreams erotic and terrible, dreams of damp flesh, and I would wake aroused against the sheets, feeling all at once thrillingly alive in my skin, and ashamed.

7

One bright morning I was leaving my rooming house to go out to work when she came to me.

Medwin was sitting out on the porch, his shirt half-unbuttoned in the tender morning heat. His skin was light brown, the hair on his chest fine black spirals. He glanced up when I opened the door, looking at me with calm, empty eyes. Slowly he turned and gestured across the way with his chin.

There she stood, at the edge of the thorny blackberry brambles, nearly in the clearing. I knew her at once: her tanned skin, her smallness, the judgment of her eyes, so that one felt their gaze even at a great distance, like a knife of sunlight.

I heard a tsk, and looked down to find Medwin shaking his head. He gathered up his rattling teacup and newspaper and stood, sighing.

"This will end in blood, you mark me," he muttered, brushing past me into the house.

Moistening my lips, I began towards her, surprised, nervous. I reached her with a feeling of dread almost, breathless.

"How did you discover where I live?" I said, trying to smile. If she could so easily find me, then it seemed even more probable that the man who'd come the other week had indeed been Willard. This small rooming house was proving no sanctuary at all.

Tanna frowned. "I am happy to see you, too."

"I am glad you are come, I am. I just did not realize I was so easily found."

"And are you lost?"

"Are we not all lost?"

"You should speak from a pulpit," she said dryly. She raised suddenly her left wrist. It was thin and quite a bit paler than the rest of her arm, the bone very pronounced.

"You have removed your bandage," said I.

"It is ghastly. Father says my wrist resembles a sea salp." She wrapped both hands around the waist of her grey dress. "I am ever so glad to have done with it. Though it still gives me some discomfort."

"Let me see." And as I took her small, thin wrist in my hands, a flash of heat went through me. I raised my face to find her embarrassed also. "Well," I said with as little expression as I could, "at least you have been spared the rigours of an amputation."

"How lovingly said." She gave a dry smile. "You know just how to speak to a lady."

"It must be all the practice."

"Mm. And where is it we are going this morning?"

I hesitated, staring a long while at her. We both knew the danger in this, in being seen alone together, a black boy and a tanned-skinned girl who might possibly be taken for a white woman. I scanned both the dead-ended road and the open one leading to the rooming house. All was silence. But the risk was foolhardy and I would not undertake it.

She seemed to understand and, lowering her face, took a step away from me. Above us, a clot of finches flickered by. The yellow light pooled on the surrounding trees, the air stirring with warmth.

The possibility of John Willard coming upon us was remote, but it existed still. What would I do then, with her at my side? Staring at her quiet, freckled face, I was filled with desire and the terrifying knowledge that I could do nothing at all to protect her.

With nervous fingers she pulled from the depth of her skirts a tattered paper. "I have written you a note." She raised her face, hesitated. "Sometimes when I am with you I have the feeling of not quite saying what I mean."

I stared at the paper she held out, feeling shame flood my face.

She studied me, lowering her hand. "You cannot read," she said quietly.

"I can read," I snapped. For I could, I had—only poorly.

She looked at her hands. "I will teach you, if you like."

I did not outwardly let on that I was bothered. It had not been her intention, but in her suggestion there seemed to be a belittlement, a setting herself above, as if my being unlettered defined my agency and character. I was flooded suddenly with memories of long, sultry evenings beneath a bleached sky, the birds crying above, Titch sounding out words and urging me to repeat them.

"Father said you were a slave," Tanna said softly. "I told him Washington Black would never be a slave, even if he was born in chains."

Again I said nothing, and the silence widened between us.

"I have offended you," she said.

I shrugged.

"What is it?" she said.

"You will *teach* me?" I shook my head irritably. "And you speak of slavery as though it is a choice. Or rather, as though it were a question of temperament. Of mettle. As if there are those who are naturally slaves, and those who are not. As if it is not a senseless outrage. A savagery."

"But you cannot have taken that as my meaning." She flushed. "What I am saying is that you are strong. You are standing on your own two feet. You are embracing your self-sufficiency. Look at you. Look at what you have made of your life after such hardship."

I puffed air bitterly through my lips. "Yes, look."

We were again silent, the sound of the surf reaching us from the side streets.

"I shall be leaving in some weeks," she said. "Father is already turning an eye to arranging our passage."

I did not know why this should surprise me—they had said many times their stay here was temporary—and yet I was shaken. I looked closely at her. "The research is finished, then?"

"There are a few specimens of which we are still in need. But Father is of course too old for a dive, and I cannot do it this time." She did not meet my eye, still chastened by her earlier offence. "My wrist is only just mended, after months and months. I cannot risk another fracture. And the water's pressure—I fear it would prove too much."

And then I understood. "You came to ask me to dive in your stead. That is why you sought me out at my rooming house."

Her face darkened. "I came to give you my note. And because I wanted to see you, and because I thought you wanted to see me. I was apparently wrong." Before I could speak, she turned in the road and began walking away.

I stood in the street with my empty hands hanging by my sides, and I understood then there was an ever-shifting world evolving inside her, and that I would forever be shut out from it.

8

I DID NOT LIKE TO FEEL MYSELF ILL-USED. AND YET THE Saturday following, under an overcast sky, I found myself travelling down to the harbour. At the end of the jetty a small seafaring vessel named the *Blue Betty* lay moored and slowly rotting. It was there, in the shadow of that boat long abandoned by its crew, that Goff and Tanna awaited me. Goff had hired it from a local friend who made his living reconstituting old vessels. The man had also told them of a recent wreckage in the shallows where Goff might find the specimens he desired.

When I reached the Goffs down on the beach, their mule-drawn cart holding their apparatus in crates beside them, Goff stared fiercely at me, as though he did not recognize me. Then he gave me a long, slow grin.

"Been keeping well?" said he.

"Still breathing, in any case, sir," I said. I did not look at Tanna. "And you?"

"Ah, very well, son, very well. Eager to complete my work here." He exhaled. "I am ever so relieved that you agreed to help us out with this. Tanna is our diver, but her wrist, you see. If we were back home, we could ask one of my sisters—Judith, or even Henrietta would come over, from France. But such is life, such are the circumstances. Well, now, are you ready for me to throw you overboard?"

"As ready as one can ever be, sir."

"Good, good. You have done this before?"

"Never."

"Well, the main thing is to try not to die. I shall give you some advice on how to best bring that about."

Talking all the while, he led me onto the boat to prepare. I passed Tanna, and was aware of her anxiously avoiding my eye. I did not understand her, these strange twists of mood. I had agonized over the possibilities of her note for days, suffered for my lack of education. And now I had arrived to ostensibly help her father out—though anyone could see, even Goff himself, I suspect, that I had come only because she'd asked it of me. But now I was here, she was behaving so elusively. I felt exhausted, done with it. I could not tolerate any more.

And yet the curve of her neck, the soft, dark hairs matted there—I saw them and felt longing and desire wash through me.

Goff himself was in the best of spirits. There was none of the tension of these last weeks and he smiled all about at nothing much. It was already after ten o'clock when we had finished unpacking and carrying the pump, bellows and coils of breathing hose onto the deck. The morning sky looked hollowed, featureless, without a line of cloud.

Goff dismissed Tanna, sending her below deck so that she would not glimpse me undressing. His old hands trembling softly, he helped me into the diving suit, arranged its copper helmet and awkward leather air hose. He had ordered it some two years before, he explained, a patched and partial sample that had been used for salvage off Whitstable some years earlier.

"Careful with the helmet, son," said he. "You don't want water getting through."

As we were affixing it into place on my head, he said, "She is so young, my Tanna."

I paused, peering down at him, the glister of his dark black eyes. "I am the younger, sir."

"In years, yes," he said, smiling pleasantly.

I understood. He meant that I had been a slave, and that the savagery of that past left me a ruined being, like some wretched thing pulled smoking from a fire. It did not matter that he accepted me as a thinking man, that he respected my mind, or even that he was in the midst of taking a favour from me. I was black-skinned and burnt, as disfigured inside as without, and though he took me seriously enough as an illustrator and a scientist, he did not want me for his daughter.

I clutched at the rim where it met my neck, the metal hot from the sun.

WITH A COLD punch the air left my lungs, and the freezing black waters sucked at my body. The first few seconds were utterly shocking, and in the wavering shadows I felt both strangely weightless and like a pile of iron, my legs in their canvas suit stirring the waters, my head solid and leaden in its helmet. There was a surge of noise in my ears, a kind of constant sucking, and I blinked against the smatter of bubbles flooding the glass window of my helmet, bubbles generated by my breathing tube. I was dropped lower and lower, feeling with each descent a tug in my stomach. The intense scent of wet leather filled my head. Craning my neck gently back, I saw above me the rocking bottom of the boat. It floated there like a coffin in the pale, sun-cut waters.

How luminous the world was, in the shallows. I could see all the golden light of the dying morning, I could see the debris in it stirring, coming alive. Blue, purple, gold cilia turned in the watery yellow shafts of light slicing down. In the gilded blur I caught the flashing eyes of shrimp, alien and sinewy.

The quality of light shifted above me, and I glanced up to watch something like a momentary dusk come over the surface. I turned my head; a rivet dug painfully into my collarbone, so that I paused to adjust the helmet. The minutes were slowing now, drawing out in the cold. I glanced down and saw a flash of white, and I thought it must be another creature, only to realize it was my own eyes, their reflection in the viewing glass of my helmet. And it was then that some deep tolling went through me, an enormous throb, as though someone had struck a large bell beside me. And all at once I felt my body dropping away, all of the clenching and the anger and the terror, the scorch of Goff's black, disapproving eyes, and the touch of Big Kit's skin; the image of Titch walking backwards over the ice, the smell of Arctic timber, the shudder of the Cloud-cutter, it all fell away; the blood on the blackened grass in the clearing, the pain on Philip's face, I let it all fall away; Willard's small, constant shadow—all this I let drop away, so that I hung with my arms suspended at my sides, the soft current tugging at me. The cold sucked at me and the light weakened, and I was finally, mercifully, nothing.

A white veil grazed my helmet. I gave a start, and propelled myself backwards. It was a jellyfish, perilously close. I recognized it as poisonous, and I kicked away, watching its tentacles retreat in a flash of tattered lace. I began to propel myself along, careful to keep myself upright lest the helmet begin to leak. I trudged towards a low rock formation, through the hazy water, among the crags. This had to be the barque.

The wreck lay upright, furred with weed, its iron railings rusted and gnarled. There were fish drifting through its opened portholes. I began to search. The water was cold. I was staring at a brown-and-red outcropping, hearing the bubbling of my breath in my ears, when a shape flashed bright orange, before transforming again into brown rust.

I paused. Very slowly I began to wade closer, passing through a last bright spot of sun cutting through the waters. I squinted; nothing moved, nothing stirred. Then, in a series of hallucinations, the rock became a slick blue smudge, then a bumpy red crag of meat, then a mottled brown rag, then a vile red slash.

Again I went very slowly towards it, extending my arms in their thick hide. The creature shot up from its rock, its orange arms boiling all around it, the suckers very white. Its gaze seemed to churn up out of its soft mantle and burn through me, seeing, I suppose, the sad rigidity of a boy, the uselessness of his hard, inflexible bones. I stared at the bulb of its pendulous head, the crags that made it look ancient, and a hot, glorious feeling rushed through me, a bright, radiating hope.

I could see by the tentacles on the third arm that she was a female. She was wondrous and brilliantly vivid, and when I thought of Goff killing her to crate up as a specimen for his exhibition, a twist of nausea went through me. How wrong it all felt. Could she not, I thought, be brought to England alive, to be seen as the breathing miracle she was? Was that so impossible? In fact, could not they all—the anemones and the comatulids and the nudibranchs and the octopus—be taken in their living state to be viewed by a public who would never have the chance to see such creatures up close?

I knew it was impossible. The science was wanting. What would you house them in? Which ones could be housed together, and how? Could plants also be transported without their rotting? How, indeed, would you keep the marine life itself alive? It was hopeless, futile. And yet the certainty of its failure convinced me fully that it should be attempted.

The octopus arranged itself in a smatter of algae, its body hanging blackly before me. When I came forward to touch it, it sent out a surge of dark ink. We paused, watching each other, the grey rag of ink hanging between us. Then it shot off through the water, stopping short to radiate like a cloth set afire, its arms unfurling and vibrating. There was something playful in the pause, as if it expected me to ink it back. I held my hands out towards it, gently; the creature hovered in the dark waters, almost totally still. Then, shyly, it began to pulse towards me, stopping just inches away, its small, gelatinous eyes taking me in. Then it swam directly into my hands.

THE SUN WAS low and without fire when I surfaced.

I could not get warm. The Goffs had lit the lanterns, and by the flickering light I could see Tanna getting the boat under way. I fell exhausted onto the deck, letting Goff drag me clear, my breathing tube slapping wetly behind me. Goff heaved off my helmet; I gasped at the raw air, my body shuddering, a sensation of sparks popping under my skin. It was excruciating. In the fading afternoon light Goff's face loomed greenish and pocked above me.

"How was the bath?" he said with his crooked grin. "Clean enough yet?"

I gasped for him to unhook the trap from my back, in which I had gathered the unknown octopus and several *Glaucus atlanticus* and comatulids and sipunculid worms. Goff helped me from the suit with a look of some sympathy. He handed me a brown wool blanket from a box of personal effects. It stunk of wood char and naphthalene, but I was grateful all the same. I sat in shivering silence, then went below deck to dress myself before going up to study the catch in the dripping cages.

"What is it? What did you get?" said Goff, peering over my shoulder.

When finally Tanna joined us, she appeared anxious, nervous.

I studied her face; I could not tell if she had been crying. "You are unwell?"

"I am fine, Mister Black, thank you."

"What did you manage, eh?" said Goff impatiently. "Open them already."

Turning from Tanna, I opened a cage with great care and took out the flaring orange creature, the octopus.

"It rather resembles the *Bathypolypus arcticus*," he observed with soft fascination, "but it is far too large for that."

"It inked me, sir," said I. "I do not believe the *Bathypolypus* has ink." As I hefted its glutinous body in my hands, it slowly wrapped itself around my arm, the touch of its suckers shocking, like cold little mouths. It felt so intimate. I would unwind one arm only to find it glued back in place by the time I had liberated a second.

"It likes you," said Goff.

Crouched there on the deck, with the octopus braided over my arms, I could see the late afternoon lanterns of the cove approaching in the distance, and I felt very calm, very far from the rough, scoured-out life I had made for myself. And I began to laugh.

9

We settled the animals in a row of tin buckets filled with sea water just behind the Goffs' little blue house, then went inside to eat.

I entered the dark dining room to discover that even here was an explosion of papers and pickling jars and specimen cases. A tiny squid had dried to a brown tangle on the table's bare surface. Goff swept it aside, onto the crumb-strewn floor.

"We took the house furnished, and added to it our own disarray," he grumbled.

"I do hope you like fried mackerel," called Tanna from the next room. She appeared in the doorway, her smile curiously anxious, as though she feared my disappointment. I did not understand her strange, tentative manner all this day. But it did seem to me now that in her father's allowing me into their home, she saw the possibility of his acceptance of me.

"Modest food for modest people," Goff grunted, scratching at the side of his nose.

"Is that what we are?" said Tanna.

"It smells wonderfully fresh, thank you." I sat on a pine chair, and it shivered unsteadily under my weight. Despite the mess I thought the room charming, with its long mahogany sideboard overhung with rows of tiny oil portraits in rusted gilt frames.

"Are these yours?" I gestured, turning to Tanna.

"That depends," she said vaguely, taking my plate to serve me. "Do you like them?"

Suddenly the plate snapped in half, and she fumbled to catch the pieces. She managed to grab one, the second half clattering unharmed to the floor. "Truly?" she said, flustered. "The hardwood floor is soft enough, but my hands too hard?"

I half-rose from my seat. "You are hurt?"

"Oh, for god's sake," she said. "Life is not a Venetian opera, Mister Black." I did not understand her meaning, but I could see she had a cut on the inside of her wrist, and that she was embarrassed. She went alone to the scullery to patch it up.

"Your daughter is a fine painter," I said to Goff, who all this time had sat silently. I stared boldly at his face, awaiting his reaction to the compliment. When he said nothing, I continued, "One of her many charms."

"You seem to have taken a great interest in her charms," he said, his black eyes steady.

I felt my heart in my throat. I knew I was being too forward, but I was filled with an impulsive irritation and could not help myself. I moistened my lips. "She is an admirable woman."

"She is no woman. She is a girl."

"She is *twenty*."

"She *is* twenty."

I could see now a strange sheen on his hardened eyes, like a second darkness, so that I stopped abruptly as though I had reached a rocky precipice. "Well, then," I murmured, letting my voice taper off.

Goff took a deep sip of his wine, and I could see he was relieved I had stopped. He turned the stem of the glass in his hands. "Life has been more difficult for Tanna than I ever imagined it would be," he said softly. "You would never know it—she is so self-possessed. But she has never been accepted in English society, and this has wounded her deeply. I will say she does not make things easier on herself by being always drawn to strangeness. Mark me—you put twelve people in a room and Tanna will always gravitate towards the most eccentric of them. Even as a child she was this way. It is touching, and big-hearted of her, but it has rarely served her well. I would not wish her any more hardship."

He peered softly across at me, and I understood then that what he feared for her, for us both, was social disdain. He seemed to be saying that had circumstances been different, he would certainly have accepted me.

He cleared his throat. "Her drawings, yes. Well, Tanna does try. But your own paintings, Mister Black—now those are things of beauty. I have never seen an artist be so meticulous and still bring life to it."

The praise was not new; Goff had often commented on the grace and elegance of my line.

"You are too kind," I said.

"We both know I am not." He flashed a dry, crooked smile. "But I have been meaning to ask you for some days now—would you do me the honour of illustrating my new tract?"

I felt my cheeks warm with embarrassment. "You tease me?"

"It does not appeal to you?"

"It would be an absolute pleasure, sir." Despite all that lay between us he was still a legend to me, and I saw this for the deep honour that it was.

He frowned. "What's that? Speak louder."

Tanna returned with a chipped, gold-rimmed white plate. When she set it down before me, a wet-eyed ginger cat oozed from beneath the table and leapt directly onto it.

"Ah," said Goff, swatting at it. "You're in her seat, that's what." He clapped his hands sharply. "Away with you, Medusa."

"You see the state we live in," said Tanna.

Goff puffed air through his lips, as though this was nothing to apologize for. Then he began to gobble up his fish in quick, rabbit-like bites, his eyes always on his plate.

"I said I would be honoured to do it, sir," I said. "How *is* the writing proceeding?"

"Do what?" said Tanna.

"Ah, the writing," Goff grumbled, and shook his head, the flesh of the mackerel flashing in his small, bright teeth.

"Illustrate the new book," I said, turning to Tanna.

She glanced at her father. "I see." She took her seat across from us, and the candles shuddered as she bumped the table, grey shadows passing like moths over the pale fabric of her dress. She looked at her fork some moments, then raised her face with a smile. "It will be beautiful, I have no doubt."

Goff continued to eat heartily. "I would do it myself, but the eyesight, you know. In any case, I grow rather less and less interested in drawing these days. In writing, even. The exhibition—that is the thing."

I had not intended to mention it, and yet all that had come to me on the dive rose now to mind, and I felt I must speak or lose the opportunity. "Have you given any thought to making your exhibition a live one?"

Goff frowned at me. "A live one, Mister Black?"

I paused, going on only when I had their full attention. "Imagine a large hall, a gallery, but filled not with benches. There are instead large tanks holding all manner of aquatic life. Enormous tanks. Perhaps there are open-air terrariums with toads and turtles and lizards. And people could come and press their faces right against the glass. Learn the habits of the animals first-hand. It could be permanent, like an indoor park."

"A menagerie of the sea," murmured Tanna.

Goff gave a flustered grunt, shoving some boiled potatoes into his mouth, but I could see he was interested. "Such a thing is not possible."

I peered quietly at him. "Nothing is possible, sir, until it is made so."

He studied me, his expression softening. "Well, it would be a marvel, son."

"But how?" said Tanna, and I could see she too was giving it serious thought. "The tanks would need to be sealed utterly, leak-proof over the long term, and yet—"

"The animals would be in ready need of oxygen," said I.

"Precisely. And how would you begin to house such a collection? It is one thing to organize a temporary exhibition of dead specimens, and quite another to nurture living organisms over a period of years. Would one be able to repurpose a building for such a use, which might prove less costly, or must a building be specifically designed for the purpose?"

"It is a fascinating conundrum, in any case," Goff grunted.

We began to speak at length of the problems of balancing carbonic acid and oxygen, of the decay of vegetation and the temperamental acidity of water. It was bracing, and intimate, the three of us weighing each other's words with true enthusiasm and consideration. So absorbed were we in our talk that when finally I rose to go out to the water closet, long shadows had deepened across the table.

I returned to find Goff staring thoughtfully at his gravy-stained plate; something was just now occurring to him. I expected some new point on oxygen levels, but he only said, gruffly, "I will have to leave you two to sort out the crinoids next Saturday. I am travelling up the coast, to a little hamlet some thirty miles from here. Seems a fisherman there caught a white-skinned fish with wings. They say it is a strange and alien thing, not of this world. Who knows if this is not some exaggeration—if it is a common-enough genus that has suffered a trauma altering its externals. But perhaps it truly is something rare, something new. In any case, shouldn't take but a day or two. I will take a room, and I hope to be back the following evening."

Tanna looked calmly, coolly at him. "This is the first I'm hearing of this."

I lowered my eyes, took an uneasy sip of my water.

"You are upset I have not asked you to accompany me, my dear," said Goff. "It will not be a pleasant journey. I did not think you would mind."

"Do what you must," said Tanna.

And she stood and began to clear the table in silence, leaving in a clatter of clinking dishes, her dress rustling.

Goff turned to me, unruffled. "Will you take a port, son?"

10

Some days later it came to me.

I'd awoken that morning to a dreadful chill in my room, feeling strange, unhappy. I hobbled down the hall to the water bucket, shirttails drooping. There I splashed my face and armpits, trying to take no notice of the sounds emanating from the room directly opposite. Its occupant was a tiny, sway-backed man with no teeth who smoked incessantly, and every morning he would wake to the world with a violent, racking cough.

I returned to my rooms, tending to the seedlings I grew in soup platters on my windowsill. I was pouring out the greening water from my stoneware cask when all at once it struck me. I started to tremble. I set the cask down with a click and, without even fastening my waistcoat, went out to the shores to dredge specimens. When I returned, my apartment was dark, smelling of chalk and damp. I placed the rotifera and infusoria I had gathered, along with some sea water, in my cask, by the window. After much nurturing I was crestfallen to find them dead two days later. But then I thought it through, and went again to the shores to collect more sea organisms and plants, placing them this time in an entirely clear glass receptacle.

For what had struck me was this: marine animals absorb oxygen and exhale carbonic acid; plants do the opposite—absorb carbonic acid and throw off oxygen. So perhaps, then, the way to make them thrive in captivity was to house them together.

What had been missing from my first experiment, with the clay urn, was light. In the clear glass tank, the vegetation could get what it needed for synthesis.

In this way my new specimens survived a long while. The natural decay and excretions of both the plants and the animals were fended off by my occasional stirring and syringing out of the tank's salt water.

I held off rushing to the Goffs. Instead, on one of Medwin's trips to Halifax, I travelled in the safety of his company to the constructions on the main square there. Trundling across the dirt and fallen lumber of half-erected warehouses, I began to ask after their builders. At a warehouse some two blocks from the ocean a foreman walked out from the shadow of a cast-iron frame and irritably agreed to answer my questions. It did not take long for his impatience to turn to curiosity. We conversed nearly an hour, and I went happily away to make calculations.

I am no great mathematician. But the Cloud-cutter had required some very precise mensuration, and with this knowledge I was able, over the coming days, to design what I thought might be a viable large-scale tank. I drew plate-glass walls of several dimensions, with parallel sides to prevent distortion. I experimented with many bonding putties, deciding finally on a mixture concocted of white lead.

It took me three evenings to build. I spoke to no one outside work and ate little and laboured until the joints of my hands clicked painfully. I built a tank two feet long, one and a half feet wide and a half foot deep; for the base I used a one-inch slab of slate. Medwin brought me some cast-off birchwood from his friend's lumber operation, and this I lathed into pillars with knobs at the top, joining them with a bar. I attached everything together, then sought out a glass-blower who owed Medwin money and had him cut me four pieces of glass at no charge. These I slid into grooves notched into the slate and the wood, securing them with my white-lead putty. I was careful, however, knowing how murderous lead was to sea life: When it had set, I filled up the tank with shell-lac dissolved in naphtha to make a paste with whiting. When the mixture solidified, it would stop the water from coming into contact with the lead, which constantly gives off small doses of oxide.

I held my breath and prayed it would all come together, prayed that in the end I could give her something to draw out the astonishment in her fine, sharp face.

An early dusk was falling when I left the dry goods store the next evening. Crisp leaves rasped in the wind, and I noted with surprise that autumn was upon us again. There was a charge in the air; it smelled strongly of damp, of mud. I passed many cancelled-out lodgings, the windows black, and I passed also many brightly lit ones, so that I could see in clear detail the pleasure or the irritation or the disappointment in the gestures of the people at their windows. I passed a home in which a man sat at a crude pine desk, his head in his hands.

Nearing a coloured grill-house, I paused, inhaling the scent of burnt onions and spiced meat. Impulsively, I counted the money in my billfold, then went inside.

It was a rundown little establishment, the air hazy with grease, the tables filled with men hunched over plates in which their faces were reflected greyly back up at them. I trod over the flaking wooden boards to an empty stool at the far edge of the bar, feeling the slow weight of men's stares on my burns. It was always so, especially in eateries. And though I had long grown used to it, I felt no less alien and apart.

I withdrew a small ledger from my satchel and began to make calculations to do with water composition and temperature and volume. The barman approached to take my order of hodgepodge and went away again. I glanced at the spattered windows at the end of the dining room. The light was darkening, cooling. I rubbed at my eyes, wondering, not for the first time, if I was in need of ocular assistance. I sighed, my gaze drifting to a tall, corpulent man in a clean new suit just as he glanced up and met my eyes. He was a stranger to me; I looked quickly away.

My stew came, and I ate absently, chewing on one side of my mouth, scratching away at the ledger. I was reaching for my spoon when there came a damp click on the counter and I saw by the side of my eye a glass of clouded whisky. I shifted slightly on my stool, making space for the man settling in beside me. I drew two columns on the page, tallying, frowning. In the far corner a drunk barked out ugly laughter.

"You enjoy equations," said the man beside me.

The voice so obviously belonged to a Scotsman that I looked up in puzzlement.

It was a white man.

"I used to fiddle with numbers myself," said he, and I froze to see those eyes behind their smudged spectacles, so light they were nearly colourless. "I still do have the fascination of it. Calculations, proofs." He paused. "I suppose one never loses the knack of a childhood passion."

I had the feeling of being slowly submerged underwater, as if I wore the weight of the diving suit, though I was light-headed, dizzy. I stared at him, and I was astonished at how different it all felt from how I had supposed it would be, how quiet and familiar.

The barman watched us warily.

The white man paid the barkeep no heed, only peered gently at me from behind his lenses, curious. He wore his sooty blond hair pomaded into place, his side part severe as a scar above his right ear, and his face was tanned, calm, a trace of purple veins in his cheeks. It was a thin face, a pleasant face, with high cheekbones and a slow, lipless mouth shadowed by a line of tidy blond hairs. He appeared relaxed, at ease.

"Please do not get up," he said softly, though I had made no move to do so, not risen at all. "Go on with your meal, eat."

I swallowed; it was as though sand had caught in my throat. Even seated, I could see he was much shorter than myself, Goff's height perhaps, and he was lean and rangy, his forearms hard with veins.

"Please," he said again, and there was the faint suggestion of a smile. His left eye squinted nearly shut then, and the defect was off-putting, as if his eye had never properly formed. "You need your sustenance."

I would never have imagined such a voice. Light, soft, but not effeminate. Rather, he sounded like a man easily respected, a man who need not press his will to be heard. He could not, I thought, be more than forty years old.

"What would you recommend of the food?" he said, unhooking his spectacles. "I do not eat fish."

I only stared, feeling the punch of my heart in my ribs.

"You can vouch for nothing? Well, now. That stew of yours smells good."

When I made no answer, he slowly took up his whisky and drank. I could see through the smudged glass a mouthful of bright, crooked teeth. Despite the shiver in my hands a hard calm came over me, as with Philip in the clearing all those years ago. The noise of the eatery—knives scraping, coughing, muttering—grew sharper, icier. I was filled with a bitter sense of inevitability.

My eyes came somehow to rest on his clothes. I noticed threads hanging from his left cuff and the patched elbow of his very poor suit, the fabric cheap and threadbare. It was as though he had lately been brought down in the world, and fallen hard.

He chuckled softly to see me take his measure. "My tailor died, if you can believe it. Now, there was a fine man. He knew his craft as men today don't care to. Every seam, every stitch had its name and its purpose. Such men pass from the world and are replaced by dilettantes. Dabblers. I tell you, there are few of this new generation who have the patience to learn an art truly. And so nothing lasts, and all crumbles and is impermanent. The world rots before our eyes." He smiled, his eye squinting. "I sound old." He shrugged. "I *am* old. Or so my daughter tells me. I do not see the changes myself."

I did not even glance at the exit, knowing I could never reach it. I gripped my ledger, the paper cutting into my hands, thinking of this man's daughter, trying to picture a new line with the same colourless eyes, the same rough red chin.

"Of course, she was born with every advantage," he said, studying his drink. "Cotillions, fine dresses. Me, I was a St. Joseph's boy. Raised in the spike. You don't know work until you know the spike." He shook his head imperceptibly. "There is nothing, *nothing* worse than it. No greater anguish."

I recalled my last moments with Philip, his conclusion that my life was easy, simplified by slavery. I peered stiffly ahead.

"I suppose modernity will have its way, whatever our desires." He paused, thoughtful. "Have you seen the new steam locomotives? The Stockton and Darlington rail?"

I stared at his small eyes, said nothing.

He smiled dryly. "Don't you talk? I asked, have you seen the new public rail lines of England?"

"I have not," I said, hearing the brittleness of my voice, the suppressed contempt.

"Oh, as a lover of equations you would surely find them wonderful. The calculation involved. The art. They are true marvels of propulsion. But mark my words when I say they will bring about the desecration of all that we know and rightly hold sacred. Distances grow ever shorter, the lands are more closely drawn together, and distinctions become blurred." He spoke slowly and with great measure, so that I almost could not hear him. "I myself will always go by carriage, even when it ceases to be fashionable and other men accept strange means of conveyance—steam engines and such. Unholy aerial contraptions."

I studied him quietly; he was speaking of the Cloud-cutter, of course. Behind me a man cried hoarsely out for more drink and was hissed down by his companion. A glass clattered to the floor but did not break.

"I made the most fascinating journey recently, in America. I passed for hours through the countryside. Outside, the grass was grey and dry, went on for miles and miles. You see, one misses such things when one travels by other means—you don't get the sense of dimension. I had always supposed America to be a land of mountains. Well, I tell you, that is not so. Not always. This I have witnessed with my own eyes. You can rumble about for days without seeing so much as a bearded hill. So much as a bump.

"I came to a final stop in a village I did not know. I hadn't wanted to disembark, but the driver would no longer have me. It was full dark, and I began to walk but saw no landmarks. I was well and truly lost. I noticed then a figure on a far-off bench—a lady in dark skirts. How odd, I thought, a lady out alone at night. I called out to her, but she did not answer, and so I approached.

"Imagine my surprise. She was not human; she was a doll, life-sized, sewn up out of sacking with little black rocks for her eyes. The deeper I walked into that village the more dolls I came upon, as though some deranged old woman had spent a lifetime sewing them. I saw no living soul. A village inhabited only by scarecrows."

I felt my grip giving on my ledger and I adjusted my wet palms.

"What do you make of that?" said he.

I did not answer. Behind me a man coughed softly.

"At an inn some two miles beyond the village," he continued, "I found a living man to tell me the story. It was strange, sad, as such stories usually are. Some twenty years before, the village's children had begun to sicken. At first it had seemed the usual maladies: headache, grippe, sore bellies. But then came the bruising, the boils, the fits. It was as if some perverse disturbance were playing itself out, a shift unnatural and not right. The local doctor's knowledge did not extend to these mysteries. And so the children were sent away, to be cared for elsewhere.

"They never returned. Only the old were left. And they began to die off. Those who did not die left the village by other means. In the end there was only one widow left, a dressmaker, and she began to sew the visages of those who had vanished. She hand-stitched the bodies and the clothes; she perfected the faces. Each and every doll was a precise replica of someone who once lived there."

He stared quietly down at the table. "And so it is that the true and the living disappear, and in their place rise the disfigured and the unnatural and the damned."

He paused, raising to me eyes calm and water-blue. He seemed to be awaiting some answer.

"That is a fine fable," I said.

"It is no fable."

I glanced at the exit.

"Do you think it is natural, what I have said?"

"I think it is unnatural that you have said it."

He gave a vague smile. "Your manner of speech, even." He shook his head. "In the dark you might be taken for an Englishman." He paused. "Is that natural, Mister Black?"

I stared steadily at him. I betrayed no alarm, no fear.

"Is it natural to sever low beings from their true and rightful destinies? From their natural-born purpose? To give them a false sense of agency? As if some creatures are not put here in the service of others. As if cows don't exist to be eaten." He turned his glass in his hands. "Nothing is accidental in the works of nature. Do you know who said that? Aristotle. He said, Nothing is accidental, everything is, absolutely, for the sake of something else."

I smiled bitterly. I knew I should better hide my contempt, but the man struck me as ridiculous, beyond fraudulent, memorizing fine quotations from the Greeks in order to twist their meaning. I glanced at his face. The sight of his clear, placid eyes made my stomach plummet.

"Do I amuse you?"

I made no comment.

"Do you know Aristotle?"

I did not answer.

"He was a great thinker. A European."

Again I said nothing, studying his face.

"It is not for you that I have come," said John Willard softly, and it was as if in speaking it he was unsettled anew by the fact, the oddness of it. "You could not be further from my thoughts these days."

"You have been to my rooming house," said I.

And then this man whom I had feared, this hunter from my past, smiled vaguely, so that his crooked white incisor peeked over his thin lip. "I did not even know you were in the country, Mister Black."

I wondered what to make of this.

"I am in insurance now," said he.

I almost failed to take his meaning, so outlandish did this strike me. I searched his face for irony.

"Erasmus Wilde is dead. Though I will say he was getting more and more difficult to work for. You might imagine how the work dried up after that."

I was shocked, taken aback; I could not speak, though the truth of it seemed plain. And yet a part of me would not believe it.

"I am still an investigator of, shall we say, human errors, but for a business venture that insures cargo being shipped overseas. It is fine work."

"How did he die?" said I. "Master Wilde, I mean?"

"Of course, you would be surprised at how many attempt fraudulent claims. It is rampant. Men lying about the cheapest of goods."

"How did he die?" I said again.

"Some illness or other, I do not know. Putrid fever, perhaps. It has been two years now." He shrugged. "I earn more money in insurance than was ever paid me scrambling after niggers and misfits."

I recalled Erasmus, his thatch of white hair and his pale eyes like steel shavings, the refined, almost cultured cruelty. I did not understand how he could be granted so merciful a death as a fever. However painfully it had struck him down, the release seemed too easy—like a betrayal of the countless men and women and children whose fates he had ended on a whim, because the sky on that day was too blue or they moved too slowly through the field or the moon had kept him up the night previous.

"I *was* shocked to discover you here, in Nova Scotia," he continued. "Imagine. To leave the docks after hours of inspection and encounter you at once, right in the street, strolling about like you owned all creation. Now, mind, you almost don't look like yourself, grown so old now—I will admit that at first I was not certain. But that scar will betray you each and every time. Lord. For *years* I looked for you. Years. And when I finally give it up? You appear."

He glanced sidelong at me, his pupils flinty, black and fine. "You caused me a lot of embarrassment, you and your master," he said with a dim smile. "I was told, dead or alive. You can take apart a piece of furniture and pack it up in a crate, or you can transport it whole, it's all the same. But you must acquire it first." He stared at his glass without expression. "What does a boy like you know of the world? What can you understand of its workings? You should have been easier to find than a spoon in a bowl.

"I did not hold such a fine reputation after losing you and your master." His voice was soft. "I was not, shall we say, sought after. I lost considerable business. When I was last in England, Mister Wilde himself passed me in the street without so much as a glance. For years I hunted the two of you. For years that man ran from me. In the end? I might have been a street sweeper, for all his acknowledgement." He paused, thoughtful. "If that is not failure, I do not know what is. If that is not defeat—" He fell silent.

I was slow to take in his words. "Christopher?" I said. "You mean Christopher?"

"Your owner," said he.

"Christopher," I said again. "He is in London?"

"Liverpool. I was inspecting a cargo of mahogany chests arrived from the Indies. March of last year—no, two years ago. I would not have remarked upon him at all but that I heard someone talking loudly to himself in the street, and I glanced up to see if he might be avoided."

A heat radiated through my chest, a weight warm and almost liquid.

Willard was studying me. "You did not know," he said.

I was picturing the impossibility of Titch shuffling the streets of that unknown city, mumbling to himself—alive, saved, whole.

"Did you run from him too, once you were clear of Faith? Is that what happened?" Willard gave me a curious look. "Oh, do not tell me he released you?" He shook his head. "Erasmus was right. There was always a madness in that man."

I sat in a haze, hearing his lips on the glass of whisky, the moist sound of his swallowing.

A long moment seemed to pass between us.

"The moon has a strange aspect here," Willard said, setting down his glass. "It is so different from how it appears in the southern hemisphere." He peered beyond me to the window. "When it touches stone, it has the quality of water. Of dirty water."

I glanced at the window, at the hard yellow light pooled on the gravel path. Calmly, Willard set his spectacles on his small nose, pushing them into place with his thumb. He stood, and with great delicacy placed change enough for his drink on the counter, arranging it with his tan, veined hands.

"I'll leave you to your meal," said he.

And he stepped between the tables and was gone.

11

So this was him: my ghost. This man small and calm and emboldened by outlandish morality tales and borrowed quotations. This was he, the one from whom I had been running these three years, the creature of nightmare who had driven me through landscapes of heat and wind and snow, whose shadow had forced me aboard boats and carriages and even a shuddering Cloud-cutter by night, whose face I'd pictured so many waking days and imagined so many sleepless nights, the man who'd forced me away from all I had known, so that I was obliged to claw out a life for myself in a country that did not want me, a country vast and ferocious and crusted in hard snow, with little space, little peace for me.

I sat in the roar of the grill-house, my sticky bowl touching the back of my hand. My throat was very dry, and I felt a great fear spreading through me, and it was a fear touched with wonder.

Was it some madness on my part to believe he might actually have encountered Titch in Liverpool? Willard was obviously a sinister creature, not worth the believing. And yet. I sensed the possibility of it, the way I had always known in my blood that Big Kit was dead. But perhaps these feelings had no basis, were only superstition, hope or the absence of it.

No; I did not believe it.

Nor did I believe that Willard had tracked me down in all this fashion simply to talk. He was no longer interested in my flesh, he'd said; he was a claimsman now. And yet there had been such a tension underlying all he uttered that even now I felt the heat of his hatred, his contempt. I despaired to think of him in the streets, roaming, restless.

I rose to find my legs shaking, and I had to sit. Breathing deeply, I stood again and placed my own money on the counter alongside his. I gathered my ledger and satchel and went out.

The evening was quiet, the vacant streets echoing distantly with the clattering of far-off carriages. I looked constantly over my shoulder, staying close to the buildings. The wind was soft and smelled of lavender, and I could hear my shoes stirring the gravel on the uneven path. Dry leaves rasped in the gutters. My mind was afire, going in all directions. Big Kit, Philip, Mister Wilde; I had suddenly the image of Titch at the window of his residence, leaning over his long steel scope. And I thought of Willard quoting Aristotle.

I had long seen science as the great equalizer. No matter one's race, or sex, or faith—there were facts in the world waiting to be discovered. How little thought I'd given to the ways in which it might be corrupted.

I passed now a blackened alley. It ended in a bricked-up wall before which a heap of trash had been dumped. A small shadow broke off with a squeal, went dashing across; a large rat, or a cat. The wind filled an old canning jar with a deep hum, and I was flooded by a memory, of myself in the field at four years, climbing up to sit on an old fence I'd sat on many times before, a fence weathered and aged, the wood so grey and flaking it looked like bones half-rotted, and all at once I was filled with presentiment, a feeling the fence would break beneath me, and though I told myself the fear was stupid, unfounded, a dread entered me as I clambered up, my knees swinging, and seconds later came the angry snap, and I was falling, falling at the field's edge, the pale screech of restless birds above as the old familiar fence gave way, driving its wreckage and splinters into my thigh.

I was turning away from the alley's dark mouth when the blow fell hard on my forehead. I staggered, the crack resounding in my teeth, my nose filling with the stench of hot tin. Above me the moonlight swayed crazily between the rooftops and I planted my feet to stop from falling when a blow dropped on my collarbone, the pain flaring up my arm in a wave of fire, and I fell, the gravel spraying from under my knees. I could hear him heaving up there, swinging some hard object down, and I rolled instinctively out of his path, so that the hammer or baton or board struck the dust in a shimmer of grit.

All was darkness. I blinked the blood out to see the frenzy of his small white hands grabbing at me, the claws of them as he dug viciously into my cheeks so that I felt my hardened skin tearing away, the scars of many years, and I cried out, shocked, shaking, sickened at the rope of blood pouring down my face, filling my mouth with a taste of rust. I struggled away, smelling his milky stink of sweet unwashed skin and whisky, hearing the moisture of his mouth as he began to curse in a stream as I drove my own nails into his face. I was afraid he would take up his weapon again and I sought his neck, praying I might grip it strongly enough to cut his breath.

A bird hooted in the masonry; wind rustled the trash. I flailed for his neck, trying to shift my own body so he could not get at me, praying beyond all hope for some drunk to stumble from the eatery and aid me.

"Audacious nigger," hissed Willard, his right hand grasping my throat as he groped with the other for the weapon tossed somewhere in the dust. "You will not humiliate me. You will not embarrass me."

I shifted back and forth on the gravel, the stones grinding into my spine so that I felt my back bleeding. There was the smell of primrose and whisky, of blood and rotted leaves and clean rock dust. He fastened his hands at my throat, hot and callused, and I kicked out, my legs sprawling, my hands clenching at his own throat as I felt my breath choking off. In that moment I could see the gleam of his crooked white teeth, the sheen on his dirty spectacles. I felt the bulk of his body on my abdomen and was surprised by the lightness of him, the thin, wiry weight of his power.

The knife, I suddenly remembered it—the ivory-handled kitchen knife I'd taken from a sideboard drawer and carried daily in my forepocket. I tried to take my hands from his sweating neck but found myself overpowered, breathless, and had to put them back on. We lay in the dust choking each other, his left hand feeling wildly for the weapon in the thin moonlight. Slowly I eased a hand free, and in a single swift motion I groped the blade from my front pocket, cutting my own thumb, and swung it briskly up under his spectacles, driving the tip in as deeply as I could.

His scream I will never forget. Rearing back, he clutched in anguish at his face and I shoved him off then, kicking at him, crawling to my knees and panting fiercely for breath. We kneeled side by side, like worshippers at an altar, him screaming in agony and me just breathing. And then I stood, retching, broken-shouldered, blood coursing down my face, and, gripping the side timber of the building, stumbled slowly away.

12

I SHOULD HAVE SOUGHT OUT MEDWIN. MEDWIN WHO HAD always the thirst for a fight, a desire to leave other men in ruins. Instead I found myself at the door of the small blue saltbox house, my blood staining the welcome mat.

When she answered the door, her hair was pinned sloppily at her nape with a series of laboratory clips. I was startled to see her dressed in her nightgown, a white, billowing gust of cloth, the edges of the sleeves soiled with ink.

I lowered my eyes. I had not realized she would be sleeping.

She came out to me at once. "Heaven's sake, Wash," she cried. "What has happened? Good lord, do come in." Her voice sounded hollowed out, shaken.

I entered the reception hall, with its familiar comforting smell of lemons and fixative. I tried not to further hurt her modesty by looking at her dress, though the instinct was silly—here I stood bleeding and broken before her, my shirt torn. "Your father is not—?"

"Come in, come. Come into the drawing room. Let me fetch the medical bag."

I remembered then that Goff was from home, to see after the rumoured existence of a winged fish.

She turned and bid me follow her to the parlour. The lamps caught her form, and I could see the trace of her body through the fabric. I glanced away, the scuff of my shoes loud in the hall, and I thought of the blood I must be trailing on the boards. But ever so slightly my eye was drawn back, and as I watched the soft undulation of her hips, a heat flooded through me, despite all.

As we entered the chaos of her parlour, the light from the low fire caught my face and she gasped, drawing shocked hands to her face. All at once she began to cry.

"Don't cry, Tanna," I said softly, but the words were slurred, distorted with blood.

Clearing her throat, she led me across to the settee under the dusty window and went to fetch her father's bag of medical supplies. The embers of a fire hissed in the hearth, heavy, half-burnt logs crushing it into smoke, a smell of char and menthol in the room. Beneath me, the settee was strewn with patchwork blankets. Stacked by its side was a pile of stained, warped books, as though tea had been poured over them.

She returned and, crouching before me in her sheer nightgown, began to sort wildly through the leather sack's tangle of bandages and salves and threads. "Do you need sutures?" she said, still in a haze of shock. "You will need sutures."

I moistened my lips, tried to focus on breathing.

I could hear her own ragged breath passing dryly over her lips. Kneeled before me there, I could see the fine sheen of sweat on her forehead. She bit at her lip in concentration. When she raised her hands to dab at my cheek with a cotton, I could smell the vague sweat in her armpits.

"Bastards," she said, sniffling. She began to heat a needle for the suturing.

"What?"

"My god, they are vicious to Negroes here. It's appalling."

I said nothing, adjusted my chin.

She began to stitch my torn face. Her fingers were gentle, soft, and she worked unhurriedly. I tried not to flinch, gazing upon her tensed brow. Finally she said, "You think I've made a bad job of it."

I touched at my face.

"Not the sutures—my sutures are perfect. I am talking of my fire. I saw the look of contempt you gave it when you came in. I have been giving it that look myself all day. Well, I am a zoologist's daughter, not a lumberjack's. What do I know of fires?"

I cleared my throat. "Would you like me to fix it for you?"

"No, no, of course not. You must rest."

But I stood from the dishevelled settee, the springs creaking. She protested, but fell silent when it seemed clear I would not listen.

"What is it?" said I, seeing her look at me strangely.

"It is not a good look for you, these new wounds," she said.

I touched my battered face gingerly, tried to smile.

"You are like an interruption in a novel, Wash. The agent that sets things off course. Like a hailstorm. Or a wedding."

"I do not read novels."

"Do not let my endorsement dissuade you. They are not all as I describe." She rose swiftly from her place on the floor, so that her gown slid up and I could see the golden sheen of her kneecaps shining there in the poor light. I turned back to the fire.

"That is enough," she said softly. "You will injure yourself further."

But I kept at my work, turning my back to her.

"Something is blowing in," she murmured, and from the direction of her voice I understood she was facing the window. "Father will surely be waylaid."

Finally the flint began to spark, and I turned the logs aside and reached out for the kindling to feed the little flame.

"This timber is still damp," I said, turning to her. "Has it not been brought inside to dry?"

She gave a helpless little shrug of her shoulders. "I'm hopeless."

I stood, dusting the flakes of bark from my knees.

"Why do you insist on worsening your injuries? Sit down, Wash. Rest."

"Is there anything else you need before I leave you?"

"Leave me? You are in no state to leave."

But I shuddered at the idea of Goff finding us here alone, together.

She nodded, and it was clear she too had thoughts of her father. "Yes."

"I had better go."

"Yes." But she did not stir from her place; she made no move to see me out. She said, instead, "You are a gentleman, George Washington. Perhaps too much so."

I could see the glow of her body through the thin fabric of her gown. I did not feel like a gentleman.

"I have disturbed you, Tanna," I said.

"Yes," she said again, but it was as though she was answering a different meaning.

Her eyes were narrowed. I felt my heart quicken, a heat radiating through me. As I stared at the dark shadow of her body through the cloth, the clean hollow at the base of her throat, the fine, hard bones of her ribs, the crest between her thighs, I wanted to rest my hands on her, to place my mouth on all that was hidden from me.

"Washington," she said softly.

That was all. And then slowly she stepped forward and, looking boldly at me, she began to unfasten the bone buttons of her gown. I heard only the sputtering of the hearth behind me, the scratch of the cat in a far-off room. She looked for a moment to the hall, as if she had heard a sound, and then quite silently the cloth dropped to the floor.

SOMETIME DURING THE hour a harsh rain began to fall. In the darkness we lay watching the long silver threads slamming down past the window, chewing up the earth. Water roared and overflowed the ditches. The porch groaned, as though ghosts walked back and forth upon it. I thought of Willard, still out there, the knife in his eye.

Tanna lay with her hair strewn across my good arm, the strands of it black, soft. We were on the floor before the settee, the rug under us gritty with crumbs. I was filled with an elation beyond all pain, still shocked at how natural it had all felt, at how much we'd already understood of each other's bodies.

I kissed at her forehead. "You were to illustrate your father's tract, weren't you?" I said softly. "The one he has asked me to illustrate?"

"No." Her smile was vague. "I had hoped he would ask. It is why I have spent these months improving my skill." She shrugged one shoulder. "But it is right. You are the wiser choice."

"I'll decline, Tanna."

"And punish yourself? No."

"We could illustrate together, then. There will be more than enough plates."

"Father's book will be a success, I am sure, and much more so with your hand at work in it than my own. And I think you must do it, my dear poor Washington Black. If not for yourself, then for those like you who would never get the chance of it. Men as talented as you, who will never get the chance of anything."

"What difference does that make?"

"I think it makes a great difference."

"No one will know my origins from looking at my drawings, Tanna."

"Truth has a way of coming clear," said she. She put a finger to my lips, to silence any further protest. Then she turned from me in the flickering light, reaching for a cup of cold tea balanced on a stack of books. The bones of her spine pried through her skin. Above her backside were three large, dark, circular birthmarks.

"And what are these?" said I, mischievously.

"Oh, I hate them," she cried, wriggling away from me. "Don't you look at them. Bind your eyes."

"They remind me of low tide. Of the patches of earth that surface when the water retreats."

She rolled towards me, planting a kiss on my nose. "You make an awful poet, George Washington Black."

I lay thoughtfully some moments. "What is your favourite marine organism?"

"I beg your pardon?" she murmured, gently kissing my neck. "That is *not* what you wish to talk about."

"Mine is the nudibranch."

"Because it is nude?"

"Because it will steal the harpoon off a jellyfish or anemone, then mount it to its own back as a weapon."

She leaned back. "Is that some comment on my character? Come, we needn't speak in these metaphors." The expression on my face made her pause, and laugh. "Oh, for goodness' sake. You are in earnest? I could not say, perhaps the octopus. If I were forced to choose."

But I was not to be put off. "The octopus?" said I, smiling. "Wonderful."

"All right."

"Because it is so strange?"

"Strange? An animal that can change itself to match its surroundings, just by contracting its skin? That can weigh as many stone as a man and stretch the length of a carriage, and yet fold its body through a crevice? Whose brain is wrapped about its throat—a brain no larger than a pea—but who is clever enough to play actual games? An animal with this much ingenuity, this much intelligence, who will sadly die within five years? I would not call that strange, but magisterial. Your nudibranch is nothing, dear George Washington Black. Octopodes are the gods of the sea."

"I think it is octopi."

"And I think your Greek and your Latin are confused."

She turned to me with a vague smile, so that I could see the smatter of raised black freckles peppering her cheeks.

I kissed her ear. "They have three hearts," I murmured, smiling.

She grimaced. "Oh, dear god. I fear there is more poetry in you after all."

There came then a scratching from beyond the door. "Medusa wants in," I said.

"Let her wait."

I gathered her in closer, feeling the cold dampness of her skin. I grabbed a blanket off the settee to cover us, and a sudden taste of fresh blood filled my mouth, as though I had torn something anew. The wool was rough and stank of camphor.

"I have always felt myself to be different from everyone, to be apart," she said with a pale smile. "I know you do too. I could sense it on that first day, on the beach." She paused, raising her face to me. "I meant you no ill will when I said you were a slave," she said softly.

Somehow, when she said it, all the desperate pain of these last hours rose up in me and I feared I would cry. I lay in silence, breathing.

She raised a thin hand, gently traced the knotted scar of the *F* on my chest. "Your master was cruel to you."

I did not want to speak of it. And yet I found myself going back to Faith Plantation, to Big Kit, to the strange, miraculous arrival of Christopher Wilde. I started to speak, slowly, methodically, something tightening all the while in my chest. How young I'd been then, how very different I now felt myself to be. I told her of the cruelties before Titch took me up, and of the unbelievable wonder of my time with him, when life had seemed to stretch the limits of reality. I spoke of Philip's suicide and of the hasty trip to the Arctic, Titch's final words as he walked into the snow.

"He sounds an apparition," she said. "He sounds a ghost."

"Then I am not describing it well," I said, but without reproach. For in truth I did sometimes have the feeling that I had dreamed him. "Life with Titch," I continued, "it was not real, Tanna, it was not the world. That is not a kindness for a slave boy. There were times, I am ashamed to say, when I just shut my heart to all the cruelty going on out there, beyond our door. I simply stopped seeing it. I was so afraid of returning to it. Does that not sound monstrous? But what Titch offered me, my own deliverance, was of worth *because* of the horror that was going on around me. I turned away from Big Kit. From all I had once known."

She was silent, staring into the nearly dead fire. "It was John Willard, wasn't it?" she said. "Who attacked you. It was no random incident. John Willard or one of his agents."

I lay my head back, stared up at the cracked plaster in the near dark. I sighed.

A long silence passed before she asked, softly, "Was it fatal, Washington? Did you kill him?"

"He is not killed." For though I had used all my might, the angle had been awkward, my purchase on the knife askew. He would no doubt lose his eye, but it would surprise me to learn of worse. And in some strange way it was a mercy to me, accepting that I had spared him. To be certain that I would never become what he had hunted these long years, a murderer.

Tanna raised her head. "Well, you must come with us to London at once, Wash. You cannot stay here. He will find you."

"It is over, Tanna."

"In London you will have more protections."

"Titch argued differently. In any case, it is over."

"Why would he argue differently? I do not understand. Surely it is obvious that you would." She paused. "You will not like to hear this, but from everything you have told me, it is clear to me that this Christopher Wilde had not your best interests at heart. You were a cause to him, not a person—however much he protested otherwise. You were something to be used to further his own crusade, his own sense of goodness."

"That is not so."

"It is, frankly. You have intimated that he first chose you because of your size. Because you would make for good ballast. And then he had you scrambling all about as his assistant, picking things up, drawing for him." She grimaced. "But were you anything nearing his equal, Wash? I doubt very much that he saw anything in you beyond your immediate usefulness to him. How could he, given the imbalance in your statures?"

I moistened my lips. I did not think it so, but did not dispute it.

"Even the Cloud-cutter," Tanna continued. "Did it ever occur to Wilde that having those poor souls drag and assemble his contraption up on the hill was likely as physically gruelling to them as their regular field work?"

I said nothing, my mind casting back to the sight of the slaves' pale clothes shadowed against the brighter sky.

Tanna rose onto one elbow. "Father and I recently visited New York City. Have you seen it? Oh, Wash, it is a dream. We lodged with a friend of my father's, a Quaker. One evening he took us to a meeting at the Society of Friends. I knew nothing of what any of it was, but I sat there just smiling and listening. Well, they talked and talked—and it was all poor Negro this, poor Negro that. And wouldn't you know, there were three Negroes in attendance, and they were made to sit on separate benches, away from everyone else. I could scarcely believe it—the irony. And none of the Quakers seemed in the least conscious of it."

I lay there, feeling a pain shoot through my shoulder. I let out a long, slow breath. "Erasmus Wilde is dead now. Willard said it. It is over."

Tanna looked sharply at me. "And you believe him?"

I thought some moments. "I do."

Tanna was silent.

"He also said something else. He said he had seen Titch in Liverpool two years ago. In the street."

"Alive?"

"One would imagine so."

Tanna gazed up at me from the tangle of blankets, staring a long while. "But he *would* say such a thing, wouldn't he? To confuse you, to put you off your guard? It is a lie, Washington."

"And if it is not?"

"What does it matter? What would it matter if he is still alive? You are your own man, Washington. You owe nothing to Christopher Wilde. You have been standing on your own two feet. Now keep going. Save yourself. Come with us to London. Come with me." She looked up at me. "I cannot bear to think of you staying here."

"Willard will not come after me again, Tanna."

"You have struck a white man. It would not be difficult for him."

I said nothing.

She tried to smile. "And tell me, good Mister Black, to whom shall I direct my abuse if you are not near? And who shall hold my robe for me while I undress?" She peered up at me. "If these are not temptations enough, think of the specimens. How will we manage them without you?"

I remembered my tanks then, wanting badly to describe what I'd discovered, to describe the prototype of wood and glass. But I was so tired, and instead I closed my eyes. There would be time enough later.

She kissed my forehead.

I asked, "Why do you smell always of tobacco?"

"You can smell it?" She pinched up a strand of hair and sniffed. "I had thought I concealed it well." She glanced up at me. "You don't suppose my father has noticed, do you?"

At the mention of Goff I fell silent, pressing my face into her hair.

PART FOUR

England
1836

1

The building was lovely enough: tall, wooden, narrow, set in a grove of black poplar rambling gently down a slope in the zoological gardens. But the grounds were poor, the grass spotty and ash-strewn; some three years earlier the building's left wing had exploded in the night, the boards flung burning into the black sky. An overturned candle, they'd said. It took months to reconstruct, and had only been completed the previous year. The timber on that side was yet pale, gleaming like a scar against the weathered planks.

This was no complaint. I was amazed we had been granted anything at all, given how outlandish our plan must have initially struck them as. Before leaving for London, Goff had pitched to the Zoological Committee our idea for a permanent exhibition of aquatic life in that city; we had been accepted enthusiastically. We could scarcely believe it. For days we went about dazed, half-believing it would all be wrenched from us. The city offered the land, and allowed for the repurposing of an old timber building in the gardens. If all went swiftly, we could open our doors to the public the following year. It would be called Ocean House.

Oh, what this meant to me, seeing my idea come into the world. Even the Cloud-cutter had not moved me as much—it had never been mine, despite all my work on it; it had always been Titch's vision. But here, finally, was a thing of my own making—the invention of a boy born for obliteration, for toil and for death. What vindication, to think I might leave this mark.

Even if I alone would know it. For I was not naive. My name, I understood, would never be known in the history of the place. It would be Goff, not a slight, disfigured black man, who would forever be celebrated as the father of Ocean House. When I allowed myself to truly think of it, a tightness rose behind my eyes. Goff was not a bad man—he did not like to take credit for my discoveries in principle, but I understood he was getting older, and that the desire to make a late sensation burned deep in him. And I understood too the greater conundrum—for how could I, a Negro eighteen years old, with no formal scientific training, approach the committee on my own, or even be seen as an equal in the enterprise?

I did not dwell on it, in these slow, hazy days. London narrowed the hours, so that my life became gauzy, drifting, strange. The Goffs kept a small house edging the city, and they offered me the smaller garden house behind it, once storage for Goff's lesser-used instruments. It was cramped and stank of mud but bright and pleasant enough. I adored it. Its four walls solid and final; my life made private, finally my own. To me the house felt inviolate. I knew that for any who would seek me I could still be discovered, but the shade of its tall Norway maples made me feel walled off from the world. For the first time in all remembering, I felt truly invisible.

It was no slight to me to be kept from the main house. I understood Goff was eager to maintain the illusion that Tanna and I were not lovers, though the fact must have been uncomfortably clear to him. I was happy to indulge the falsehood if it allowed me to live so near.

He had of course resisted my accompanying them to London. It was only in my laying bare all my troubles that he relented. But he remained gruff and unfriendly in the journey's first week, so that I kept my distance. And yet, somehow, things began to shift during the long days at sea. We started to talk more and to joke again as we cared for the live specimens, and soon we were often together, changing and aerating the water, feeding our creatures. A bond took shape, something richer than the uneasy truce of Nova Scotia. I respected his mind and he mine, I believe, and this seemed, finally, enough.

There had also been his shock at how others treated me. Goff grew daily more uneasy with this. One evening a lady in dark, expensive finery paused at our bench on the viewing deck. Curling her lip, she stared at me with theatrical astonishment. When Goff asked sharply what she meant by this performance, she said, "Your nigger is best kept with the other animals below deck."

I had never seen him so outraged. It was only through Tanna's cautioning that some larger incident was not made of it. After that, when each new insult arose, he'd speak roughly to the aggressor, low-voiced and shivering, as if he were the slighted.

The winter crossing was rough, and some of the less hardy genera began to die off. When the octopus I'd caught in the cove grew colourless, lethargic, we stopped paying the steward to bring us sea water. Instead, Goff and I descended to the clanging, grim lower hold on the rare days we were in port and, stepping out into the blanched air, we'd disembark alongside a crewman to gather clean sea water into fir-wood casks. Using some rude instrument of my devising, we tested for impurities. The breeze would lift my hat, and I'd crouch there with my sticks and papers, sometimes cupping the water to my face to taste for deadly metals. Occasionally, a small, curious crowd would gather at the boat's glistening rail to peer down at the strange old man and his ugly burnt slave who drank straight from the sea.

IN THE DARK, rain-drenched afternoons Tanna would steal onto the deck and, sitting beside me on my damp blankets, open a book across our laps and listen to me read. She made no corrections; it was not a lesson but rather a recitation, and somehow my reading became fluid. Weeks before we reached England, I could comprehend the complex sentences of all my cherished books; and their drawings, which I had long admired as depictions, came newly alive for me, like remembered conversations. They went beyond mere likeness now; they were blood and wing and cell and breath.

And so the hours at sea were rich and peaceful, and I thought with a kind of longing of those strange months of drifting towards the Arctic, when the days turned endlessly white and freedom seemed a thing I might live in, like a coat, a warmth I could draw around myself as some armour against the world. How far away it all felt, that journey with Titch. As if a hard crust had grown over the loss of him.

2

And yet, I was not convinced he was lost.

Some weeks after we arrived in London, during a brisk walk in Blackfriars along the northern bank of the Thames, I caught a chill. Within hours I was too weak to stand, even to lift my head. I shivered and shivered, my teeth clicking in my jaw. And what filled my mind in that wretched state were scenes from the past: Willard's attack, that last sad dinner at which I'd caught my final glimpse of Big Kit, the flash of Titch's eyes as the pane of hydrogen exploded in shards between us. And I thought also of Titch still alive somewhere among these green fields of his country, pacing the same London streets with their laughter and dirty-cheeked children, their ill-lit alleyways alive with the bright hiss of rats. And a strange fog settled across my mind, a kind of dull, fireless anger.

Tanna crept in every few hours and set the iron kettle on the coals. I sensed her presence flitting about the darkness, the pale weight of her lying beside me on the bed. I felt the warmth of her hand on my brow, and it was like a touch of sun seeping through the linens nailed at the window. Faintly, I called out, "Kit."

There was a rasping sound as of a machete being sharpened.

"Kit," I said again.

"Shh. You must eat something."

The sound of the machete thinned, became, strangely, the sound of boiling water.

"This is no evening," I said. "Not now, not tonight. The moon is too low."

Her breath was close on my face. "Wash?"

I felt myself surface a little, aware now that the voice was Tanna's. She sounded distant, as if she were in another room, and when I raised my hand to touch her I felt only the unpleasantness of my own skin slick with sweat.

I felt my shoes and socks quietly being removed, and I began to murmur, something about ashes in water, about winter.

"Rest, Wash." All at once there was a damp scrap of cloth across my eyes. "You will never recover unless you rest."

I do not know how many nights I lay delirious, only that I felt hot, then cold, then hot, my skin wet and my breath tasting of paper.

I began to remember the weekend before last, when we had made the long, slow trek out to Weymouth, to the shoreline; and suddenly I was there again, wading into the cold waters. The dawn was calm, the beach deserted, and I removed my waistcoat and set to floating on my back, the sea plants shivering blackly on the surface all about me. I lay weightless with the water filling my ears, staring high above me at the brittle stars fading in the rising sun.

I WOKE WITH a heaviness, as if a large cat had leapt upon my ribs. Around me the cottage's wood creaked in the damp weather. I turned and twisted in the wet sheets, bleary-eyed, my head aching still. But the fever had finally broken. At the window the horizon burned redly over the dead grey grasses. I stood and I wetted my face and scraped at my teeth with the harsh brush, dressing without care. Then I pulled on my boots and coat and went out.

I knew I should not venture outside, so shortly after recovering from my chill. But the cottage felt dark, close; I had been confined too long. The day was overcast, clouded, a thin fog silvering the maples. I waded through the brambles and mud, my boots squelching. Breath threaded from my mouth like vapour.

How was it that I had lately given more thought to the possibility of his being alive than to Big Kit's death? It was shameful. But my sense of betrayal shook me deeply—the idea that Titch had cut, rather casually, my tie to him, which was all I'd had in the world, my lifeblood. I trod past a grove of dead elms and then into a grove of live ones, their leaves glistening. It seemed too early in the season for so great a rain, but here it was, vast and hanging over the fields in a mist. I felt as though I were passing through a canvas, a landscape of grey strokes.

It struck me that his disappearance had been nothing but another desperate act to rid himself of me. That he had survived, and walked quite comfortably into another life.

And yet what lengths, to shuck off one small, hopeless innocent. Perhaps he did not like to think of me unprotected in the world, and so was finally relieved to see how I might make a life with his father and Peter House. I thought of all the protections he had offered, his speeches that my humanity should be everywhere known and accepted. And yet Tanna's objections to him bore some truth, I now saw. Titch's actions were the truer measure, and he had abandoned me, in the end. Once he'd finished his papers on aerostation and the treatment of slaves on Faith, I had lost some value for him. I had become, perhaps, too solid, too heavy, too real—

an object to be got rid of. He had mounted a frail Cloud-cutter, crossed a heaving black sea and walked vulnerable into a wall of snow, as though even the risking of his own life were worth being shed of me.

How could he have treated me so, he who congratulated himself on his belief that I was his equal? I had never been his equal. To him, perhaps, any deep acceptance of equality was impossible. He saw only those who were there to be saved, and those who did the saving.

I RETURNED TO find a smudged note pinned to my cottage door. Tanna had come to seek me out; when I returned, I should come to the main house to dine, if I felt myself so recovered that I could go out in this weather. The sharpness of her words made me, despite myself, smile. I set the note aside, and folding my coat on my cot, I sat instead at my tiny wooden table to draw.

I drew and I drew, and I thought irritably of Titch. It turned black at the window and my hands began to ache, and still I drew, the lines fine and threadlike, taking on great dimension. Never, since leaving Faith, had I been compelled to depict it. Yet here it was, all that I could remember of it, in brisk, vicious detail. There were the huts, their roofs stripped half-bare by decades of hurricane weather, the Spanish cedars nearby and the great royal palm with its wondrous purple-and-yellow berries. There were the bright frogs croaking in the underbrush, and the old sugar boiler, its stone chimney piercing the aquamarine sky. There was the dry, stony path leading up to Wilde Hall, its canopy of redwoods eerie with moss that hung like white men's hair, the sun's glow red in the strands.

There were the four tall walls of the hothouse I had lived in after Big Kit had broken my ribs as a child, the stone traced with water stains like large maps. There were the bullfinches that creaked from a high-up crater. And there was the tablet mounted above the hothouse's entrance, the Latin script upon it: *Not Unmindful of the Sick and Wretched.*

There were the fanged metal jaws of a mantrap meant to catch runaways, and the blood-blackened boulder upon which several men had been whipped dead, and there was the solitary redwood wide as a carriage, from which a weathered noose hung. And there were knife marks in the tree's bark, where men had been pinned through the throat and left to perish, and there were the raw patches where the grass had not grown back since the bodies of the old and infirm had been set there to rot.

And above it all, pristine and untroubled, sat Wilde Hall, with its clear view to the sea—a sea turquoise and glistening with phosphorus, the miles of sand pure and white as salt.

3

At last I understood what was working its way through me: I desired, despite every apprehension, to find Titch. The need was strong in me; to know if he lived still, and to confront him. My life had been one life before he had taken me up; this he had wrenched off course into a thing of wonder and then loneliness and destitution. My current life, I realized, was constructed around an absence; for all its richness I still felt as if the floors might give way, as if its core were only a covering of leaves, and I would slip through, falling endlessly, never again to get my footing.

I could delay it no longer. I would go to Granbourne. I would seek him out there.

Would I find him in residence? I did not know. But it only made sense for him to have returned to its halls. He had griped and complained and hated it with a passion. And yet it struck me as his only true sanctuary from a rough world that misunderstood him, the seat of his wealth and his privilege, a place he would forever be drawn to as water is drawn to its source. And so I addressed a letter to him there and received, surprisingly, a response from his mother, inviting me to afternoon tea.

The reply made me uneasy. Why had not Titch himself written? Was it as Tanna had foretold? Was he dead?

Over a cold herring lunch the next afternoon I mentioned my intentions to the Goffs.

Tanna quietly set down her fork. She did not frown, but there was something of that harshness on her brow.

"But why?" she said. "Why seek him out? Where is the sense in it?"

Goff sat chewing with swift, squirrel-like bites, clearing his throat gruffly but not speaking. As usual he seemed unaware of his daughter's annoyance.

I had grown flustered; Tanna seemed, in that moment, incapable of all understanding. "I would just like to speak with him again. To have him explain where he went."

In truth, my reasons proved as murky to me as they did to her. I suppose I wanted an apology, some expression of his remorse. Or at the very least, an explanation. I wanted him to tell me why he had plucked me from my life of toil in the first place, if anything had existed for him beyond the possibilities of my being useful to his cause. I wanted to know why my loyalty had moved him so little that he'd abruptly abandoned me. Perhaps his words would never be enough, in the end. Perhaps it was stupid to seek any peace from him. But I wanted very much to hear him speak my name, and to read in his face the guilt, the shame. And if there was no guilt or shame, I wanted to see that too.

"What good will it do, seeing him?" said Tanna. "What will it resolve?"

I made no answer.

"Does it not seem more likely that Willard lied to you? That Christopher Wilde is dead?"

"It does. But that still does not mean it is impossible."

"Who?" said Goff suddenly, abruptly. He gave a sharp cough. "Oh, yes, I remember."

"And in any event, why should Wilde go to Granbourne?" said Tanna. "Why would he retreat there? He despised the place. You said it yourself."

"It was his home. He hated it, but he was tied to it in a way I think he himself little understood. I know him. If he is not there currently, he will have recently passed through it."

"If he is still alive."

"If he is alive, yes."

Tanna drew a breath, as though to calm herself. "The truth of the matter is that Wilde did nothing to further your cause that did not further his own. You were a convenience for him."

I rubbed at my face in frustration.

Her cheeks reddened. "Well, you cannot go Tuesday next. We promised Father we'd source the Portland cement for the artificial rocks." She glanced over at Goff, who was wholly absorbed in his meal. "Father?"

"What's that?" said Goff.

"Surely it can wait a day, no?" I turned to Goff. "Or perhaps you might go yourself, sir?"

"We've also to drop the plans for the tanks at Wolcott and Sons," said Tanna. "He will need us to explain them."

After months of searching we had finally found engineers competent enough to build my complex designs.

"Mister Wolcott likes and respects you," I said testily. "He will not mistreat you if you go alone."

She appeared wounded by the suggestion. "Finding Christopher Wilde is important to you. Surely I should be at your side."

Something twisted in me. I had been anxious about going alone, and yet I did not wish to be accompanied by her criticism, by her vocal insistence that my search was foolish and futile. My nerves, I was surprised to learn, were raw already.

"I will bite my tongue in silence," said she. "I promise."

"Bite your tongue in silence," Goff grumbled. "It will be a bloody stump before you're halfway down the lane."

She smiled nervously across at me, and I lowered my eyes.

WE WERE DAYS in preparation. The visit to Wolcott and Sons was delayed until our return, and Goff was left unhappily with the task of sourcing eelgrass. And then we set out, the cool morning still damp with the evening rains.

We spoke little on the journey. I sensed Tanna's confusion, her lack of understanding that we should be going at all. I was tired, and did not wish to defend myself. We leaned softly against each other, silent, watching the city thin out and fall away.

Finally we reached the edge of the great estate. Driving up the gravel path, through the silver maples, we glimpsed buildings so rotted it was impossible they should be standing. I could see a gathering of thatch-roofed cottages, and a crumbling gardener's shack seemingly held together by vines grown through the stone. Against a rain-soaked carriage house someone had lined up broken axles, black as burnt bones.

I felt myself nearing the centre of a great darkness, a world from which my childhood, Faith—the endless suffering and labour there—was but a single spoke on a vast wheel. Here was the source, the beginning and the end of a power that asserted itself over life, death, the very birth of children. We cantered through a grove of low-hanging branches. I listened to the horse's shoes biting into the gravel, mud grinding under the carriage wheels. The air tasted of metal, and I remembered suddenly the Far North, the ferocity of the cold.

A silver band in the distance began to widen, to glisten. An artificial pond. Crystalline pins winked across its pale blue surface, so that it seemed to have some alarming sentience, like the eye of a blind man.

I remembered then something Titch had once said, during one of his rare quiet tirades against his mother—that she had no tolerance for anything not English. That, despite her having lived an unconventional life with Mister Wilde, and been herself an unconventional young woman, her sense of the world was old and rigid and unforgiving.

Would I actually find him here, behind these crumbling, moss-strewn walls? The grounds had a feeling of plenitude, of growth and richness, but there was also a sense of vacancy, as though the place had been abandoned not only by its people but by progress itself. One felt great age, and a silence like a held pause; it was as though everything that could happen here had already occurred, as though you were wading into an aftermath.

I sighed and brought my head to rest on Tanna's shoulder, feeling the pulse of the wheels clattering on the gravel under us. For nights I had thought of what I might say to Titch; staring now upon the grey fields, my mind grew empty, hazy. Tanna gently took my hand, but there was a hardness in her eyes as she gazed upon the acres of dead grass.

We slipped from under a canopy of bare branches, and it was

then I glimpsed it: the grand, forbidding, illustrious old house, the great manor of Granbourne. I saw its several unlit wings, I saw the ancient scars of weather and wars upon its facade. It was this from which the Wilde men had fled. The pillars and pediments were crumbling, the pavilion choked with moss. I could smell, on the surrounding air, the bitter, offal-like stench of dead garden beds.

The facade was black with cold ivy. The stonework was incut with unwashed, green-tinted, leaded windows. As our carriage approached, the landscape rose up watery and ethereal in them.

All at once the doors were opened and an old manservant stepped out onto the high landing. I could not see his face, but he clasped his hands behind him and became absolutely still. He was of average stature, slightly corpulent, but the stillness of his bearing, as if he were sucking all the surrounding silence into himself, gave him a natural authority. He looked very much as I imagined a parent might look to an infant from the depths of his crib.

We were shown into the high-ceilinged reception hall, where Tanna stood rubbing her hands together, as though she could not get warm, as though the weather had followed us inside. The air smelled of wet tea leaves and dust, of burnt wood. I peered at a large, unlit stone hearth, the intricate scrollwork overhanging it. No fire had been lit.

THE MANSERVANT LED us through darkened corridors, then out onto a great terrace of weathered chairs and large, cracked stone pots grey with long-dead roses. I looked to the sky; the birds appeared like shreds of cloth, distant, faint. The air felt very cold, the sky strewn with clouds so thin in the atmosphere they could barely be seen. And yet they seemed to block out all warmth; I could feel Tanna shivering beside me, and I rubbed at her back, its fine, hard bones. Yet for all this cold, the air still felt much warmer than inside the house, as if the years of Hampshire winters had accumulated in the old stone walls.

The servant stood unspeaking near the doorway, waiting.

Tanna hesitated; we looked nervously at one another. Finally she leaned forward and said, "Is Mister Wilde currently in residence?"

The servant appeared at first not to hear her. Then, very slowly, he gave a grave shake of the head. The vagueness of her question made his answer unclear—which Mister Wilde was from home?—but it was obvious that even to shake his head caused this man great strain, and that we should tax him no further. How very old he was. He had likely been a fixture in this house for decades—indeed, the manor might have been built around him. He had a wrecked, creviced face, and the stiffness of his carriage appeared to pain him. He would, I thought, have been witness to Titch's earliest days here, and I longed to ask him about them.

There came a rustling from inside the house, and a woman appeared from the darkness, magisterially tall in her damp riding dress, her hem muddy. She paused at the threshold, blinking at us. Her stature was extravagant—nearly Titch's height—with just the faintest curve in her upper spine, a soft hump between her shoulder blades. Her face looked waxen but for a stain-like flush across her broad nose. She clasped her hands before her, the forefingers adorned with heavy, identical jade rings; and I remembered Titch's hands, the emerald rings poised just above his knuckles.

She stared a long while. "Mister Black?" she said finally, and it was less a welcome than a statement of disappointment, as though she had expected another man. And yet in my letter I had explained all to her: that I had once been a slave on her plantation, had been stolen away by her youngest son and journeyed north with him. I had even warned her of my disfigurement, in case it should startle her.

Sparing Tanna no glance, Mrs. Wilde said, with great forbearance, "You are very welcome."

"Mrs. Wilde," said I with a bow. "What a pleasure to make your acquaintance, finally. I have heard much about you."

She looked me slowly over, her eyes resting on my burns. She said nothing.

I continued to smile, but it was as though the weather had entered my bones.

With no word more she crossed the wind-pitted terrace, its leaves skittering across the tiles, and stationed herself on a bench at a vast stone table. She said nothing, made no gesture that we should join her, merely sat looking over the far-ranging greyness of all she owned. Tanna gave me an irritable look, but together we went to her, brushing at the dirt on the cold bench across from her to sit.

With her light-brown eyes Mrs. Wilde studied us. There was a faint wheezing in her chest from the morning's ride, but even this seemed less a weakness than some mark of privilege.

"My man here cautions me against riding," said she, gesturing vaguely at the manservant still at the door. "Idleness is the worse danger at my age, as far as I am concerned. What is a broken bone?"

"Exercise *is* beneficial, at any age," offered Tanna.

Mrs. Wilde frowned faintly and did not look at her. "The weather has been most uncooperative of late."

The manservant stepped forward and, taking a white woollen shawl from a far-off chair, settled it across Mrs. Wilde's shoulders.

"I do hope you managed to have something to eat before travelling all this way," said she, and I thought this surprising, given her invitation to tea. "I would have offered a lunch, but I did not know if you enjoyed English food." Her eyes roamed vaguely about the terrace as if determined not to rest on anything. "I certainly know that when I am abroad I suffer much."

"I am English," Tanna said.

For the first time Mrs. Wilde allowed her eyes to settle on Tanna. She gave a faint smile.

"My father is Geoffrey Michael Goff, the marine zoologist."

She studied Tanna, her smile still vague. "My husband was somewhat interested in all that. I care nothing for the subjects."

"Mister Goff has made major achievements in the field," I said, though I felt a twinge as I spoke. "He is a fellow of the Royal Society, as I believe your late husband was?"

Mrs. Wilde clasped her jewelled hands upon the table, her expression unchanged.

"We have come in search of your son Christopher Wilde," said Tanna, having exhausted her pleasantries. "Is he here?"

Something entered Mrs. Wilde's face then, some indefinable hardness, and I could not say whether we were its source, or Titch. "I have not seen my son these three years."

Three years. *Three.* Willard had not lied: Titch *had* survived. He had walked through a pane of snow into an open, free life. I sat numbly, absorbing the news. It still did not strike me as true.

"How long did he stay?" Tanna asked. "Where did he go?"

Mrs. Wilde let her eyes drift over my face. I seemed, despite her better impulses, to compel her. "We no longer have the plantation. It is no longer in the family. It has been sold."

We sat some moments in silence as this new detail sunk in.

"And what happened to the slaves there?" said I, thinking painfully of Big Kit, of Gaius. "Surely they were not sold off with the property?"

Mrs. Wilde frowned. "Sold? But they were no longer slaves to sell. They had not been slaves many a year. They were apprentices, workers. Paid to do some grounds-work. Paid handsomely, I might add. They were even given lodgings for free. But it was never enough for them."

I could feel Tanna stiffen at this, but she made no remark.

"What happened to them?" I said again.

Mrs. Wilde sat back and breathed lightly out, her eyes roaming. "They were there of their own volition—they left of their own volition too, I imagine. Went on to other work, elsewhere."

"Is your son here in England?" said Tanna. I could see she was growing impatient.

Mrs. Wilde paused. She pressed the palms of her hands deliberately together, and turned her eyes on me. "You were with my husband when he died, yes?"

I paused. "I was."

She moistened her wrinkled lips, hesitating, and in that moment I understood why I had been invited here. It was nothing to do with Titch; as she'd said, she had not seen him in years. She wanted to know all about her husband's death—his last hours on the cold, lustrous plains of ice, among races of men unimaginable to her and therefore inhuman. She wanted to ask the question that had unsettled her these long years. She wanted to know, I believe, about Peter House.

But the longer she did not ask it, the more she became unable to. We sat in the long silence of her indecision, the leaves rattling across the terrace, the patter of rain starting in the distant trees. I was aware of the manservant slowly nearing her chair, watching her every gesture for signs he should intervene.

"Your son Christopher is most definitely still alive?" asked Tanna.

Mrs. Wilde paused, her smile full of strained patience. "Last I saw him, he was. But as I say, it has been years. No one, however, has written me to tell me otherwise." She cleared her throat. "I shall certainly let him know you are looking for him, if I do hear from him." She turned to me, expressionless. "In the meantime, perhaps you might try him at Grosvenor." She gave a raise of the eyebrow, as if feigning innocence. "At his cousin Philip's house. Philip's mother lives there still. Alone."

I understood then that she knew it all—my witness to Philip's death, my possible hand in it. I said nothing, felt Tanna grip my fist under the stone table.

"And do you mean to stay long in England?" Mrs. Wilde rose slowly from the bench. The manservant slid her falling shawl back onto her shoulders.

I glanced at Tanna. "Forever, perhaps. Certainly a good long while. Miss Goff and myself are helping her father with the new exhibition going into Regent's Park. Perhaps you have heard of it—Ocean House? It is a display of living aquatic organisms."

Mrs. Wilde gave her faint smile. "Well, I do hope you will get to see some of the city while you are here, Mister Black. This is your first excursion in London?"

"It is."

"Regent's Park," she said, frowning. "The Zoo is there, is it not?

I daresay you should feel quite at home." Again, she smiled. "In London, that is."

We had passed back through the house and were descending the grand staircase to our carriage when the manservant came out to us.

He stood against the wind as though it would fold him in half, clutching at the stone banister. We glanced up in alarm, and watched him take the stairs deliberately and one at a time, like a child learning to walk.

"You will catch cold, sir," I said with concern.

He pulled his coat about him and placed a steadying hand on the banister. "Christopher was here some two years ago, or less."

I was surprised, and showed it.

"He left quite upset," the manservant continued. "But then it was always so, between Mrs. Wilde and her sons. I do not know what troubled him. But I understand he meant to sail out of Liverpool on behalf of the Anti-Slavery Society. What for, I do not know. But he was always at their offices, always at their behest, desiring to aid them any way he could. He had placed the plantation's papers there, after poor Erasmus's death. And so he went daily there to help with the sorting of them." He glanced over his shoulder, but not nervously. "I am not certain if he actually managed to sail out—I do know he had some apprehension of doing so. But he did not return to Granbourne, and we heard no more of him. You might do well, I think, to inquire at the Society as to his whereabouts—they must certainly have some information."

"Oh, bless you," breathed Tanna. "Where would we find their offices?"

As he explained the location to Tanna, I thought of Titch having the wherewithal to place Faith's papers securely in London, and was somewhat disturbed. After hearing Willard's story of him mumbling in the street, a part of me had believed him half-mad.

"You have been most helpful," said I.

And he smiled, a down-turned, crooked smile that showed his surprisingly strong white teeth.

4

THE MANSERVANT HAD GOT THE NAME WRONG: IT WAS THE Abolitionist Society for the Betterment and Integration of Former Slaves. And on the morning we were to visit its offices, the octopus fell sick.

She was a new and unknown genus, and we were thrilled to be able to name her, and to put her on display in all her rareness. But she was growing sicker with the days, more lethargic, so that death even seemed a possibility. When I circulated her waters, she no longer playfully grasped the stick. I lowered fresh prawns into her tank by the cords of their seed-like eyes; I might have been placing rocks in there, for all her interest. She lay curled in a pale ball in the corner, one arm tepidly fingering the surface.

As I stared into the makeshift tank, watching her, a strangeness came over me: I began to feel that everything I put my hand to ended just this way, in ashes. I had been a slave, I had been a fugitive, I had been extravagantly abandoned in the Arctic as though trapped in some strange primal dream, and I had survived it only to let the best of my creations be taken from me, the gallery of aquatic life. And I felt then a sudden urge to reject it, to cast all of this away, as if the great effort it was taking, and the knowledge that it would never in the end be mine, obliterated its worth. I looked at the octopus, and I saw not the miraculous animal but my own slow, relentless extinction.

Tanna was staring at me; I had missed something.

She gestured again at the tank. "What do you suppose ails her?"

I squatted down, studying the softly boiling form behind the distorted glass. "God forbid she's been exposed to copper in her water," I murmured, feeling still unsettled, not quite in my skin. "We'll get to the bottom of it."

But I stared at the grey knot of her body, and was convinced of nothing.

5

"Oh, Miss Goff, lovely, wonderful. And this must be Mister Black. We have already pulled the documents. You have use of the room until noon."

I was slightly taken aback; I had not asked for any documents to be pulled. I was about to object when Tanna placed a hand on my wrist.

"Excellent," she said, "thank you."

She did not seem surprised and I understood then that she had made arrangements.

"Do let me know if you are in need of anything further." The woman smiled, and it was as though she had suddenly passed a window, so dazzlingly did it illuminate her tired face. Behind her the gallery of dark rooms buzzed with men scratching at papers and voices calling out and footsteps shuffling. The building had once been a printing shop, and even now there were faded splashes of ink on the concrete floors, once black and now aged to a lustreless grey. The rooms smelled heavily of wet paper, like a library in winter.

Tanna put a hand on the woman's arm. "We did mean to ask you—we are also looking for Christopher Wilde. His brother was Erasmus Wilde, the last owner of Faith Plantation in Barbados.

We understand Mister Wilde was to sail out of Liverpool on behalf of your organization." She hesitated. "Perhaps you might tell us where he was going? What was the mission?"

The woman frowned. "I know of no such mission. Indeed, such an excursion would be beyond the reach of our mandate, I'd think. I do recall Mister Wilde's being here, two or so years ago, to drop off Faith's records, help organize them. But I know nothing more beyond that. Mister Solander would certainly be able to help you." She paused. "He is not in for another hour. If you are still here, perhaps I might send him in? He was a great supporter of Mister Wilde's."

"Oh yes, do," said Tanna.

Glancing behind her to the short, dark corridor we had just come from, the woman explained that the organization was not just a repository of records but was in fact still very much engaged in combatting slavery, even after Emancipation in the Indies. "America is still an area of darkness," said she. "It is unrelenting."

I stared into the room before us. There, upon a wood table whitened by old water stains, sat a large wooden box of bound records.

"I realize they are many," said the woman, hesitating. "As I said, you have use of the room until noon." Then she turned and left us.

Was I shocked to find that the world of my childhood could be contained in a single crate? It was not easy to accept. I stared uneasily at it, glanced at Tanna.

"I thought you might like to know," she said softly. "Of course, we do not have to go through them, if you'd prefer not to. I just wanted to give you the possibility."

I stepped into the small room, into its hushed glow. Three gleaming lanterns blazed on the table before the crate, alongside two steaming cups of tea. Clearly, some pains had been taken to ensure our comfort here, and seeing this, I felt suddenly drained, ill again. The books in the crate were brown with age, the pages warped. I imagined I could smell stale water in the paper, the scent of decay. The table was flooded with yellow light, and I walked slowly into the illumination to take a volume from the crate, the wood creaking faintly at my touch.

I pulled back a chair, sensing Tanna take the chair opposite. I did not see her, felt only my hands on the crusted paper, the fragility of it, as if the lives described here might break apart in my clumsy fingers; as if I would destroy these people's sole commemoration, however awful it was.

I turned slowly through the records, the pages gaping away from the binding. Dust rose invisibly; I sneezed once, twice. I set it down, then picked up a kind of scrapbook, yellow with old newspaper notices. The notices related to slaves lost, slaves for sale, cotillion balls on neighbouring plantations. I ran my eyes nervously along the clippings. And then I saw it: the advertisement Titch and I had seen posted in Virginia.

> *A Reward of One Thousand Pounds will be paid for the capture of GEORGE WASHINGTON BLACK, a Negro Boy of small stature, his countenance marked with Burns; a Slave for life. His Clothing is a new Felt Hat, black Cotton Frockcoat and Breeches, and new Stockings and Shoes. He may be travelling alongside an Abolitionist White Man not his lawful owner, with Green Eyes and Black Hair, of tall stature. Whoever secures the Murderous Slave so that I get him Dead or Alive shall have ONE THOUSAND POUNDS Reward.*

JOHN FRANCIS WILLARD, acting agent for
ERASMUS WILDE
Faith Plantation, Barbadoes, British West India

I shivered softly. How strange to see it again, with the knowledge now of how everything had ended. I had been so frightened then; these words had reduced my boyhood to a further terror. The memory of that fear entered me now like a shadow. I had been nothing but an object to Erasmus Wilde, nothing but an expression of his wealth in the world. My escape was his diminishment; I understood what he had lost was respect—that is, power.

The lamplight passed in flickers across my hands. When I raised my eyes, Tanna was staring anxiously at me.

I gestured for her to slide across the volumes she held.

The first was a log of apprentices, detailing those men still working on the plantation after Emancipation; it was a list of their names and death dates. I stared a long while at its cover, and that black certainty that had been in me since leaving Faith, the knowledge that Kit was dead, entered me sharply. I opened to the page Tanna had marked, running my eyes down the columns, but I did not find her name, neither the true one she had been born with, Nawi, nor the new one she'd been given upon her arrival in the Indies. Then all at once I caught sight of it, her death date inscribed in a fine hand. Slowly I set the book down, and was silent.

I had always known it; she had been old even before I first met her. Her field work had not lessened in apprenticeship, and if she'd still had that boy in her care, she would have been completing some of his work too, to spare him the brutality of so long a labour. And yet to see her name logged so plainly here, as if it were a list of stored goods I looked at, or weekly sugar yields—it was peculiarly agonizing. I felt the wrongness, the disgustingness of the life granted her; I imagined her body taken from the fields with no more ceremony than would be given a dead plough horse. And I wanted to smash something with my fists, to destroy everything around me. I sensed Tanna's eyes on me, and in that moment I hated her presence, hated this foolish attempt to give me back my past, as if the blackness of it could simply be boxed back up and left behind in this cold room with no more thought.

With trembling hands I opened the second book. On the marked page was a very tidily kept log, penned in the hand of my first master, Titch's uncle, Richard Black. His writing was difficult to decipher, the letters like sutures stitched into the page. I squinted at the words.

Mother's Name	*Child's Sex*	*Child's Name*	*Time & Place of Birth*
Maria Cunitz	*Female*	*Eleanor Anne*	*May 21, 1817, Faith*
Eleanor Glanville	*Female*	*Maria Clara*	*June 12, 1817, Faith*
Catherine MacCauley	*Male*	*George Washington*	*April 19, 1818, Faith*

Catherine MacCauley.

Kit.

Big Kit had been my mother.

All the light seemed to leave the room. I stared at the table, the white rings left by cups, my hands dark and calm upon them.

For years she had ignored me, until I had turned up suddenly in her hut, and then with a ferocity that terrified she'd fought off all who would cause me harm. She had cared for me and cursed me and cracked my ribs and clutched me so tight in her love that

I thought she might break them again. She'd damned my father as cruel and my mother as foolish, and when I said she could know nothing of their natures she struck me hard in the face. When I got up the courage to again muse about who they might be, she would cackle furiously and tell me I had been born of a goat and a god, of a sheep and a chicken, of the good strong winds and the blackness that dropped swiftly across the crops in the cold season. She told me I was born of stupidity, that it must be blood-deep, and also that I was brilliant, that there would never again be a mind like mine. She loved me with a viciousness that kept me from ever feeling complacent, with the reminder that nothing was permanent, that we would one day be lost to each other. She loved me with the terror of separation, as someone who had lost all the riches of a scorched life. She loved me in spite of those past losses, as if to say, I will not surrender this time, you will not take this from me.

She had been born one person on the far side of Africa, and had walked out of the wretched hold of the slaver's boat a second person, an alien on the white sand shores of an alien land. What had she seen on that terrible journey; what had she survived? I saw the cool monsoon morning, Kit captured in a dusty yard under a windy sky. I saw her long walk of weeks, months, to the coast. The stories she told herself along the way, stories of birds turning into men, of men turning into trees, of anthills devouring goats whole. The memory of a grandmother who'd come to her hut two years after she died, to tell her she had grown too thin.

Perhaps the bright ocean frightened her, its endless light, the white roll of the breakers far out on the sandbars. Perhaps she was terrified at the sight of the vicious pink men, hollering, drinking, sprawled out sweating in the sand. And when she was penned downstairs, darkness gathering in her crowded cell, perhaps she did not cry, had no tears left by then.

In my mind I saw the awfulness of the officers at the fort, their savagery, their casual violence. How they spat in her face, or dumped scraps on her scalp, beat and raped her for sport. I saw her selected to wash the corpses of the officers who died, how at night she talked to these men on the wrong side of life, how they spoke back to her. *Does my wife know I have passed? Will any write to her? Does my father know I have passed?*

And the horrors of the crossing, when it came? The stench of the holds, all of them roiling naked and ill in the dark stomach of the barquentine. The urine and excrement and vomit, men clawing their own throats open with ragged fingernails, bloodied women leaping the deck rail into waters sharp with the fins of sharks. I saw the dozens who had died on the way to Barbados, and I saw those who died once ashore. I saw my Kit grow sick, fattened on rich, strange food, and only just recover. And I saw how I left her behind to the cane and the punishing sun, in favour of Titch, and began gradually to forget her face, the sound of her voice.

I felt then Tanna's warm hand on my shoulder, and I realized I was crying.

6

WHEN TANNA PULLED AWAY, I RAISED MY HEAD, TOUCHING a sleeve to my eyes. A man was standing in the doorway, hesitant.

"Forgive the intrusion," he said, his eyes shifting uncomfortably about the room. "Forgive me." He slowly, almost unwillingly, stepped forward, and I became conscious of my burns. "Robert Solander. I was told you sought information on Christopher Wilde?"

He was a balding, red-faced man of minute stature. I tried to picture him alongside Titch, dwarfed in that man's shadow.

I cleared my throat, collected myself. "His mother mentioned you might have knowledge of his whereabouts."

"I have not seen him recently," said Solander, with an odd wince of apology. His was a small, square face in which the bones sat high and prominent, and the gesture seemed to thrust his skull to the very surface of his brow. "Though I do suppose it depends on what you would consider recent. He appeared here some two years ago, with records from his family plantation, which had been sold. The sale had taken place just months earlier—I believe his brother had just died. He worked tirelessly, helped us to catalogue everything."

"He must still have been in mourning," said Tanna.

"Indeed." Solander paused. "Though outwardly he was his usual self—amiable, smiling, full of jokes. I do not mean to suggest he was not saddened—certainly there were moments when he was less excitable, melancholy. But still we had a riotous time. He is excellent company, as you must yourself know." Solander's smile sat awkwardly on his face, as though a mask had been overlaid there. "He had been recently to France, to Cormeilles-en-Parisis, to visit a friend there. They had apparently spent the months fussing about with camera obscura. Mister Wilde—well, he has the gift of being both scrupulous and funny. He tried to explain the science to me, and I did not understand a word of it. But it was all still extremely diverting."

My mind was still half on Big Kit; in my distraction the description of Titch as funny struck me as not right, as though he were speaking of a different man entirely. I gave a hard smile. "Is there anything else you might tell us, Mister Solander?"

Solander shook his head no. Then he paused, his brow furrowing. "Yes," he said, "yes." He cleared his throat, uncertain.

We looked expectantly at him.

He hesitated. "As I said, his brother had recently passed away, and so I put it all down to mourning. But near the end of Mister Wilde's time here, his dress became increasingly peculiar. He is a tall man and, as you know, slender, slim. And yet in those last weeks, his attire appeared much too small for him—his wrists sticking out of the cuffs, his trouser hems much too high." He gave a nervous shrug. "It was odd."

Tanna and I exchanged a glance.

"He was wearing another man's clothes?" said I.

"No. It seemed they were his, somehow. And yet they did not fit him."

"As if he had grown taller?" said Tanna.

"No," said Solander. He struggled to arrive at the right words. Finally he said again, "No."

"As if what, then?" Tanna said.

Solander only shook his head.

"Did you question him about it?" I asked.

"I was disinclined to. I did not wish to embarrass him. As I said, he was in mourning."

"And he was otherwise himself?" said I.

"Yes," said Solander. "Entirely."

"And you did not see him again after that?"

Solander pulled from his pocket a neatly folded envelope, its paper pristine. "I received this some fifteen months ago."

Tanna accepted the envelope, parting it with her delicate fingers. "The letter itself is lost?"

Solander flushed. "When last I saw him, I had been having problems of a personal nature. Of a marital nature. Mister Wilde remembered this, and he wrote to me some advice." He gave a smile like a grimace. "Things were put to me in that letter that are not for strangers' eyes. You understand, I hope?"

"Of course," I said, though I longed to see the letter. I glanced over Tanna's shoulder, observing the postmark of fifteen months past. I saw Titch's beautiful penmanship, and then I saw the return address, and was startled. It had been posted from a home in Amsterdam, care of a Mister Peter Haas.

Tanna noticed almost in the same moment. She glanced up at me. "Peter Haas. Is this not your man from the Arctic—Mister Wilde's assistant?" She furrowed her brow at the address penned there. "I thought he was House."

"House," I murmured. "Haas." Perhaps in my naivety I had got it wrong. It did strike me as unlikely that Titch would know both a Peter House and a Peter Haas. Though it was not impossible.

"Amsterdam," said Tanna thoughtfully.

"You are welcome to keep that," said Solander, apparently relieved to have something concrete to give us. "I am sorry I could not be of more help."

I gripped the envelope, the warmth of Tanna's hand still in the paper's folds.

7

The next weeks passed painfully, with the confirmation of Kit's death still weighing on me, the acceptance that she was my mother. Tanna was overwhelmed in her concern for me; and her eagerness to heal me, to never let me alone, annoyed and distressed me. We fought bitterly all the next week, so that she began to avoid spending time in my cottage. I did not seek her out, knowing that any gesture begun in love inevitably turned to poison; every good speech, every clean overture, died on the air. I thought constantly of Amsterdam, but I was blind to myself; only a full week after speaking to Mister Solander did I realize I longed to write to Mister Haas, to seek him out—that indeed I was irritable precisely because I knew I needed to.

And so, one evening, after a full day's work at Ocean House, I sat at my creaking desk and wrote out a long, searching letter. I posted it the next morning and still weeks later had received no response. And so I wrote again, following it quickly with a third letter—and again, nothing came. How disappointed I was, how shaken. I was desperate to speak of it, but did not feel I could confide in Tanna; I knew she would criticize me for putting so much effort into seeking out a man who after all might have been a ghost. Her contempt for Titch was obvious, though she had never met him. Her displeasure at my need to see him again was really her displeasure at what she perceived to be the worst of my faults: my habit of expending my energies on those things and people least worthy of them—herself and her father exempted. In my desperation to find Titch she saw a fear of accepting my own power, a mindless surrender. It disgusted her, though she never spoke so.

But then, gradually, miraculously, things began to clear between us. We were able to speak as we'd once done, with great love and little calculation. We began to go almost daily into the city together, to inspect new specimens or pieces of equipment. We sourced Portland and Roman cement to build artificial rocks, and purchased Thames river sand from a stone wharf to line the tanks' bottoms. We sought out annelids and crabs; we talked constantly of light, its shifting properties throughout the seasons. The windows of Ocean House were very large and poorly blown, and we feared what the summer months would bring, when the solar rays would energize the plants but lay waste to the animals.

And finally the tanks for the main floor were completed, and we were invited to go to Wolcott and Sons to examine them. On our way there, we passed damp stone buildings abutting the road, the facades black with last night's rain. As we entered Guilford Street, I finally spoke of my failure to reach Haas.

I steeled myself for Tanna's disapproval. Instead she hesitated, and with some reluctance, as if she'd been hiding a secret, said, "Father has a distant colleague in Amsterdam, in Jordaan—Kees Visser. Some months ago Mister Visser wrote with news of a specimen he thought perfect for Ocean House but did not entrust to the post. He could not bring it himself, being permanently confined to a Bath chair. But he said he would cold-store it, in the hopes that

Father might have a chance to go and collect it." She peered warily at me. "If I'm only mentioning it now, Wash, it's because Father had no notion of going. We do not know Mister Visser well, whether he is trustworthy or not. But the nature of his claim, it's so unlikely. We get many such claims, as you know."

I paused, absorbing this news. She stood before me nervous, as though expecting a dressing-down. Very calmly I said, "What does he say he has?"

"A two-headed cetacean."

"Born live?"

"Stillborn."

"It would be a triumph to display such a thing."

"I myself do not believe him."

"Conjoined twins do exist in nature, Tanna, though admittedly they are rare."

"He says it is a beast of two heads yet one brain, with the limbic system divided perfectly between them."

"Astounding."

She made no reply, kept walking.

We continued some paces, a spit of rain now in the air. I was not angry with her for withholding this information; I understood the great risk she took in telling me. For here was what I had been awaiting, in my bones—a tangible, feasible reason to visit Amsterdam, something more concrete than the rumour of a lost man.

We shoved open the grimy door of Wolcott and Sons, the bell ringing tinnily. Wood shavings scuttled across the floor, pale as gull's feathers. Almost instantly Mister Saunders stepped from behind the dark curtain, his hair flecked with lathe shavings, a smile on his pocked face. He was Wolcott's son-in-law, a tall, lanky redhead from Midlothian, and though he spoke with no trace of accent, one had a sense of his difference. With a boyish wave of the hand he bid us pass through the curtains and led us mumbling to the workshop in back. In this large room stinking of burnt glue, its tables strewn with bottles of paste and great cement plates, a small, begrimed man in a black apron squinted quietly at his work.

"Good morning, Mister Wolcott," Tanna called out.

Wolcott grunted but did not glance up. Yet we both saw the strong blush cross his cheeks, and were careful not to look at each other. The old man admired Tanna desperately, and in her presence he became abashed, abrupt. I had seen him once socially among only men and he was quite lively then, and talkative.

"And what do you think?" said Mister Saunders, leading us to the wall at the far back. In a tidy line our tanks sat stacked, clean and new and gleaming. They ranged in size from sixteen inches to nearly eight feet, their bottoms made of slate and their framework of iron.

"They are wonderful!" said Tanna, kneeling to touch at the glass, her skirts pooling on the wood shavings. "I wish I could live in one myself."

Mister Saunders smiled, a single crooked tooth creeping over his bottom lip. "Said Mister Wolcott here, We must endeavour to get them *right*, Saunders. These are for Miss Goff."

Wolcott frowned at his labours and did not look up.

"Well, I am ever so grateful for the extra care taken," said Tanna. "I can already see the small worlds they will hold."

"Ah now, we were glad of your business, dear. And we welcomed the challenge." He laughed lightly. "The design I will say was quite complicated. I see you are very modern and do nothing by half measures." Saunders glanced over to me. "You will take them away on Wednesday?"

"A week Wednesday," said I. "We must return with the proper transport."

"Aye, yes. Just as well, with that business out at Newgate. The streets will be black with people."

"Another one?" frowned Tanna. "It is as though they mean to save on food, the rate they are dispensing with those poor men."

"Indeed," said Saunders. "But you mustn't be so modern as to forget they are robbers and killers."

"How many this time?" said Tanna. "What are their crimes?"

Saunders hesitated, as if he hated to speak so before a lady. Treading over the slippery wood shavings, he plucked a newspaper from a counter strewn with stained and discarded papers and handed it to me.

"Here, give this to Mister Goff," he laughed. "It's a father's prerogative to tell a daughter, if he chooses."

Tanna smiled politely, but in the dim light I could see Wolcott set his lips, as though he was displeased she should be exposed to such iniquities.

Tanna bade them good day and I led us out. Stepping into the cool, grey air, I felt I could breathe again, the breeze fresh and biting.

"You are happy with the tanks, I hope?" Tanna looked up at me, and a soft anxiety entered her face. "You are thinking of Amsterdam."

But I was scanning the newspaper, and seeing his name I stopped short in the street and could find no words.

8

Goff had declared that morning that he desired a winter picnic. And though we were in no mood for it, still we found ourselves dining, impossibly, that evening at Regent's Park.

The air was already golden with the faltering light. It had been a milder afternoon than the previous, though still cold. Tanna and I had spent the rest of the day wandering the city aimlessly, in a silence that deepened by the hour. We did not speak of the upcoming hanging, but it stayed uneasily between us, a web. I was quiet, gloomy; I went about in a stupor, hardly knowing how to hold my body. The shock of it was too much: seeing his name printed with such matter-of-factness on the finger-smeared page, as if he could as easily have been a Member of Parliament as a criminal. I did not want to have to go and share a casual meal with Goff; I urged Tanna to beg off. But she did not want to disappoint her father, and so we went, filled with our quiet horror.

We arrived in Regent's Park to find, laid out before a bone-white copse of birches, a simple picnic on a checkered blanket in the damp grass. There were cold meats, salads, a frosted and unevenly tiered white cake. Seeing the bounty, I was relieved we had not abandoned Goff alone to his meal. He lay sidelong on the blanket, like a Roman senator. He had already begun eating.

"Now what is all this?" said Tanna with a soft, tired smile. "Surely you did not make all this food yourself?"

"Eliza was in this afternoon. She cooked and she brought it down for us."

"We are late," said I. "Forgive us, the fault is mine."

"Nonsense," said Goff, smiling. "Now tell me, how were the tanks? Did Wolcott succeed?"

Tanna settled down on the grass, pulling her shawls around her. "This is hardly the season for a picnic." She shook her head. "Of course you would not hear of it, Father. Truth is, you love the cold and feel at your liveliest in this weather."

Goff grunted. "Well, I am old. And I will be dead soon. What's a little inconvenience for you young ones, to allow an old man a late pleasure? Eh?"

As Tanna began to describe the tanks, she glanced sadly across at me. I could see it exhausted her, this having to perform for her father. But still she did it. It struck me that her whole life had something of this theatre, this desire to shelter Goff's happiness at all costs. I constituted, I thought, her sole rebellion.

I tried to smile. "I see you have brought spirits and good wine to warm us, sir. Very thoughtful."

"Do help yourselves," said Goff.

"We have been walking along the Thames," I continued. "I was afraid we would not be back in time. Tanna has been a most accommodating guide. I think there is not a sight in London that she does not know the history of. It is an impressive city."

"And an ugly one." Goff shrugged. "But there is enough goodness in its people to make it worth the saving. Some of its people, at least."

Taking up our plates, we began to eat. But I tasted nothing, feeling myself entirely elsewhere, absent, as though another man had taken my place.

"It is pleasant, is it not, my dear?" said Goff. "Having a winter picnic again?"

"I do miss Henrietta." Tanna turned to me. "Sometimes, when we would dine outside in winter, we would be joined by my favourite aunt, Madame Lemieux."

"She is French?" I said.

"Her husband was French," said Tanna.

"Her *last* husband," said Goff with a grin. "There have been four."

"So many?" said I.

"Four so far," said Goff. "French all but one. Henrietta is in Paris now, likely hunting for a fifth. Otherwise I would insist on introducing you."

"If you would like an example of the extraordinary English temperament," said Tanna, though somewhat distractedly, "you could not do better than Madame Lemieux. I daresay you will not encounter a more accomplished woman."

"That is arguable," I said with a gentle smile.

"She would tell you so herself, if she were here," said Goff. "Though accomplished in *what* is the real question."

Tanna smiled reproachfully at her father. "Madame Lemieux is a respectable woman, Wash. Do not let my father mislead you. She has been ninety-eight times to Paris, has ridden camelback in the East, and was once nearly killed by a flying horseshoe in the streets of New York City."

"Ninety-eight visits to Paris?" said I.

"You are impressed."

"Impressed that she has not lost count."

Tanna gave me a tired smile. "In addition to her four marriages, she has declined no fewer than five proposals. The last, an industrialist by the name of Horne—you may have heard of him? Horne's Confectioneries?—she turned down because, one evening, he removed his shoe in her presence."

"She is very proper?" I said.

"Henrietta has been married to Frenchmen half her life, Washington," said Goff. "She is most certainly not proper. It was the man's foot she objected to."

"Would you like to tell it, Father?" asked Tanna. But Goff waved her on. She continued, "It seems Mister Horne inadvertently pulled off a sock with his shoe. And in the strong candlelight she saw he had very small, hairless, finely made white feet. Like the feet of a young girl."

"Tell him about Dover," said Goff.

"Dover?" I said.

"My sister has sworn to never again set foot in Dover," said Goff.

"When last there, it seems, every woman she met was named Lemieux. No relation, of course," said Tanna. "A coincidence, it seems. Mrs. Adele Lemieux, Miss Martha Lemieux, Mrs. Margaret Lemieux . . ."

"I did not know there were so many in England," said I.

"Nor did she," said Goff. "Some of them were holidaying from the Continent. But some were English through and through. I think she means to get married again, just to rid herself of the name."

"She fled Dover just as fast as she could," said Tanna. "When we saw her, she looked like she had seen a ghost."

"And this had never occurred, on any of her ninety-eight visits to Paris?" said I.

"My sister amuses us," said Goff dryly. "I think she does it out of pity for our modest lives."

"She has actually been a great help," said Tanna after a moment. "There was a time when we could not get on without her. She used to accompany us to the seashore—she is a wonder at the keer-drag. Though of late she has been rather more interested in her glass-blowing."

"And her husbands," said Goff.

"Glass-blowing is an art and a wonder," I said, somewhat absently. My mind was exhausted, drained; I wanted nothing but a good bath, the comforts of my warm cot. "I have always longed to learn it."

"Madame Lemieux makes tiny glass trees," said Tanna. "Tiny glass winter trees, leafless ones. They are astonishingly beautiful."

We fell silent then. And as she smiled across at me, sadly, tiredly, I was relieved to understand we had finally come to the end of our performance. Goff smiled all about, chewing his food, happy.

9

WEDNESDAY ARRIVED WITH EXCRUCIATING SLOWNESS. Only then did Tanna and I reach our final, mute conclusion, staring across at each other over dishes of cold mince and pickled smelts. We would go to the hanging; how could I fail to? I would never accept the death if I did not myself see it.

We sat in silence on the drive over, the sound of our breath filling the carriage as it swayed and rumbled under us. Tanna removed her gloves to clutch my hand in her damp grip.

We heard the crowd at Newgate long before we saw it. As we rounded the corner, the crowd seemed to rise out of the muck like some rabid hallucination. There were so many people we did not argue when the driver barked for us to climb down long before we'd actually reached the prison. My mind was afire, my limbs sluggish, and I trod silent through the rain-damp streets, Tanna studying me nervously. By my own rough count there were no fewer than four hundred souls churning through the mud.

I was of goodly height, and despite my thinness there was a power to my wide shoulders, so that I was able to shove open a clear path for us through the crowd. The people gathered here were rough, men who but for God's grace might themselves be hanged; sailors; a few ex-slaves; but also women in tattered hats, their dresses ugly with torn stitching. The stench of onions and sour wine clung to the air. Even the children, the many children, darted among the gathered, slicing pockets and collecting a good day's earnings.

In my seven months in London, I had never set eyes on Newgate Prison. Nothing had brought me to its gates. I saw now a hideous brick building, tall and looming, before which had been erected a large platform with a gallows. The platform was surrounded by a low wooden fence barely strong enough to fend back a dog. And it was behind this fence that the crowd surged, hissing and laughing, gazing up at the nooses swaying there, as if already savouring the spectacle.

We pushed onwards. I felt a growing anxiety as I listened to the low roar of the crowd. I glanced back at Tanna, at her quiet, nervous face. I should not have brought her here, I thought. As we neared the scaffold, something—a strong nausea—cut through me. I understood that what I was nearing might be the final scene in the terrible drama that had ravaged these last five years of my life. Was it really to be? Was this truly how it would end? The newspaper had stated that two were to be hanged: Louis Hazzard, a Negro, for the crimes of theft and arson; and John Francis Willard, a Scotsman, for the crime of murder of a Freeman. And so what had happened to him, in these intervening months? Had he been unable in the end to swallow his vengeance and killed another man, believing him me? Or had it been a more random act, a striking out at a black man whose freedom seemed unnatural to him? I stood in the cool air, watching the great irony of it—his indictment for the crime of killing my double, and his sharing of this legislated death with yet another black man.

Vendors cried out their wares; men carried trays of hot chestnuts slung about their necks. A group of fiddlers stepped over the thin fence and began tuning up to play. We continued to push our way forward.

I could see the scaffold clearly now, a grey, rickety wooden structure, the steps half-buckled on the far side. Guards stood in a loose semicircle around the works, their weapons at the ready. The crowd was tense, but not angry. There was an air of holidaying to it all.

At last, on the stroke of noon, the two men were led out.

I strained to catch sight of them. The black man came first, and though he resembled no one I knew, I started at the sight of him, as if I were gazing upon a familiar. He was neither young nor old, his hair shorn and his face squinting. He wore no boots. He walked slowly, as though savouring the damp brick on the soles of his feet—or perhaps as though he feared collapsing. He appeared momentarily confused.

Peering at the second man, an anguish came over me. How was it we stood on opposing sides of this fence, as if it were the dividing line between death and life? I began to shiver; Tanna gripped my arm harder. I saw clearly the damaged eye behind the glinting spectacles, white and sightless. I saw his grey prison shirt immaculate as if just pressed, and I saw the blond head with its air of a scholar as he stared out over the crowd, seeming to seek someone. He looked terribly, impossibly tired.

When I'd caught sight of his name in the paper, I had been filled with relief. Now, seeing him standing so straight-backed there, as if trying to maintain a dignity long ago lost, revulsion washed over me, an astonishment at my own blood lust. I had not killed him all those months ago in Nova Scotia because I had not wanted to take a life. It had been a badge to me, a triumph of decency. Seeing him now, I understood how false was my self-congratulation, my high moral stance. I had been afraid, that is all. The true mercy would have been to kill him, to give him the death he had been thirsting after all these years. For that had been the true prize in all his years of hunting me: the gift of a death at my hands, a death befitting his ideals, a martyrdom.

I held my breath as the men were led to the scaffold. Without any theatrics a young hangman came forward and shuffled the prisoners into place, drew the nooses down from the beam and loosened them, then set bags over the prisoners' heads. In the seconds before it was covered, I saw Willard's face, fleetingly. He flinched in panic, his eyes white with terror.

A man of God stepped forward with a Bible held before him like an open hand. When he lifted his face, I saw a large purple birthmark under his chin. He said some words I did not hear, and the young guard nodded. The crowd had begun to hoot and jeer, as though they were a single animal, all teeth and vicious anticipation.

Dread filled me; I clutched Tanna's face to my chest, so that she might not see. The preacher stepped back, and the hangman took his position. He drew hard on a pulley; the floor swung noiselessly away. The two men kicked and struggled, and then were still. The crowd had fallen terribly silent. From where I stood, I could hear the creak of the ropes. The hangman made his unhurried way down the scaffold, ducking underneath. He gripped first the legs of Hazzard, then Willard, and pulled with all his strength, holding them for two minutes each to be sure of their deaths.

The crowd erupted in cheering, laughter and singing. Then it turned away from the spectacle and upon itself: fist fights broke out, men yelled and scuffled. A guard was standing nearby, bored.

And so it was truly over, done.

I stood among the crowd, rocked on all sides. Tanna lifted her face to stare grimly at the lifeless legs swaying there, the trousers darkening with urine. Watching her fascination, I felt a mild irritation at her interest, though it was only natural. And then, just beyond her head, I caught a strong flicker of colour, and I glanced past her to see.

A figure stood half-obscured by the crowd, gazing up at the gallows. He was tall and slightly corpulent, with a long, equine face. He wore a lovingly tailored blue frock coat with a sunflower-yellow waistcoat underneath. In his hands, naked and unadorned, he held a black top hat, which he turned and turned by the brim.

My body drained of all blood, and I felt myself going cold. I stared as the man angled his head to restore his hat. Then he began to turn away.

I stepped forward into the crowd, yelling out, shoving past.

"Titch!" I cried.

I could hear dimly behind me Tanna calling my name, but I did not stop, clawing my way past sweat-laced men, their breath stinking of beer and foul meat. The bright-blue coat was swallowed cleanly by the sea of bodies, then became suddenly visible again. I pushed and shoved my way closer, repeating his name. Just when I believed him altogether lost, he turned, gazing past my head to the gallows beyond. And I saw then the general shape of his face—the bulbous nose, the cheeks rounded and bloated with drink. He was, I understood, another man entirely, a stranger unknown to me.

10

Over the next days I could not get the hanging from my mind—the fear in Willard's eyes before the hood was lowered; the vicious, feral crowd; the sight of Hazzard peering about as if he couldn't understand how everyone could fail to accept that he was not guilty. There was but a thread between life and death, and he had stumbled blamelessly onto the wrong side of it. I felt for him, and was surprised at how intensely I felt for Willard also. He was a wretched man, a pox, but I did not rejoice at the brutality of his end, however well deserved. He too had been a boy once, desirous of understanding the world. And how he had wasted all his talents, all his obvious facility for learning, twisting every new fact and arranging it into senselessness and cruelty. He had spent years trying to cultivate an ethos, and despite possessing a clear intelligence, he had lived his whole life in avoidable savagery.

How easy it is, to waste a life.

I thought of the man I'd followed away, the one I'd thought was Titch. He had not, after all, been him. Given his blunt features I was astonished I could ever have believed it so. And yet the sight of his double had left a shadow on my thoughts, a stain.

I felt then, more strongly than ever, that I must go to Amsterdam. Who knew what I would discover there. But I needed to do myself the justice of at least looking.

I told Tanna she needn't accompany me, but she insisted, and despite my trepidation I was overjoyed. Amsterdam was a city we had heard much spoken of for its unusual aquatic specimens. And the thought of going away without Goff gave an extra excitement to the trip. We began to whisper of it as a lovers' holiday.

We did not of course explain to Goff that Tanna was to come with me. Instead, Tanna told him of her desire to see her aunt Judith again—Goff's other living sister after Henrietta. Tanna told Goff that she'd already written to Judith, and that her aunt had graciously invited her to stay at her house in the countryside. As usual she would be met at the station by Judith's own manservant, an impoverished Hungarian count, and cared for in the utmost luxury and safety.

In all truth Tanna had written no such letter. She trusted that, Goff and Judith being distant in address if not in affection, the two would not meet for years.

I did not understand the pleasure this lie seemed to give to Tanna; but she laughed and was fast-tongued and buzzing with the secrecy of it, and I was delighted to see the return of her good spirits after the previous dark weeks.

And so Goff granted her permission to go to the countryside, and I promised to bring him back from Amsterdam the specimen of the two-headed cetacean, if indeed it existed. Tanna and I would leave separately and meet later at the port.

+ + +

It was a rainy afternoon. The light had gathered like oil on the surface of the Prinsengracht, so that its waters held a lustreless glow, like tea. Tall, narrow houses lined the canal, and we walked before these through the cobbled streets, seeking out Peter Haas's address. I had never received a letter back from him, and so it was with great apprehension that I wandered here, fearing in my heart he was dead. Tanna and I paced the narrow roads with their soaked trees, blinking against a rain that seemed to drain all colour from the landscape.

The journey had so far been miraculous. The day before, we had entered Kees Visser's small laboratory, a shack edging the harbour, and found a man small and pale and grey-browed in his Bath chair, his gaze vicious as a bird's. He had already laid out the specimen. As we approached the bare wooden table smeared with solvents, an instinctive silence fell over us. There, under the ashen light of a flickering lantern, lay the black glob of a stillborn nightmare: two harbour porpoises conjoined in utero, fetuses sharing a single body. They were like some impossible breach in the normality of life, like a sudden vicious murder. We stared in quiet shock at the black, rubbery flesh glistening there. Visser's preservation methods had been flawless, so that the creature seemed as fresh as on the day he had first discovered it. We gathered it into a receptacle made especially for the task and, after much conversation about long-term preservation, returned it for safekeeping to our hotel.

Then, still reeling from the wonder of it, we went out to walk the great city.

So this, I thought, was Amsterdam—city of shadows, in which the Old Masters had sought to capture light as though it were a living thing. I remembered Titch's description of the way those men had painted skin, especially women's skin—the flesh so luminous it had the concentrated lustre of honey. I thought of my own art, of my desire to represent through force of line rather than shade. And I wanted to gather all of this light into myself, to remember and to draw it.

FINALLY, LIKE A plain face asserting itself in a crowd, Peter Haas's house stood out—tall, blue, with a small garden in front. There was a fierce staircase, steep and narrow, and a door very like the door of a crypt, old and black. We glanced in nervousness at each other, dropped the knocker.

A manservant answered, and it was evident he was most unimpressed. He stared up at us with roaming, shining black eyes, and as he studied my scars, he seemed inclined to shut the door.

"Forgive our intrusion," I said, "but we are seeking a Mister Peter Haas? I believe he might have lived here, once upon a time?"

The manservant moistened his colourless lips, frowned.

Someone entered the foyer behind him, a man impeccably and fashionably dressed: the master of the house, clearly, with his air of casual authority. He was very young, his face lineless, his eyes a little vacant-looking, his auburn hair combed in a high peak. Obviously, this was not my Peter House.

I felt sick, terribly embarrassed and disappointed. I did not know why I'd had any notion at all of finding the man here, given his silence at my letters. How far we had travelled for all this. I was struggling with how to explain our presence when Tanna spoke up.

"We were just asking after a Peter Haas. We believe he was the previous resident. Perhaps you might know where he went?"

The young man had been studying my face, taking in my burns, and he glanced now at Tanna, arrested suddenly. I understood the instant attraction—I had felt it once myself—the curiosity of her tan skin, her flinty eyes. He smiled almost imperceptibly, a false lack of interest in his face.

"I am Peter Haas," said he in his thick accent, the voice rich, sonorous, deep.

Hesitation passed between us, and then he said, "My father is Peter Haas also."

I stared at him, his fine good looks and his dazzling clothes, feeling still somehow unconvinced this could be the right home. "Do you know—did your father ever work with a Mister James Wilde?"

The man's eyes drew sharply back to me, and he looked a long while. He spoke briskly with the servant, who turned and, with a courtly brush of the arm, whisked us in.

THE DINING HALL was long and narrow, with age-darkened windows and mahogany panelling. I was surprised to find the table extravagantly laid as though we had been expected. There were game pies, pâtés, potted meats, roasted beef, cold fish. A large bowl of hock-negus shivered at the table's centre.

"Forgive us, you are expecting company," I said. "We shan't stay long."

The young man waved his hand. "It is only our usual lunch. Please, join us."

Before we could say anything more, the young man followed the servant from the room. I glanced nervously at Tanna, listening to his rushed passage through the hall. The light in the room was greenish, and it streamed through the leaded windows with a weight almost like cloth. On the walls hung small oil portraits mounted without frames. The most arresting was of an older woman laid out in white silks in a casket. How stern her face looked, as if she had wrestled death to the last. There came now some noise from a side door, and the young man returned with an older man on his arm.

The older man's eyes were a stark grey, his thin hands traced with veins dark as subterranean streams. On his long, pale face were the brutal brown moles I remembered so well from our days on the cold plains of the North, those bits of flesh that had sometimes struck me as the only spots of colour in an otherwise featureless place.

He grasped me in his arms, and his embrace was like slow-running water, it lacked all strength. He smelled strongly of wet wool. And I was taken back to the snow, the ferocity and the obliterating whiteness.

He stepped back, and began to sign furiously with his hands.

As if cued, his son orated. "You survived. My good dear Washington Black."

I was jarred by this—to hear Peter's words in this thick Dutch accent emanating from the other side of the room, as if the essence of his voice had drifted from his body and taken root outside him, in the form of this boy.

I kept my eyes on Peter's face. "I am so shocked to find you," I said, and it was as though I could barely get my breath. I stared and stared at the face so familiar yet so different. "I did not expect this."

"I'm so glad you are come," said the son, his eyes listing every few seconds from his father's hands to Tanna's face. "However did you find me?"

I explained the strange, halting search, how we had finally discovered him. He nodded and frowned in turn, his face the face of an ancient, a statue. He began to move his hands.

"I did not receive any letters," the younger Haas said for his father. "How odd that they should all go astray."

I shook my head; I could not myself account for it.

"Titch is not here," he continued. "He did come a year and a half ago, or thereabouts, and stay some weeks. But he is long gone."

The disappointment was bitter. "Where did he go?" I said.

With his long, rootlike fingers Peter gestured for us to sit at table. His thinness was astonishing, cadaverous, and it seemed a great irony that with the piles of food laid out here he should appear gaunt and starving. He settled slowly in the wooden chair with its embroidered cushion on the seat, and the rest of us joined him.

"Forgive me—may I present Tanna Goff?" said I. "Her father is G.M. Goff."

Peter's face lit up, and he went into great effusions about her father's contributions to marine zoology, as I had myself once done upon meeting Goff. It was she who directed the conversation back to its source, back to Titch.

Peter sighed gravely. We sat in silence some moments, the room seeming to darken; it was as if he did not want to lift his hands to speak.

"He was not himself, when he arrived." Again he paused. "Rather, he was a new self you would not easily recognize."

I sat forward in my chair; it creaked plaintively beneath me, and it was as though the sound were emanating from inside myself. "His mother's steward said something to the same effect, as did his friend Robert Solander of the Abolitionist Society in London. And yet neither could tell us *how* he was changed. Only that he was."

"Why do you seek him out?" said Peter, frowning.

I hesitated. I felt Tanna's eyes on me, which only increased my nervousness. "I thought him dead."

Peter moistened his lips, but it was a while before he moved his hands. "That Titch, the one you knew—" He paused. "As I said, he is greatly changed."

"How so, sir?" said Tanna, and her voice was like the sudden opening of a window, a shift in temperature.

Peter turned to her. "It is difficult to characterize."

There came a silence in which the son looked openly at Tanna.

"I would say . . . ," said Peter. "I would say that he passed from a place of inquiry to a place of uncontested belief."

We waited for him to elaborate, but his silence was resolute.

"You are saying he became a man of faith?" said Tanna.

Peter smiled. "My dear, he was always a man of faith—his faith was simply in what was measurable. It lacked a god."

"And now he has found one," said I. "A god."

Peter shook his head. "No, I would not say that."

Tanna leaned to ask another question, but I interrupted softly.

"Where did Titch go, in the snow that day?" I said. "Did he say how he survived?"

"That is it, that is my very meaning," said Peter. "We finally spoke of it when he came to Amsterdam all those months ago. He told me, when I asked him, that he was there."

I paused. "Where?"

"He said he returned to us, that he was among us there, at our encampment."

Tanna lifted a soft eyebrow at me.

"I do not understand," I said.

"He did not understand it himself, but he said he was there, at the camp. As if he were returned there and yet not present, as though he lived alongside us in a second realm."

The silence was thick then, as fog. I could smell the cold herring on the table between us, its reek of salt and dill.

"Absurd," muttered Tanna. When we looked to her, she shrugged softly.

"I do not believe it myself," said Peter. "Of course not. And yet he was able to speak with staggering accuracy of our days there after his disappearance—the long search through neighbouring encampments, his father's worsening distress." He turned his eyes to me, grey, sharp. "He spoke of you, Washington. He said that when James fell ill, you spent the afternoons drawing at his bedside. He said you were present at the moment of his last breath."

A fine shiver rose up in me, and I could feel the chair biting into my thighs. I shifted on the seat and could not get comfortable.

"It is not possible, I know," said Peter quietly.

"I do not understand." I shook my head. "He was a man of science."

"And still he is. I would argue that he is more invested in it now than ever before. And yet that interest is in the pursuit of something rather beyond us."

I said nothing; I knew not what to say.

"Things were complicated by his brother's death," said Peter in his son's low, clear voice. "His father's he seemed to tolerate well enough, but Erasmus's . . ." He shook his head.

"Where is he now?" said Tanna, and I felt a soft shock at her voice, as though she had arrived suddenly from some far-off place.

Peter studied her. "He became obsessed with capturing images on paper. He spoke on and on about light, about using sunlight to burn images of faces onto paper. Shadow grams, he called them. He wanted to use the process to capture astral features." He paused, his smile dim. "Frankly, I could not follow the trail of all that he said—his ideas were frenzied and not entirely intelligible. I thought him very tired."

"Did he mention where he was going?" I asked.

"Last I had a letter from him, he was in Morocco, in an area on the outskirts of Marrakesh. I have the address, you might write to him there. I do not know that he's in any mindset to offer a response, but it might be worth the trying."

"Morocco," said I, astonished.

"How long ago did you receive his letter?" said Tanna.

"Some eight or so weeks past. I imagine he is there still. He was very specific in his calculations about the best place to undertake the project."

I peered solemnly about the room, and it was as though I did not recognize objects I had been staring at this long hour; the clocks, the tablecloth—all looked so very different.

"I have something for you," Peter said, standing abruptly.

The three of us were left sitting rather uncomfortably: Tanna glancing from young Peter to me; Peter looking openly at Tanna; and me trying to keep my eyes from the both of them, staring at my chapped hands.

Peter returned carrying a large wood case in his fists. His son rushed to take it from him. "On the chance that you seek him out, please do give him this. It might prove useful to him, from the little I'd understood."

"We are certainly not going to Morocco," said I, baffled. "You would do well to hold on to it, sir."

Peter smiled. "Keep it yourself, then. Please. So fine an instrument is useless in my care. And my son, for all his charms, is no man of science. It is wasted here."

"What is it?"

His smile widened, so that I saw in his features again that impassioned man so devoted to Mister Wilde that he had lived out the entirety of his days in the great man's affection, abandoning a young son and following the scientist through plains of heat and fields of ice into a final ennobled solitude that even a late forgiveness could not brighten.

"My first expedition as a young man," said Peter, "was as a botanist on the *Deliverance*. We travelled to Tahiti, to study the Transit of Venus across the face of the sun. We needed to observe the precise second at which the silhouette of Venus entered, then exited, the sun's disc. It was our chance to map the distance of the sun from the earth. Such an opportunity would not occur again for one hundred years.

"Well, the very night before the transit, our quadrant was stolen. Without it, we could not measure the astronomical angles—the whole expedition would be worthless. I resolved to go immediately in search of the thief.

"This, I tell you, was very unwise. Only the week previous there had been a misunderstanding between a member of our group and one of the Tahitians—a musket had been purloined, and a Tahitian nearly killed by one of our guards. The situation was perilous. We did not understand each other's differing notions of property.

"And so I made my slow way, unarmed, through the narrow trails far up into the hills, accompanied only by an interpreter. The heat was dizzying, suffocating. Finally we reached a small village among the trees, and from each side the people poured out like smoke, jostling and yelling at us. I knew then we were in grave peril.

"By instinct, I drew about me a quick circle in the grass, and everyone began to crowd around, watching. Then, with my interpreter giving me voice, I began to negotiate, to ask and to explain. And wouldn't you know? Very slowly, beginning with this heavy deal case, the quadrant was returned to me, piece by piece." He thumped the large wooden box and grinned. "Me, the only man there without a voice. I spoke for us all. And it all came tumbling back."

11

Tanna and I lay in the grey light of our room in Haarlem, listening to the traffic pass by the open window. There was the clatter of carriages, the low moan of an aged horse. From somewhere far off, so that it carried only faintly to us, came the cry of a child. Ice broke up softly in the water urn on the washstand across the room. In the corner, the two-headed specimen sat hidden in its case.

I kissed her still-damp skin, the hollow at her throat. She tasted of salt. Naked and with her hair spilling about her, she appeared smaller, vulnerable.

"I adore your naturalness," I said, kissing her breast.

She gave a lazy smile. "Is that a euphemism to say I'm plain?"

"I admire your lack of adornment."

"So I *am* plain."

"Surely you noticed Peter Haas staring at you. You augment your beauty gently, with small things, so that your actual features are the more noticeable."

"You have been reading a manual on how to make love to a woman, I see. God save us." She smiled faintly. "The irony is that for years and years I begged my father to allow me to wear jewels, and to paint my face, and to dress in the latest fashions. And he resisted me a long time, long past the point when such a thing was natural for girls my age. When finally he allowed it, I was given a purse of money and told I could purchase the four items I most desired: a dress of pale muslin; a handbag with a single emerald clasp; a skin powder; and a very red lipstick. I put them on at once."

"And you looked garish, like a street mime."

"I looked breathtaking—very like a living doll. My father was so astounded by the transformation that he apologized for having so long refused me. I think he saw at once the fine match I could make, the easy life I might have as a beauty. And yet. Something happened to me, dressed so. I became emphasized in the world, sharpened. I stood out, and felt the constant touch of others' eyes. And the more people looked, the more effaced I felt, as if I were disappearing. It was the strangest feeling. I did not feel as though all those glances were scraping away some essence, though that is possibly a part of it. It's more that the heightened expectation made me retreat deeper into myself. I had a feeling as of physical obstruction, as though I were standing in front of myself—I needed to shove this second self away, to open the view to the true self. I was so dull in those months, Wash. At every conversation, a great vacancy would fill my eyes, an air of departure, as if I'd already left the room. I began to get a reputation for being stupid. Pretty and stupid."

"No one could think you stupid, Tanna."

"Silly, then. Trivial."

"Well, now you are silly and plain," I said teasingly, kissing at her hair, "what purpose do you serve?"

"To stop you acting out stupid whims."

I smiled, but felt softly criticized. I settled back onto the pillows.

"Mister Haas's story about his stolen instrument took on quite the opposite resonance for me from the one he'd intended, I think," she said. "I kept thinking, but what of the poor Tahitians? Being shot at, having to suffer the condescension of these strange arrivals and their frightening tools." She shrugged.

"Morocco," I said. "I would never have thought it. I wonder what it is that drew him there."

"Shadow grams, wasn't it?"

"Why say it that way?"

"What way?"

"Disdainfully."

She breathed out deeply. "Your obsession is grown so relentless you have even begun seeing him in strangers." She rolled onto her side. "At Newgate, when you ran from me in the crowd—you thought you saw him, didn't you? And now you are already thinking of rushing off again."

"Rushing off?" I said.

She gave a bitter shake of the head, a few fine strands clinging damply to her forehead. "Must we pretend? Must we entertain this ruse?"

I said nothing, watching the light drift in a slow creep across the ceiling.

"I used to believe it was only a matter of finding the source of your origins. That Titch represented your early life, that there was something unresolved there. But we did that, we went to the Abolitionist Society. Kit was your mother. And yet here we find ourselves, in Amsterdam." She raised her softly rounded thighs, hooking her arms across them. I stared at the back of her matted head as she mumbled something. Realizing she had not been heard, she turned her face to me. "Do you mean to kill him? Is that it?"

I glanced at her, taken aback.

"Of course you do not—I say it only to show you how senseless all this has been. How confusing and strange it all seems to me. I do not understand it—I have tried and tried and I do not. Why do you hunt him so? Do you imagine you will be made stronger by this?" She shook her head. "You will be weakened. You will be wrecked."

I was flooded with anxiety, with sadness. I knew in some measure she was right. But something in me would not cease—a great lunging forward, a striving rooted as deeply in me as the thirst for water. I had gone this far, seeking a truth that might not exist; I could only go on.

"Is it because you feel my father stole your idea?" said Tanna, her voice anguished, her face calm. "Is that why you run from us? Ocean House was taken from you, and now you are moving farther and farther away from it, as if to rid yourself of the loss."

I knew I should bite my tongue. Instead, rising up on one elbow, I said, "Well, was it not taken from me? I've spent over a year working out the science of it—even now I work on it. And what will it bring me in the end? Nothing. My name nowhere."

She was trembling softly. "Is it a question of your name?"

"No," I said, and it was the truth, though it also wasn't. I knew only that I had believed the project would be a testament to my contributions in the world, and that this, somehow, would mark my passage through it, confirm that my existence had been meaningful, and worthy. But already that certainty was fading; I did not know what to believe anymore.

"Washington," she said.

"I am tired," I said softly.

She hesitated.

The room was darkening, cooling, and in the moist air the whine of a fly could be heard.

"My father's brother," Tanna began, and her voice was so quiet I almost could not hear her. "Uncle Sunshine, we called him. He was very morose. When he would visit my father, I had only to see his carriage in the distance to begin running away. He came and he moped and was gloomy. I suppose it's the Goff temperament—even Henrietta and Judith are often melancholy. Father, too. And of course Aunt Miranda killed herself. But Uncle Sunshine, he seemed to delight in his misery. My laughter only seemed to sadden him further—all children saddened him, as if they were but small reminders of an age when he was truly happy.

"When my grandmother died, she left him a sum of money, as she did to all her children—three hundred pounds each. My father spent his immediately on scientific instruments. My uncle? He bought himself a grand headstone for his plot in the family cemetery.

"He went every day to visit his own gravestone, leaving flowers upon it. Any small purchase he allowed himself would be tied in ribbons and laid chastely on the grave. Once he left himself the dark Portuguese figs we'd given him from our trip to the Serra da Estrela. How I'd wanted him to taste those figs. But onto the grave they went. In the end, he visited that grave more than he visited us. It became his sole destination. When finally he died, it was like a homecoming."

I smiled, sadly. "Did he even exist?"

Tanna rested her damp head on my chest. "The world is large, larger than we sometimes allow it to be." She breathed shallowly, her face pressed against my skin.

How exhausted I felt, how drained.

"I will go with you," she said.

I had already closed my eyes, and falling asleep, I felt myself reach out for her fingers.

12

We returned together to England with our specimen, and it was never a question that I would again be leaving.

I did not want to bring her to Morocco, to a place possibly inhospitable and dangerous to her. There was also Ocean House to prepare, and the frailty of her father to consider. For though Goff was hearty and in the best of health, he was still sixty-six years old, and we did not want him climbing ladders and lifting heavy equipment. His was a peculiar old age in which the outward strength of his body seemed to signal an inner weakness. It was as though some hidden thing lay waiting to break out, as though he would wake suddenly one morning white-haired, blind, deaf and stumbling, in an explosion of old age.

And yet, to our surprise, Goff gave his blessing, even insisted. He had discovered almost at once that Tanna had accompanied me to Amsterdam. Wandering in New Bond Street one afternoon to clear his head, he'd glanced up and spied his sister Judith herself leaving Savory and Moore's Pharmacy. He accosted her, and the bewildered woman wept openly in the street, confused at his anger. He followed her to her carriage, ranting and raving as she cried great loud thespian sobs, pleading that she knew nothing of the matter, so that at last a man tried to intervene, thinking Goff was a random harasser. Goff returned home, and was just then making plans to hunt us down when we arrived with the porpoise in tow, glistening like onyx on its freshened bed of ice.

He was too shocked by the creature to scream at us. Staring down at it, his face blanched and he was silent a long while. Finally he said, "I have never seen such beauty in such ugliness."

We were scolded for our lie, but that was all. The next days were spent making arrangements for the two-headed creature, testing Visser's suggested methods of long-term preservation, discussing the ways in which it might best be displayed. If our octopus from Nova Scotia did not recover, this, perhaps, might be our centrepiece.

Goff began to speak of another colleague of his, a marine zoologist in Marrakesh. "He wrote of a very rare squid." He spent the evening mapping out the location where we might find the man.

And so the weeks passed in making preparations for our journey, and in hard work. A silence reigned at Ocean House, the outside world dropping away. With the door shut tight, the air reeked greenly of preservative fluid and rotted plants, of stagnant, murky water. Sun streamed through the dirty windows, dust spinning in its glow. I turned all about, seeing our tanks of Aesop prawns and molluscs and crabs and sea worms and polyps. A display of velvet fiddlers writhed silently in the corner.

I felt, in those moments of looking around, ferociously proud—of this strange, exquisite place where people could come to view creatures they believed nightmarish, to understand these animals were in fact beautiful and nothing to fear. But a part of me felt also somehow anguished, ravaged, torn at. For I glimpsed, in each and every display, all my elaborate calculations, my late nights of feverish labour. I saw my hand in everything—in the size and material of the tanks, in the choice of animal specimens, even in the arrangement of the aquatic plants. I had sweated and made gut-wrenching mistakes, and in the end my name would be nowhere. Did it matter? I did not know if it mattered. I understood only that I would have to find a way to make peace with the loss, or I would have to leave the whole enterprise behind and everyone connected with it.

One tank held the drifting pink rag of a jellyfish, and next to it I watched one filled entirely with nudibranchia. Very slowly I went to it, and I pressed my hand to the cool glass.

13

The light was dazzling; it shuddered in waves off the rooftops dotting the white plain. So grand was it, so powerful, that we raised constant hands to our eyes, blinded by the haze.

It had all been a great mistake. Peter had arranged for a guide to meet us, but that man was nowhere to be discovered at the loud, bustling port. And so we were obliged to take rooms in Marrakesh while I wrote to Peter of the error, begging his assistance in procuring a second guide. There was little to do but wait.

In the slow, hot days we made several attempts to find Goff's marine zoologist. We were led on many twisted routes, the last ending in confrontation with a man demanding heavy compensation. And so we gave up the hunt. Instead we began to explore the city, with its smells of clementine and dried leather and fresh plums, the stench of donkey excrement and the sweating pelts of camels penned at market. We passed a man pulling at a rope threaded through the nose of a furious camel, blood spilling from its head in dark-red stripes. How indignantly the beast lifted its jaw. It kicked and bucked and gave out guttural roars, and this made no impression at all on the noise and bright laughter of the bustling outpost. Tanna looked away, and seeing her turn her face, an onlooker came over to us with his shuffling gait and began to mime an explanation. But we could not understand him and finally, with a look of profound disappointment, he went away.

Later we strolled the markets, wondering about a possible return to England, though this struck me as a defeat. The stalls were all distinct: some were overhung with beautifully woven baskets, some with dusty red peppers, some with dyed wool bursting forth in a riot of crimsons and yellows and blues. In the rope stalls several rope makers sat fast at work, their hands flitting quickly over the hemp. The jewellers had a courtyard all their own, and from beneath the shadowed awnings their gems winked like human glances.

I discovered a jeweller who spoke broken English. All at once I began to ask after the strange Englishman in the desert, if he had any knowledge of this man. I asked also after Goff's colleague. He peered out at me from his dark robes, his face vacant as a freshly washed plate. Then he broke into a sudden smile and, in a shiver of shuddering shrugs, said no, no, no, no.

All this we took in with the nervousness of having left the known world behind, of moving blindly forward. With each day I became more convinced that Titch was here no longer. We grew exhausted, and though I was careful not to show Tanna my fearfulness, she could no doubt sense it.

One morning I paused by the side of a market to wash my hands in a basin. I felt a man's gaze on me, and lifted my face.

He stepped forward as though summoned. I stood and dried my hands uneasily on my pant legs. He was a slight fellow with an angular, jutting jaw, so that he appeared to always be disagreeing with something, though his eyes were kind.

He stood before me, the sun behind me gilding his brown eyes the colour of burnt butter. Tanna looked nervously across at me from the folds of her blue shawl.

"Washington Black?" said he, flattening the *a*'s to *e*'s.

To our surprise he was the very man who was to have led us to Titch in the first place. He had been sick these last days, he explained in his broken English. Now recovered, he had come to the city with the dim hope of finding us. How astonishing that it should actually come to pass.

And so he led us in a small, rattling caravan towards a seemingly empty horizon. The paths carved from the desert were vast and twisted, and as we creaked along the sandy passageways, away from the great noise of Marrakesh, I felt a sense of diminishment, as if we were disappearing in the heat and the light. The air felt very tight, full of salt. My eyes began to itch at their corners, and as the hours lengthened, a fine trace of blood leaked through a crack in my lower lip. I held a damp cloth across my nose, breathing.

"I promised your father I'd return you safely," said I.

"And you shall keep the promise," Tanna murmured, half-asleep.

I peered across the hazy plain. "How far do you suppose Dahomey is from here?"

But she was barely listening. Her blue shawl was draped over her head and face, and from the dark folds her eyes shone out incredibly clear, almost orange in the light. As we cantered through the landscape, all speech seemed to drain from us, so that even the instinct for it died. With each mile the terrain shifted, brightening and darkening, and every hour I became convinced we were lost, that even our driver must be disoriented by the changing light. I peered out at the plain, exhausted. Here again, through no volition of his own, Titch had brought me to a place of great unfamiliarity.

The hours passed. We stopped to eat and relieve ourselves, still not much speaking. In the arid wind I began to hear sounds, though there was no life for miles. Strangely I could not place the origins of the noises—the ones from the west seeming to emanate from the east, the ones in the south drifting from the north. My skull felt dry in my head; I drank. The heat was all at once suffocating, then dropped away in layers.

Abruptly, night fell. It was as though someone had set a lid over the earth, so quickly did it happen. The stars came suddenly, like sparks, illuminating the plain. And just then, what looked like small buildings rose up in the distance; they were so much what I wanted to see in that moment that I felt I had imagined them. Mute, we cantered up to a series of sudden walls; it was some time before I realized the walls were actual houses. There were few windows to the street. I could just make out, through the narrow buildings, the wide circle of a darkening courtyard. We disembarked, our legs stiff, as the driver cut down our belongings in an explosion of dust.

It did not seem we could have come to the right place. This was no town as Peter had described it, but rather a few scattered dwellings, built almost as an afterthought at the desert's edge. It was difficult to picture survival here, so far from the lushness of the city. There was a feel of desolation and abandonment, of darkening distances.

Just then a boy stepped out from the courtyard. He could not have been more than nine years old, his bones thin as ropes, prying from beneath the skin. He had an oblong but delicately made face in which the eyes were sunken deeply. He appeared both tired and fresh, like someone made privy to a damaging truth before he could fully make sense of it. Dust threaded the strands of his glossy black hair.

Our guide beckoned the boy in a sharp voice, and in an exchange that struck me as both plaintive and tender, something was understood, some agreement reached. The boy finally gestured for us to follow, and I glanced questioningly back at our guide, at the folds of sweat in his dust-caked face. He gave his friendly smile, nodded.

I began to drag our bags by the rope, so that an eerie sound echoed off the ground. We followed the boy in the direction of the courtyard. In the evening shadows I could see little before me, and an uneasiness rose in me, the hard knowledge of having arrived in a country in which I could not even speak to ask for water, into which I had brought Tanna unthinkingly and without defences. I stared at her veiled shape there, her body tiny and fragile.

It was as though the courtyard contained its own weather; the air was suddenly stiller, cooler. There was a smell of boiled peppers, of clean fabric hung in the wind to dry. The dusk seemed younger here somehow, and in the open yard, its swept stone so white it had the sheen of a frozen pond, a great covered object loomed darkly. We paused, startled by the enormousness of the shadow's size. It was silhouetted against the starlit sky and the walls of the compound like a natural obstruction, yet one could see that whatever lay beneath the tarp was not natural. My eyes adjusted, and still I could not make out what it was.

There came some movement from the side of the courtyard. A man had stepped from a doorway, a live hen struggling in his hands. He held the bird by its legs, and in the darkness its feathers appeared very white, like wax. It was clear that the man meant to kill it for his evening meal; indeed, that it should have been brought inside alive in the first place struck me as strange. We watched in silence as he crossed the courtyard pinching and prodding at the chicken, testing for the meaty places.

He shifted, and in the dim light of the moon I saw him, saw his face. And before I even understood, a great pain passed through my body and I called out, "Titch."

The man turned; in his surprise he let go of the hen. The bird flapped madly away, its free limbs scuttling across the courtyard and into the shadows.

He watched after it some moments, his harsh breathing filling the yard.

"You are late for supper," he called back, but in the thin grey light I stepped forward and saw he was trembling.

14

The door was made of four weathered planks hammered together with metal, and he led us through this inside, into the yellow candlelight of his front room. It was cool in here, though warmer than outside, the walls thick, the few windows tiny. The room was small and fastidiously clean, and among the local tapestries and baskets were chairs and tables very much in the European style, as though he'd sought to bring order to this world through the familiar.

We passed through this place to the smaller room in back, and it was this low-ceilinged space, with its doorway he had to dip his head to get through, that was evidently where he did his true living. There was a cot upon which the greyed sheets were strewn like a sleeping dog. Books had been stacked at the lone window; by the far wall, on a wooden block notched by scratches, sat a half-cut red pepper, spilling its seeds.

He paused at the room's centre, and it was as if he did not want to—as if he wished to keep moving so as to avoid our eyes. He turned to us with a tired smile, and at this full glimpse of his body, this full sight of his face, tears rose to my eyes at the great familiarity and difference in him. He was as he had ever been, his green eyes bright and inquisitive, the white scar rising like a thread from either side of his mouth. His dress was casual, and English, wrinkled white linen shirt-tails and pale trousers, and though he did appear different in them, older, they were not what jarred. Rather, some indefinable thing had shifted in his features, his eyes especially—there was beneath his gaze such concentrated pain that for a moment I thought, It is not him, we have come to the wrong place. He was like someone only slowly becoming aware of a malady taking root inside him, confused by the first stirrings of tiredness. It was as though, in the four years of his absence, he had come closer to an understanding of darkness, closer to knowing what his cousin Philip had always accepted, that destruction was within us, and nothing we could hide from.

"Washington," said he in his soft, low voice. "I dreamed you would come. How grown you are."

So empty a comment, after what felt a lifetime of being lost to each other. The urge was strong in me to embrace him, and yet I held back, I could not do it, I could not close the warm, dim distance between us.

We sat in the flickering shadows of the front room—Titch, Tanna, our guide, the young boy and myself—cupping warm bowls of vegetable stew in our hands. For all my hunger I couldn't eat, couldn't take my eyes from the changed and familiar face. In the orange light his jaw appeared long, horselike, and he chewed every bite with great consideration. He seemed to be feeling out each vegetable with his tongue. When he caught sight of me watching him, he smiled pathetically.

"Toothache," said he, abashed. "I have not the courage to pull it out."

"There are no doctors here?" said Tanna.

Titch was chewing by one side of his mouth. "I fear their medicine."

I listened to the others eat, searching his face. He seemed not to look at me, to speak generally to everyone, his eyes meeting mine rarely. And though it had been but four years, I found I could not read him; if he was astonished or saddened or irritated at our appearance here, I did not know. His manners were elegant, and it was as though they created a barrier around him.

"How serendipitous, then, that we arrived just in time to scare away your chicken," Tanna smiled. "There are no bones to contend with in vegetables."

"A very merciful act."

His comment somehow brought to Tanna's mind the scene of the bleeding camel, and she began to describe it.

"It was rabid, perhaps," said Titch. "When one goes rabid it must be killed, or it will kill people."

"Kill people?"

"They crouch on the chests of sleeping men, suffocating them."

Tanna brought a hand to her mouth, but the gruesomeness of the story obviously interested her.

How strange all this was—that after months of speaking harshly of Titch, Tanna was as gentle and polite with him as I'd ever known her to be with anyone. I had watched the slow transformation taking place within her—the coldness with which she'd first given her name, then the growing interest in his formidable presence, as if she could not help herself; and finally her apparent pity at his outcast circumstances, as though he had not himself chosen them. Perhaps it was a question of his mental fortitude: she too saw the anguish in his eyes and did not wish to tax him further, knowing that our surprise arrival here would be strain enough. And she was right to be kind. But I did feel as though she'd left me standing alone, in a resentment I alone would carry. I stared at Titch's face and a great sadness rose up in me, but I felt wounded too, angry, adrift.

Outside, the tarp thrummed in a sudden wind.

"Your arrival could not have been better timed," said Titch. "We are awaiting a storm. You would not have wished to be caught out in it."

"And yet there was so little wind earlier," said Tanna.

"Change here is swift. It burns hot and then cold. Bright and then dark."

"I've heard it said there is no weather like African weather."

"The regions differ vastly. Though I suppose it could be said generally."

I peered across at the boy, at his thin, intelligent face. The traces of dust in his hair gave him an air of age, but he was so very young, and hopelessly at sea in our English conversation. He had not been formally introduced to us and it began to seem he would not be. Titch looked at him rarely, and always with an instructive frown; I sensed a tenderness there, so that a pain rose in my throat and I looked swiftly away.

"What is that outside, under the tarp?" Tanna said. "We had such a fright."

Titch was chewing thoughtfully. I sensed again his great effort not to look at me. "You called at Granbourne, you mentioned. My mother was well?"

"Extremely well," said Tanna. "She had just returned from a ride."

"So her bile was up. Was she perfectly horrid?"

Tanna paused. "I believe she was tired."

"She is my mother, and you are therefore too polite to impugn her. But your good manners do not make her bad ones any less awful." Titch sighed. "Did she feed you, at the very least? I do hope you got a good supper."

Tanna shrugged helplessly. "It was for the best, I believe. We might have found ourselves on the menu."

Titch smiled. "Well, I do apologize for anything she might have said to upset you."

How eager he was to accept responsibility for a slight done by his mother; but where was the remorse towards me, the guilt?

"At the very least she let you know of my whereabouts, and so I am grateful to her," said he.

Tanna paused, then explained how we had come to find him.

Titch laughed. "Well, all the same, you are here. I cannot believe you came all this way." For the first time since our arrival he looked squarely at me. And to my surprise I thought I glimpsed, in the sheen of his eyes by the dim candlelight, an uneasiness nearing fear.

"You said you dreamed me," I said abruptly. They were the first words I had spoken and I felt the others turn towards me in surprise. "What did you mean?"

"Dreamed you?" said Titch.

"When I arrived. That you had dreamed I would come."

"Did I?" Titch shook his head, as if genuinely puzzled. "I cannot imagine my meaning."

15

The hour grew late. Titch insisted Tanna take the back room with the cot; I was invited to sleep on the settee in the front room we'd eaten in. He himself would sleep alongside the boy in a tent pitched outside. When Tanna objected, Titch explained, "We might have done so anyway, on a night such as this. To observe the stars."

"You said there was a storm coming."

"It is well-sheltered from the weather," Titch said. "I'm more concerned about scorpions and snakes."

"Dear god."

"Rest easy." Titch smiled tiredly. "Do stay off the floor."

And taking the boy by the shoulder, he went out, our driver following quietly behind.

I could not get comfortable for the sensation that I was lying where Titch's own body sat, day after day. I twisted and turned. There was also the cold; how surprising that such cold should exist in the desert. When finally I did drift off I dreamed of Ocean House. But it was no grey wood building half-salvaged from a fire. It was a huge glass structure, an enormous greenhouse, its sides all windows, reflecting the frenzied trees around it. Everything was shimmer and light. I stood staring, my eyes wincing up at the bright, rattling panes.

All at once Big Kit was beside me. I felt no tension from her, no pain—she appeared to be in a state of resolute calm, as if the hard layer of fury she'd worn about her like an armour had been scraped away. Her cheeks looked hollowed in the dusk, her face speckled with the late afternoon light sieving through the trees. She seemed in her silence neither fully awake nor sleeping, nor even dead or alive. She had outgrown such borders, passed through them into some murkier place. There was in her orange eyes a brightness like copper, a hot, lucent sheen. But she did not glance at me. I thought I should reach out, take her hand as I'd always done. Instead I only stood quietly beside her, feeling the heat pouring from her skin, the good living warmth of it. The wind held a smell of rain, of mud, though the sun lingered. Our reflections shivered in the mirrored panes like spectres.

And then I awoke.

My BAD RIBS ached, so that I rose from the settee and paced the small room. I wanted to go outside, to take the air. The cold was as suffocating as any heat. I flattened my palm along the wall, guiding my slow way forward by the coarse plaster. The room smelled still of boiled vegetables.

I was disoriented, and found myself instead in the back room with the cot. How I could get lost in a two-room dwelling I did not understand. In the dark I could see Tanna's sleeping form breathing softly. It was the smaller of the rooms, the walls painted stark white and left bare of portraiture. There were thin cracks in the plaster and I could hear small creatures scuttling in and out of these breaches.

I was feeling my way towards the door when I heard Tanna call out, "Who's there?"

"You are awake?" I said, going to sit by her cot. Moonlight fell in a large pane on the wall above her prone body. "Forgive me, I did not mean to frighten you."

I felt her soft grip on my shoulder, and I pressed my lips to her moist hand.

"You could not sleep?" she yawned.

"I had a dream," said I.

"What was it?"

I kissed her hand again, patted it. The moonlight began to drift slowly across the stippled whitewash, so that the wall appeared almost lunar.

"England feels very far away," she murmured.

"It does."

"Ocean House feels very far away."

Indeed, it was as though many years had passed, so much another life did that seem.

"Do you despise me?" she said softly. I turned to her in the darkness, not understanding. "For being kind to him?"

"Of course not—you are decent, merciful. It is why I love you."

She hesitated. "His eyes—never in all my life have I seen such pain in a man's eyes. You did not tell me he looked like that."

"He did not always. When I knew him he was different."

"It must be so shocking to you."

I said nothing, brushing grit from my hand.

"Is it as you imagined?" she said, yawning again. "All this? Is it what you had pictured?"

"One could hardly imagine this."

"No." She fell suddenly silent.

"What is it?"

I sensed her turning away in the dark. "Nothing."

But I thought I understood what she would not ask. I understood she desired to know if I had found what I was seeking, if this trip would finally satisfy my erratic pursuit of an unanswerable truth, if it would calm my sense of rootlessness, solve the chaos of my origins for me. She wanted to know if anything would be laid to rest, or if we'd continue to drift through the world together, going from place to place until I made her like me, so lacking a foothold anywhere that nowhere felt like home.

"It was a madness, coming here," I said quietly. "I am sorry."

But she had already softened into sleep.

I NOTICED THEN a door just beyond her cot, leading outside. I went forward slowly and opened it, the breeze rushing in. Above the low roof the heavens were vast, filled with bright stars. I could hear a thrumming in the distance, and I thought it must be the large tarp in the courtyard out front, shuddering in the strong wind. The air was even cooler, denser, and I shivered. I looked up into the illuminated plate of the sky.

I saw a door to the very right of me, as if there were another room. It was half-open and spilling with light, as in a dream. Uneasy, I went towards it.

Going in, I stepped instantly back.

Dozens of scientific instruments had been piled here, so many papers and scales and scopes that the door could only open partway before striking a desk on which a candle was set. It was as if a single obsessive thought had been made manifest in these tools; each steel piece seemed an idea cast aside, each glass scope a possible answer.

Nailed to the walls were several glossy black sheets; in the middle of them, like drops of milk dissolving in ink, were blots of the purest white. They were ghostly, strange, like phantoms of the human brain. I stood mesmerized before them, so that it was some time before my eyes roamed to the picture pinned beside them. It was a portrait of the boy, his eyes clear and dark-lashed, his right cheek distorted by poor fixatives. It was as if light had attacked one side of his face, as if the chemicals had been unstable.

"Those are the moon."

I turned to find Titch still dressed in his clothes from the evening. He appeared less nervous, though the uneasiness was there still. He stepped forward. "I attempted to capture an image of the moon by polishing sheets of silver-plated copper, treating them with fumes and exposing them at midnight." He traced his slender, emerald-ringed finger from the white blots to the child's face. "The process works much better with human faces than astral features, as you see. But my goal is to have them be equally sharp. I think it is a question of distance. Of distance from one's subject."

I searched his face, feeling there was something now more recognizable in it.

"But human faces are so interesting," said I.

"Yes, to be sure. But when you are looking at one face, you are not looking at another. You are privileging that face. You are deciding who is worthy of observation and who is not. You are choosing who is worth preserving." He shook his head, and it was as though he was too tired to hear the irony in his words.

I gestured at the portrait of the young boy. "He is your assistant?"

Titch hesitated. “He is learning.” He glanced away. “It comes, though slowly.”

I nodded.

“I did not—” said he, and I turned to find him flushed. “I was afraid you might think . . . I did not want you to think I had merely replaced you.”

Silence passed between us; strange birdcall echoed from beyond the walls.

“You are happy here?” I said.

He looked warily at me. “There are several kinds of happiness, Washington. Sometimes it is not for us to choose, or even understand, the one granted us.”

It was supposed to be a wisdom; it sounded instead like something he said to comfort himself these cold nights when only the sound of wind and strange cries could be heard.

I felt the cold running into my bones. I shivered, gripping my coat close around me.

“Shall we go inside?” said Titch.

“Where did you go, when you left your father’s camp?” I said. “Peter said you spoke some madness about it—that you had been there among us the whole time, that you could see us. But where did you truly go?”

He moistened his lips, but said nothing.

“A search party was sent out to find you, from your father’s encampment. Did you never chance to cross paths? How is it they never discovered you?”

Again he seemed disinclined to say anything.

“I have travelled all this way,” I said.

He exhaled a slow breath, and I thought he would speak, but

he was silent a long while. Finally he said, "I knew you would never leave me." He paused. "I could not go in a simple way."

"So it was a ruse? You only made it look as if you left?"

"I left." He frowned out at the air before us, as though he saw something in it. But he said nothing more.

"I might have died there," I said.

"You had Peter, you had my father. I would not have left you otherwise. I knew you would be well cared for." He turned to me. "You were with my father, when he died?"

I stared, nodded rigidly.

"That was always a great comfort to me, that you were there. My brother died also, some two years ago. I had thought his death would shatter me, but it did not. I was shocked at myself, at the callousness I could feel. We were boys together, we were blood. And yet, nothing."

What would he have me say to this? His brother had been a cruel, evil man and it struck me as only just that no one should cry at his passing. I was only surprised that Haas and Solander had spoken so differently, had said Titch had been devastated.

"I went some years ago to clean up Faith. I put all its records in London, as you know." He glanced in pity at me. "I saw your Kit on the list of the deceased. I had not known it then, that she was your mother." He frowned softly. "She died naturally, I understood."

I knew it was a kindness he was trying to extend, an attempt to bridge the distance he sensed between us. And yet I did not wish to share this wound with him; I did not wish to share it with anyone.

"You told me once, when I was drawing, 'Be faithful to what you see, and not what you are supposed to see.'"

"Did I say that?" Titch seemed genuinely surprised.

"You did. And yet it always did seem to me that you never lived by it yourself."

He paused. "What do you mean?"

"You did not see me—you did not look at me, and see me. You wanted to, but you didn't, you failed. You saw, in the end, what every other white man saw when he looked at me."

He frowned softly. "That is untrue."

I moistened my lips, and it was as though I could finally ask it, the question that had twisted and defined my life.

But he wanted to go, and starting to walk ahead, he said, "Come, there is something I would show you."

"Titch," I said sharply, and it surprised me, the depth of the anguish in my voice.

He stopped. There was an expression of sad warning in his face, as if he wished to ward off what I might say.

I stepped forward, my heart punching in my rib cage. "Why did you choose me?"

He stood expressionless.

"That first evening, when Big Kit and I were serving dinner for your brother. You chose me quite deliberately that night. I remember it. You said I was just the right size for your Cloud-cutter. You chose me because I would make the perfect ballast."

There was a curious look on his face.

"Do you deny it?"

He frowned. "Why do you ask me this?"

"That is your answer?"

He shook his head. "I said it quite plainly at the time. Your size is indeed why I chose you. I made no secret of it."

I smiled angrily, feeling both vindicated and desperately heartsick.

"What else would I have had to go on, not knowing you at the time? It is why I chose you, but it is not why I engaged you to help with my experiments. It is not why I befriended you. Do you suppose just anybody could have grasped the complexity of those equations? You were a rare thing."

"Thing?"

"Person. A rare person."

"Not so rare that I could not be abandoned. Not be replaced." I felt a pain high up in my throat, and when I spoke, there was a pressure in my voice I could not control. "And so you took in a young black boy, and you educated him as if he were an English boy. For his benefit, though? Or so that you might write about it?"

He looked quietly shocked. "I have never written about it."

"You took me on because I was helpful in your political cause. Because I could aid in your experiments. Beyond that I was of no use to you, and so you abandoned me." I struggled to get my breath. "I was nothing to you. You never saw me as equal. You were more concerned that slavery should be a moral stain upon white men than by the actual damage it wreaks on black men."

Even as I spoke these words, I could hear what a false picture they painted, and also how they were painfully true.

He stared at me. Slowly, ever so slowly, he shook his head. He peered calmly at me with his dark-green eyes.

I stood, my mouth dry, waiting.

Again he shook his head. "I treated you as family."

How strange, I thought, looking upon his sad, kind face, that this man had once been my entire world, and yet we could come to no final understanding of one another. He was a man who'd done far more than most to end the suffering of a people whose toil was the very source of his power; he had risked his own good comfort, the love of his family, his name. He had saved my very flesh, taken me away from certain death. His harm, I thought, was in not understanding that he still had the ability to cause it.

"Please," said he, "just let me show it to you."

I felt the blood shifting in my body, a heat rising to my cool skin.

"Washington," he said.

I looked upon his pained face, and I went.

16

He led me back to the passageway I'd come from, through the twisting, fragrant halls of the house and into the courtyard outside.

It took my eyes some moments to adjust to this new darkness. And I glimpsed in the courtyard, rising blackly into the sky, the shadow Tanna and I had passed upon first entering. It had been uncovered, and squinting, I could just make out a tangle of wood and cloth and metal rods. And then at once I was struck silent.

For there, lying sideways on the pale ground, was the elegant shape of a small two-man boat. Its strong white masts rose at a slant towards the sky. I saw, stretching from either side of its hull, wings of prehistoric proportions—the wings of a creature frightening and mythic.

I stood aghast, the masts thrumming above me in the high wind.

"I have been constructing this some years now," Titch said, frowning up at the masts. "I still mean to cross the Atlantic. I had been thinking, actually, of Barbados as a destination. It would seem to me fitting to take the craft to the shores there."

I stared at him, and every account of his madness came flooding back. And yet I knew he was not mad—I knew he was simply re-enacting his past as a form of comfort, conveniently forgetting all that had been bad and wrong about it. And I understood too that he was setting himself up for a second failure, that this craft would not take him even halfway to that lost island, that he would either have to give it up or die in the trying.

As I peered at the glorious white masts, the hull's dark, polished wood, the wings splaying from either side, I felt again the wet winds from the turquoise sea, the touch of the royal palm's leaves in bloom, the fine, dry grass under my heels. I felt the damp of cane toads and leaf-toed geckos in my fists; I smelled the hot rust of machetes in the heat; and a bright pain came into my head then, filling it, so that I grimaced and shut my eyes.

17

We sat on opposite sides of the floor, drinking mint tea in the near dark. Outside, the wind had picked up, blew in powder-white gusts against the windows. The boy had wandered sleepily inside, lay snoring softly on the floor in the far corner.

Titch dredged a bent spoon through the leaves in his glass, silent. We had lit a single candle, its flame so little that our hands and faces were just visible. I noticed a sore on the back of his thin white hand, saw he had been troubling it much; it looked weeping and raw.

"How far are we from Dahomey?" said I.

He yawned, rubbed at an eye. "Dahomey?" He paused, searching my face.

"What is it?"

"When your face was injured," he said softly. "I remember you mentioning Dahomey. You thought you had been reborn there." He sensed he had embarrassed me, and ventured, "It is not near. The journey would be most dangerous for one such as you. I would not risk it."

We were silent some moments. He gave a great yawn.

"You should go to bed," I said.

He regarded me sleepily some moments. "Do you remember Mister Edgar Farrow?"

"I do."

"He is dead. I only just had the news."

I struggled to remember that strange man's face. I recalled his kindness, how it bore no correlation to his darker, unsavoury hobbies. "I am very sorry."

"He had been ill. Indeed, I was surprised to find him still able in body when we last saw him."

"He did look ill."

"He was a great man. All that he did for people."

Silence passed. Then, in some surprise at myself, I began to speak of Ocean House, of what I hoped it would be, in the end. And I knew then, in my very mention of it, that I would return to London and fight to undo the expunging of my name, that I would devote myself wholly to the project and seek some credit for it.

As he listened, I could see in Titch's face something of the ferocious interest of his days at Faith, when the sight of even a beetle sent him rushing for his magnifiers, to lose the whole day following its trail on an ironwood leaf. "I know you do not desire my affirmation, Wash," he said, "but what you are building—it sounds astonishing."

I looked momentarily down at my hands, glanced back up.

Titch was hesitating. "When I said outside that you were family—" He paused. "That was always my feeling towards you, at least. I hadn't any idea of mistreating you. I tried to be kind."

I looked at his tired, anxious face, saying nothing.

It seemed as if he would speak something more, but he fell silent.

"John Willard died," I said.

Titch glanced up warily. "I had heard that as well. And that it was no pretty death."

"You hear much here at the edge of the world."

"Indeed—I am more abreast of things here than I ever was in England."

I thought of his father, Mister Wilde, at his outpost in the North. How long ago that life seemed. "I was there, at John Willard's hanging."

Titch looked surprised. "You might have spared yourself, Wash."

"It was as though I had been fated to see it." I stirred my tea, felt the soft resistance of the mint leaves. I raised my eyes. "I thought I saw you there. In the crowd. I even followed you."

He smiled exhaustedly. "Perhaps it was my spirit," he said, and I thought of what he'd told Peter Haas, his explanation for where he had gone in the snow.

"Peter Haas gave me his old quadrant to give to you."

"But that is much too large an instrument to transport. However did you manage it?"

"I didn't. It's back in Amsterdam, I'm afraid. As you said, it was simply too big. I paid to have it delivered back to him." I shrugged. "It did not seem right to take it from him, in any case. Even if he will never use it, it marks his life."

Titch took a slow sip of his tea. "And how was he?"

"Very well." I hesitated, adding, "Concerned for your sanity, I think."

Titch appeared surprised.

"Robert Solander, too. He said your clothes were too tight."

"My clothes too tight? What the devil?"

And I described what Solander had said, about his arriving at the Abolitionist Society wearing what seemed to be another's clothes. Titch began to laugh.

"I had sent my luggage ahead to Amsterdam, in anticipation of my visit to Peter," Titch said. "I was left only with what was on hand at Granbourne. As I had been many years away, not much fit me. I was forced to make do."

"That is just what a madman would argue to save face."

Titch smiled again, though it did not touch his eyes. "All the while I was wearing them, I kept thinking, what would Philip think to see me dressed so? He who prized his clothing so much."

Hearing that name, I was flooded with images: The slow white fingers on the hunting rifle; the way, after a great meal, he would lick those same fingers thoughtfully, as if considering again each herb and spice and vinegar. The tiredness of his ever-darkening face throughout the days of autumn. The look of him on the field that evening.

I did not know why Titch would mention him, if not to wound me. But I could see now, in his face, the desire to explain.

"Earlier, outside, you asked about the North, what happened." He rubbed at the sore on his hand. "I was not myself, walking into that storm, I did not feel myself at all. I was so—" He paused as though he knew not how to begin. "Erasmus, Philip and I—we were very close as boys. We played together like brothers, all three. And yet Erasmus and I, we did not quite see Philip as our equal. His family was poorer, his manners less refined—all the things boys find to twit each other over. We teased him mercilessly." He lifted his eyes, abashed. "But then things seemed to go rather beyond that."

I peered across at him, silent.

"It was little things, at first. We'd speak of Granbourne's being haunted, then lock him up in one of the disused rooms overnight. We'd take him off into the woods on the estate as if on a leisurely hike, then suddenly we'd turn on him, demanding he remove all his clothing. When he began to cry, we would strip him bare and leave him to walk naked home." He looked uneasily at me. "I am not proud of this.

"Things, they began to take a grimmer turn. We began to beat him, Erasmus especially, he would punch and punch and punch and Philip would drop to the ground, and Erasmus would kneel and keep beating him. Only when Philip lost consciousness would it all come to an end.

"We had the taste of it, we simply could not stop. The violence was in us. I sometimes wonder if that is not where it all began for Erasmus, with Philip."

I shifted on the floor where I sat, said nothing.

"Me, I never felt I understood Philip. He seemed always a being from another world. As we age, most men solidify, become more of what they are. Not so Philip. He seemed to only grow more obscure. There were so many odd things about him, so many details that made no sense. After he died, we had many surprises, things no one had ever suspected of him. Every month he donated half his income to a ladies' aid society that had established a home for orphaned children. Why? I cannot begin to fathom. And this while he owed significant gambling debts in Whitechapel, debts that could easily have been repaid with his charitable contributions. Why did he do it—did he secretly have children somewhere? I do know that he used to brag about being engaged to a widow in Lisbon, but she turned out to be a phantom—no record was ever found of her. He loved fine food and fine clothes but frequented the most disreputable clubs, places one could never mention in daylight. He socialized, spent wildly. He had not a friend in the world.

"We were so awful to him." Titch glanced at me, but would not let his eyes come to rest. "On the very night his father would die, Erasmus and I insisted Philip join us on an outing to a public house, though he resisted and resisted. His father had been sick for weeks, you see, and Philip never left his bedside. Well, finally we convinced him. Philip returned to Grosvenor that night half-blind with drink, to learn his father had passed.

"When he took his life at Faith—" Titch shook his head, let the sentence drop away.

I sat in the blackness on the hard stone floor, feeling the events of the past shift and splinter. I remembered Titch's silence on that night I'd run to him in his study, speechless and shaking and drenched in blood. How responsible I had felt for that death, though I had laid no hand on Philip. I had felt so helpless at what I could not stop.

"Retrieving his body from the field that night," Titch said, "I could not do it, I could not touch him. I thought only, these pieces, this flesh, this is not Philip." He shrugged softly. "It suddenly seemed that the physical properties of the world were not all there is, that there is more."

The boy stirred in the corner. I spared him no glance. I looked instead to my hands, thinking of the years spent running, after Philip's death. And I thought of what it was I had been running from, my own certain death at the hands of Erasmus. I thought of my existence before Titch's arrival, the brutal hours in the field under the crushing sun, the screams, the casual finality edging every slave's life, as though each day could very easily be the last. And that, it seemed to me clearly, was the more obvious anguish—that life had never belonged to any of us, even when we'd sought to reclaim it by ending it. We had been estranged from the potential of our own bodies, from the revelation of everything our bodies and minds could accomplish.

"You are disgusted to hear how awful I was," said Titch. "As you should be." He looked at me, his face lost in the dark.

I glanced at him, silent.

"We were so cruel to him."

I looked at the dusty floor some moments. "What is the truth of any life, Titch? I doubt even the man who lives it can say." I raised my face. "You cannot know the true nature of another's suffering."

"No. But you can try your damnedest not to worsen it."

We fell silent. Then, with little sound, I rose to my feet. Titch did not glance up. I went towards him and, very slowly, very gently, placed a soft hand on his shoulder.

WIND BATTERED THE house. I stepped away, letting my hand drop. Titch sat silent some moments. We both said nothing. Finally he rose and, setting his cup on a tower of books piled at the window, went and lay down to sleep beside the boy. I sat quietly there in the dark, my mind blank, empty. Within minutes Titch was asleep, breathing exhaustedly. In the outer dark, the sand hissed against the windows like human whispers.

I thought I could hear Tanna stirring in the other room, but then I knew it was only the wind. I raised myself up to a crouch. The windows held a soft orange glow, as if the sun were trying to rise through the roar of sand. I watched shadows beat like black birds at the panes. There came a long howl from the east, and then a clicking, as though pebbles had been thrown at the glass.

How astonishing to have discovered Titch here, among these meagre possessions, his only companion the boy. His guilt was nothing to do with me—all these years I had lain easy on his conscience. But what did it matter anymore. He had suffered other sorrows. And these wounds had arrested him in boyhood, in a single draining urge to re-create our years at Faith, despite their brutality. Someone else might have looked upon his life here and seen only how different it was from all that had come before. I saw only what remained the same: the scattered furniture, as if no real home could ever be made here; the mess of instruments that would only measure and never draw a single conclusion; the friendship with a boy who, in days, months, years, would find himself abandoned in a place so far from where he had begun that he'd hardly recognize himself, would struggle to build a second life. I imagined the boy nameless and afraid, clawing his way through a world of ice.

There came a sound from the other room, and I thought I heard Tanna rising, her soft, girlish steps. I stilled myself, waiting for her to come through the doorway, but she never arrived. At the window I could see the great sky emptying, as though it could no longer sustain anything—no bird, no cloud.

Through the badly nailed boards of the door a hissing threaded in like voices. Exhausted, I rose unthinkingly to my feet. I pressed my palm to the door, felt its vibrations. And then I was dragging it open, so that the grand yellow air rose before me, buzzing. A tree's branch whipped past, splintered apart against the harsh stone house. The wind was furious, rasping and singing over the pale ground, whipping sprays of sand into the whitening east. There was no trace of human presence anywhere, neither trail nor footstep. It was so cold I expected to see my breath.

I stepped out onto the threshold, the sand stinging me, blinding my eyes. Behind me I thought I heard Tanna call my name, but I did not turn, could not take my gaze from the orange blur of the horizon. I gripped my arms about myself, went a few steps forward. The wind across my forehead was like a living thing.

ACKNOWLEDGEMENTS

THANKS ARE DUE to Ellen Levine at Trident Media, Patrick Crean and Iris Tupholme at HarperCollins, Rebecca Gray and Hannah Westland at Serpent's Tail, Diana Miller at Alfred A. Knopf, Peter Straus at RCW, John Sweet, Noelle Zitzer and the Athabasca Writer-in-Residence Program.

And thank you also to Peggy and Bob Price, Jacqueline Baker, Jeff Mireau, the Edugyans, and especially to Steven Price, my dearest partner in this madness.